VALLEY
OF THE
SHADOW

Also by Franklin Allen Leib
Fire Arrow
Fire Dream
Sea Lion

VALLEY
OF THE
SHADOW

A NOVEL BY
FRANKLIN ALLEN LEIB

PRESIDIO

Valley of the Shadow is a work of fiction. Any resemblance between characters in this novel and persons living or dead, other than historical figures, is coincidental and unintended.

Copyright © 1991 by Franklin Allen Leib

Published by Presidio Press
31 Pamaron Way, Novato CA 94949

Library of Congress Cataloging-in-Publication Data

Leib, Franklin Allen, 1944-
    Valley of the shadow / by Franklin Allen Leib.
       p.   cm.
    ISBN 0-89141-337-5
    1. Vietnamese Conflict, 1961-1975--Fiction. I. Title.
PS3562.E447V35 1991
813' .54–dc20   90-25438
                                                              CIP

Typography by ProImage

Printed in the United States of America

This story is dedicated to the missing in action
and the prisoners of war in Indochina, and to the long
riders who went in to look for them.

Greater love hath no man than this,
that a man lay down his life for his friends.

John 15:13

The author wishes to thank several friends who helped with details in the story, first among them John Donahue, Huong diRocco, Bao Nga Duc Am, John Ehrlichman, Mike Kennett, and Katrine van Houten.

Valley of the Shadow

1. Trai tren Nui Cao

2. Trai o Bo Song

3. Xieng Mi (NVA Concentration Point)

4. Gorge of the Nam Mang

5. Lower Nam Mang

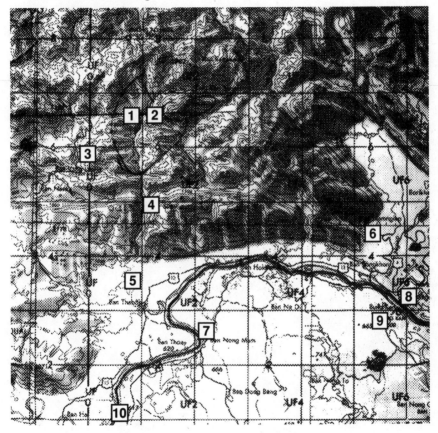

6. Ban Namngiap (NVA Concentration Point)

7. Ban Nong Mum (Thai Special Forces Camp)

8. Pak Sane (NVA Regional Headquarters)

9. Bung Kan (Thai Border Patrol Police)

10. Mekong River

PROLOGUE

The Air France DC-8 jetliner roared down the runway and rose into
the haze. The sound of its engines was lost immediately, even before
the plane lifted off; Tan Son Nhut was filled with noise twenty-four
hours a day. Heavy lift aircraft of the Air Force Military Airlift Command—turboprop C-130s ferrying cargo inland and back, jet C-141s,
and the giant C-5s long-hauling materiel in and wounded and dead
out—took off and landed constantly, delayed at times by the weather,
and occasionally by rocket attacks from the uncontrolled swamps to
the south and west, but never halted. Tan Son Nhut was the busiest
airport in the world.

Lt. Philip Hooper, USN, a tall, red-faced blond man in a black and
green cammie uniform, threw his arm around Lt. William Stuart, also
navy, and pushed him away from the runway and toward two waiting
vehicles, a black jeep with no markings that belonged to the SEAL
detachment assigned to Newport Docks in Saigon and an olive-drab
van with U.S. Army markings. Stuart resisted being pulled away, and
watched the French airliner lift out, wishing it safely away and wishing
it would return at the same time. Hooper and his SEALs, and Stuart
and a man of his ANGLICO detachment had come down from Danang
like a whirlwind, summoned by a girl Stuart had known briefly and
perhaps loved through the ever-increasing pain in his soul, the pain
of Nam. The girl and her family were gone now, safely on their way

1

to Paris and new lives. Stuart wondered how it felt to take that final step, to lose one's country, finally and irretrievably.

So much death, he thought. So much suffering and sorrow. Vietnam took so much from all of them and simply remained, at once charred black and riotous with color, beautiful, seductive, alluring, and deadly. Stuart sighed as Hooper tugged at his sleeve again with greater force. Khanh and her family were gone, escaped, taking away Stuart's last remaining illusion: that the Americans were saving the country for its people. He watched the smoky trail until it disappeared. Hooper shook him roughly and dragged him toward the jeep.

"Time to go, Willie," Hooper said, firmly but not unkindly. Stuart continued to stare at the place in the dirty sky into which the airliner had gone. "We have to check the jeep back in with my friend in Saigon, ditch the truck, and get back up to Danang. We got a war to run; a war my every instinct tells me is about to get busy."

Three members of Hooper's Danang SEAL detachment stood around the vehicles, armed with Stoner carbines, an upgraded version of the M-16 standard military weapon of U.S. forces, talking softly and watching the officers nervously. They knew they had no business in the security area where they were, and were anxious to leave. Lieutenant Hooper had arranged helicopter transport back to Danang without orders, but they were used to that. Standing a bit apart from the SEALs was a black-haired, black-eyed, mean-looking giant of a man they didn't know; he had shown up two days before with Stuart, whom they also didn't know. The giant gave his name as Moser, and had said precious little else. He carried, almost nonchalantly, an M-2 machine gun, .50 calibre and weighing eighty-four pounds empty, and he had carried it all day while this Lieutenant Stuart had gathered up the scared family of Vietnamese civilians, a mother and four young women, from central Saigon, and they all had brought them out to the airport and seen them off on the Air France jet to Paris.

"Come on, now, Willie," said Hooper, releasing the other lieutenant's arm and climbing into the army van. "She's safe; her family's going to be all right. We got to git."

Stuart nodded and strode slowly toward the jeep. As they approached the SEALs mounted up. Moser waited. "It was a good thing to do, Hoop," said Stuart. "It's nice to actually help some of these gentle people escape from all this."

"You done good, laddie," said Hooper, watching his friend, feeling his sadness. Two jeeps painted Air Police blue with red rotating beacons were headed toward them from the direction of the terminal, trailing red clouds of dust in the bright sky of late afternoon.

Moser, six feet five inches tall and 260 pounds of hard muscle, moved close to Stuart, crowding Lieutenant Hooper away, protecting his own officer as he had since they had first gone in–country together seven months before. Stuart was to Moser the finest human being he had ever known, and a man who genuinely cared. It was sad he suffered so, thought Moser, but it seemed bound to happen. He felt he should say something to the lieutenant, who still stared at the pinkish western sky, the hole in the atmosphere through which the lieutenant's girl and her family had escaped. Moser was never sure of himself with words; he had had little schooling at his home in the mountains of northern Georgia. Still, say something, he thought sadly, to show you understand at least a little. He put his machine gun on his shoulder and bent to address Stuart. "Let's go, Mr. Stuart. You done all you could."

Stuart wiped the dust from his eyes with a bandanna and nodded, then climbed into the backseat of the jeep. Moser got in beside him without a word, shipping the machine gun under the seat.

In twenty minutes the little party was airborne in an army Huey and in three hours they were back in Danang, waiting for the war, which had left them alone for over a week, to fall back in on them.

I
THE
RIVER

ONE

Trai tren Nui Cao (The High Camp), Thung Lung Toi, Laos
14 December 1968

What could he say about the river?

Douglas MacArthur Moser squatted in the dusty street in front of the camp commandant's hootch with the other thirty-three prisoners who were healthy, squatted the way the Vietnamese squatted, knees high and head forward for balance. Moser scratched a scab on his stringy, muscled thigh. He had lost nearly forty pounds since being brought to the camp, but he still felt strong. Most of the other prisoners, even the ones in camp less time than he, looked weaker. Moser wondered if some of the prisoners, all but himself officers and aviators, had sufficient will to survive. Surviving was the only way to beat the cruel, dead-eyed Vietnamese guards who scorned the prisoners and called them by the names of animals. Moser fought them with silence and his pride as an American fighting man who would not be broken.

Each man held a single piece of paper and a ball-point pen supplied by the thin, nervous woman in the gray Red Cross uniform who stood, chain-smoking, beside the commandant, Major Nan, who smiled with amusement at his prisoners and at their apparent bewilderment with the papers and pens. The white Alouette helicopter with the large red crosses on its doors and belly sat silently at the edge of the camp, its Swiss crew drinking beer bought from the hill people who lived in cleared patches in the forest along the river and who hauled the bottles of "33" Export and Tiger up from the cities of the great river, five or six at a time.

Nan shifted in his canvas chair. He lacked an arm and a leg and was in constant pain. The Swiss woman paced the wooden deck in front of Nan's hootch, crouching down and encouraging the prisoners, most of whom had laid their single sheet of paper on the step in front of the deck or smoothed it onto a knee. Moser could see she was impatient to complete the "inspection of the living conditions of the prisoners of war" she had announced on her arrival. Every prisoner was given the paper and pen so that he could write home through the Red Cross, but few had written a word.

What could he say about the river?

Moser's letter had gotten as far as "Dear Momma." He guessed there should be a thousand things he should have to say but he couldn't even begin to find words enough to fill the little sheet of lined paper.

The only good thing in this place was the river. It had a name, the Nam Mang, and it lay between the High Camp the prisoners had built for Major Nan and the abandoned River Camp on the other bank and the rice fields below. It ran dark and slow between high rock walls. It was always there just as the prisoners were always there, and yet it came from some place and it went away some place. It moved in the morning beneath its shroud of mist and glowed reddish brown in the sun of midday. In the afternoon its waters turned black in shadow. The river was serene and it was beautiful, and it alone of all the things and men of this place meant the prisoners no harm. It beckoned to Moser and called him home, and mocked him because he knew neither where the river ran nor which way was home.

"Please finish your letters," said the Red Cross woman with her harsh, insistent accent. "We must visit other camps."

Moser printed carefully the words he hoped might touch his mother and filled in the address block. It was so little to send to her; he had been gone nearly two years, although he didn't know that exactly. The woman took his letter and two or three others. She handed them to the scowling, owl-faced North Vietnamese Army officer who had flown with her from Hanoi, who sat at the table in the doorway to Nan's hootch. The officer read English, and he ran his finger under each word of each letter, his hand poised with a thick black pen to censor any detail that might be of use to the Americans if the letters were ever delivered. He made a long smear across one letter before handing them to the Red Cross woman. Moser hoped it wasn't his.

The prisoners were dismissed and sent back to the fields. Moser wondered what the woman would say about their living conditions; she had walked straight from the helicopter to the commandant's office and now walked straight back. The men watched wistfully as the little French helicopter lifted off smoothly.

The Red Cross visit hadn't changed their lives. Perhaps it had brought some faint hope but it had left none behind. Two days later another aircraft came and changed the life of every prisoner in the High Camp, though none so much as Moser's.

15 December 1968

Major Nan had been awake for an hour or more, since before the sun slanted through the mist onto the bare plateau that held the High Camp, but he did not rise from his stretched canvas cot. The night-damp brought terrible pain to his right arm and leg, the ones that were no longer there. The major listened as the guards harangued the thirty-four prisoners from their pallets in the woven nipa shelters, formed them up, and shouted them through their listless Tai Chi exercises.

Every day in this place I die a little, thought Nan. The thought came to him each morning, but brought no sorrow. I have been dead since the aftermath of the Great Tet Offensive, almost a year ago, when the American claymore mine took my right limbs and nearly my life from me as I marched my battalion away from the angry American marines who chased us after they had driven us from Quang Tri City and across the A Shau Valley. Nan's mixed force of Viet Cong and North Vietnamese regulars had driven off the marine patrol that had set the ambush, and Nan had been carried on his men's backs for two days until they had reached a field hospital across the Ben Hai River. At the same hospital, in the very next bed, Major Nan had found the prisoner Moser, called by all the Water Buffalo because of his improbable size. Moser had been shot in the thigh and burned when the medevac helicopter he had been riding had been shot down. An NVA antiaircraft unit on their own retreat across the Ben Hai River, had carried him, still strapped in the steel-cage stretcher in which they had found him. The river marked the treaty border between North and South Vietnam.

I began my life as a soldier with a fighter's purity of purpose, thought Nan, rubbing the remaining sleep from his eyes. I did what I did with the clearest of consciences and my only reward was to be opposed by an ever more brutal and implacable enemy. The French were soft— not the soldiers, and certainly not the paras, who almost turned the war around before the glorious encirclement of Dien Bien Phu—but their leaders, fat *colons* in Hanoi and Paris terrified by the lessons the Japanese had taught them about the ability of Asians to fight and defeat European armies. The puppets the French left behind in Saigon were too busy lining their pockets with American dollars, which they shipped off to banks in Europe and Singapore, to take much interest in fighting a war.

But then the American soldiers came, and even worse, their marines. Men who came to fight and who were willing to take the war away from the safe enclaves of the coastal cities and into the countryside, men who fought day and night, units that took losses and replaced them with ever more big, ugly, rudely grinning kids who killed and died and kept coming, finally forcing the NVA to begin the general offensive a year early: too early because the supplies had not been gathered in sufficient quantity but perhaps already too late because each day the Americans shipped in more young boys to kill and die. Men like the water buffalo. Tough ground troops, mud marines like the ones who shattered my body and left me a dishonored warder of prisoners. Moser was so unlike the rest of the prisoners, the pampered and now defeated aviators out in the exercise yard. Moser had the mad light in his eyes, eyes black as a Vietnamese's, and the hard silence of a soldier. His strength reminded Nan daily of his own weakness and shame. We are the two halves of divided harmony which must be joined, even if only in death.

We are linked, this Moser and I, thought Nan, painfully swinging his left leg off the cot and pushing himself into a sitting position with his left arm. Linked in anger and in disgrace, and one day even in shame.

Nan had been a legend in Vietnam, especially in the South. He had fought the French as a boy, first offering himself as a prostitute to their perverse officers and then slitting their throats with an upward thrust as they covered him. Later he had led smaller boys, attacking French houses with satchel charges and grenades as the occupants lounged or ate or slept.

Nan was originally from Vinh, in the North, but when the war began against the corrupt puppet brothers Diem, he had gone south. He had been a captain then, a *dai-uy* in the North Vietnamese Army, but in the South he had operated a team of assassins, killing off the vermin who represented the puppet government in the villages and hamlets, and on two occasions, once in Hue and once in Phu Bai, killing puppet generals as well. He was famous throughout the First Military Region, the part of South Vietnam the Americans called I Corps. His appearance was well known: tall, nearly a meter eighty-five, handsome and strong. He always wore black sunglasses, day or night, until in time his disguise became a trademark. He was called in French *l'homme sans yeux*, the Man with No Eyes. The Vietnamese of the resistance, both North and South, adopted the name and rendered it into Vietnamese as *Nguoi Mu*, the Blind One. Blind people were considered powerful connections to the spirit world, and Nguoi Mu was powerful magic since everyone knew he was not blind at all. He was so sought after by the assassins of the American *Phoang Hoang* (Phoenix) program that he recruited a dozen doubles: it was said that wherever any of the doubles appeared the puppet officials fled.

Nan reached beneath the canvas cot and retrieved the crude prosthetic leg, made of gray plastic in East Germany, that he had been given in the receiving hospital in Vinh to which both he and Water Buffalo had been taken. He had hobbled around the hospital ward each day, and when he could manage the thirty meters to the prison enclosure he would go and stare at Water Buffalo, then enclosed in the prison ward, as the giant recovered steadily from his burns and his bullet wound. Later the doctors had fitted the stump of Nan's arm, severed just below the elbow, with an even cruder device of North Vietnamese manufacture that ended in two steel hooks that could be separated by pressure on the hooks themselves and could then grasp small objects, much like chopsticks. Nan attached the leg over his stump, using his left hand only, then got the hooks in place using his left hand and his teeth. Getting into his artificial limbs and subsequently his simple black pajama uniform left him fatigued and dizzy. Shrapnel from the claymore had struck the back of his head as well, and he tired easily.

Nan had been released from the hospital in six weeks, not recovered, but well enough. The beds were needed for the terribly wounded NVA regulars who returned from the South after the furious American counterattacks that followed Tet, as well as for the very few Viet Cong who survived. Nan was deemed too badly injured and too conspicuous to be returned to field operations, and was given a desk in the supply transfer center in Vinh, coordinating transshipment of Soviet and Warsaw Pact materiel from the port of Vinh down Highway 12 through the Mu Gia Pass to the Laotian town of Na Phac, where the supplies were delivered to the thousands of bicycle and wheelbarrow runners on the Ho Chi Minh Trail. Nan hated the work because it was in the rear and nonoperational. Nan had been in the front of the fighting since his tenth birthday and could think of no other way of life. He also hated the people he had to work with because they wouldn't look at him. To a Vietnamese mutilation was a great disgrace, and his soul would be denied access to the next life. Major Nan was no longer tall and handsome.

Nan had asked for another assignment and had been given the River Camp, as commandant. He had found the camp badly organized and inefficient. The previous commandant, fat, lazy Lieutenant Mounh, had allowed the production of opium poppy on the high, sunny plateau to decline, and nearly all the thirty-eight prisoners were too sick and weak to work. Major Nan was galled to relieve a lieutenant, and more galled to discover that a major portion of the camp's dwindling poppy production had been diverted to buyers from the Shan tribes who hiked in from northern Thailand and even from Burma, the profits deposited to Mounh's bank accounts in Singapore. Nan had written a scathing report of Mounh's embezzlement and sent it to Vinh but he doubted anything had been done. Mounh's father was a high party official in Hanoi.

Nan had forced the prisoners to clean the camp and had persuaded the district headquarters in Vinh to send medicines and to provide weekly visits by the region's barefoot medical worker, and both medical maintenance and poppy production had risen sharply. The raw opium was shipped to the processor in Na Phac for later sale to American soldiers in the South, and the profits properly accounted for and deposited in the treasury of the People's Republic. Nan's bitter sense of irony was pleased to witness the cultivation by American prisoners of the drugs that were sold at great profit to their comrades in the South, weakening them and often killing them. The profits bought bullets from the parsimonious Russians that allowed the penniless North Vietnamese government to continue the war.

The listless shouting outside diminished and Nan knew the prisoners had been marched off to the fields, which were laid out on the open plateau. Nan had directed the construction of the High Camp, partially to move the workers closer to the poppy cultivation, partially to get them away from the mosquito-infested river, and also to get himself up out of the gorge's eternal damp.

The prisoners Nan inherited were aviators except for the silent giant, Moser, a Navy man who had been attached to the marines who had taken Nan's limbs. Nan wondered why Water Buffalo's spirit had been attached to his, virtually since the day of his mutilation. The aviators were mostly docile, dispirited, and tractable, but Moser had been difficult from his first days. Was it karma, wondered Nan, or false karma that Moser was always with him, dragging his spirit back to the agony of his maiming and the continued shame of his mutilation? One never knew.

And yet one must know, or at least assume, thought Nan, as he hobbled into the misty sunlight of the Annamite Mountains. How I wish for the wet heat of the coastal plain! Leave these dreadful highlands to the *moi*, the Montagnards who wish to live in the cold.

Nan limped to the center of the camp. The acting senior American officer awaited him as he did every morning, shrunken and gaunt but still defiant. The senior American officer was a docile air force colonel, but he had sickened three months ago, and then Nan had endured without interest or pity the elevation of Maj. Carter Peters, USAF, to the sorry, prideless office. Peters pestered Nan daily with his absurd talk of Geneva Conventions and rights of prisoners.

Nan walked to the latrine and washed carefully. He went to the mess shelter and received his morning meal of cold rice with fish and tea. There was little for the commandant to do: once he had reestablished discipline around Sergeants Minh and Vo the camp ran itself. There were ten guards and thirty-four prisoners now; four had died since Nan had taken over—weak, easily broken men who could not take the work of the fields. The men had to grow rice for the camp in a plot down by the River Camp, but the field was small and the work not hard. Working the poppy field was even easier, just weeding and every month the careful collecting of the white, sticky sap from the pods. Clumsy prisoners who damaged the plants while cutting in for the sap were severely beaten. Ironically, the biggest man, the shambling water buffalo, had the best hands and harvested twice as fast as the best of the others, and he almost never damaged a plant. Moser was close to the earth, and in that respect as well he was closer to Nan than to his compatriots. Karma.

Major Nan hobbled to the highest limestone outcropping on the plateau as the morning warmed. The tropical sun rose swiftly, already topping the east mountain, giving it a coppery halo in the morning mist. Nan looked down at the High Camp. Two rows of one-story buildings, built on raised floors of rough-sawn hardwood, roofed with nipa thatch and with walls made of the same material but woven. The guards' barracks, his own hut, and the cookhouse and mess hut were on the left as he looked at them from the east. The right row was comprised of the three huts where the prisoners slept, the small, ill-equipped infirmary, and the latrine. There were no fences and no guard stations. At night the prisoners' ankles were locked into wooden blocks, each held by a single pin, and they were handcuffed with ancient French cuffs, two men together. Nan knew the men could get out of the blocks, but none had dared try an escape, having no idea where they were and, with the exception of a very few, lacking the courage to try.

The prisoners shambled up the hill in two ragged lines from the broad swept-dirt area between the lines of huts, going to work among the poppies. The shouting of Sergeant Vo and the other guards could be heard but their words were lost in the mist, muffled by the distance. Major Nan stretched and twisted his body as best he could, the sun's growing warmth soothing the aches in his missing limbs, but only a little. Why do I yet live? he wondered. Why could I not have had a soldier's grave? Instead I am humiliated, as these prideless American pilots are. Why do they live? Why, most of all, does Water Buffalo survive, clinging to a life without merit?

TWO

16 December 1968

Moser and the other prisoners deemed adequately skilled were cutting the poppy pods and milking out the sticky white opium sap under the lazy watchfulness of Sergeant Vo when Moser's keen ears picked up the sound of a distant airplane engine. The sound grew to a grinding scream as the unseen craft approached. Sergeant Vo jumped up and menaced the prisoners with his carbine, gesturing and shouting for them to hurry beneath the trees. The only aircraft that ever overflew the camp were American, and Vo didn't want to chance a lucky sighting by an American pilot, who might see the shambling skeletons as Americans and not Laotian peasants.

The aircraft engine popped and the scream subsided, then there was a loud explosion in the river valley. Moser, squatting beneath a tall palm, saw a fireball topped in smoke rise to the east. Then he saw the parachute, almost directly above the poppy field. The pilot in the harness seemed to hang as though unconscious or dead. Moser could see that the light easterly breeze would carry the pilot into the jungle just below the poppy field.

Maj. Carter Peters got up slowly, keeping his eyes on Sergeant Vo, who watched the parachute slowly pass overhead. "Two men," said Peters, softly. "Moser, Lieutenant Morse, come with me."

Moser followed the big black Navy lieutenant and the major across the field and into the woods. Sergeant Vo began to shout, *"Dung lai! Dung lai!* You prisna stop!" Moser tensed his shoulders for the bullet, but he didn't expect Vo to shoot. As the three Americans entered the dark jungle, Moser could hear Sergeant Vo crashing along after them, cursing and shouting as he came.

Major Peters reached the downed pilot first. He bobbed against the bole of a giant mahogany, still partially supported by the shrouds of his parachute, his head lolling and his arms jerking like those of a broken marionette. Moser and Morse supported the man, an air force captain with "Burchard" on his name-tag, while Peters cut the risers with the pilot's own shroud-cutter knife. Sergeant Vo caught up, panting and sweating, and gestured for Peters to toss the knife to his feet, followed by the pilot's .38 revolver. Moser pointed to Vo's canteen and was surprised when the guard gave it to him without protest.

Carter Peters took the canteen and poured a little water into the corner of the pilot's mouth. The man choked and opened his eyes. "Who?" he said, blinking at the gaunt, dirty men, who were obviously not Asians.

"Americans," said Peters, giving the man more water. "Prisoners. You landed in Laos, sorry."

"Laos!" the pilot struggled to sit upright, but sagged back, his face twisted with pain.

"Don't move, Captain," said Morse. "I think you broke both legs."

"Laos! Fuck me! If I coulda held that crate together for another fucking *minute* I'd have made Thailand!" The pilot made another attempt to sit up and fell back once again. "Another *twenty minutes* and I'd have made Udorn!" The pilot blinked at the gaunt, uncomprehending faces. "We have to get going! Do you guys have any idea how close you are to the Thai border? That river over there, where the Thud finally crapped out and I ejected, flows into the Mekong, and the other side of the Mekong is fucking Thailand!"

Sergeant Vo forced himself to the center of the circle and thrust the barrel of his AK under the pilot's chin. "*Im lang di!*"

Captain Burchard looked at the fat Vietnamese guard with his yellow snarl and his carbine and his expression changed from pain to fear. "What?" he croaked.

"*IM LANG DI!*" shouted the sergeant, stifling Burchard's cry with a thrust of the muzzle of the gun into his throat.

"Be quiet, Captain," said Major Peters, softly. "*Im lang di* means silence, and the guards will expect you to remember that."

"Oh, sweet Jesus," said the pilot, his voice gone soft and hopeless.

"Bring," said Vo, pointing to the pilot. "Bring; we go Major Nan."

"We can't carry him, Trung-si," said Major Peters to the sergeant. "Legs broken," he made a chopping motion with his hands at his own. "Need make stretcher."

Vo pointed at Moser. "Water Buffalo bring, can carry over shoulder."

Peters and Morse hoisted Burchard up on Moser's broad back as gently as they could. Moser took the pilot in a fireman's lift, with his head hanging down Moser's back and his broken legs in front. Moser held Burchard across the buttocks and calves as tightly as he could to keep his legs from swinging.

"*Di-di*," said Sergeant Vo. "Go."

At Moser's first step he heard a sigh from the pilot on his back, and on the second step a little yip. By the time they reached the camp, each step brought out a howl of pain which nothing Vo shouted could suppress. When Moser knelt and set the pilot down on a mat in front of the thieu-ta's hootch Burchard gave a choked gurgle and finally passed out.

Major Nan hobbled out onto the covered porch of his hootch and looked at the bleeding pilot and his escort. "Sergeant Vo, lock these prisoners down. Send Private Thieu to guard the prisoners in the poppy field. Then return to me."

Vo saluted and turned to herd Moser, Peters, and Morse to their hootch. Major Peters held up his hand. "Major Nan," he said, "let us take the new man with us; make him comfortable."

"Thank you, Major," said Nan, with a thin smile. "I will look after this pilot, and I will try to locate the barefoot doctor."

"But at least let us take him to our hootch and get him out of the sun."

Major Nan looked at the pilot in his bloodstained gray flight suit. His face was white around the lips and his cheeks and brow were pasty and damp. Deep shock, thought Nan. "He will stay with me until I find the doctor," said Nan. "You may bring out my own cot and lift him onto it, then carry him inside, and then Sergeant Vo will lock you down."

"But—" protested Major Peters.

"Do it *now*, Major!" shouted the commandant, stepping aside and pointing into his hootch. "*Di-di!*"

Vo marched the three prisoners back to the hootch and watched as they inserted their legs into the wooden blocks. He inserted the long iron rod that locked the blocks, handcuffed each prisoner, and then left them in the stifling, fetid air of the hootch.

Carter Peters watched Vo walk back toward Major Nan's tent through a tear in the woven nipa mat outer wall of the hootch. He turned to Moser and Morse and whispered, "Moser, you talk a little gook with Vo and he practices his English on you. How much of what Captain Burchard said would Vo have understood?"

Moser shrugged. "Next to none of it, sir."

"Okay," said Peters. "Look, if he is right, and I think he would be, we are a few klicks from Thailand! We never had any idea where we were before."

"We could escape. All of us," said Lieutenant Morse.

"Just *di-di mau* down the river," grinned Moser.

"Well, it won't likely be that easy," said Peters, wiping his streaming brow with the backs of his manacled hands. "The border must be guarded, and for all we know there are other camps downriver, and patrols."

"Send one man," said Morse. "He gets out; he tells U.S. authorities where we are."

"They will likely kill him if they get him," said the major. "And we would never know."

"Chance to take. Army or Air Force from Udorn could get here in a matter of hours if they got off their asses," said Morse. "Gooks couldn't get us all out that quick."

"They could kill us all in reprisal," said Peters. Through the hole in the wall he saw Vo returning.

"You ain't just a little bit dead already, Major?" said Lieutenant Morse. "I'll go."

"'Scuse me, sirs," said Moser, softly. In his mind Moser saw and felt the dark river that flowed below the camp, and its deep afternoon shadows beckoned. He had no idea how he could make the journey, but even the slightest possibility of getting free and striking back at Major Nan and the other gooks excited him as nothing had in months. "I'm a mountain man, from Georgia, and I am still strong. I'd stand a better chance to get through."

"I'll talk to the colonel," said Peters. "In the meantime we have to convince Nan that Burchard told us nothing of value, or he will chain us up and prevent us from telling the others." He peered through the hole in the mat just as Vo, striding as always in his slow, tropical pace, reached the front of the hootch. "Let's get our stories straight.

He was raving, delirious. He told us he was flying out to sea to bail out."

Morse and Moser nodded as Vo pulled the door open and entered. He unlocked the cuffs and the ankle blocks and beckoned. "Come Major Nan talk. *Di-di.*"

Major Nan hobbled back and forth inside his hootch, looking alternately at the snoring form of Captain Burchard, stripped to his underwear, and at the fat, slovenly sergeant. "Vo, you are sure you understood nothing of what this pilot said before you silenced him?"

"No—no, Thieu-ta," stammered Vo, knowing he should not have allowed the American to say anything. He had been delighted with the airman's shiny pistol, which now was hidden in the small of his back, under his loose black shirt. "A couple of words he spoke amid cries of pain, and then I shut him up."

Nan continued his lurching pacing. "The Americans tell me the same: that the pilot was raving, thought he was flying toward the sea. Damn!" Nan rounded on the frightened sergeant. "I should have interrogated them immediately! That Major Peters is a clever bastard. He could have concocted that story and told the others to tell it as well."

"B—but Major," said Vo, "what does it matter?"

"How did you come to this camp, Sergeant?" demanded Nan, pointing his finger like a pistol at the bridge of Vo's flat nose.

"We walked from Vinh," said Vo, shrinking from the major's anger. "It took a long time and many prisoners died on the route."

"And you have no idea where we are now, nor why this place was chosen for a camp?"

"No, Thieu-ta," said Vo.

"We are here because the soil and the shade are good for the poppies, Vo. We are but a few kilometers from the Thai border."

"But if the pilot was raving—he was crying out all the way when he was carried here—"

"I examined him, Vo. I opened his flight suit and checked his entire body. His only wounds are fractures of both thighs: compound fractures, very bad with much blood loss. But they are fresh wounds, blackening only now, as you can see." Nan pointed to the hugely swollen black bruises of the pilot's exposed thighs. Vo did not move from the farthest corner of the hootch. "Wounds due to impact, Vo, not to the bullets of our gallant air defense forces. In all probability he struck his legs on some part of his aircraft when he ejected."

"But why is that important?"

"He would have been in pain when he landed, Vo, but he shouldn't have been raving, although he is now, when he wakes. And he is a pilot, Vo, probably trying to reach the base at Udorn. He must have known at least his approximate position, and he could have told the others."

Vo hung his head. "I am sure he said only a few words, Major."

"You should have allowed him to say nothing! Shot him, if need be!" shouted the major, hobbling toward Vo and forcing him to back farther into the corner. "If the Americans now know Thailand is a few kilometers downriver they may overpower you and your slovenly comrades and escape!"

Vo drew himself up. "Surely, Major, we can handle these spiritless *cho de*, these sons of dogs."

Nan looked at the sergeant, his face showing utter contempt. "Keep those three isolated from the other prisoners. Now get out of here; I have to decide what to do."

Nan watched as Vo scuttled out the door like the rat he resembled. He turned and looked at the American pilot who might—or might not—have brought a fatal infection of knowledge into his camp. If this man knew his approximate location and told Major Peters and the others, I should isolate them from all the other prisoners and keep them locked up. But if I do that they are more likely to give credence to whatever this man told them, or to the mere suggestion of his plane's course, and the word would eventually get out anyway. And besides, this prison has never had walls; the despair of the prisoners alone has always been sufficient to keep them here. Nan looked at Captain Burchard and shook his head. Whatever knowledge he had would leave with him when he left. The pilot's lips moved but no sound emerged. Nan had radioed for the district doctor, but she wouldn't come until tomorrow. Nan doubted that Captain Burchard would last through the night.

Major Peters, Lieutenant Morse, and Moser were let out of their hootch and reunited with the rest of the prisoners when they were brought in from the poppy fields and up from the hidden rice paddies down near the River Camp. Vo had said nothing when he had released them from the hootch. Either Nan bought our act that the pilot was raving and told us nothing of value, thought Peters, or perhaps the pilot really had no idea of his position before he crashed. Peters himself had been an F-105 "Thud" pilot flying out of Nakhon Phanon in 1965 and 1966, and at Korat in 1968, until he had been shot down while dropping bombs on a P.O.L. dump near the port city of Vinh. He knew the jungle all looked pretty much alike from the air and that the pilots had trouble returning to bases in Thailand without assistance from the radio beacons at the bases, and sometimes from the radar operators. Burchard would have had his hands too full trying to keep his aircraft in the air to worry much about navigation; he would just have flown in the general direction of Thailand and would have known he was there when he passed over the Mekong River, which was just too big a landmark to miss. But he never made the Mekong, thought Peters, and maybe we are hundreds of kilometers away, not just a few. Maybe Burchard repeated his story to Nan, and Nan knows it is wrong. I could be condemning Moser to certain death if I let him try to escape. Peters was glad the dying colonel would have to decide. Nan had Colonel Manzini in a separate hootch, bedridden and weak from the fevers and the parasites the barefoot doctor's herb medicines and very rare doses of precious quinine could do nothing to cure. Nan allowed Peters to see the colonel for a few minutes each evening after chow, occasionally sitting in on the meetings but never restricting the conversations. Peters hoped Nan would not come in tonight; the old man had to be told about the escape plan and grant his approval as senior American officer.

Moser walked slowly around the perimeter of the High Camp at the end of a ragged detail of six prisoners flanked by two guards. Each evening before chow a similar detail was sent out to police up any litter, natural or man-made, and then the bare earth was swept by the men with brooms made of palm fronds. Moser stretched his muscles as he walked. He was not tired from the fields, nor from carrying Captain Burchard. Moser had been six feet five inches tall and almost 250 pounds the day he was captured, but like the rest of the captives he had become stooped from the work and had lost much weight. He had no real idea how much he had lost, but he felt a little thinner than the 190 he had weighed when he had enlisted in the navy, a skinny ridge runner from northeast Georgia. He had filled out rapidly on the navy chow and had grown his last three inches in his first year on the ship. Now his muscles stood out like ropes beneath his slack skin and the bones of his previously round face stretched against his cheeks, but his muscles still had great strength and he had energy reserves the aviators lacked. Moser didn't think much about it, but he guessed growing up dirt poor and working hard every day with never enough food to fill him had accustomed his body to making the best of the little food the prisoners received. He felt he could make it down the river if any of them could, and he hoped the colonel and the major would let him go.

Moser paid close attention to the ground in front of him. The guards had just turned the prisoners back toward the center of the camp when Moser stooped and picked up a rusty object, and with the other hand two stones. Flipping the larger stone into the jungle, Moser palmed the rusted object, a piece of the stiff wire that had been used to reinforce the corners of the hootches. When both guards were looking away he concealed the piece of wire and the second stone in a pocket he had made in the hem of his black shirt. Moser, trained in the navy as a master gunsmith, had the makings of a tool.

THREE

Moser squatted in the latrine, working quickly on his tool. He needed a few minutes of skillful work out of sight of the guards, and then he could polish and refine his work after lockdown.

Moser first used the stiff piece of wire he had picked up to knap the stone he had taken from the same part of the yard. The stone was a piece of fine-grained chert, a hard, flintlike rock. Pressing carefully at the stone with the sharp end of the wire, Moser quickly formed a crude scraping edge. The opposite side of the stone was rounded, and Moser knapped it flat to be used as either a hammer or an anvil. Moser held the wire by one end against one of the flat stones that surrounded the latrine trench and struck it twice with his crude hammer stone, padding the sharp edge against his palm with his shirttail. Despite the padding each blow made a sharp click. Moser examined the wire: it was nicely flattened. A little more pressure, then polishing with the edge of his stone, and it should function to pick the ancient French handcuffs.

Moser folded his tools into his loincloth and wrapped it around his waist. He pulled up his trousers and pulled aside the flap of the latrine. Only one prisoner was waiting and the nearest guards took no apparent interest. Moser breathed easily as he crossed the yard to the mess hootch. He hadn't taken too long in the latrine, and now he had only to wait for Major Peters to tell him to go.

* * *

Carter Peters was allowed in to see Colonel Manzini after chow, and spent the first fifteen minutes of his visit feeding the emaciated man his rice gruel and tea. Major Nan had made no move to accompany Peters, and indeed had been nearly cordial, reporting sadly that the new arrival, Captain Burchard, had not regained consciousness and was running a high fever.

Peters told the colonel about the conditions in the camp, numbers of men sick, and so on. Colonel Manzini stared straight up from the small sack of dried rice stalks that made his pillow, breathing in shallow gasps. Every day he loses strength, thought Peters; the fever sucks him dry. When we lift him off this cot for burial he will weigh no more than his mattress of dry rice stalks. Peters stood and looked around the small hootch, looking for signs or shadows that someone might be listening. He took a small breath and squatted next to the colonel. "Colonel, a pilot crashed here today: a Thud driver heading for Udorn. He says Thailand is just a few klicks downriver. Moser wants to try to get out."

Colonel Manzini's eyes lost their listless look and burned briefly through the fever. Spots of faint pink appeared on his gray cheeks. He looked at Peters for the first time since the major had entered the hootch. His chin quivered as he tried to breathe harder, and he licked his lips.

Peters thought the old man wanted to speak, so he leaned closer. The colonel's face worked but no sound came out. "Colonel," asked Peters in an urgent whisper, "do you authorize the attempt? The enemy could take reprisals."

Tears started in the corners of the old man's eyes. "Tell—" he mouthed, making almost no sound. Even this seemed to tire him, and the glassy cast drew back over his eyes.

"Tell what, Colonel?" whispered Peters. His visit with the colonel would be interrupted by the guards at any time.

"Tell Moser Godspeed." The colonel's eyes closed and the color on his cheeks faded into the gray. His breathing slowed to its former rhythm.

Peters stood and backed away from the bed. Sergeant Vo stood at the open door of the hootch, beckoning.

Major Nan replaced the damp cloth on the forehead of the unconscious pilot in his bed. The man was burning with fever now; an hour earlier his teeth had been chattering as the fever broke in streams of sweat.

Major Nan felt genuine regret that the camp was allowed so few medicines, but the troops needed all that could be begged from the East Bloc or stolen from the puppets and the Americans. This man will master his fever from within, thought Nan, or he will die. Karma.

Nan hobbled to the door of his hootch, taking his staff from his chair. I will find a guard to make a pallet for me on the floor and then I will walk up to the little hill to the east, and think about what this man means and what effect his tale might have upon the harmony of the camp, if indeed he had told the prisoners anything at all. Karma.

Sergeant Minh watched silently as the prisoners sat in the hootch and arranged the blocks around their ankles. He gave them a few more minutes to adjust hips and shoulders against the rice stalks that covered the wood floor, and against each other. It would be a long, cool night and the men would be unable to shift positions once locked down. After the men settled Minh put down his carbine and his lantern, came forward to insert the metal pins that held the ankle blocks closed, then handcuffed the men to each other. There were four men in this room: Thieu-ta Peters, two pilots who had no names of which Minh was aware, and the giant Moser, whom the guards called *Con Trau Duc*, the Water Buffalo.

Minh clicked the cuffs, tugged on them to make sure they were fast, and then let himself out into the gathering darkness.

"Moser," said Major Peters, to the dark interior of the hootch.

"Yes, sir," replied Moser, his voice soft and eager.

"The colonel says you can try it, if you want, if you volunteer."

"Yes, sir. Good to go, sir."

"You will have to make mental notes of your passage. If you make it to Thailand you will have to tell them where we are."

"I understand, sir." Moser pulled the cuffs toward him. Lieutenant Dalby next to him stretched his arms to allow Moser room to reach his loincloth and recover his wire and his tool stone. Moser braced the wire against his thigh and turned it flat side down. He laid the stone tool's sharp edge against the wire and began planing with slow, careful strokes. The faint scraping sound mimicked the singing of the black crickets that infested the rice stalks.

"We will begin hoarding rice at chow tomorrow," said Peters. "A few grains a day from each man and we will have a few good-sized balls in a couple of days."

The scraping sound ceased. Moser tried the wire in the lock of his handcuffs, holding it carefully with his fingertips in order to reach. The shim fit into the lock but was too tight to allow sufficient movement. He withdrew the wire, returned it to his thigh, and once again began planing, first one flat side and then the other. "The guards might see that, Major," said Moser. "Everybody gathering up rice."

"Well, perhaps just a few men. You have to have food."

"I reckon," said Moser, holding the shim between his blunt fingertips, gauging the smoothness of the finish, "they gonna be watching for things like that, Major. Major Nan gonna figure that pilot mighta tole us what he did, about bein' close to Thailand."

Major Peters nodded in the darkness. "You're right, Moser."

"That's why just one man, sir." Moser tried the wire in the lock again. It fitted smoothly and worked easily. "That's why no preparation the guards can see." He probed the old lock carefully. The wire was barely long enough. He held his breath and twisted, willing his fingertips to grip tightly and not to slip. He forced himself to stifle his impatience to be free, knowing that if he dropped the piece of wire into the straw he would never find it in the darkness. He strained for one last degree of twist, and the old lock surrendered with a soft click. "That's why it has to be tonight, sir."

The men squeezed together to allow Moser room to sit up. He pulled the pins from the leg blocks, crawled to the nipa mat that served as a door to the hootch, and looked out at the sleeping camp. "Moon should set in about an hour, Major."

Carter Peters felt a tightness in his chest and he fought the urge to weep. "Godspeed, Moser."

"Thank you, sir," whispered the dark form crouched in the corner.

Major Nan watched the moon set behind the dense wall of trees beyond the camp. The evening cooled rapidly and the mist rose from the river to the east. I look upon this camp of ruined men, he thought. The Americans are weak and have no honor, and I, their master, am beyond honor because no honorable man would look at me, pulled apart as I am. We are all here to await death, and then our shades will stay in this valley forever, denied the next life. For the first time since he had come to the valley Nan felt harmony, *hua*. He smiled to himself in the darkness. There will be no escape; these men haven't the will, or perhaps they understood as he understood that all must remain, enriching the poor red soil with their ashes and then haunting the forest with their shades. Nan would instruct the guards to watch for suspicious behaviour from the prisoners, and he himself would watch, but there would be no escape. The wheel of time was complete; every man here would stay. Karma.

Moser slipped out of the hootch just after midnight. He spent the hour after moonset studying the movements of the two guards, one at the western end of the camp and one near the path that led down to the bridge and the River Camp below. Moser recognized the man by the path as the fat, indolent Private Thieu. The other guard was nearly invisible in the gloom, but he gave his position away several times by lighting the rough, dry cigarettes the gooks smoked. He was apparently walking in a tight circle.

The entire camp was dark except for a light in the small shack next to Major Nan's hootch. Moser knew that the two sergeants slept in that shack, and that the light must mean that one of them was standing a watch. That was unusual, and Moser wondered whether Nan had set up an alert after all. The long hootch that served as housing for the remaining guards was dark, but Moser had no way of knowing if the guards were actually inside.

I will wait an hour, thought Moser, and become the night. As he watched and waited for the night to become darker and the guards sleepier he reminisced about the path that had brought him here, so far from Breaker's Holler, Georgia. He had joined the navy at a judge's order, barely seventeen years old, to avoid prosecution for assaulting three older men. He had only been defending himself, but the judge had to listen to three against one. He had served on an assault carrier, the old *Valley Forge*, where he had met Lt. William Stuart, the only man Moser ever felt had really taken an interest in him. Moser had been just a big strong kid, good with his hands but barely able to read, but Mr. Stuart had gotten him to believe in himself, gotten him to study and take the test for Third Class Gunner's Mate, and Moser had passed. Mr. Stuart had been ordered off the *Valley* in 1967 to take charge of an Air and Naval Liaison Company, spotting aircraft bombs and naval gunfire for the army and marines, and Moser had asked to go along. Stuart had let him, and he brought an old .50 calibre machine gun he had restored personally. Moser smiled in the blackness. They had been in some good fights together, him and Mr. Stuart, that wild Billy Hunter who taught Moser jungle craft, and the big black sergeant with all the schooling, Bobby Coles. Hunter was dead and Moser couldn't conjure up much of a picture of Coles, so maybe he was too. Moser's smile faded. He watched the guards a while more, feeling anxious to go, but forcing himself to wait.

Moser had held a single thought in his mind since his capture, and the thought had kept his spirits up, no matter how low those of the aviator officers around him fell. A man as good as Lieutenant Stuart would never leave Moser here if he could find him. Moser's only worry, which crept up on him in the night, especially if the malaria was on him, was that Stuart might think he was dead. Moser had been shot in the leg in one of the long clearing operations after Tet, a minor wound— he hadn't wanted to leave Mr. Stuart. Moser was more afraid of letting his officer down than of any danger to himself, but Mr. Stuart had ordered him to go. The helo he was being taken back in had been shot down and he had been thrown clear and then carried away by the NVA, but maybe he was written off as dead. Moser told himself every night that that could be the only thing that would prevent Mr. Stuart from coming after him. Every night before he slept he concentrated real hard on Mr. Stuart and all the shit they had done together, and then he said his name, in his mind. It's Moser, sir, he said silently. I'm alive.

Moser reckoned an hour had passed. The night was getting cooler, and dark, low clouds blew up from the south, bringing a fine rain that silenced the insects and created a soft background of sound. Good, thought Moser. The guards will want to get out of the rain and the sound will cover any slip I make. He knew the guards had been on duty at least since he had first looked from the hootch; he wondered why they hadn't been relieved.

Moser dropped silently to his hands and knees and began to crawl along the deep shadow of the prison hootches, using the opposite hand and foot, knee and elbow movement that his friend Sergeant Hunter had taught him in the old ANGLICO. Gook sappers used the swaying, rhythmic crawl, and with it a mental discipline, a heightened concentration that allowed them to feel the texture of every patch of light and shadow. Hunter had called the crawl the "lizard," and Moser willed his body to be silent and his mind to probe the darkness as he passed the last prison hootch and crept with patient slowness across the inky darkness of the swept area out to the perimeter of the camp.

The guard Thieu was invisible in the steady rain but he had to be near the path. Moser expected Thieu would be sheltering among the huge roots of an old and broken teak that stood next to the path. Moser would parallel the narrow path, though the going would be very slow through the dense forest and down the slippery slope to the old iron bridge that crossed to the River Camp, but he would have to leave concealment to cross the bridge and reach the river.

Sergeant Vo rubbed his eyes and sat up in his cot in the hootch he shared with Sergeant Minh. He had dozed off again despite Major Nan's order that he and the other guards watch all night against the slim chance that one or more of the Americans might try to escape. Vo had seen no movement of any kind from the prison hootches across the compound, and he thought resentfully that Nan's order was more to punish and humiliate him because he had let the new American utter a few words before he had silenced him.

Vo stretched and looked at his rusty Czech wristwatch. He was already late to relieve Sergeant Minh and his squad, and he knew Minh would be angry. In addition to the normal guard at either end of the camp Minh and two more men waited along the path to the bridge, concealed in the forest. The Vietnamese knew of no way to leave the High Camp except across the bridge, and saw no reason the Americans would find one.

Vo slid his dirty feet into his sandals and stood. A smirk crossed his face. I hope one of the stupid long-noses does try to escape, he thought. Nan would have to allow Vo to administer a good beating to the unlucky one. Nan allowed far fewer beatings of the prisoners than had his predecessor, Lieutenant Mounh. The rat-faced sergeant thought beating prisoners one of the few rewards of his job.

Vo picked up his carbine and the lantern and went to the guards' barrack to rouse the remaining four guards to relieve the watch.

Moser made the trees without spotting Private Thieu and began slipping quietly through the dense undergrowth. He was completely soaked by the steady rain and he shivered. The shivering would bring on fever, but perhaps not for a while. Moser started downslope, five meters to the left of the path, planning to come back to the path beyond the big blasted teak if and only if he spotted Thieu. The wind blew strongly from the southeast, and Moser expected to find Thieu sheltering on the northwest side of the tree. Moser was coming from the northeast. Once past Thieu Moser could move quickly to the bridge and across, down to the deserted River Camp below, and then down the river. If Captain Burchard was right the river would carry him to Thailand.

Moser spotted the guard huddled among the exposed roots of the teak tree. His weapon was propped against the tree beside him and his head was down on his chest. Moser dropped to hands and knees and resumed the lizard. The wind would carry his scent away from Thieu; Moser had heard the gooks could track by smell. Moser had hunted enough back home to know how to use the wind.

The dense undergrowth forced Moser very close to the tree, at his closest approach barely two meters from Thieu, who didn't move and might have been asleep. At every pause Moser gathered tension in his legs like a runner in starting blocks, ready to charge Thieu and his weapon if the guard stirred. It took Moser ten full minutes to cover the five or so meters until he was able to pass the tree and angle back toward the trail. He began to move faster. He wanted to be as far downriver as possible before he was discovered missing at reveille.

Vo sent the first guard who emerged from the barrack to relieve the man at the north end of camp. The other three men stumbled out into the night, grumbling as they shrugged into their black pajamas and attached canteens and ammo packs to their web harnesses. Vo cursed them in a harsh whisper and told them to get ready and that if they awakened Major Nan he would cut off their ears.

Moser half-walked, half-slid down the slick wet clay of the path to the bridge. When he could see the bridge pathway and the iron arches beneath it he stopped, lowered himself to the jungle floor next to the path, and watched and listened. He saw nothing and he heard nothing except the pounding of his heart. I just have to cross that bridge, he thought, willing his heart to slow. Get down to the River Camp, get hold of the old rice storage platform, and get into the river. Moser listened for another minute, then rose slowly and stepped toward the path.

And froze. From the near end of the bridge Moser heard a man laugh, a high, girlish squeak. Then another man spoke. Moser sank back to his hiding place as the two men got up and stretched. They had been sitting against the parapets on either side of the path across the bridge, concealed in the shadows. They were less than ten meters from where Moser crouched.

Damn, he thought. I will have to pass right between them to cross the bridge, which surely and purely could not be done. Moser rubbed the sweat from his eyes. His fever was coming on and his head ached. What to do? Wait, he decided, and if those guards didn't move away in an hour or so, try to make it back to the compound, back to his hootch and his ankle blocks and handcuffs.

Moser heard the sound of another man approaching. The guards near the bridge picked up their AKs and tried to look alert. Moser recognized the weasel profile of Sergeant Minh as he approached. The sergeant addressed his men in low tones. Moser caught only the last of the conversation; he had only begun to teach himself gook. Minh's last comment was that he was going to cross the river and have a good shit before that lazy bastard Vo got around to relieving the watch. The two guards tittered and began walking around, trying to look like real sentries.

Moser had observed that the gooks were funny about relieving themselves, almost ashamed that they had to go at all. He had seen the guards walk deep into the bush, out of anyone's sight, just to take a piss. And they all made little jokes about it, like children. Moser suspected that Minh would be gone a long time. The guards, now moving about and up the trail, were less of a threat to him than they had been dozing by the parapet. Moser began to crawl forward. It was a long shot, but if he could make the bridge undetected he could lizard-walk in the deep shadow of the parapet. And if Minh took as much time over his shit as the gooks usually did, he would cross before Minh returned. Moser knew the odds were stacked against him, but he also knew that if he returned to the hootch his heart would break and he wouldn't try again.

Moser swayed along, his belly resting on the ground only during pauses in the deeper shadows. The guards wandered about, looking up the trail and never to the side. Out of deference for or fear of their sergeant they never looked back toward the bridge. Moser recited the mantra Billy Hunter had taught him. I do not walk, I flow. In the shadows I become the shadow. In the light I am a rock or a tree, only seeming to move. I flow, seeking water.

Moser paused two meters from the bridge. The nearest guard was the one the Americans called Greaseball. He stopped, leaned his AK against the parapet, and picked his nose thoroughly. Moser's nose, stock still as the rest of him, could pick up the faint smell of gun oil. Greaseball picked up the carbine and started another aimless circle up the trail, then stopped abruptly just as Moser was tensing to move. Moser heard the sounds of a group of men slipping and sliding down the trail. Sergeant Vo led them, a gas lantern in his hand. Greaseball took a step away from the bridge. Moser looked for the other guard but couldn't see him. He took a look across the bridge: no sign of Sergeant Minh returning. It must be now, he decided, and slipped like a silent reptile around the parapet and onto the bridge.

Sergeant Vo deployed his two men at intervals along the path and told them to walk around, check the bushes. The guards grumbled and shambled about, poking their carbine barrels a few centimeters into the undergrowth next to the path. Vo approached the two guards of Minh's detail, who stood more or less at attention, carbines grounded beside them. "Where is Trung-si Minh?"

Tranh, the one the Americans called Greaseball, answered. "He crossed the bridge, Trung-si, to, ah, be alone."

Vo laughed, a single high-pitched yip. "Well, you two get along back up the hill, then. No telling how long he will want to be 'alone.'"

"Yes, Trung-si," chorused the two men, and began the slippery climb back up to the High Camp.

Sergeant Minh sat across a log just outside the formerly cleared perimeter of the deserted River Camp. He listened to the rain and the sound of the wind in the trees, and hoped the music of the night would bring serenity, as the Buddhist monks who had been his teachers had taught him. He faced south, into the wind. The damp smell of the jungle was far preferable to the stinking mess accumulating behind him as he suffered through the slow and painful bowel movement. The Buddhists had been right, he thought, just as right as the Communists were wrong. There is serenity only in letting go of the world, not in struggling to change it. Nirvana, literally the state of no wind, perfect nothingness. He closed his eyes and listened to the wind, willing it to cease.

Moser emerged from the shadow of the parapet on the River Camp side of the bridge, still in the lizard posture, still silent and alert. Carefully he wiped the coarse grit from the bridge surface from the palms of his hands. He turned his head first one way and then the other, listening. Nothing but the wind and the rain, but Minh had to be around somewhere. Moser crawled two meters to a dense growth of ferns, which had grown up in an area that had been swept earth before the camp had been abandoned. He stopped again and listened, then moved on to another clump near the hollow stump where the guards had threshed the rice. Just beyond, in a clear space three or four meters across, was the rice storage platform, left behind because of the still-powerful sap of the *lua* bush daubed on the vertical posts. The sap of the fire bush could burn away the skin of a man's hands, and no insect, rodent, or snake would climb through it to reach the stored rice.

Moser stopped again, his heart pounding and his head throbbing. I cannot let the fever take over now, he thought. I have to concentrate, to keep one with the night. He studied the shape of the rice storage platform. It was roughly three meters long and two wide, made of woven reeds and supported by four stout bamboo poles. When in use it had had a pitched roof of nipa mat, but that had blown away. I hope it isn't waterlogged, he thought, for it was to be his raft to float to Thailand.

Because of his great height Moser would be able to reach the platform without the aid of the plank steps, which had been removed to the High Camp. He planned to use his stone tool to cut the split-bamboo lashings that held the platform to the posts, then lift it off and carry it to the river. If it was very heavy he would know it was waterlogged, but then what would he do? He had no other plan. His head throbbed and tears came to his eyes. He shook them away and began to crawl toward the platform.

He stopped. A sharp, foul smell washed into his nose and was immediately blown away by the wind. Moser shook himself to clear his brain. He had forgotten all about Sergeant Minh.

Sergeant Minh finished his business and stood, tying up the black trousers with the simple drawstring. He felt better despite the sharp pain in his lower gut. Must get some more worm pills from the barefoot doctor, he thought. He took a few steps forward, into the wind, and then circled wide away from his mess and through the center of the old camp. He had left his AK propped against one of the poles that supported the old rice storage platform. As he reached for the carbine he detected a slight movement in the undergrowth to his right. More curious than alarmed, he peered intently at the spot. There was no further movement, but the center of the bush seemed unusually dense. He stepped forward carefully, pointing the AK. The denseness in the bush seemed to flow to the right like a drop of oil behind the foliage. What jungle spirit can this be, thought Minh, lowering the weapon and feeling a crawling sensation rise up his back. He opened his mouth to speak and the apparition sprang from the bush, its rush carrying it onto Minh's head and chest, bowling him backward. Minh tried to raise his weapon, but the beast snatched it away with a clawlike hand. The other hand had Minh by the throat. Minh wanted to cry out but was too afraid. The giant placed a knee in Minh's gut and pressed down hard. All of Minh's breath was taken away and his head swam. He sank into a soft darkness, his last memory that of the beast's foul breath.

Moser realized the sergeant had fainted, and he rolled the little man over onto his stomach. Moser's heart was pounding again and he was dizzy with the fever. With a single motion he tore off Minh's loose shirt and ripped it into shreds. Minh did not move as Moser tied and gagged him, using a whole sleeve as the gag. Moser tugged Minh out of the clear area and concealed him under some giant ferns in a shallow gully. On the way back he found the sergeant's AK where he had thrown it. He thought for a moment of taking it along, but rejected the idea. Just staying afloat on the river would be difficult enough without the impediment, and his only chance of survival and escape lay in avoiding the gooks, not fighting them. Moser took the magazine off the bottom of the carbine, checked to see that there was no round in the chamber, then threw the AK and the magazine into different parts of the forest.

The rice storage platform proved a bit more difficult to dislodge than he had thought, as the wood frame of the reed platform was nailed as well as lashed to the posts. Moser was panicky now, and he rushed. He cut himself once with the stone tool and he got *lua* sap on both hands and arms. The sap burned his skin and made his fingers feel numb, but he got the platform loose and carried it to the edge of the river. The platform felt light and supple; Moser had thought that reed wouldn't soak up water until it rotted, but he was relieved nonetheless.

He went back for a quick look at Minh. The sergeant lay still as Moser felt for a pulse, which was strong. Moser hadn't wanted to kill or hurt Minh, since that would certainly worsen reprisals against the other prisoners. Moser wondered how long the gooks would respect

Minh's sense of privacy before they came to look for him. Moser took a look across the bridge, but saw no one. Time to go, he thought. He realized he had never expected to get even this far, and he was excited and scared. He went to the riverbank and launched his raft, wading in afterward and then flopping aboard. Water flowed in around his body but the raft seemed stable. The gentle current pulled him out into the stream.

FOUR

The Mang River, Laos, 17 December 1968

The current pulled Moser and his raft more strongly as he neared the middle of the river. At first the raft rotated slowly like a floating leaf as it drifted downstream, but Moser learned to control it somewhat by dragging his feet on one side and then the other. The raft settled beneath his weight and the edges curled up on both sides of him. He could see clearly only ahead, and he didn't think anyone on the banks would be able to tell there was a man on the thick woven mat.

The river was about twenty meters wide at the River Camp, and it widened in places and narrowed in others as Moser drifted south, he hoped toward Thailand. The rain stopped, the clouds drifted up and away to the northeast, and the night became lighter. He could see the banks of the river, higher in the narrow spots. He tried to gauge his speed as the forest swept past: about twice the pace of a man walking on a clear road, he guessed. The pilot had said the Mekong was about twenty klicks to the south, but then Moser knew a river wouldn't run in a straight line. The journey could take days.

Now that he was on the river Moser began to plan how he would travel. Holing up during daylight seemed to make sense; the gooks didn't move around much at night and the hill peoples were said to be deathly afraid of the forest spirits, who they believed danced and sang and stole men's souls in the night. A problem would be choosing a place to hide and rest before daylight; he could easily pull up right in front of a village or a camp in the darkness, and he had to

avoid people at all costs. He decided to try to guide his raft to shore
and managed to do so with some difficulty. After lying quietly, listening while holding onto an exposed tree root, he dragged the raft
into the undergrowth. Crawling, feeling ahead of him with his hands,
Moser found a piece of bamboo, dry and split but not rotten, which
would serve as a crude paddle or pole. He launched the raft, placed
the pole in the center, and sprawled on top of it, pushing back into
the stream. He guessed he had at least two more hours of darkness.

The sky began to lighten as Moser's raft entered a wide turn of
the river. The pace of the current slowed, and there was a broad beach
on the right bank on the inside of the turn. Moser could see two steep
hills up ahead and he heard a sound like rushing wind. Time to find
a place to hide, he thought, steering the raft to allow himself to scan
the banks. He looked at the dense jungle on the left bank, where the
current ran swiftly. The bank was undercut and steep. Dragging his
feet to the right of the raft, Moser turned the raft toward the right bank.
When the slot formed by the curled-up sides of the mat faced the beach
he looked out. He caught his breath and his heart thumped. Not five
meters away was a young girl, naked except for her heavy bead jewelry,
bathing in the shallows. Her skin was very dark and her hair was bobbed
short. Languidly she dipped water in her cupped hands and poured it
over her head and down over her small breasts. She did not look up.
Beyond her at the tree line was a small village of nipa huts. Moser
could see no one else moving about.

Hill people, thought Moser, as he steered his raft back toward the
middle of the stream. Hmong or Meo. Moser had seen them come into
the camp to trade with the guards, usually trinkets or raw jade for rice,
sometimes sex for rice and beer.

Moser decided to press on around the bend, even though the sky
was now becoming quite bright. The sound like rushing wind ahead
of him grew in volume and the current under the raft increased. The
mountains were a jumble here, confining the stream between high cliffs.
No place to stop, thought Moser, as the raft rushed on, pitching and
bucking over short waves. Moser got out his paddle to help him steer.
The rushing sound ahead grew louder and Moser knew that when he
rounded the bend ahead, where the cliffs to the left were nearly vertical, he would enter a rapid. Desperately he looked for an eddy or a
tiny cove or even a fallen tree he could grasp, but there was nothing.

The raft was swept around the bend, spinning and caroming off the cliffs despite Moser's frantic efforts to steer. He pushed off a huge boulder that was surrounded by racing white froth. The next boulder snatched his oar away and he was reduced to wrapping his arms around the raft and hanging on as it was tossed high on the plunging water and then turned over and dragged under. Like many sailors Moser had never learned to swim, and had passed the test in boot camp only because his platoon mates had half-dragged him across the pool while the instructor turned a blind eye.

The raft twisted and tumbled underwater, tugged violently in different directions as though in the jaws of unseen monsters. Moser closed his eyes and held his breath, though his lungs cried out for air. Sweet Jesus, gather and protect me, he thought, and then the raft shot to the surface and he spluttered and gasped a deep breath. The raft planed on over the surging black water, facing downstream. The high cliffs squeezed the river as far ahead as he could see. Huge rocks protruded from the river, dividing the stream like jagged teeth. Moser hung on, his hands clasped under the raft, and waited to be torn in half by the boulders, but the white water surged between the rocks and the pressure waves of leaping foam pushed him away from them as the current tugged and spun the raft. Ahead the river was pressed into an ever-narrowing gorge, and the noise of the racing water became deafening. In his mind's eye Moser saw a giant waterfall, a chasm of enormous depth, and he thought of dying. I wonder, he thought as the raft once again turned over and dragged him under, if Major Nan knew of this place and let me go to my death. For the first time since his capture his fear became hatred, and he wished he could go back to camp and tell the others of the major's trap.

The raft surged into the narrowest part of the gorge, bucking and rolling over, and once again emerged facing downstream. Moser could see the river tilting sharply downward, a flume but not a waterfall, a few hundred meters ahead a pool, and then the river spreading out broad and slow and passing through plowed fields. The raft was sucked into a narrow pass between two large rocks; Moser received a blow on his left shoulder and another on his right hip. The shock and the pain caused him to gasp, and then he felt the fire of the deep bruises. Hang on, he thought, please, Baby Jesus, let me hang on. If I make the river below I can stop and hide. Hang on. Once again the river rolled him under, and he held his breath. He was thrown hard against the bottom and almost lost his grip, then the raft rose, spinning, and broke the surface just in time to vault over a submerged boulder and crash down onto the next. Moser buried his head in the reed mat to protect himself and once again closed his eyes. The raft flipped and he felt a blow like the kick of a mule on his right knee. He gasped and got a mouthful of water, then the raft caromed off another rock and rolled, he felt a shot as from an axe handle on the side of his head, and his grip under the raft loosened and broke as the world faded out slowly to a wet, roaring blackness.

Moser woke up slowly into a world filled with pain. His head boomed with every beat of his heart and the bruises on his body added their own aches. His eyes, mouth, and nose were gritty with sand and he was burning with fever. With a great effort he managed to get his right arm underneath him, and he rolled onto his back. He opened his eyes and more sand fell in. He tried to brush the sand away, but his fingers were coated with more sand. He forced himself to sit up and look around.

The sun was well down to the west and the day was hot and still. Insects hummed and buzzed in the jungle, some ten meters away across a sandy beach. Three meters in the other direction a broad lake lapped at the beach. Moser stood, swaying, and hobbled into the water. He had no recollection of crawling onto the beach, but he was well up from the water's edge.

The water in the lake was a muddy reddish brown, and when he scooped several handfuls into his eyes to clear the sand a finer grit remained. He blinked and tears gradually cleared his vision. The warm water eased the pain in his head and in the bruises on his legs and shoulder. He touched the wounds; he found no signs of broken bones.

The waters of the lake were calm, unruffled by any breeze. Mosquitoes and flies skimmed the smooth surface in clouds. Moser climbed out of the water, sat on the sand, and rinsed his loincloth and his torn shirt. The black pajama trousers were gone. His stone tool and his wire key were also missing, and there was no sign of the rice storage platform that had been his raft. A strange sense of lassitude held him. He could sit by this broad lake forever, he thought, and then his fears returned. He must find a place to rest and then somehow build a raft. He must get away, to Thailand.

Moser looked upstream for the rapids that had tried to kill him, but the lake seemed to stretch on forever in both directions, placid and flowing east.

The realization hit Moser like another blow from the rocks in the rapids. This flowing body of water was no lake, it was a huge river. The stream from the camps must have come virtually straight down the mountains. This river had to be the Mekong, and if Captain Burchard was right the right bank would be Thailand.

Trai tren Nui Cao, 18 December 1968

Major Nan sat alone in his hootch, his brain boiling. How could Water Buffalo have done this to me? Could he not know that we are linked unto death? If any other prisoner had gone he almost would not have cared; they were all of value only to the extent they cultivated the rice and the opium. But Con Trau Duc had been with Nan, had been *attached* to Nan, ever since the Americans had torn and ripped his body. Nan pounded his fist on the small camp table. He must return. I must have him back, even if it is only to clutch him to me as we die.

Nan remembered the terrified look on Sergeant Minh's face as he had been half-helped, half-carried into the camp at dawn by two guards Sergeant Vo had finally sent to look for him. Gasping for breath, Minh had blurted out a tale of being attacked by a jungle beast who had trussed him up to eat later. Nan asked the guards what they had found, and they said Minh had been bound and gagged with pieces of his own clothing. Nan immediately ordered the guards to fetch Sergeant Vo and all his team back to camp, and then told the shivering Minh to get some tea and go to bed. When Vo returned he had him turn out all the prisoners, and then they found that Moser, and only Moser, had gone.

Nan had ordered the prisoners locked down again, except Major Peters and one other who were sent to bury the new pilot, who had died during the night. Nan had paraded his scruffy little force save the one-armed guard, who accompanied the grave digging detail, and cursed them for their incompetence and their laxness. To think that Con Trau Duc had eluded as many as five of them to cross the bridge they all knew was his only avenue of escape and then managed to attack Trung-si Minh almost literally with his pants down. This last remark evoked a few giggles that Nan silenced with a bellow. He sent Sergeant Vo with four guards down to the River Camp to try to determine where Moser might have gone. Neither the guards nor the prisoners would receive any morning meal.

Nan radioed the NVA garrison at Xieng Mi and asked for help. The commandant was unsympathetic; the prisoner was not worth the effort to find him, and he would likely die in the jungle anyway. Nan did not tell him that Water Buffalo was special, and he didn't tell him about the pilot who had come in yesterday and what Nan was now sure he must have told the Americans. The commandant said he would tell the local Pathet Lao leaders and the tribal elders that the usual reward of rice and ammunition would be paid on the return of the prisoner or his body, but would do no more. It was Nan's problem. Karma.

Vo returned and reported that the rice storage platform was missing. So he went down the river, thought Nan. He didn't know what the river was like, but he assumed it must be rapid since the elevation dropped from 600 meters at the River Camp to 160 at the Mekong, less than forty kilometers away. It hardly seemed possible that Moser could reach the Mekong and cross it, but if he did he would be gone and Nan's soul would be mutilated yet again. If only we both could have died that day so long ago in Quang Tri Province. Nan's brain seethed with powerful emotions: anger, sorrow, and fear. I must have him back. The circle must be completed so my soul can go onward when I die.

FIVE

The Northern Bank of the Mekong

Moser stood, fighting the dizziness caused by the blow to his head, his fever, and his gnawing hunger. The water flowed east, away from the setting sun, to Moser's left. He was still in Laos. The river's far bank was invisible in the haze, but there was just a slight suggestion of tall trees in the distance. Moser could only guess at the width of the river: a mile, perhaps even more. But he had to get across. He had to have another raft.

Moser began walking downstream, looking for materials to build a raft. He moved slowly through the jungle, trying to be silent, hoping to find some fruit he could eat. He wondered if the hill people would feed him if they found him, or simply turn him in to the Laotian or North Vietnamese authorities. He couldn't risk it; he would have to find a place and hide until full darkness. The thought of hiding made him feel very tired, and soon he found a dry grassy spot partially concealed by a fallen tree. He matted the grass down the way a dog would, by walking in circles. He slipped down to the river and drank deeply of the silty brown water, then retreated to his shelter and went to sleep despite the clouds of biting midges that set upon him.

Moser was awakened by the sound of laughter and shouted conversation. He had slept curled in a ball to protect his face from the midges, and he uncoiled slowly and looked around. There was no one in sight and the sounds seemed to come from the river. Moser felt stiff and sore as he crawled toward the riverbank. His head felt a little better and his fever had subsided, but his hunger had reached the point of actual pain in his gut. He knew he should be avoiding people at all costs, but he had to find something to eat before he lost all strength.

As he drew closer to the river Moser could hear splashing in addition to conversation. He didn't understand the language, but he was sure it wasn't Vietnamese. He crawled silently into a bamboo thicket that grew right to the water's edge. A small, brown-skinned man stood in the shallows about three meters out from the bank, casting with a net into the current. A long, narrow boat with a slender outrigger was pulled up on the beach, and two small boys played and splashed in the water next to the boat.

Moser studied the group for several minutes without moving. It was apparent that they were unaware of his presence. About every third cast the man caught a fish, usually an orange one about twelve inches long, but occasionally some smaller brown ones. He pulled the fish from his net and dropped them into what looked like a gunnysack that was tied to his waist and trailed in the water behind him. The man wasn't armed, but Moser could see the handle of a machete rising above the gunwale of the boat. I could rush the boat and get that machete before the man could wade in, thought Moser, and then I could take the fish and the boat. Could I kill him? The man turned and answered a question from one of the little boys. The man smiled. If the man spoke gook, maybe I could treat him as my enemy and kill him, thought Moser. Maybe I could just jump in the boat and push off, leaving the family alone. But Moser was no boatman and he knew the man would come after him, and he might have another weapon. Still, he thought, clutching his aching stomach, I need that boat and I need food. Moser looked at the little brown children, happy and slick with water, and he knew he couldn't just attack these people. If only the man hadn't brought his kids.

The man wrapped his net around his forearm and waded back to the boat. He dropped in the net and the gunnysack, which moved jerkily as the fish struggled within. The man gestured to the west, where the light was going quickly, and then shouted at the children, who clambered into the boat. Moser lay paralyzed in his hiding place, his mouth watering at the thought of the fish. The man pulled the boat off the beach and then climbed into the stern. He took a long paddle with a pointed blade and steered the boat expertly into the sluggish current. Moser watched until the boat was perhaps sixty meters from the bank and a half mile downstream, and then he emerged onto the bank. The boat looked to be heading back into shore, and as Moser watched another joined it from the east and both disappeared into the bank. A cove? he thought. Perhaps a village? Moser began to walk along the bank, downstream. If there was a village, perhaps he could enter at night and steal some food. Right now nothing was more important than food.

Bannerman (corporal) Phatang of the Pathet Lao steered his heavy-framed bicycle toward the village of Ban Cha Kay on the edge of the Mekong River. It was a prosperous village and Phatang decided to spend the night there. He had ridden all day from Xieng Mi, first on the barely cleared track through the forest and through the villages of Ban Van Luong and Ban Vasay, and then onward, often walking the bike as the path all but disappeared. Phatang rolled up his purple trousers and took off his shirt, the better to spot the leeches as they set upon him, but he kept his kerchief of parachute cloth carefully tied around his neck. It was both his badge of authority as an NCO in the Pathet Lao and evidence that he had captured or killed an enemy flier.

He left the mountains and the forest for the broad, cultivated flood-plain of the Mekong and picked up the improved, packed-dirt roadway of Highway 13, where he turned east. He was very weary from the long ride, but he had orders to spread the word of the escape of the American from Major Nan's camp to the villages along the Mekong. At least in Ban Cha Kay the bannerman could expect a good meal of fresh river fish, although the people in that area usually ate a fine-grained bread made from the tapioca plant rather than rice. The fine rice they grew they sold; the price had risen sharply since the war had drastically decreased production in Vietnam.

Phatang reached the village just at nightfall. He leaned his bicycle against the raised deck of the main building, then removed his ancient French Modèle 1892 revolver from the bag that hung from the handlebars and put it in the back of his waistband, along his spine. The village elder came out onto the deck, greeted Phatang, and invited him into the communal longhouse to refresh himself and to eat with the fifteen or so large families who lived in the village.

Moser found that the thick jungle dwindled almost as soon as he began walking toward the place where the boats had disappeared. The land was cultivated, the paddies near the river flooded and planted with rice and the fields inland planted in something he did not recognize. The paths between the fields were well defined and maintained and lined with trees, mostly palms. There were very few places of concealment, but Moser saw no people in the fields. The tropical night fell quickly, but the paths were easy to follow in the moonlight. The night was warm and damp, and the sound of distant thunder blew up from the southeast. Moser could smell the village before he could see it: human smells and animals, and over them all the powerful, wonderful aroma of fish being cooked in oil. Moser put his hand to his face and found he was actually drooling. As he approached the village he lowered himself to a crawl on the edge of the path and slipped into a stand of hardwoods that stood next to the shallow stream that divided the village in two. Six boats, all the same design as the one he had seen earlier, were drawn up on the beach, each tied to a carved pole stuck into the sand. Nipa huts with sides rolled up held rice in baskets and what looked to be yams racked for drying. The major building of the place was a longhouse with a thatched roof and woven nipa sides with many doorways. The floor of the longhouse was raised up three feet on pilings and there was a little stairway before each entrance. Between the longhouse and the boats were racks where split fish were drying over low fires. Moser saw no people but could hear voices and laughter from the longhouse, and smoke fragrant with fish drifted out from beneath the eaves. A lone bicycle was propped against the raised floor of the building.

Moser studied the tranquil scene and wished he were home in Georgia or back on the old *Valley Forge*, among friends and eating good food. He thought to sneak across the moonlit beach to grab some of the drying fish, but he was afraid of being seen, of being caught. The night grew darker but not cooler, and clouds obscured the moon and dropped a light rain. People came out of the longhouse in mixed groups of men and women and children. Some went into the river and squatted, others just strolled and chatted. Two women in short purple skirts and black tops added several sticks of wood to the shallow, dug-in fires under the fish; Moser supposed that was to keep animals away during the night. The women each tasted a fish at the end of the sticks, and then they removed several sticks from the rack and carried them into one of the outbuildings. These same women rolled down and lashed the woven sides of the various storehouses. Moser was relieved to see plenty of fish were left out. His stomach growled loudly.

The fine rain stopped. A single man came out of the longhouse and smoked a cigarette. He was wearing dusty purple-blue uniform trousers and almost matching shirt, and he had a revolver thrust into the waistband of his trousers. Moser's practiced eye had never seen one like it, but it looked very old. The man straightened the bicycle against the raised floor, finished his cigarette, and went back inside. Gradually the people all returned to the longhouse, and soon the lights coming from the doorways and the sound of voices both faded. Moser guessed it was about 2100 before he had the night to himself.

Moser waited for what seemed about another hour. No one left the longhouse, and he was close enough even to hear the sound of snoring. Moser crawled to the edge of the stream and took a drink. His mouth was parched from salivating over the fish. He took a careful step into the water, and then another. It remained shallow and in a few minutes he gained the other bank. Forcing himself to go slowly, he dropped into the lizard and approached the nearest smoking pit. Trying to remain as still as possible, he reached up and pulled off the nearest fish. It wasn't really smoked enough and it had an unpleasant, oily taste, but Moser ate it carefully, sucking the meat off the fine bones. He ate another, and part of a third. The rain began again and the thunder grew louder on the wind.

Moser stood. He hoped the rain would cover any noise he might make. He reached out over the fire and grasped one of the sticks as near to its center as he could, then raised it off the rack and backed away. The stick held about thirty fish and should last him for days. Keeping one eye on the darkened longhouse, Moser backed down to the beach. He looked into the first boat and saw that it held a paddle and a tin can, presumably for bailing. There was a net in the prow. Moser folded his fish into the net to keep them out of the bilge and as dry as possible, and then went to the next boat and removed the paddle. Best to have two, he thought, remembering the rapids. He untied the boat, pushed it out into the Mekong until he was waist-deep, and then tried to climb aboard. The boat tilted suddenly, pulling its outrigger on the opposite side out of the water. Moser let go barely in time to avoid capsizing the tender craft, and the outrigger fell back with a loud splash. Moser was puzzled—how to get in?—and then he remembered. The man he had seen fishing, and even the tiny kids, had ducked under the outrigger and boarded from the same side. Moser made his way around the stern to the opposite midships-point and carefully rolled aboard. The boat drifted out into the rising, gusty wind.

Moser had paddled canoes in the dark rivers of Georgia, but this boat was ungainly and heavy by comparison. The hull was hollowed and burned out of a single log and the outrigger, a thick piece of bamboo turned up at the ends, was suspended on two booms of the same material some twenty feet long. The boat with its outrigger was as wide as it was long, and it wanted to go sideways in the increasing wind. The current carried him slowly downstream to the northeast, but the wind kept pushing him from the southeast, pinning him to the Laotian bank of the river.

Moser looked back at the village. No sign of anyone moving in the driving rain. He knelt in the bottom of the boat and began to paddle steadily, one stroke to starboard and then two or three strokes on the port side where the outrigger was, to compensate for the drag. The wind eased a bit and he began to find his rhythm. Slowly the village disappeared behind him as he pulled into the dark river. Lightning flashed brightly in the black clouds, quite near, and thunder crashed close behind. The lightning revealed the whole river; the southern bank was much farther away than the northern. Moser paddled and paddled, angling across the current. Despite the cold, despite the storm, he grinned to himself. He would get across if he had to paddle all night, and then he would locate Thai or U.S. military and lead them back to the High Camp. He stopped only once, when a stroke of lightning showed him to be about halfway across the big river, and quickly ate two small fish, washed down with rainwater he caught in his cupped hands. He paddled until his shoulders burned, and then more. Almost there, he thought, almost there, he repeated with every stroke, and then he began to hum, the old hymn "Amazing Grace," stressing every second syllable with a downstroke of the paddle. A series of three lightning strikes, one on top of the next, lit up the river as bright as day, and Moser could see the tall trees and the open fields of the south bank, the *Thai* bank, now no more than a hundred meters away. He felt the current underneath the dugout decreasing as he approached the shore.

Moser sang the hymn in his rich, deep bass voice, every verse he remembered, and then he improvised one for himself:

> Amazing Grace, how sweet the sound
> God shed his grace on me!
>
> I once was lost, but now I'm found
> I was chained, but now I'm free!

And then the storm wind came, spun the boat around, and tossed it on steep, leaping waves away from Thailand and back toward the middle of the Mekong.

SIX

The Mekong River, between Laos and Thailand,
18 December 1968

The first rush of roiled water spun the outrigger around and tore Moser's
paddle from his hands. Because the river was broad and shallow the
waves, driven by gale-force winds, quickly built to irregular shapes
six or eight feet high and no more than fifteen feet from crest to crest.
The canoe rapidly filled to the gunwales as wavetops fell in and the
rain became an opaque curtain. Moser lay in the bottom of the boat,
bailing with the rusty tin can and continuing to hum his hymn through
gritted teeth. Before the storm had crashed upon him he had been praying
happily for deliverance; now he prayed quietly for his soul. The river
tore at the boat and spun it uncontrollably as lightning zapped and smoked,
leaving a strong scent of electrical discharge in the air. The thunder
rolled and cracked without pause.

Then there was a lull as the wind dropped to nearly nothing, and
the night once again became hot and still. Thunder growled in the middle
distance. Moser bailed the boat out completely and checked the fittings.
The forward lashing on the outrigger had broken loose and he rewrapped
it with bits of the net. The fish had washed away save for two that
lay in the bilge. Moser threw those away; his stomach was queasy from
the ones he had eaten earlier, nearly raw. He unshipped his second
paddle and once again began to pull at an angle across the current.
Then the rain returned and the wind filled in from the opposite direction,
from the northwest. Pushed by wind and current, Moser once again

saw the Thai bank closing in the flashes of lightning. He pulled on, cursing and praying and fighting against the pain in his body and the fatigue in his head. The waves that towered and crashed in the middle of the river became more tortured and confused as they were met by the opposing wind. Once again the boat began to fill and Moser had to stop paddling and bail for his life. The southern shore rushed up in the lightning flashes and the boat pounded on the bottom in the troughs of waves.

The river roared and spat at Moser as the volume of the rain quickened the current. The bank in front of him was steep, with giant trees growing right down to the water's edge, their branches and exposed roots reaching out toward his boat. The boar caught on a root as it rushed along, spinning out of control, and the outrigger tore off with hardly a sound. The dugout immediately capsized, throwing Moser under the churning water. He held his breath in the total darkness as the current rolled him. He felt the roots under the river grapple for him, trying to hold him down. He struck the bottom frequently, and then suddenly he was lying on his back on a sand beach, his head and chest out of the water. He blinked his eyes as the rain rinsed them free of the river's grit, then dug the heels of his hands into the sand and pulled his legs free of the pull of the current. The wind continued to howl overhead and once again swung around to the southeast. Moser rolled over and crawled to the edge of the trees, then huddled in between the roots of an old trunk. It must have been a waterspout that pushed me across, he thought. Or the hand of the blessed Lord. He knew from the way the current had pushed him that he had been beached on the right bank of the Mekong, in Thailand. He was completely exhausted and wanted only to sleep, but he felt he should say a prayer of thanksgiving. He could think of nothing except a prayer from distant childhood:

> Now I lay me down to sleep, I pray the Lord my soul to keep,
> And if I die before I wake, I pray the Lord my soul to take.

Moser pulled his knees up against his chest. When the morning comes, he thought, I will find Thais and then Americans, and then I will go and gather the others for Jesus' sake. He thought then of Lieutenant Stuart, and he said his message to him aloud: It's Moser, sir. I'm alive.

Moser's head fell slowly to his knees and he slept as the storm boomed away to the northeast mountains and blew itself out.

*   *   *

Bannerman Phatang was roused early by a group of the village elders. It was barely light and the bannerman felt a little the worse for the large meal and the plentiful local rice brew from the night before. He would have preferred to sleep, but the elders told him excitedly that the escaped prisoner he sought had been in their camp the night before and stolen a boat. Phatang pulled his high-topped sneakers on over his bare feet and followed his hosts to the river's edge, where several people were gathered around one of the carved wooden posts that were used to tether the boats but that now stood clear. "Could the boat not simply have blown away in the storm?" asked Phatang of the headman.

"Oh, no, Phatang," said the old man, tapping the top of the carved pole with his gnarled hand. "The poles are driven deep, and join the earth spirit with the river spirit where the water flows beneath the sand. When the river spirit fights with the earth spirit and takes a boat he takes the pole as well, or at least breaks the rope and leaves a piece to show his anger."

Phatang squatted and gripped the pole and pushed. It certainly seemed well enough set, and there was no remnant of the boat's rope painter. "Perhaps the wind untied the knot?"

The people laughed, a bit nervously. No one wanted to offend the Pathet Lao, especially not the district NCO. The elder spoke carefully. "Bannerman, the knot is a secret of our tribe. It is so clever only the initiated can tie it, and even the forest spirits can't untie it."

Phatang smiled. Ignorant savages, he thought, forgetting that before he had joined the Pathet Lao forces he had lived in a village much like this one, albeit in the mountains. All this nonsense about spirits! Still, these people were skilled fishermen, and it stood to reason that people who could build boats and make nets could tie up a boat securely. Nonetheless, it seemed far-fetched that an escaped prisoner could have come this far so quickly and that he would be in the very village Phatang had chosen to spend the night.

"He took fish," said an old crone in her high-pitched voice. "He took a whole stick of drying fish."

Phatang stood up. "Couldn't it simply have blown down in the wind, Old Aunt?" he asked.

"I came out in the night before the wind," said the woman loudly, as though talking to a simple child. "I took all into the storehouse; there was one stick missing."

Phatang considered. It made sense that an escaped prisoner might try to cross to Thailand, where Phatang had heard the imperialists had many bases and airplanes. He turned back to the elder. "Could he have crossed over in that boat?"

"Oh, yes," replied the elder, making a sweeping gesture over the river with his hand palm-downward. "On a fine, smooth day like this, yes, yes. But last night the Old Man of the South blew all night; surely the river would have claimed him."

"I will have to look for his body," said Phatang. "Will you help?"

"The reward you spoke of, Bannerman," said the old man, a cunning smile tickling the corners of his mouth. "Is it for the body, even though the life spirit is gone?"

"Yes, at least part of the reward would be paid for the body," said Phatang. "But the Vietnamese pig Major Nan will pay more if he is returned alive."

The villagers chuckled nervously. They feared the Vietnamese, whom they rarely saw, even more than the Pathet Lao. "We will help, Bannerman," said the elder, "and you will allow us to share the reward?"

"Of course. Now, do you have any idea where he might have washed ashore?"

"Most probably on this bank somewhere downstream," said the elder, and several others nodded. "Because the wind blew so hard from the south. Otherwise on the Long Sand Islands, where the river divides and the current flows over shallow shoals. We will send the women and children to walk down the shore, and the men will go to the islands."

"Good, Old Uncle," said Phatang, grinning. "I will accompany you in the boats."

Moser slept well into the heat of the morning, tossing and turning as insects buzzed and bit and pestered his nose and mouth. He knew he should be up and moving, but lack of food and sleep, plus the battering he had received in the storm, had sapped the very last of his energy. Soon he would get up, as soon as he felt just a little stronger. Now that he was in Thailand he could move in daylight and on roads, and soon he would find a village and people. Just a little more sleep, he thought, swiping ineffectually at the flies with his hand. A bird trilled nearby, very loud, a harsh, repeated sound. Moser willed it to leave him in peace, but it trilled and trilled. I might as well get up and start moving, he thought. I have to find food, and then people. Thais, and then Americans. He uncoiled his body out of the damp hollow at the base of the tree and forced his leaden eyes to open. The bird trilled loudly, from very close. Moser's eyes focussed and he saw a wizened old man dressed only in a blue loincloth squatting six feet away on the sand, making the trilling sound with his mouth through cupped hands. When the man saw Moser's eyes open the man stood up and drew a machete from the woven grass sheath belted around his waist. Moser stood, swaying slightly as he became fully awake. Three other men came running up the beach, all small and brown and dressed in loincloths like the first. A somewhat taller man, dressed in a shirt and pants of purple-blue that didn't quite match and high-topped sneakers, walked slowly up to join the group of men in loincloths, who pointed to Moser and chattered like happy monkeys. The bigger man grinned and nodded. Moser saw that he had a revolver in his waistband. The man looked somehow familiar, but Moser's exhausted brain couldn't place him. Moser pointed to the big man and said, "Thai? Thailand?"

The men all laughed. The uniformed man said something in a soft, musical language and two of the others approached Moser with pieces of twisted rope. Moser stepped back and struck the tree behind him. He tried to resist but the little men were strong and quickly had his arms bound behind him. It shouldn't matter, he thought. The Thais would recognize him as an American, and they would contact their American allies. "Thai?" he repeated.

"Lao," said the man in the uniform, with a grin. "Lao."

"No!" shouted Moser, as the two men who had tied him began marching him along the beach. He looked at the river, which flowed strongly from his left to his right as it went east toward Vietnam. He was certainly on the right bank. "Thailand!" There had to be a mistake.

The men marched him a hundred yards or so to a spit of land where there were three dugouts pulled up on the sand. The man in uniform took Moser's elbow and gestured he should walk a little farther, to a place where the riverbank seemed to end. Moser found himself on the end of the land, and he could see the great river flowing around both sides. The south bank was across a channel perhaps three hundred yards wide and the north much farther away, barely discernible in the haze. The man in the purple uniform grinned and pointed to the north. "Laos," he said, and then pointed to the ground beneath his feet. "Laos," he said again, and then waved at the south bank. "*Thai-ko.*" The man in the uniform shook his head and grinned, then led Moser back to the boats where the others waited.

Moser had little precise memory of the long march from the Mekong back to the High Camp. His arms were bound at all times and in each village he was paraded before the people and often beaten. Stops were infrequent, though; the Pathet Lao were anxious to receive the promised large reward, and the last day they even marched into the evening, reaching the High Camp well after dark. When they reached Nan's camp the Pathet Lao troops were paid and told to leave. Moser was dumped like a sack of rice in the center of the camp, bound and blindfolded. He heard the guards shouting and pushing the other prisoners into formation, felt the heat of a large fire, and smelled the burning thatch. Then Nan had begun speaking, his voice edged with rage, high-pitched and stuttering. It seemed to Moser that Nan was afraid, as he ranted on in English and sometimes French and Vietnamese. *Pour encourager les autres*, he raved, over and over again. *Pour encourager les autres*, and then a Vietnamese word or phrase Moser had never heard, *cac rach nat*, and then repeated, *cac rach nat*. And then Moser had been jerked off his feet and hog-tied, his loincloth torn away. He had felt the steel of Sergeant Minh's knife, cold against his skin, and then the pain that seared throughout his body to the ends of his fingers and toes, to the lids of his eyes and the skin of his scalp. *Pour encourager les autres, cac rach nat*. To give courage to the others, mutilation.

II
THE CRAZY MAN'S PLACE

SEVEN

Lt. William McGowen Stuart, USNR, parked his four-year-old Chevy convertible in the parking lot behind the Officers' Open Mess. He straightened the blouse of his service dress blue uniform and walked around to the side entrance. A steady stream of officers from all four armed services entered and left the club, many of high rank and many in dress uniforms, including fancy, nineteenth-century-looking Army Dress Blue. Snappy salutes were rendered by juniors and returned with studied John Wayne laziness by colonels, navy captains, and even a few generals and admirals. Stuart saluted his way up the path and inside, and was glad to be relieved of his cap and further ceremonial responsibility at the coat-check.

What a contrast to Vietnam, thought Stuart, where a nasty war with men in green or camouflage uniforms soaked with sweat and covered with mud continued despite less and less agreement in Washington and the nation as to its reason or even its goal. Stuart was jostled by a beefy army colonel in the narrow passageway and shrank respectfully into the coatrack to let him pass with a whispered "Good morning, Colonel." The noon stampede to the bar continued to swell and the young lieutenant was carried along.

William Stuart had been serving in Washington at the Naval Investigative Service, a branch of the Naval Intelligence Command, for just over a year, after leaving Vietnam wounded in body and spirit. His extended tour had been completed in a hospital in Danang not long after the Tet Offensive of January–February 1968. Tet had cost the American military effort its credibility, Lyndon Johnson his presidency, and some said it had cost America its first defeat in a foreign war. That it had also cost the Viet Cong nearly all of its main force units and the North Vietnamese Army three and a half of its eighteen divisions had received little notice in the American press.

Tet held a special sadness mixed with anger for William Stuart, the commander at the time of an Air and Naval Liaison Company (ANGLICO) detachment operating from Danang. During Tet and the marine and army clearing operations that followed, when all Viet Cong and NVA troops in the South had been smashed or forced to flee to their sanctuaries in North Vietnam, Laos, and Cambodia, Stuart had lost three of his noncommissioned officers, three of the finest men he had ever known: Billy Hunter, Douglas Moser, and Bobby Coles. Sgt. Billy Hunter, USMC, the cheerful country boy from Arkansas with an unspoken tragedy in his memory had been the first, killed the night the assault began, shot down in a dusty yard at Camp Tien Shaw while trying to get a message through to headquarters that Stuart and the others were trapped by the assault; Billy died alone after enduring great pain from his wound. Thirty days later, as the marines followed the fleeing NVA north and west, Douglas MacArthur Moser, Gunner's Mate (Guns) Third Class, USN, the confused and exploited brawler from the mountains of Georgia whom Stuart had started on a path to self-knowledge and self-respect, and who had assigned himself the role of Stuart's personal protector and even his conscience, had taken a bullet aimed at the lieutenant. The wound had been serious but not life-threatening if treated quickly, but the helicopter that carried Moser to safety on the casualty treatment ship had been shot down. Moser and everybody in it had been burned beyond recognition.

Stuart sighed, glad of his anonymity in the Fort Myer crowd as he waited in line for the cafeteria service in the informal mess where the junior officers usually had lunch. The field and flag grade officers disappeared into the larger dining room. Stuart's eyes burned and salt tears collected in his throat every time he thought of his fallen men, his friends, and he thought of them almost every day and certainly every night. Marine Staff Sergeant Bobby Coles, a fiercely proud black man from the Watts ghetto in Los Angeles, a university graduate who wanted to play pro football and be a lawyer, a man of infinite promise, had fallen last, gutshot, and died all night on the edge of a stream with Stuart holding him against the cold of his ebbing strength. Stuart was in the hospital and then out of the war after that, and Vietnam was frozen inside him, as real as when he smelled and tasted and felt it every day, but locked away in a space in his mind, a large space, a major part of him still, but locked away, for the moment secure. Stuart was reminded of those dark houses in zoos where the people stumble about in inky blackness watching bats and other wide-eyed night creatures crawling around in dim yellow light behind thick glass. Nam was packed away in his brain, sealed off, but all the night eyes were still there and still watching.

William passed through the cafeteria line, receiving a cheeseburger and serving himself a large salad. He added a pint glass of beer, paid the cashier, and carried his tray into the informal dining area of the Officers' Open Mess. Maj. Harry MacAndrew, the head of the Naval Investigative Service—Code 41, Foreign Counterintelligence—waved to him, motioning him to a table in a corner where MacAndrew sat alone. Stuart set his tray down and sat across from the section leader.

"Glad your duties permitted you to join me, Lieutenant," said MacAndrew, a smile crinkling his ruddy face around his clear blue eyes. MacAndrew was a short man and stocky, with iron-gray hair cut close to his scalp. He was dressed in sharply creased gray trousers and a blue blazer, and wore a Chevy Chase Club tie.

"Glad to come, Major," said Stuart, who worked as an analyst-supervisor in Code 42, Domestic Counterintelligence. "Though Tom remarked as I signed out, and not for the first time, that I spend far too much time with you." Tom Miller, the head of 42, was a civilian, as were all the section heads at NIS. MacAndrew had been in the Marine Corps, serving in World War II and Korea. He had been invalided out of the marines, all his toes and half his right foot lost to frostbite in the breakout and withdrawal from the Chosen Reservoir in 1950. MacAndrew was treated as military and therefore significant by the naval officers on the staff, while Miller was not.

MacAndrew laughed. "Doubtless he fears my evil influence, and not necessarily without cause. But I wanted to talk to you before I talked to him. I have a job for you to do."

"Great, if Tom will let me do it. I have been trying to get over to 41 since I landed here last year."

"This time you will, if you want to." MacAndrew looked at the tall young man, and let his gaze flow across the serious ribbons on his chest. Maybe this man has done enough, he thought. "Do you? It may mean a short extension."

Stuart winced. His extra time in Nam had entitled him to get out of the navy next month. He was close to taking a job on "the outside." "What is it, Major?"

"Douglas MacArthur Moser is alive."

Stuart had a sip of beer in his mouth and almost choked. He set the glass down hurriedly. A thundering roar echoed inside his head as he felt the thick glass that sealed off Nam shatter and the memories surge into the rest of his brain. He fought the urge to gag at the stench of death and rot and he suddenly heard a gabble of voices, among them those of his fallen comrades. Flashes of light assaulted his eyes from within and then the explosion retreated, slithering back to its own corner and rebuilding the barrier as it went. Stuart felt that his panic must have lasted minutes and have been written all over his face, but he knew it had taken less than a heartbeat, and he forced himself to speak calmly. "M–Moser died in a helo crash, Major, in February '68, in Quang Tri Province."

MacAndrew took an envelope from his inside pocket and carefully withdrew a single sheet of shiny, greasy paper, lined in blue like a page from a child's exercise book. He passed it across to Stuart, who pushed his plates aside to smooth it out on the table. It had obviously been through many hands. The writing was faded, in gray ink, but Stuart immediately recognized the careful block printing as Moser's.

DEAR MOMMA
THERE LETTIN US WRITE THROUGH THE RED CROSS. I'M A PRISNER BUT I AM OK. ITS REAL PRETTY HERE, AND IN THE EVENING IT REMINDS ME OF THE CRAZY MAN'S PLACE NEAR THE BRIDGE. WE ONLY GIT 50 WORDS. TELL MR STUART. LOVE YOU MOMMA DONT WORRY.
DOUGLAS MOSER GMG 3 USN, B 80 42 42.

Stuart stared at the simple message, reading it over and over, trying to imagine the writer as a prisoner. Moser had been so big and so full of strength and life, and once he had got his shit together and made third class, had shown quiet purpose. Moser had fiercely protected Stuart's back until the lieutenant's carelessness had gotten the big man killed.

Stuart had never doubted the report of Moser's death, and yet here was his handwriting, and the cryptic note. "How did you get this, Major?" he asked.

"His mother got it through the Red Cross. She had sense enough to inform the local sheriff, who called the Georgia State Police, who notified the FBI. The Bureau gave it to me this morning."

"Do you have any idea how old it is?"

"Months, certainly. Maybe even close to a year. The Red Cross gets very little cooperation out of the North Vietnamese."

"So he could have been moved from wherever he wrote this." Stuart sensed that Moser was trying to tell him something about his location, the stuff about the crazy man's place. If so, he had been clever to phrase it to get it past the censor.

"Almost certainly," said Harry MacAndrew quietly. "It is also possible that he has died."

No, thought Stuart. If he survived the bullet and the helo crash, and made it all the way to a camp far enough in the rear to get a visit from the Red Cross, he would live. "But it is possible that he is alive, Major, and still in the same place." Stuart knew that the North Vietnamese held many more prisoners than could be accounted for in the camps the CIA claimed to have located.

"It is possible. Will you try to find out?"

"Of course. But how? Where do we start?" The letter is addressed to me, he thought, suddenly energized by the thought of a rescue mission. I'd be eating fire again, not paper dust, he felt, his heart racing. I'd be doing something *real*.

Harry MacAndrew pushed back his chair and stood, awkwardly. He still walked with a pronounced limp from his injuries. "We start by getting you transferred to me and, I am sorry to say, extended for an extra ninety days. I'll see Tom this afternoon as soon as we get back to Arlington; I don't think he will fight me on this one, but if he does I'll go to the old man. Are you willing to extend?"

"Jesus, Major, the man saved my life at least twice." Stuart got up and followed MacAndrew's fast, rolling gait. "I will want to work on this full time, Major."

MacAndrew stopped at the door and patted Stuart's shoulder. "I knew you would. You are a good analyst and you might get lucky. Go clean out your desk, and then you and I should plan on calling on Moser's mother."

Stuart grinned, holding the greasy letter in front of him. "Then you see it too. This letter is trying to tell us something about his location."

"Right," nodded MacAndrew. "We have to get her to show us this crazy man's place near a bridge."

Northern Georgia, 8 May 1969

Stuart dozed in the back of the gray Ford van, swaying in his seat as the vehicle ground up the rutted mountain road in four-wheel drive. Harry MacAndrew sat in front with the NIS special agent from the Atlanta field office who had picked them up after their very early flight from National Airport in Washington. The agent, who introduced himself as Tom Cox, had said little, other than that he had called Mrs. Moser and she would be waiting. Cox headed north on U.S. 19, estimating the hundred-mile drive would take three hours, with the last fifteen miles after the paved roads petered out taking an hour by itself. The agent was a cheerful man with a back-country Southern accent who seemed happy to get out of his office and spend a day in the woods.

Stuart pressed his head against the pillow he had made of his ski parka against the side of the van. The morning was chilly in the mountain mists but the van was overheated. Stuart had dressed for the trip in jeans, short boots, and a woollen shirt. He felt hot and wished he had a window to open to get some air. He was tired and a little hung over. At the party in Georgetown the previous evening he had found himself drifting into corners, away from the other guests, wanting to be alone, his mind racing with memories of Vietnam. To think that Moser could be alive gave his spirits a sudden lift. To think of that big, proud man rotting in a North Vietnamese prison immediately brought him back down. As the depressing scenes inside his head had multiplied, he had thought the application of a little more booze might drive them away. But, if anything, the scotch reinforced his inner concentration on the rapidly spinning kaleidoscope of terrible images. Alcohol hadn't eased his pain; it never did.

William Stuart had grown up in genteel conditions on the large horse farm his family owned in northern Virginia. William and his sister had grown up riding with their father and playing games in the vast formal gardens overseen by his mother. Stuart was graduated from Georgia Tech in 1966 with a degree in engineering and an ROTC commission in the Naval Reserve. He had figured to do his three years in the navy as a kind of obligatory national service. He had never thought about the war in Vietnam one way or another until one day it was all around him. It stayed around him for two years, focussing him and hardening him as no previous experience had done. By the time he came home to the cold hostility and cruel jeers of an ungrateful nation he felt he was a leader of proven abilities, sobered yet strengthened by the intimate experiences of killing and death. He hated the war with all his being because of what it had taken from him and how it was tearing at the country, but at the same time it was the most important event in his young life and he couldn't let it go.

Stuart's mind returned to Douglas MacArthur Moser. Moser was a huge man of phenomenal physical strength with a reputation for fighting and getting into trouble. When Stuart joined the *Valley Forge* he was assigned by the gunnery division officer, Philip Hooper, to straighten Moser out. Stuart had worked cautiously to penetrate the big man's shyness and eventually a strong bond, never spoken of, formed between the two men. Moser ran the ship's armory, where the small arms were kept. He had a natural dexterity and skill with guns. Stuart had encouraged him to strike for gunner's mate and helped him through the written material required for the third class test. Stuart smiled as he remembered how badly Moser had wanted that third class Crow, and how diligently he had worked despite the ridicule of his division mates. Moser had passed, and day by day had become more sure of himself and more effective as a petty officer. Moser, for his part, had assigned himself the duty of becoming Stuart's personal guardian, going along with his .50 calibre machine gun whenever Stuart drew duty in the landing craft.

Stuart shifted his position in his seat and smiled. In retrospect, he considered his war had been relatively sane and comprehensible through 1967. His ANGLICO unit would be attached periodically to various army maneuver units, rarely smaller than a battalion, and would spot naval gunfire and occasionally air strikes. It was a challenging job and sometimes frightening, but Stuart and his men rode with the command staff and were rarely in personal danger. The war went crazy for the ANGLICO with the Tet Offensive and the Marine counterattacks that followed. A month after Tet Stuart woke up in a hospital with wounds in both legs, and with the searing nightmare memories of the deaths of all three of his unit's noncommissioned officers. Stuart returned to the world, and now he sat in his office at NIS in Arlington, keeping tabs on the radicals in the SDS, the Panthers and dozens of other antiwar groups, watching and making lists of persons of counterintelligence interest, watching as the war continued to kill Americans in Vietnam and claw at the vitals of the nation at home. Every day he fought within himself to prevent his anger and his sorrow from becoming bitterness and cynicism. He felt he had an obligation, although on some days he wasn't sure to whom, but he knew for sure he owed his men, and the men he served with who had sacrificed so much more than he had.

But now Moser was alive again and had called to him. Tell Mr. Stuart to come back for me, the letter said. The message was personal, just as the war was personal, as service to a country or a cause was personal. Tell Mr. Stuart I'm alive.

A particularly savage lurch of the van caused him to bang his head against the side panel and woke him up. "How much longer to Breaker's Holler?" he shouted up to the special agent.

"'Bout two miles. Nearly there," the man called back, still cheerful.

Stuart rubbed the knot on his head and sat back. He remembered the last time he had come up here, a year ago when he had just got back from Nam. He had driven down from Virginia as soon as he had checked in for his new assignment at NIS and sat with Moser's mother, Jean-Ann, trying to tell her how much Moser had meant to him and how he had covered Stuart's back in the troop landing craft he had piloted up the dark channel of the Cua Viet River in I Corps, and later with the ANGLICO in the bush. Stuart had talked for about an hour, holding both of Jean-Ann's hands in his. She had cried and thanked him for coming, and then asked about Moser's back pay and insurance. He had left in the afternoon and driven back as far as Greenville, South Carolina, before he found a motel for the night.

Stuart remembered Jean-Ann as a pretty woman, with soft red hair and a slim but curvy body poured into tight jeans. She couldn't have been more than thirty-five or -six, but looked older. A pretty woman who could have been beautiful if she had had an easier life.

The truck bumped off the dirt track and turned into a barely visible path into the woods. The special agent pulled up in front of a small log shack with a tar paper roof and immediately jumped down. A yellow hound with a lame back leg gave a mournful howl and hopped down from the porch. Harry MacAndrew climbed slowly from the passenger seat, his back and legs painfully stiff from the long ride. He opened the side door of the van and let Stuart out. The three men walked toward the porch. The dog snuffled and crouched in the damp earth.

"It's not the same place she lived last year," said Stuart, looking around at the rusted shells of two old pickups and an ancient refrigerator with a coil on top that littered the yard beside the house.

"I checked the directions with her when I called," said Cox. "She said she been here about six months."

Harry MacAndrew fondled the old dog's floppy ears and stepped carefully past. He rapped sharply on the doorjamb. The cabin echoed back with a hollow sound. "There wouldn't appear to be anybody here," he said, trying to peer through the dirty window next to the heavy wooden door.

"We are a mite early," said Cox. "I told her noon or a little after." Stuart's stomach growled as he looked at his watch. Eleven-thirty. He regretted that he had passed up the doughnut and coffee on the flight. "I got coffee and sandwiches in the van, hey," continued the special agent. Bless you, thought Stuart.

The hound gave out a low, keening sound without rising. A voice from behind the NIS officers said softly, "You boys lost?" Stuart turned and saw a big, powerfully built man dressed in a wool shirt, filthy overalls, and high boots. He held a double-barreled shotgun loosely in both hands, the muzzle pointed approximately at Stuart's feet.

Cox held his hands in front of him, palms open and outward. "Could be that we are, sir. We are looking for Jean-Ann Moser."

"Who wants her?" said the man, expressionless and unmoving.

"We are from the Naval Investigative Service," said Cox, not visibly worried about the gun. "It's about her son, Douglas."

"Government men," the man sneered.

"Right," said Cox, with no hint of apology. "We called. She's agreed to talk to us."

"Jean-Ann!" the man bellowed, his head cocked over his shoulder. "Government men for you!"

The clearing was silent after the shout, and then a blue pickup, scarcely less rusty than the wrecks in the yard, rolled down the path into the clearing, its motor off. Stuart recognized the driver as Moser's mother.

Jean-Ann slid down from the truck's high seat. Stuart saw she still fitted the tight blue jeans. She wore a short jacket of ratty fur and her red hair was tied in a blue scarf. She smiled at Stuart, a coy and somewhat provocative look. "Hello, Lieutenant. It's nice to see you again." Her voice was low and she sounded genuinely pleased. The man with the shotgun looked at her sharply as she walked past him to shake Stuart's hand. "Put the gun down, Clem, this is Douglas's officer."

"Government men," said Clem, pushing past MacAndrew to open the door of the cabin. "I reckon you'll be wanting to come inside."

"Right neighborly," said Cox, with a ghost of a smile. Jean-Ann followed Clem inside and the three NIS officers trooped in afterward.

The inside of the cabin had a different air than the dilapidated exterior, displaying, Stuart guessed, the different personalities of Clem and Jean-Ann. The floor of broad white-pine boards was well swept and covered in spots by bright handwoven rugs. The furniture was simple, bare wood except one long couch whose faded cover had been carefully mended. The kitchen to one side had a huge woodstove of black iron, a deep sink with a hand pump, and a new electric refrigerator. The counters in the kitchen and the deal table that separated it from the rest of the room were scrubbed clean.

Cox introduced himself and Major MacAndrew. Jean-Ann smiled pleasantly and introduced the man as Clem Watkins. Clem grunted, set the shotgun on two hooks on the lintel of the front door, pulled a chair into a corner, and propped its back against the wall. Jean-Ann set out cups and saucers on the table and put a kettle on the stove, then took a fresh-baked loaf of bread, sliced it onto a cracked blue plate, and got butter from the fridge. Stuart felt his mouth water as he sat and waited while Jean-Ann poured boiling water directly onto coffee grounds in a chipped enamel pot, added an egg and some chicory, and brought it to the table. She asked about their drive up from Atlanta as she worked and Cox answered cheerfully. Stuart noticed that the agent's accent had become more pronounced as he talked first to Clem and then to Jean-Ann. I am glad we brought him, Stuart thought. Jean-Ann finally sat, and pushed the plate of sliced bread and the butter toward Stuart with her slow, inviting smile. Stuart buttered a slice and ate it quickly; he immediately began to feel better. The coffee helped as well. Jean-Ann refilled his cup.

Harry MacAndrew cleared his throat. "Mrs. Moser, we have come to ask your help. We are going to try to locate your son."

"Sure." Jean-Ann looked suddenly uncertain and glanced uneasily at Clem, silent in the corner.

"Mrs. Moser—" continued the major, following the glance.

"Jean-Ann, please," she said. "Just call me Jean-Ann."

"Jean-Ann." MacAndrew smiled his most charming foxy-grandpa smile. "I'm Harry." Jean-Ann nodded and once again glanced toward Clem. "We have the letter your son sent to you. In it he mentions a place, a crazy man's place near a bridge. Does that mean anything to you?"

Jean-Ann nodded. "I know where it is."

"Not that you'd be wantin' to take no government men up there," growled Clem.

Cox turned to look at Clem, smiling his homeboy grin. "Now, sir, I want you both to understand, we ain't the police, and we ain't Treasury ATF. Y'all got something y'all don't want the government to see, we ain't gonna see it. All we want to find out is whether the place young Moser wrote about in his letter could maybe help us figure out where he might be a prisoner. We do that, and we be gone."

Clem rocked forward, letting the chair legs fall to the floor. He looked at Cox, and then at Stuart and MacAndrew. "That right by you, Major?"

"It is," said MacAndrew, evenly.

"The crazy man's place is in the Chestatee Gorge," said Jean-Ann, quickly, as though she feared being cut off by the scowling Clem. "Maybe ten miles from here."

"How can we find it?" asked Cox.

Clem got up slowly. "You never would. I'll have to show you."

"We'd sure appreciate that," said Major MacAndrew.

Clem smiled slightly. "I was thinkin' y'all'd pay me for the guidin'."

"A fair price," said Major MacAndrew, his face taut.

"Done. Two ways to go," said Clem, retrieving the shotgun. "We can get a boat at Bull's Landing and go on the river and climb up, or walk in from Bow's Crossing and climb down."

"Let's go by boat," said MacAndrew. "I'll let these younger men do the climbing."

"And then y'all be gone, and we don't see no more government men," said Clem, thrusting his face close to the major's.

"That's our deal," said MacAndrew, pushing back his chair. Stuart could see he was getting angry.

"Then let's get her done," said Clem. "That van o' yourn four-wheel?"

"Yeah," answered Cox.

Stuart took another slice of the fragrant bread as he stood. Jean-Ann put a hand on his arm as Clem led the other men out the cabin door. "Lieutenant?"

"Yes, Jean-Ann."

"Um. Now that Douglas's alive again," she flushed pink and bowed her head. "I gotta give back the insurance?"

Jesus, thought Stuart, fighting disgust. But hell, these people are poor. "I don't think so, Jean-Ann. Don't you worry about it unless I call you."

"Thanks." She still averted her face. "You gonna go get him?"

"I am going to sure try."

"God, I really miss him." Tears started quickly. Stuart put his arm across her shoulders and hugged her lightly. She blotted her tears on his shirt, and nodded vigorously. "I think he knows you will come. He always trusted you."

"I owe him, Jean-Ann, you know that. I think I'd go even if I didn't, but owing him means I have to."

"Nobody cares about those boys over there. Everybody just hates the war."

Stuart nodded, wishing he had something comforting to say. "I'd better get on, Jean-Ann. Don't forget, you need anything, you have my number."

She squeezed his arm and stepped back. He let his arm fall, walked through the open door, and climbed in the back of the van next to the rank-smelling, scowling Clem Watkins. Cox reversed the van past the blue truck and back onto the dirt road.

Bull's Landing

Major MacAndrew paid the man called Bull twenty dollars to rent an aluminum skiff with a twenty-five horsepower motor for two hours, and another fifty "deposit." MacAndrew thought sourly that the chances of the same man being there to return his fifty when they got back were between slim and none. Clem climbed into the stern and started the motor, which ran roughly while putting out a cloud of blue smoke that settled on the smooth-flowing black water of the river. Stuart and Cox climbed into the bow thwart with the camera bag. Stuart stood and took MacAndrew's arm, steadying him as he struggled aboard and took his seat in the middle thwart. Without comment Clem put the stuttering motor in gear and the boat shot forward, pulling swiftly into the center of the stream.

Stuart sat facing forward, watching the heavily wooded banks of the river slide by, their silence shattered by the sound and the echo of the engine. Well, Moser, we know we are talking about a river bridge. You are near a river. It wouldn't look like the Chestatee, of course. Water in tropical rivers was green from growth or reddish brown from sediment, while the acid from leaf litter and runoff made this river's water black. The trees would be different: at a similar altitude there tropical hardwoods, tamarind, teak and tropical oaks, thick with undergrowth and creepers. Here we have tall Southern pine and a few live oak, widely separated and with almost no vegetation pushing through the thick carpet of needles on the ground.

The boat rounded a headland and the river narrowed abruptly, hemmed in by walls of exposed granite that rose on either bank to a height above the river of sixty feet. The river's rhythm quickened as the boat entered the gorge, and the banks went by more slowly as the old motor fought the current. They rounded another bend and Clem headed for a fallen tree on the right bank that shielded a dark pool. Above stretched an arched trestle of rusted iron with weathered stone footings. The bridge had no road crossing it, and from below they could see rotted railroad ties and twisted rails. Clem shouted for Cox to tie the boat's painter to the fallen tree, then gunned the motor to kick the stern toward the shore and shut it off. Clem jumped out onto the narrow sand beach and pulled the stern in. The three NIS men climbed out, MacAndrew leaning on Stuart's shoulder.

"Where is the crazy man's place?" asked MacAndrew.

"'Bout halfway up," said Clem, suddenly cheerful. "Worth the climb, too. Who's gonna climb?"

"Stuart and Cox, go ahead. Take one camera and leave one," said MacAndrew. "I'll try to get this place inside me from down here."

Stuart and Cox followed Clem, who set a fast pace up an invisible trail. Stuart estimated that the bridge was about fifty feet above the river, with the highest points of the cliffs perhaps twenty feet farther up. The trail wound around trees and rock outcrops and switched back on itself many times, and Stuart soon found himself breathing hard as he watched Clem's broad back, with the shotgun slung muzzle-down, always seeming about to disappear and lose him. Cox's labored breathing from behind cheered Stuart as his city boots slipped in the damp earth and gravel and his elbows and knees gathered bruises.

Clem raised his hand to halt them at a point where the trail passed along a cliff of decomposed granite on a crumbling ledge no more than eighteen inches wide. Stuart looked at the dark river far below, and his stomach tightened at the prospect of negotiating the narrow ledge with its surface of weathered flakes of stone. Clem spoke softly. "Better I go on ahead. The crazy man be just that, and he prob'ly ain't seen a stranger in thirty, forty years."

"We nearly there?" wheezed Cox, breathing and swallowing as he looked over the cliff.

"Just around here. You got money?" said Clem, grinning.

"What the hell do we need money for?" asked Stuart.

"Crazy man sells whiskey. Stranger-man, 'specially city man come up, bother him, and then don' *buy* nothin', he gonna take exception." Clem reached back and patted the stock of his shotgun. "Likely take exception with one o' these."

Stuart took a ten-dollar bill from his pocket. "Try to get some change back. I guess that would buy more moonshine than we could carry down this hill."

"Whiskey, not moonshine. *Good* whiskey, and by the time we do get it down, it'll be twice as old as when he sells it." Clem snapped the ten out of Stuart's hand with two fingers. "Y'all come when I call you, hear?" He turned and walked rapidly along the ledge and out of sight around the bend without taking any apparent notice of the footing or the river far below.

"You get the feeling we are following a wild goose?" said Cox softly, as his breathing became more even.

"Well, Clem is surely enjoying himself," replied Stuart, taking off a boot and rubbing his bruised toes. "But we have to see the place. Moser had to mean something."

"This Moser was some friend of yours, hey?"

Stuart sighed. He still hadn't gotten fully used to the big man's death, let alone his apparent resurrection. "He was a good sailor, he was fiercely loyal to me, and he protected me in the field, Cox. Given the way this country treats Vietnam vets, his loyalty and courage make him seem all the more important."

Cox nodded. A shout came from beyond the ledge. "Y'all come!"

Stuart shrugged. "I'll go first, Cox, and kick loose a few stones."

"I'd appreciate that, sir," said Cox. "I'm a hick and proud of it, but I ain't no mountain man."

Stuart slid along the ledge, moving quickly and forcing himself to look not down at the river or his boots but forward along the trail. He rounded the blind bend of the cliff and entered a broad clearing. Cox followed, a second behind. Clem stood with a twisted old man, his hand holding the man's shoulder in what looked like a restraining grip. The old man squirmed, his eyes darting. He had snow white hair and a beard that flowed to his waist. Behind them both Stuart could see a small cabin with gray smoke seeping from a fieldstone chimney, and beside it an open-sided shed that covered a copper still. There was a large, well-tended vegetable garden and a chicken coop full of noisy birds. The end of the arched bridge was thirty meters beyond.

"Strangers, Clem!" rasped the old man. "Flatlanders! City folk!"

"Be easy, Ben. They just come to look around." Clem grinned, toasted Stuart and Cox with a tin cup, and then drank.

"Po–lice? Revenuers?" the old man quailed.

"Just visitors, sir," said Cox, his accent grown yet thicker. "We mean no harm, and will soon be gone."

Stuart looked at the camp and at the bridge. What are you trying to tell me, Moser? he thought. He unslung the Nikon camera and took pictures of the camp and the bridge, then walked to the bridge itself and took more. The bridge was clearly impassable and seemed ready to fall into the river in the next good blow. The crazy man continued to wail behind him.

"Seen what you want?" Clem spoke from directly behind him and Stuart jumped. Clem chuckled. "Come have a taste, an' we'll get on down this hill."

"Where does that bridge lead?" asked Stuart, sharply. I don't like the way this man creeps up, he thought. I am getting soft in Washington. In the field, people who crept up without you knowing it usually killed you.

"Old mine, I think," said Clem. "'Tain't been used in years. We go now?"

"Give me a few minutes, Clem," said Stuart, feeling the anger in his voice. Clem chuckled again and returned to the still.

I must take this place in, thought Stuart. Moser was a visual man, never good with words. He had become a master gunsmith because he could absorb diagrams the way many sailors could only read comics. In the field he had carried a sketchpad, drawing cartoons of the other men, and sometimes strangely beautiful line drawings of trees, flowers—and rivers. There is a picture here, and I have to see it.

The clearing suddenly became dark, as though a thick cloud had covered the sun. Stuart looked up through the trees, but the sky was still bright blue and cloudless. Nevertheless, the darkness deepened. "Hey, Clem?"

"Yo, government man." Clem sauntered to the bridge.

"Why has it gotten so dark all of a sudden?"

"There's a mountain to the west. Highest in Georgia, I heard, called Brasstown Bald. Throws a shadow over the whole valley. You want to see it, we gotta climb some more."

Stuart nodded. "Let's go."

Clem grinned, and hitched his shotgun higher on his back. "Follow me, boss." He set off along another trail along the cliff face without a backward glance. Stuart followed, slinging the camera.

The trail upward to the top of the cliff was much easier than the one from the river to the crazy man's camp. Clem loped along in an easy gait. He spoke over his shoulder. "Jean-Ann wanted me to ask you: now young Bubba Moser be alive again, we be gettin' his back pay?"

Stuart stared at the big man's back, suddenly angry. "I don't know. We will make sure *Jean-Ann* gets whatever is coming to her."

Clem stopped in a small clearing and turned, unslinging the shotgun in an easy, practiced movement. He held it at port-arms, across his broad chest. His face held an expression of pure meanness. "I want to tell you something, boss."

"Go ahead, Clem." Stuart walked closer, watching Clem's thick, dirty thumb touch the safety switch behind the twin breeches of the gun.

"I never much liked that boy," said Clem, raising the muzzle slightly. "We had us a fight, once."

"Bet he whipped you," said Stuart, easing a step closer.

"He did. Wasn't a fair fight, of course."

"You don't say."

"I do. You really gonna bring him back here?" Clem's breath was foul.

"We aim to find him if we can." Another inch closer. "And I expect he would come back here to his home."

Clem looked uneasy. "He might take exception—"

"Don't worry, Clem," said Stuart, amiably. "We'll see you get twenty-four hours warning so you can clear out of his mother's bed."

Clem's face darkened to mottled red. He started to bring the gun up. "Why you city son-of—"

Stuart snatched the gun from Clem's hands and with the same lunge shouldered the bigger man back. It was much the same movement with which a drill sergeant would take a rifle from a boot camp trainee for inspection. Clem didn't release the weapon as a proper boot would, and received a long gash on his finger from the trigger guard. Stuart stepped back. Clem looked startled as well as angry. He sucked his cut finger as Stuart jacked the gun open and palmed the shells, slipping them into the pocket of his parka.

"You got no call to take my gun!" shrieked Clem.

"Oh, I'm not taking it, Clem." Stuart smiled broadly. He felt pleased with his quickness and a little light-headed from the adrenaline rush. "I'll just tote it for you a while. Be rude to let you carry this heavy iron all the way up and down this mountain."

Clem sneered. "I could just walk off and lose you. You would never get off this mountain."

"I doubt I'd get lost this close to the river, Clem," said Stuart, still grinning as he slung the weapon over his shoulder. "I've been in the woods before, a lot darker than these. Besides, since I got your iron and you haven't been paid yet, I reckon you will want to stay close."

"Fuckin' smart-ass city man, I oughta break you in two."

"Let's just get on up to the summit, Clem; then we can all go home."

Clem turned and started up the rocky path, still cursing. In ten minutes they broke out of the thick woods onto the granite knoll that capped the cliff. Clem pointed to the west, where a high, conical mountain jutted a thousand feet higher than the surrounding hills. "That's Brasstown Bald." He walked twenty feet away from Stuart, sat on a rock, and began to cut a chew of tobacco from a thick plug with a wicked-looking narrow-bladed knife he pulled from his boot.

Stuart looked at the mountain and guessed it to be about two miles away. Bright sunlight shone around the peak, and the inky shadow of the mountain stretched to where he was standing and beyond. A somewhat smaller cone was barely visible in the shadow, perhaps a mile closer.

What is Moser telling us? he wondered. The bend of the river? The gorge? Maybe the bridge. Maybe he just made an observation for his mother, a touch of home to say he was all right, with no hidden meaning at all.

Stuart rejected the thought. It's something, and it is *here*. Moser would see the place he was in as a whole and try to describe the *feeling*. That eerie shadow, falling so quickly over the place at least two hours before the spring sunset, certainly would have affected Moser's sense of color and texture.

Stuart turned back toward the silent Clem. The terrain fell away to the east into a saddle, and beyond was another mountain, seeming taller than Brasstown Bald because it was much nearer, perhaps a half mile away. The deep shadow had just reached the cliff face, and the sharp silhouette of the western peak was projected on the granite cliff of the mountain to the east like a black arrowhead. Stuart looked back and forth. The two mountains were in a perfectly straight line, west to east, with the lower peak in the shadow in the same line. This has to matter, thought Stuart, getting excited. He took a series of photographs, knowing they would be of little use. Moser always read the topographic maps the unit carried in the field. Three mountains in a line with a river in the middle would stand out in the jumbled ranges of Southeast Asia. Moser is giving me an aerial view.

"We 'bout done? Better to be outta here 'fore dark," said Clem, rising.

"Yeah, we can go. Clem, does this place, this area have any special name?"

Clem shrugged. "Some folks call it like the Indians done. The Valley of the Shadow."

Night had fallen by the time the van pulled away from Clem and Jean-Ann's shack, and the dark woods were spooky in the sweep of the headlights. The noise of the truck grinding in low gear and the bouncing of the vehicle prevented much conversation. The van reached the paved road in less than an hour, and Cox drove swiftly south.

"Slow down, Tom," said Major MacAndrew. "We aren't going to make that last flight."

"Okay. You want to go to a hotel?"

"It would seem the best," said MacAndrew.

"Hey, great!" cheered Stuart. "A night on the town in sultry Atlanta, and all at government expense."

"Restrain yourself, Lieutenant," growled the major. "I don't even have funding for this mission yet."

"But you will get it," shouted Stuart from the back. "Hell, even the antiwar pukes in Washington won't begrudge prisoners of war their return."

MacAndrew twisted in his seat to look at the younger man. Stuart's face wore a broad grin, far different from his listless expression at the beginning of the long day. "You are really sure you saw something significant?"

"I think so. Moser would remember that place and those mountains marching from west to east in the setting sun. Remember his letter says *in the evening*. We are going to need aerial photos of the area, a full map work-up, then we go looking for a similar pattern in North Vietnam and Laos and Cambodia."

"Which is going to take special funding, which I will begin to seek as soon as we get home. By the way, I didn't see fit to ask before, but how did you happen to take possession of the charming Clem's shotgun?"

"He kept half-pointing it at me. I didn't like it so I took it away from him."

"Just like that?"

"Sure."

Stuart continued to look immensely pleased with himself. He really believes he can find Moser, mused MacAndrew. The major chuckled. Stuart was six feet one or so, about 190 pounds and clearly not in fighting trim. "I'd guess old Clem had two inches on you and twenty pounds, and I would guess he gets a lot more exercise than you have lately."

"Don't mean nothing," Stuart grinned. "I am cat-quick."

MacAndrew turned back in his seat, shaking his head. I have got to get that funding; Stuart has me convinced.

EIGHT

Trai o Bo Song (The River Camp), Thung Lung Toi, Laos,
9 May 1969

Douglas MacArthur Moser woke slowly in the still night, the snakes
in his dreams slipping naturally out of his head to join the snakes in
his tiger cage. There was no light yet, only the slight chill breeze that
always preceded the sun. Moser shifted slowly in the cramped pit, feeling
the waking reptiles as they slid away from his skin. Moser knew that
most of the snakes were deadly poisonous, but also that they meant
him no harm, wanting only to share the warmth of his body in his hole
in the ground. When he had first been brought here he had wished
for one to bite him, to kill him and end his sorrow, but that had been
when Major Nan had shamed him and despair seemed the only feeling left in his soul. Sergeant Minh had put him here alone as an example *pour encourager les autres* while his wound still burned and
his head still swam with madness and pain. Since then Moser had clung
to life despite privation, despite disease and his heavy labor, and despite
the daily reminders of his shame. Moser lived for the day when he
would catch the sergeant off guard and kill him. Then Moser would
lie and wait near the bridge like a cobra, and Major Nan would die,
and then Moser himself would be free to die. Moser had no idea how
these things might come about, but he lived on, knowing that he could
never go to rest a complete man until Major Nan was dead by his hands.

There was a faint light of dawn now, visible through the thick bamboo
bars that formed the ceiling of his cage. No light yet entered the pit

in which Trung-si Minh locked him every night. The snakes sensed the warming day and climbed silently up the damp earth walls and up through the grating, iridescent and brightly colored as they reached the light. Would that I were a snake, thought Moser. I would slide out of here and wait for Sergeant Minh and strike him, then hide by the bridge and wait for Major Nan to come down from the High Camp with the other prisoners.

Moser's tiger cage was four feet deep and five feet square, a small space for the six-foot-four-inch man. He had weighed 250 pounds when he had been captured, but poor food and disease had reduced him to a hollow-eyed skeleton of 160. His skin was covered with sores, some of them inches across, which had started as insect bites or minor scratches and never healed in the constant jungle dampness. Gook sores, the soldiers called them. He had lost most of his teeth and his left eye had grown cloudy. He knew he had many diseases but couldn't name them, and that the sharp pains in his gut were from worms. Despite the fever and the aches he retained at least a portion of his great physical strength, as hard as Sergeant Minh tried to work it out of him on the pumps. He was strong and he would not die until he could take his tormentors with him. He stretched, feeling carefully around him for a late-departing snake. The morning warmed; Sergeant Minh would come soon, to scorn him and take him to the river to wash, and then to the pumps. Moser began his daily silent dialogue with himself, building his hatred, preparing for another day of waiting for death: first Minh's, then Nan's, then his own.

I am Douglas MacArthur Moser, he chanted in his mind. I am a Gunner's Mate Third Class, United States Navy. I am a man, not an animal. I think and I feel. I am Douglas MacArthur Moser. I am a man; I am not—

"Con Trau Duc! Water Buffalo!" shouted Sergeant Minh, shuffling his rubber sandal and kicking a shower of dirt into Moser's pit. "Con Trau Duc, get up! The day awaits, and the water trough is nearly dry."

I am Douglas MacArthur Moser, he thought, as Sergeant Minh unlatched the bamboo grill. Moser stood, hoping he could grab Sergeant Minh's ankles with his clawlike hands, drag him down into the foul pit, and squeeze his life out, drowning him in the wet slime of the pit's floor. But Sergeant Minh knew his mind and had stepped well back, his Makarov pistol drawn, as Moser pulled his filthy body up and out into the morning. Without a word Moser pulled himself together and shambled stiffly down the narrow path to the river twenty feet below with Sergeant Minh following ten paces behind, as he had every morning for the past 121 days, since the day of Moser's recapture and his solitary confinement in the pit.

Moser waded into the river, its waters red and slow-moving. When the water reached his waist he untied his loincloth, the only garment permitted him, and draped it across his shoulders. Sergeant Minh sat on the edge of the bank, took a small sliver of soft, greasy soap, and tossed it to Moser, two paces away. Moser caught the soap and washed carefully, starting with his nearly bald head and working down, hoping to drive the lice down into the river. He cleaned each gook sore individually, rubbing the soap in and pushing the pus out. When he finished his torso and arms he drank two double handfuls of the silty, metallic-tasting water, then walked carefully back to the bank. Sergeant Minh got up quickly, giggling and pointing at Moser's wound. Sergeant Minh backed up to regain his safe distance of three paces. Moser looked at him with his good eye. Even with your gun drawn you are afraid of me, he thought, looking at Sergeant Minh and squatting in the shallows next to the broad sandy beach. You know that we will be brothers in death one day.

Moser found two small black-and-white leeches attached to his legs and freed them with a careful, rocking movement, as he had seen the Vietnamese do, so as to prevent the leeches from leaving their infecting mouth-parts in his flesh. More gook sores, he thought. He washed his crotch carefully and then worked on the sores down his legs, squeezing and cleaning, gritting his few teeth against the pain. The soap was nearly gone, but he still had to do his feet and save a little to wash the loincloth. I am Douglas MacArthur Moser, he chanted in his brain. I am an American fighting man. A fighting man takes care of his feet, no matter what.

Moser finished with his feet. They were swollen, his toenails lifted by fungus, but he had done what he could. He had no towel to dry himself, but nothing was ever dry in the jungle anyway. He spread his loincloth on the sand and smeared the last of the soap on it, then rubbed clean sand into the soap and the cloth. He rinsed the cloth in the sand underwater, over and over, until Sergeant Minh barked at him impatiently to hurry; the morning was going. Moser rinsed clean water through the cloth, then wrung it as dry as he could. He stepped up onto the bank, watching Sergeant Minh hop back another safe meter, and wrapped the black strip of cotton first around his waist, then under his crotch, then again around his waist, and tied it in the front. He headed back up the trail without looking at Minh, who would follow as he always did.

At the edge of the cliff near Moser's pit were the pumps and the turntable that drove them. The pumps were a version of Archimedes' screw, two long columns of straight bamboo with flexible plastic hoses wrapped around them in tight spirals. The shafts turned in wooden bearings on the riverbed and on tripods near the turntable, joined to the turntable by gears with wooden teeth belowground in a chamber protected by large, flat pieces of stone. The turntable had a central shaft and a crossbeam. At each end of the crossbeam was a yoke. The pump, which brought water up from the river to pour into irrigation channels that led to the rice fields in the saddle below Moser's pit, had been designed to be turned by one or two water buffalos walking in endless circles, but now the table was turned by Moser.

Moser put his shoulders to the yoke and draped his arms over the crossbeam on either side. He knew Sergeant Minh wouldn't give him his morning meal unless he did, and unless he spread his legs wide behind him, a position from which he could not move quickly to strike at Minh. The sergeant sidled in from behind and strapped first one arm and then the other to the crossbeam with the canvas ties that were through-bolted to the stout beam. He then stepped back and smiled, feeling safe again.

"Open wide, Water Buffalo," said Sergeant Minh, reaching in his pouch and producing a ball of cooked rice with a few slivers of fish embedded in it.

Moser opened his mouth and Sergeant Minh inserted the rice ball with his dirty thumb. Moser pressed the rice between the roof of his mouth and his tongue, squeezing it rather than chewing, letting it dissolve slowly, making it last.

Sergeant Minh stepped away, nodding his head, satisfied. The gaunt, ugly giant was once again helpless. How long will it take him to die? "Begin, Water Buffalo. The trough must be filled and the paddies watered. If the fields are not flooded when Major Nan comes there will be no rice in the evening."

Moser looked at Sergeant Minh with all of his hatred. I am not Water Buffalo, he thought, I am Douglas MacArthur Moser, an American fighting man. I will work because I must eat, and I must eat to gain the strength to squeeze the life from you and Major Nan. Moser bunched the ravaged muscles in his legs and shoulders and heaved against the yoke. The turntable began to move, and after five revolutions water pulsed from the spiral hoses and splashed into the catchment trough.

"Good Water Buffalo," said Sergeant Minh, giggling and backing away. "Water the rice well and you will be allowed to eat, and then to defecate outside your hole." Sergeant Minh holstered his pistol and turned toward the bridge, his sandals slapping in the damp earth. Moser watched his narrow back each time the slow revolution of the turntable permitted, until Minh was across the iron bridge and lost in the trees, on his way to his major at the High Camp.

NINE

Harry MacAndrew limped into Captain Willis's large office and greeted his commander. The director of the Naval Investigative Service rose from behind his desk, waving MacAndrew to a leather wing chair that the captain knew was more comfortable for MacAndrew than the lower couch, where Willis seated himself. Harry looks tired, Willis thought. He spoke first. "Well, Major, how did the visit with Mrs. Moser go?"

"I think it went well, Captain. It was damn sure tiring on my old bones, but Stuart thinks he has made some sense of Moser's letter."

"What sense?"

"Stuart believes Moser may have given us a very accurate description of the place where he is, or at least *was* being held. Apparently Moser was somewhat of an artist, and liked to read topographical maps as well. From the top of the gorge Stuart observed three distinct peaks, lined up west to east, two on the west side of the river and one to the east. The westernmost peak casts a deep shadow across the gorge, and even onto the eastern mountain. Stuart thinks that Moser is in a place that has those features."

"A river gorge and three lined-up mountains? That collection of features can't occur that often."

"No, and it would stand out prominently on a topographical map, even a fairly small-scale one. Stuart is beginning to look for it today in the archives at the Defense Intelligence Agency in Arlington."

"Good. What is the next step?"

"Funding, Captain. We don't have a budget for this."

Captain Willis grimaced. "Funding is super-tight, Major. I am long out of my small contingency kitty for this fiscal year, and I even got an argument out of BuPers when I extended Stuart. They want us to release reserve officers early."

"I know it's bad, sir, but we need to spend a few dollars to try to prove up Stuart's theory, and if we actually find something truly promising, spend a lot more."

"What has to be done and how much will it cost to get started?"

"We want an aerial survey of the area around the gorge in Georgia; photographs and work-ups as topographical maps. That won't cost much if I can pull a few strings with the Army Corps of Engineers. A lot of this won't really cost much if we can use military resources, but everybody is counting pennies and hoarding consumable supplies."

Captain Willis stood up and began to pace. He was a tall, thin man, slightly stooped by his seventy-one years, but otherwise youthful and vigorous. He wore a conservative gray suit and white shirt with a Harvard Club tie. He touched his gray crewcut as he walked. Harry MacAndrew sat in silence and watched the older man think. Willis turned and looked steadily at MacAndrew, holding the major's light blue eyes in his much darker ones. "Harry, what is your feel for this?"

"Stuart is sure Moser is out there, sir, and he wants to find him."

"But what do *you* think?"

"I think it is worth the effort. Any chance of getting any POWs out of that hellhole is worth following up."

The captain nodded. "I am going over to Washington tomorrow on another matter. I will try to see Senator Brush; he chairs the Military Intelligence Subcommittee, as well as the Foreign Relations Committee, and he might be able to get us some special funding."

"This will have to be a top secret operation, sir," said MacAndrew, carefully.

"I know. Senator Brush will live with the outlines *if* he wants to help."

Harry MacAndrew climbed slowly out of the leather chair. "Even if it's a long shot, sir—" he began.

"I know. We owe it to those poor men, budget or no budget, Major." Captain Willis smiled. "It would be the proud end of my career and yours, old soldier, to bring that boy home."

"Yes, sir," said MacAndrew, a lump in his throat. He didn't like to think of his retirement, now only six months away.

"I will get you the funds you need, at least to check Stuart's theory, one way or another, Harry."

"Thank you, sir."

"It's my job."

MacAndrew straightened against his pain and shook the captain's hand. "And you are very good at it, sir."

"We will talk tomorrow as soon as I have seen Brush and perhaps a few others."

"Yes, sir," said MacAndrew. "You might mention to the senator that the lad we seek is a Georgia boy, and therefore his constituent." He turned and left the office. A smile crossed his face. No one in the intelligence community had the connections the old man did. We will get what we need.

Washington, D.C.

Senator William Brush admitted Captain Willis after only a short wait. Willis entered the senator's large hideaway office in the Capitol. Only the most senior senators had these sumptuous office suites, far from the bustle of their official working offices in the Senate Office Building. Willis sat on a soft leather settee. Brush smiled and made an apologetic gesture with one hand; his other held a telephone. Willis looked around the room, fragrant with leather and cigar smoke. The office was softly lit by an ornate crystal chandelier. Shelves lined every wall, full of law books, leaving open only the west wall with its window overlooking the Mall and the Lincoln Memorial. The pale, washed-out winter sun was already low in the western sky.

The senior senator from Georgia spoke into the phone in low, richly colored tones, his Southern drawl as thick as cold molasses. He looked the way Willis believed a United States senator of the old school ought to look: tall, a little pot-bellied, with a great mane of silver hair and a florid face split with a happy smile as he warbled into the phone. He must be talking to a constituent down home, or perhaps another legislator from the South, thought Willis. He wasn't listening to the senator's conversation—to do so would have been rude—but Willis enjoyed the music of the man's voice. Every inch the Southern politician, thought Willis. Senator Brush had been a Rhodes Scholar; he was one of the brightest men in Congress and one of its foremost thinkers on foreign policy, but he could still talk to his folks back home about peanut and soybean prices, and he could still pull federal dollars into his state. The senator was far out on the liberal wing of the Democratic Party on foreign policy, but his mostly conservative constituency seemed not to care. William Brush was an institution, in the Senate and in Georgia.

Brush finished his conversation and rose from behind his carved walnut desk to greet his guest. Captain Willis stood to take the senator's hand. "Jake Willis, you old dog, it's been far too long. How's your lovely wife?"

"Well, Senator. Mary will be pleased that you inquired."

"Mary is one of my favorite people, Jake." Brush sat on a chair opposite the director and slapped his hands on his knees. His accent had all but disappeared, but the well-practiced smile remained. "What can I do for the navy today?"

"We have reason to believe a sailor, from Georgia as it happens, is a prisoner somewhere in Indochina and can be located. We need some funds from a discreet source."

The senator let his breath out in a whoosh. He opened the humidor on the table between them and turned it toward Willis. The director shook his head sadly; his doctor had forbidden cigars. The senator turned the box back toward himself and selected a long, thin Montecruz. Willis felt his mouth water. "Funding is very difficult, Jake. This damned war is taking so much, and this Nixon feller is squeezing everywhere, trying to make it and the Great Society just go away."

"We won't need much at first, Senator, just funds for research."

"How much?" the senator placed a finger alongside his red-veined nose. He looked cunning.

"Initially, no more than a million dollars," said Willis coolly. He had no idea what funds would be needed, and the initial research described by MacAndrew couldn't require more than a hundred thousand, but one didn't talk less than seven figures for anything with a powerful senator. "To see whether the theory of this sailor's location can be proved up. Quiet money, Senator, to augment stretched budgets in my office and in other government departments."

"I don't know, Jake," said the senator, shaking his head. "I don't suppose you can tell me any details?"

"No, Senator. This will have to be covert."

The senator raised his hands in front of himself and slapped his fat thighs. His face showed exasperation. "This damned war! Jake, you know I am against it, have been since '65."

"I know, sir, but this isn't about the war, it's about a sailor, locked in a cage far from home, and likely other American servicemen as well."

Senator Brush shook his head again. "Don't wave the flag at me, Jake; we have known each other far too long." The senator paused. He looked at Willis and frowned. "Jake, why is it I smell a little navy adventuring here? Doesn't the army have primary responsibility in the prisoner-recovery area?"

"It does, sir, but they have had no success."

"Navy do it better?" The senator allowed himself a smirk.

Willis locked his eyes on the senator's. "We believe we have a chance to locate a specific camp, Senator. We have very precise preliminary intelligence, which we can prove or disprove quickly and cheaply. Those boys deserve anything that might bring them home."

The senator got up and crossed to the window, seeming to admire the view. Willis regarded his broad back. I cannot believe, thought the director, that a senator from *Georgia* is going to turn away from a son of his own state lost in the enemy's web. If we should get him back it would be a boost in the senator's reelection campaign next year. But Brush, of course, stood no chance of losing that race.

Brush returned to the table, sweeping up a decanter of sour mash bourbon and two glasses from the sideboard as he passed, a smooth, effortless, and doubtless much-practiced maneuver. "Jake, I'm gonna be perfectly frank. I don't like this interservice rivalry, especially in respect of Veet–nam. And I don't like Veet–nam, period. I think you should turn whatever you have over to the army." Willis started to protest, knowing the army would bury the fragile report, under the Washington doctrine of NIH—Not Invented Here. The senator held up his hands to forestall the interruption. "But let me think on it, Jake, and then I'll do what I can. Meanwhile, have a little bourbon and talk to me about something else."

He will do nothing, thought Willis, smiling through his anger and accepting the cut-crystal glass half filled with the fragrant whiskey.

Willis wasn't really surprised; the war was so unpopular that no one in politics wanted to be associated with the armed forces in any way. It was a classic case of blaming the victims. But Willis didn't despair. There were many offices in Washington whose doors were open to the director of the Naval Investigative Service.

The director's limousine swept around the Ellipse into West Executive Avenue east of the Old Executive Office Building and through the southwest gate of the White House. A uniformed policeman emerged from the kiosk at the gate and examined the director's identity cards, three plastic laminated photos giving his name and position, each a picture of the captain against a different background. All the background cloths were red, but had different patterns; each showed his clearances for different facilities. Red in each case meant highest access. The guard saluted and the limo moved slowly toward the west basement entrance, where the papers would be checked again.

Captain Willis was tired. It was after seven o'clock and he had been shuttling around Washington all day. He had phoned Mary from his last stop, telling her with regret that he would be late for a small dinner party at their home in Reston, Virginia.

Willis had called and asked to see Henry Kissinger, the president's national security advisor, a man he had known for years due to their mutual association with Harvard University. Kissinger was out, but his assistant had suggested that Willis might like to meet with one of the president's special assistants who was also involved in defense and intelligence matters. The director had quickly agreed; best to get to know the new Nixon team as soon as possible. Willis didn't know John Hermann; in fact, he knew few of the Nixon people. Willis was a lifelong Democrat in his heart, but given his position in the service he was publicly nonpolitical.

As the car moved slowly through the floodlit driveway Willis thought about what he would say to the special assistant to the president. He had spoken to Hermann at the White House from the office of the last congressman he had visited, and the special assistant had agreed to see him on a "matter concerning prisoners of war."

The driver stopped at the basement entrance, got out, and opened the rear door of the Cadillac for the director. Captain Willis didn't rate a limousine in his post, but he had money of his own and he hated driving in Washington traffic, especially after dark. He pushed himself out of the plush seat, allowing the driver to take his arm. His arthritis was acting up, as it always did in the damp of Washington in the spring. The uniformed policeman took note of his credentials, entered his name on a clipboard, and directed him to the special assistant's office, down the long corridor. Willis passed the White House Mess on the left and the National Security Council situation room just beyond. The special assistant's office was next door, also on the left.

John Hermann met Captain Willis at the door of his small, cluttered office. Hermann was of medium height, tanned and balding, with a friendly smile and a feeling of great energy about him. He looked a youthful forty years old. He was in shirtsleeves, his tie undone and his sleeves rolled up, and wore a broad, carved leather belt with a silver buckle that looked Navajo. Willis wondered whether the buckle was a statement that the man had come to Washington from a long way off, from the real world.

Hermann ushered the director to an uncomfortable wooden chair and sat behind his desk. He offered coffee from a thermos jug, which the director accepted gratefully. The coffee was hot enough, and surprisingly good. "Thank you for seeing me at such short notice," said the director, studying the younger man.

Hermann smiled. He showed no fatigue despite what must have been a long day. "I am happy to meet you, Captain; I have heard a lot about you and the NIS. The president is very interested, as you know, in getting our boys out of Vietnam, and he has told us repeatedly he means all of them, including POWs. What have you to tell me?"

Willis repeated the story he had told Senator Brush and later other congressmen. Hermann nodded occasionally, holding Willis's eyes in his own intense, heavy-browed gaze. Hermann never interrupted, and Willis found himself going into greater detail with Hermann than he had with the others, although he gave away nothing of an operational nature. Hermann continued to nod and took an occasional note, but asked no questions. One of Nixon's whiz kids, thought Willis bleakly. Not like Washington insiders at all.

"How much money will be required, Captain?" said Hermann, when Willis had finally wound down to silence.

"Very little at first. A few hundred thousand for research." Willis cursed himself for the slip of asking for too little, but the man seemed

so technically oriented that he would probably know the photorecon-
naissance and map-making he had described as the first phase couldn't
cost even half a million dollars.

"And for the operation, if it comes to that?"

"A few million, sir. Less, if we are able to use units in place in
Vietnam for the extraction. Authority will be as important as money."

John Hermann stood and extended his hand. The director rose slowly,
standing erect despite the shooting pains in his lower back. "I will see
the president in the morning, Director. You will have your funding
authorization before noon if he approves, which I am confident he will."

Willis swallowed his astonishment and smiled carefully. "Thank
you, sir. And please thank the president for me."

"He may want to see you on this if it advances to the operational
stage," said Hermann, still clasping the director's hand.

"Of course. I will be at his disposal."

"In all events, Captain, please keep me informed."

"I will. And thank you."

The special assistant walked Captain Willis back to his car, waiting
by the basement entrance. In this town, you never know who your friends
are, thought the director, settling back into the soft backseat of the
limousine. He told the driver to take him home.

Fort Myer, Virginia, 9 May 1969

Major MacAndrew took his usual table in the Officers' Club at
Fort Myer with a stein of beer and a large salad. MacAndrew hated
salads, always had, but his doctor insisted he leave off the hamburgers
and chops and steaks that were hardening his arteries. MacAndrew
complied as best he could without going crazy, eating a salad every
other day at lunchtime and fish in the evening prepared by Rose Marie,
his wife of twenty years.

Lt. William Stuart placed his lunch on the table and excused himself
for being late. MacAndrew thought he looked tired and dejected, and
his eyes were decidedly red-rimmed. The major sipped his beer and
toyed with his salad, waiting for Stuart to speak. The younger man
ate in selfish silence, and MacAndrew had to ask the question. "Any
luck, William?"

Stuart shook his head, his mouth full of succulent-looking hamburger. He swallowed and chased the burger with a swig of beer. "No, Major, none. I am going cross-eyed staring at those old maps at DIA, both at headquarters at Fort Meade and more in their musty warehouses in Arlington."

"How much have you covered so far?"

"Most of North Vietnam and some of Cambodia. Nothing even resembling the three mountains in line with a river in the middle, even if we disregard the east–west lineup of the mountains, which I believe is significant." Stuart took another pull at his beer and blinked his reddened eyes. "The worst of it, Major, is that the best maps Defense Intelligence has of most of the area are DOD Evasion Charts, printed on flexible waterproof plastic sheets, intended to be carried by pilots in case they got shot down. The material is apparently deteriorating in storage. The plastic gives off a gas that irritates the eyes within an hour and leaves you ready to puke within two."

Major MacAndrew pushed his salad around in its simulated wooden bowl. "You have found nothing?"

"Nothing. Large areas of the charts are marked simply 'relief data incomplete,' with only the slightest suggestion of what the terrain might look like." Stuart paused and looked at MacAndrew, seeing the disappointment on his face. "Worst of all, DOD charts of Laos, where our colleagues at ACSI*–Army think most of the small camps are located, are small-scale and largely devoid of detail."

"So it's hard going," said MacAndrew, pushing his salad away with a final gesture. "I am going to get another beer; would you like one?"

"Yes, thanks," said Stuart, starting into his second cheeseburger. MacAndrew's stomach cried out for meat as he approached the service bar. The uniformed soldier served him quickly, and he carried the beers back to the table.

"How did the director's mission across the Potomac go?" asked Stuart, as MacAndrew sat and pushed the full stein toward him.

"He got enough funding, at least for the first phase."

"I hope he got plenty," said Stuart, leaning back and wiping his mouth with a napkin, his face flashing into a broad grin.

*ACSI: Assistant Chief of Staff for Intelligence

Major MacAndrew smiled back, his gloom dissipated by his young analyst's grin. "Why *plenty*, pray?"

"Because DIA says the only detailed maps of the area we have to search are under the care of the Archives Nationales d'Outre-Mer, in Aix-en-Provence, France."

MacAndrew laughed. "Well done, William. A trip to France, is it?"

"Yes, sir, I believe it is necessary." Stuart's grin had slipped away, replaced by the hard look he had worn when he had climbed down from the plateau in Georgia carrying Clem's shotgun. "I can leave as soon as we have the funding, and the aerial maps and photos from the Corps of Engineers."

TEN

Trai o Bo Song (The River Camp),
10 May 1969

Moser plodded in his slow circle, listening to the water splashing into the trough and hearing it gurgle away into the drilled bamboo pipes that led to the irrigation ditches below. A soft rain began to fall about noon, cooling the day and dispersing at least some of the mosquitoes and biting flies that swarmed and bit him, turning his shoulders and back and even his face bloody. The blood mixed with sweat and ran off, turning the rough wooden decking upon which he walked a wet, slippery pink. I walk to nowhere, thought Moser, his calloused soles slapping on the wet surface. And yet I walk to my destiny, my end. I will kill Major Nan, and then all can end.

Moser paused to rest, standing next to the trough, and watched the water drain away. The pain in his back and shoulders was dull and distant, barely a reminder of his existence as a living being. He walked to water the thieu-ta's rice paddy so the other prisoners could eat, and the guards could eat, and even he could eat. One hundred forty-five days since his shaming, since he had been brought down from the High Camp and roped to the wheel, the buffalo taken away to pull heavy cargo carts back and forth to and from the North Vietnamese base at Xieng Mi.

Moser breathed deeply as he rested, doing an abbreviated squatting exercise beneath the yoke to ease the cramps in his legs. A bright iridescent green and gold bird flashed by in the trees, giving its sharp warning call. Moser loved the jungle birds and he felt they spoke to him. Sometimes, listening to the birds, Moser felt his mind cleansed of human thought, even of language, and tuned to the many calls.

A sooty-black cobra slithered out from under his rotted log six feet from the edge of the turntable, raised the first quarter of his body over his coils, and flared his hood, a gesture of warning. Moser reckoned the snake to be about seven feet long: a young one. At least once a day the snake would come to Moser, display the delicate markings inside his hood, and flash his shiny black tongue, fixing Moser with his dead black eyes. The black *con ran mang xa* could take me any day, thought Moser, bunching his muscles and beginning again the endless trek. The snake rose higher in response to the movement and the squeaking of the wooden gears, then raced away on its afternoon hunt for rodents. The snake seemed to kill every second or third day, the meals showing as bulges in his stomach.

Con ran, the snake, thought Moser, walking his circle. The snake is my friend, my totem. The snake coiled in his mind, black and deadly, intertwining with the green bamboo snake, tiny and swift, and the blue racer, whose color flashed from sapphire to turquoise as it sped among the leaf litter and came without fear right onto the boards to eat the red ants that tormented Moser's feet. Moser's brain seemed to twitch and squirm as he continued his slow passage through time. He knew he was losing his mind and that little time remained for him to join his fate with Major Nan's.

Trai tren Nui Cao (The High Camp), 11 May 1969

Major Nan hobbled to the limestone outcropping on the plateau as the morning warmed. The tropical sun rose swiftly, pulling the mist up out of the canyons like rising smoke. Today I will go and visit the *con trau duc*, the water buffalo to whom my ravaged soul is linked. Today the prisoners will cut the rice harvest, tie the stalks at their bases, and hang them on the bamboo racks to dry.

Nan hobbled down to the center of the camp as the exercise period ended. The prisoners shambled to the mess hut for their rice from the fields below, perhaps enriched with fish if the weirs in the river below had trapped any. How can a nation that teaches its warriors no honor defeat us? he mused.

"Trung-si Minh," said the major. "I will descend with you today. See that my cart is pulled by prisoners who will not stumble."

Sergeant Minh saluted. The major noted that his senior sergeant's uniform was dirty, far dirtier than it needed to be, even in the jungle. Major Nan's fighting men had been clean, as proud of their appearance as of their mission, but Nan's men had been front-line regulars, not like these dregs, who were unfit physically or mentally to serve in the war in the South. "At once, Thieu-ta," said Sergeant Minh. "We will have Thieu-ta Peters pull and the black one, Dai-uy Morse, steady the cart from behind." Morse was a navy lieutenant, but *dai-uy* in Vietnamese made no distinction between the equal rank of army captain and navy lieutenant. Morse was the only aviator other than Peters who still showed the slightest resistance. He never spoke to any of the guards, but they saw violent purpose in his unblinking yellowish eyes and his skull-like black face.

"Good," said the major. "They need the extra exercise and the discipline."

It was best to harvest rice early in the morning, before the hot sun pierced the jungle and dried the fruiting tops of the plants. Sergeant Minh shouted and Major Peters and Lieutenant Morse fell out of formation, accompanied by an AK-47-toting guard, and pulled Major Nan's cart from the crude covered shed. The cart was nothing more than cloth canopy over a wooden seat with two bicycle wheels on an unsprung axle, pulled by two long traces in the front. It was excruciatingly uncomfortable to ride, but Major Nan could not walk the road down the hillside and across the bridge.

Major Peters pulled the crude rickshaw up next to Major Nan and halted. "Using prisoners in this manner contravenes the Geneva Convention, Major," he said, slowly. "Forcing prisoners to work, other than to provide their own food—"

"*Im lang di*," rasped Major Nan, climbing onto the crude seat. "*Di-di*: let's go, and carefully."

The trip down the trail to the River Camp was slow and difficult. The trail was packed red clay, always as slick as oil in the rain and morning mist, and narrow as it twisted and turned around the thick trunks of tall, vine-choked trees. Major Peters guided the cart as carefully as he could and Lieutenant Morse acted as the brake on the steeper slopes. Both prisoners knew that losing control of the cart, or even striking a tree or bouncing over a root or a rock, would bring a cry of pain and a stream of invectives from Major Nan, followed immediately by beatings from the guards who walked on either side of the cart, carrying whips of split bamboo in addition to their AK-47 carbines.

It took half an hour to reach the old iron bridge, built by the French to reach an opal mine long since played out. The single railroad track across the bridge had been overlaid with rough-sawn planks of local tropical hardwoods. Ten minutes before they could see the bridge they could hear the creaking of Moser's wheel and the splashing of water into the trough.

There were five other prisoners in the detail, each carrying an empty cloth sack. These men would collect the dried rice plants from the racks and carry them back up the hill. In the High Camp the rice would be threshed by the guards, first flailing the dried plants with their thin bamboo whips and then crushing the grains with large poles in a bowl carved from a tree stump.

The little procession shuffled across the bridge, Sergeant Minh leading, followed by Peters straining to pull the awkward cart, Major Nan seated, and Morse pushing. The three other guards were at the rear of the column, following the prisoners with the rice sacks. The guards who had walked beside the cart had been forced to fall back because the bridge was barely wide enough for the cart to pass.

Sergeant Minh stopped next to the water trough, noticing that it was well-filled. Moser looked at him but did not stop his circling. When Major Nan's cart had stopped opposite the trough Sergeant Minh waited for Moser to come around facing the major, then yelled "*Dung lai*: stop."

Moser stopped and looked over the trung-si's head at a point in the forest a thousand yards away. The guards giggled as Major Nan stuck his staff between Moser's hip and his loincloth and twisted it sharply. The loincloth fell away and the tittering guards pointed at Moser, the way children will laugh at a chained animal, disguising their fear. It didn't matter; Moser's anguish could not be greater and it could not be less until he joined the major in death.

Major Nan turned away from Water Buffalo, curtly commanding him to go on walking his cruel circle, his loincloth out of reach of his bound arms. Major Nan turned to the ragged line of prisoners and looked at their faces. All were expressionless; they had ceased to have personalities independent of their prisoner-ness, except the single black man, Morse, who looked sad, and the senior American officer, who looked angry. Major Nan hobbled to a spot a foot in front of Peters and spoke to him loudly in his quite good English. "This man is being punished for all of you, for disobedience and defiance. Mark well his example as he walks toward nowhere but his death."

Major Peters swallowed. Major Nan knew he was about to speak, and quickly raised his staff and pointed it at Peters's gut. Speaking was forbidden except in direct answer of a guard's question or command. Major Peters closed his eyes against the blow to come, and shouted loudly, "Hang in there, Moser, we are—"

Major Nan drove his staff into Peters's stomach, just below the solar plexus. Peters dropped to his knees, clutching his gut and gasping. "No talking in ranks, Major," said Major Nan, softly. He then turned to Sergeant Minh. "Trung-si, get these men to their work. I want all the dried rice put in the sacks and new plants harvested and racked. I would like it done quickly; we have much to do in the plantation above."

Moser listened to the sing-songy Vietnamese, storing Major Nan's words in his memory. I have your language, but you don't know that. More and more we are one, thought Moser, plodding carefully, watching the prisoners file off down the trail to the rice paddy in the saddle. Only Major Nan remained near the pumps, sitting in his cart and smoking a hand-rolled cigarette, apparently content to watch Moser walk his circle for hours.

ELEVEN

Paris, 13 May 1969

Lt. William Stuart entered the Defense Ministry building on rue Saint-Dominique in the seventh arrondissement at just after 1500 local time. Stuart had an appointment with a Colonel de Rennes of the French Army in fifteen minutes. The meeting had been arranged by the naval attaché at the American Embassy that morning. Colonel de Rennes was in charge of the records of all French military and Colonial Office operations in Indochina from the earliest expeditions to 1954, the year of Dien Bien Phu.

Stuart was dressed in a civilian suit that looked as though it had been slept in, which indeed it had. There hadn't been time to change between the early morning arrival at Orly Airport and his meeting with the naval and intelligence people at the embassy, and even if there had been, his room at the Hôtel Angleterre had not been ready, so he couldn't even shave. The hotel had barely agreed to look after his luggage. The embassy people had been helpful, but became chilly when he declined to tell them anything about his business other than that he was in France to examine French military and Colonial Office maps of areas of Indochina that were not well covered by maps in American archives. He had managed to purchase a razor and a toothbrush in the pharmacy in the lobby of the Hôtel Crillon next door to the embassy, and then to clean himself up in an embassy men's room.

The guard in the lobby of the Defense Ministry signed Stuart in, noted the number of his passport, and told him that Colonel de Rennes could be found "*a la troisième étage, à la bas.*" Stuart's French wasn't much good outside of restaurants, and he hoped Colonel de Rennes spoke English. Stuart straightened his wrinkled jacket as best he could, and took the lift to the third floor.

He found Colonel de Rennes's office at the end of the hall, behind a wooden door with a frosted glass panel bearing the legend "*Chef du Bureau, Documents de l'Indochine.*" An elegant, even striking woman seated behind a low antique desk looked up as he entered. About thirty or a little older, Stuart reckoned, slim but shapely, with smooth pale skin and shiny black hair cut too short for his taste. The perfectly white skin of her face framed enormous brown eyes under thin black brows and a vividly red mouth. Her expression was quizzical. Stuart told her his name and smiled. Her smile back was dazzling. She stood, smoothing her tailored blue wool dress over her thighs, turned, and opened a door into the inner office, closing it behind her and leaving Stuart alone.

Stuart sat on a hard wooden bench. Nice ass, he thought, his mind drifting in fatigue and the disorientation of the six-hour time change. Nice *derrière*. No women in the world look better in early middle age than the French, he thought, with the possible exception of well-born Vietnamese.

"*Monsieur?*"

Stuart snapped his eyes open. He had actually fallen asleep sitting up on the bench. The woman stood before him, looking slightly amused. "*Le colonel* will see you now."

Stuart mumbled his thanks and followed her to the unmarked door. She held the door open for him and he caught a scent of her perfume as he passed: light, clean, sexy, and expensive. She closed the door behind him and he found himself facing a gray-haired man with round spectacles who stood to greet him. The man looked trim and military in his carefully tailored working blue uniform. Stuart felt very conscious of his rumpled suit, but the Frenchman seemed not to notice as he waved Stuart to a chair in front of his highly polished Directoire desk. There was no other furniture in the tiny room. Outside, rain streaked the only window.

"*Bienvenue à Paris, Monsieur Stuart,*" began the colonel, smiling. "*Vous parlez français, bien sûr?*"

"*Un peu,*" struggled Stuart, "but not well. *Le Colonel parle anglais, peut-être?*" God, I will never get through this, he thought helplessly.

"I will try my English," said the colonel agreeably. "But you must not make fun of my accent, *hein?*"

"That is very kind of you, sir," said Stuart, immensely relieved. "My school French is really very weak."

"*C'est malheureuse.*" The colonel folded his pale, bony hands in front of him on the leather blotter. "*Eh bien*, how may we be of assistance to the American government?"

Stuart leaned forward and studied the colonel. The trim Frenchman's face gave away nothing. Stuart's orders were to tell everyone he spoke to in France the absolute minimum needed to get the cooperation he needed. "Colonel, I am an analyst with the Naval Investigative Service, a part of our Naval Intelligence Command. I have been sent here to seek maps, specifically topographical maps, of areas of Indochina where our own coverage is limited."

"Laos and Cambodia," said the colonel, his bland expression unchanged.

"Yes, sir," Stuart confirmed. "And parts of North Vietnam," he lied. The colonel smiled slightly and nodded for the American to continue his charade. "We hope that some of your surveys, even the earliest, when the colonial government was looking for minerals and plantation sites, might help us."

"You cannot, of course, tell me why."

"No, Colonel, I am afraid I can't."

"It's operational, of course," the colonel said, entirely sure of his opinion. "I sincerely hope you are not planning to widen the war into those territories; the people are mostly savages and the terrain is very rugged." The colonel looked up suddenly, and smiled. "But of course you know that, don't you, Lieutenant?"

"Yes, sir," said Stuart, flushing red. His brown official passport contained no reference to his service affiliation or rank. Obviously the French were onto him, and likely his whole game. But he had to stay with the script; even the French would expect him to.

The colonel stood up, and Stuart quickly rose. The colonel was six inches shorter than Stuart but his weak-looking gray eyes behind the thick spectacles were penetrating and confident, used to command. He held out his hand. "We will help you, of course, *monsieur*, because your government has asked us to, but I would like to suggest that we keep the whole matter unofficial. Your naval attaché, Captain Garand, is a friend; I am sure he told you that. He knows that a request of this kind could take weeks to filter through the red tape that clogs our official channels." The colonel paused and placed a finger alongside his long nose, an old Gallic gesture Stuart recognized as announcing a confidence.

"We have the indices of every document in our archives in this building," the colonel continued, clearly enjoying the game he was winning. "I will instruct Madame Richard to show you the cards and how the system works. Most of the documents, and nearly all of the maps, are stored in Aix-en-Provence, a lovely town near Marseilles. I will announce your coming, perhaps leaving out your exact purpose." The colonel paused, and his expression said caution. "As one military officer to another, my friend, I should tell you that the archives are under civil service rather than military control, and you should be, ah, *discreet* in your inquiries, *hein*?" Once again the long thin finger tapped the side of the colonel's nose. "The numbers you take from our catalogues here will lead you directly to the maps you need."

"Thank you, Colonel. Mme Richard is—outside?"

"Yes," said the colonel, his grin expanding. "She thinks you find her attractive. Do you?"

Stuart smiled and nodded before he could think.

"My youngest niece," said the colonel. "And she appreciated your admiring glances."

"Yes, sir. Thank you so much for your help." The lady is definitely off limits, thought Stuart, feeling oafish, clumsy, and stupid.

"Please come and see me when you return from Aix," said the colonel. "Of course, you won't be able to tell me what you found or didn't find, but at least tell me if you enjoyed the south of France."

"I will be delighted, Colonel, and thank you for your assistance, and, ah, your tact."

"Marlene will show you the indices, Lieutenant," said the colonel. Stuart closed the door behind him as he left. I feel like a schoolboy caught in a foolish prank, he thought. In the outer office the lovely, untouchable Marlene Richard awaited him with an inviting smile.

Stuart walked from the Defense Ministry toward the Hôtel Angleterre in the early evening. The rain had stopped but the air remained raw and cold, more like February than May. He belted his lined raincoat around him and turned up the collar against the wind. As he walked he swung his briefcase, which contained the precious aerial photos of the mountains and rivers around the crazy man's place in Georgia, as well as the topographical maps the Army Corps of Engineers had made. The walk was soothing after the long day and the cold made Stuart feel more alert, if still very tired. He left the Ministère des Armes by the northern entrance, crossed the boulevard Saint-Germain, and then walked slowly along the quiet rue de l'Université, a street of houses, government buildings, and antique shops. Many people were moving in the street despite the damp chill. At the rue des Saintes-Pères, the rue de l'Université became rue Jacob. The arch of the Hôtel Angleterre was at number 44. Stuart felt pleased with himself as he entered the lobby. He had gone over a lot of records, noting down map sequence numbers of the four areas he had planned to study, and his French had gotten better as he warmed in Marlene Richard's lovely smile. The walk in the damp had kindled his interest in the ancient city. He liked the feel of the narrow streets of the seventh and now the sixth arrondissements, and he felt he was a part of the experience of Paris.

The Hôtel Angleterre was near Saint-Germain-des-Près, a lovely old Romanesque church and a large square surrounded by chic cafes and restaurants. The only other time he had been in Paris was on a trip taken with his parents, a present for his graduation from high school. He remembered visiting Saint-Germain-des-Près and the famous cafe across the square, the Deux-Magots, once frequented by Hemingway and others of his circle. He and his mother and father had stayed at the Bristol, across the Seine on the very fashionable rue de Faubourg Saint-Honoré opposite the stately British Embassy and close to the official residence of the president of France, the Elysée Palace. The Bristol was one of the finest hotels in Paris and enormously expensive. Stuart had promised himself a meal there at least; the restaurant was famous throughout the world.

The Angleterre was quite different. Its room rates, while not cheap by the standards of Washington, were a third of the Bristol's and similar five-star hotels. Major MacAndrew had recommended it, reminding Stuart of the tight funding for the project. The Angleterre was clean and convenient to interesting restaurants, and only a half hour's walk from the American Embassy across the Pont du Carrousel, through the courtyard of the Louvre and the Tuileries Gardens.

Stuart's room was on the second floor, up a narrow staircase from the lobby. It was large: really two rooms, the double bed divided from a small sitting area by two tall closets. All the rooms including the attached bath had large windows overlooking the courtyard that the hotel surrounded. The hotel had no restaurant, but Stuart was anxious to explore the restaurants of the area. His father had told him that it was nearly impossible to get a bad meal in Paris, and in the three weeks he and his parents had stayed they never had.

Stuart hung up his clothes, setting aside the ones he had worn all the way from Washington to be laundered or cleaned. He took a long, very hot shower and felt instantly refreshed. He wrapped one of the huge, thick hotel towels around his waist, poured himself a small drink from the bottle of duty-free scotch he had brought from Dulles Airport, and took his address book from his briefcase.

The book was old, its morocco leather cover cracked. Stuart had carried it since his days at Georgia Tech and through his years in the navy. Many of the names were of people he no longer knew, and some were of men who had died in the steamy jungles and misty ridges of Vietnam.

He found the name he sought under V. Khanh Vu Binh, with an address on Tu Do Street and a Saigon phone number. The Saigon address and number had been crossed out and Khanh's married name, de Farge, added. Her address was now 18, avenue President Kennedy in the sixteenth arrondissement, one of Paris's most elegant quarters. He dialed the number slowly on the creaky French phone. Stuart hadn't seen Khanh since January of last year, when he had watched her and her mother and three sisters board an Air France jet at Tan Son Nhut Airport, bound for Paris. He closed his eyes and saw her, slim and graceful in a blue *ao dai*, holding his hands before she boarded, her mother scolding her to hurry and Khanh's tears streaming. He had loved her, briefly and intensely, but unsure of either her true feelings or his own. His wife had left him by letter only weeks before, and he had suspected her mother had pressed the girl on him because the family needed American friends to aid their departure. Two months later he had gotten her short note that she had married a retired French Army colonel and was living in Paris. He had recorded the name and address but had never answered the letter. She probably won't want to see me, he thought sadly, but I have to call.

The phone rang only twice before it was answered. *"La résidence de Farge, oui?"*

"Madame de Farge, s'il vous plaît," said Stuart, Khanh's married name sticking in his throat. *"C'est William Stuart, un ancien ami."*

"*Un moment, monsieur.*" The maid put the phone down with a clatter. William waited a minute that seemed like ten. Perhaps I shouldn't have called at all, he thought miserably.

"William?" Khanh's lilting voice surged through the wire, electrifying him. "Can it possibly be you?"

"Khanh," he choked. "Yes. I hope I am not disturbing you. I'm in Paris for a few days' holiday."

"I must see you. Can you meet me for dinner?"

"Yes. Can I invite you?" Stuart took a deep breath. It was almost a sob. "You and your husband, of course."

"The colonel is in Reims with his mother, who is ill. But this is my home; I will invite you." She sounded breathless, anxious to meet him. "Where are you staying?"

"The Angleterre. It is in the sixth."

"I know it. Not the best, but I suppose you are still in the Navy." William had a mental picture of Khanh wrinkling her tiny, upturned nose. "There is a very good restaurant near there, on the quai des Grands-Augustins. You can walk; it is called Laperouse."

"What is the number?" asked Stuart, uneasy about losing his way despite his earlier success in navigating through the narrow lanes of the Left Bank.

"I have no idea," laughed Khanh. "The quai des Grands-Augustins is a tiny length of the riverfront road, just opposite the Ile de la Cité. You will find it."

"Shouldn't I come and get you?" William realized he had a strong desire to see how Khanh lived.

"There is no need." Her voice was crisp and businesslike. A meeting of old friends, nothing more. He felt disappointed. "I will need time to dress, and I have my car. Nine o'clock, then?"

William looked at his watch. Barely six; he had left the ministry at five when it had closed, and was to return again in the morning to the rows of wooden cabinets and their contents of dusty, faded catalogue cards. "I will be there, Khanh."

"I am so glad," she said, her voice now sexy and alluring, as he remembered it. "If I am a moment late order our champagne."

William's throat contracted. He nodded stupidly at the phone, unable to speak, as those few days in Saigon flooded back. "Nine o'clock, then?" he finally managed.

"*A neuve heure,*" said Khanh, and hung up.

Stuart lay back on the starched sheets. I will take a short nap, he thought, lose some of the jet lag. But his mind raced, thinking of the woman he had helped flee Saigon with her family, thinking of the love they had made and the promises—

Stuart shut his eyes against the gut-wrenching feeling of loss and suddenly was deeply asleep.

Stuart dreamed of his parents, first in Paris seven years ago and then back in their home in Virginia. His father, a retired colonel of infantry had become a gentleman farmer on the old family lands and his mother, a soft, elegant woman played the piano beautifully and practically lived in the formal gardens of the estate, cultivating roses and other flowers. His mother had taken a bad fall from a horse while Stuart was in college and had been confined to a wheelchair ever since, but in his dream she walked swiftly and gracefully, directing the work of the two black gardeners, father and son, both old and wrinkled. Stuart felt small, and then he felt invisible; his mother didn't see him though he stood very close and tried to speak to her. He looked down at himself and saw he wore his jungle uniform, muddy and stained with blood. He was nearly overpowered by his own smell, compounded of rotting jungle vegetation and the death of men. He shrank back from his mother and the gardeners: she shouldn't see him like this. The younger of the two black men looked at him, apparently not seeing, but he pointed a finger and soundlessly mouthed the words, Bobby Coles, Bobby Coles.

Stuart shouted, no, no! His cry came out a muffled moan into the pillow and he struggled awake. He was soaked with sweat and his head was pounding. He shook his head to clear it and lit the bedside lamp. His watch said 1820; he had been asleep just fifteen minutes. The room was stifling, its old steam radiators banging. Stuart got up, closed the valve on the radiator in the bedroom, and cracked open the large window. The cold damp of the night rushed in, and he felt a little better.

He walked into the bathroom and took a brief cold shower, then two aspirin. He set the alarm on his watch to ring at 2030, just in case, but when he lay back down he couldn't sleep. The happy thoughts of his home in Virginia's tidewater country were pushed away by Vietnam and he was cold in the jungle, and afraid. He saw Billy Hunter, his first real comrade in the service, as he lay dead in a heap of bodies in the temporary morgue at Camp Tien Shaw the morning after the first night of the Tet Offensive of 1968. He saw the handsome black face of Sgt. Bobby Coles, twisted in agony as his life slipped away in a streambed as Stuart hugged him, trying with the heat of his own fever to drive away the chill of shock that was taking Bobby's life. And then he saw Moser, his silent, loyal guardian from the wooded mountains of north Georgia, his face streaked with tears of pain as the marines packed him into a dustoff chopper near Quang Tri City with a bullet in his hip, the day the helo crashed and Moser died.

Stuart's eyes opened again, and now he was cold. He pulled up the blankets rather than close the window. But Moser wasn't dead; he had written a letter and signalled his position. I have to find him, thought Stuart, grinding his teeth and squeezing his eyes tightly shut against the tears. Of all my ghosts, he could be alive. Stuart remembered the antiwar protestors the day he had returned from Nam at the end of his second tour, and how the spirits of his lost friends had steadied him and helped him get past the hatred and the ignorance. In Washington protest and derision swirled around him every day, but Bobby and Billy and big Moser steadied him, kept him from lashing out at the scruffy, yelling protestors or worse, falling to his knees in the street and crying for his terrible losses and his nation's. I have to go and find Moser, he thought, tossing in the soaking bed. I have to go myself.

The images left him and for a while he slept deeply. The beeping of his watch brought him up slowly. He felt almost drugged and needed another cold shower before he dressed and walked out into the cold drizzle, wrapping his raincoat around him and opening his small umbrella. The Restaurant Laperouse was only five minutes away, and he arrived ahead of Khanh, who was nonetheless expected by the grave, black-suited maître d'hôtel. Stuart sat at the bar and ordered a bottle of Veuve Cliquot Ponsardin.

Khanh Vu Binh—she never thought of herself as Madame de Farge—cursed silently as the long black Citroën sedan crawled through traffic on the Pont de la Concorde crossing the Seine. Evening traffic in Paris grew worse every year, and even the slightest rain slowed the flow across the many river crossings to a liquid, honking slither. She was sure the *embouteillage* would be worst at the intersection at the Left Bank end of the bridge, in front of the National Assembly at the entrance to the boulevard Saint-Germain, only minutes away for a fast walker.

Khanh touched her smooth, raven's-wing-black hair, pushing up the curl underneath. William had never seen her without her hair waist length and she doubted he would like it, but she was in Paris now and the modern style made her feel less a foreigner in a city that rejected foreigners. Why had William come? A Paris vacation seemed unlikely, yet what business could a naval officer possibly have in France? Has he come to see me on some sweet, innocent, and wholly American romantic quest? He had never answered her letter informing him that she had married, and she had thought he had never received it, but Lourdes, her maid, had said that the gentleman had asked for Madame de Farge.

She remembered the shy naval lieutenant who had been brought to her father's house on Tu Do Street—she still thought of that once-fashionable street by its old name, rue Catinat—by a Vietnamese army officer named Tho whose family had been allied with Khanh's for hundreds of years. Young Captain Tho was as indolent as he was rich, and he was considered by Khanh and her sisters as a pest. They had never found out how Tho had encountered the handsome young Stuart, blond and tall and blue-eyed, and so utterly ill at ease. William had been on some temporary assignment from his unit in Danang, but he never talked about it.

Khanh had seduced William quickly. She had had no real desire for the man, with his coarse, sun-reddened skin and broken French, but had made love to him because her mother ordered it. The family had finally decided to leave Saigon forever and needed powerful friends. Americans were powerful, and in the end it was Stuart and friends who managed to get the family to Tan Son Nhut and onto the plane, even though the high-level officials in the corrupt government of General Thieu had never delivered the exit visas that they had promised and for which they had been well and repeatedly paid. Stuart had driven the van himself, with Khanh and her mother and three frightened sisters huddled in the back under split-bamboo mats. William's friends, members of a special navy commando unit, accompanied the van in an armed jeep. They had easily intimidated the airfield's perimeter guards and the van had not been searched. William had driven the van directly to the ladder to the Air France jet, handing the family and their first-class tickets to a bewildered French air hostess minutes before scheduled takeoff. Americans didn't wait for visas, he had explained, his face split in a lopsided grin, open and uncovered; a vulgar display to Vietnamese eyes. Khanh saw that he grieved to see her go, even though he had encouraged her and her family to seek safety. She also realized at that moment and for the first time that in some way she loved him. She had cried as she kissed him, and cried again most of the long, twenty-four hour flight to Paris, despite her sisters' efforts to comfort her, and despite her mother's scoldings.

"*Nous sommes ici, madame,*" said Paul, her chauffeur.

Khanh came back suddenly from her reverie. Paul had the door open, his hand held out to help her. The chill mist touched her face. She pulled herself up on Paul's arm and nodded. "Go and have your dinner, Paul. We will be here at least two hours." Paul nodded and closed the door behind her. She stepped quickly across the narrow sidewalk and into the warm interior of Laperouse. The bar of the restaurant occupied the entire ground floor; the dining room was above, served by a tiny elevator. The decor was unique: mirrored ceilings and painted murals in the style of the nineteenth-century decorative school, with brilliant crystal chandeliers. Potted palms gave the bar a faintly tropical feeling and windows with cut-glass designs gave a view of the Seine and the light of the Ile de la Cité beyond.

Khanh saw William immediately, as she handed her wrap to the concierge. He jumped off his bench at the rear of the small ornate lounge and came to her, his grin a mixture of joy and sadness, exactly as it had been at Tan Son Nhut two years before. Her heart melted as he embraced her, and she felt her tears come as she buried her face in his chest.

William tried very hard to be bright and amusing as he and Khanh moved through the leisurely meal of salmon mousse, venison in cherry sauce, and a tart, crisp endive salad. The champagne had sustained them through the salmon; Khanh drank very little. The Bordeaux taken with the venison had been a suggestion of the waiter; William hadn't wanted to take his eyes off Khanh long enough to look at the wine list, which was the size of a small-town phone book.

Khanh was slim but tall for a Vietnamese, about five-six. Her skin was the color of fine white silk and her eyes were black and almond-shaped. Her mobile mouth dominated even the shining eyes, flashing with expressions of joy and sadness and disbelief as he told her sparingly of his life after she had left him at the airport. He didn't mention their brief affair.

Making conversation hadn't been easy for William. Khanh seemed to study him, searching for something in his face. He would have been happy just to look at her without speaking, the way people stared at the Mona Lisa in its glass case in the Louvre across the Seine. She hadn't changed since Saigon, except that her glossy black hair was cut short and the anxiety of the final dangerous weeks in Saigon had been replaced by a sophisticated confidence. She had told him in Vietnam that she felt more French than Vietnamese, and in Paris so she was.

It is difficult, mused William through one of the long, smiling silences they exchanged, to make conversation when you can't say anything about what you are doing or why you have suddenly come to Paris. Khanh was puzzled and showed it, but didn't press him. In that sense at least she retained the grace of Saigon; a Frenchwoman would have demanded an explanation.

Khanh felt a strange tension in the handsome American. He looked softer and paler than he had in Saigon, and his haunted expression had given way to one of strong emotion under strict control. What happened to him after I left? Was he caught up in the killing of Tet right after her family had fled? She wanted to know, but she didn't want to ask. She reached out across the small square table and stroked the back of his hand. He grasped her hand in his, quickly but gently, as if he had been waiting all evening for her to touch him. She leaned forward and kissed him lightly on his lips. "William, let's go home for a brandy," she said.

William nodded, unsure of what Khanh was offering and uncomfortable at going back to the home of her husband. He called for the check, which the captain brought and handed to Khanh, thanking her and addressing her as Madame de Farge. William resented the reminder, and decided he really should not go to *their* apartment, no matter how innocent Khanh's intent might be. "It might be better," he said, "if I took you back to your car, and then went back to my hotel and got a good night's sleep." He regretted the note of disapproval that had crept into his voice.

"But William," said Khanh, leaning forward and squeezing his hand. "You must come back with me. I want you to make love to me." She said it as though it had been understood from the moment she had asked him to dinner.

William felt a thump of his heart. He had waited since six o'clock to hear something like that, but it didn't seem right. "Khanh, I loved you once. I am sure I did, though we had so little time together—"

"Then let's go," she said, smiling and covering his hand with both of hers.

William shook his head, slowly. "Khanh, I don't think I should go with you to your husband's bed—"

"Don't be silly." Khanh's voice had an edge on it. "It is my flat, not his, and I want you to come. Besides," Khanh looked around the room, her expression chilled. "I do not wish to spend a night in the Angleterre."

"Khanh!" William gripped her delicate hands, forcing his voice to remain a whisper. "Please listen to me. You are married; our chance has gone."

Khanh kneaded the back of William's hand, forcing him to relax the tension. She watched his face as he stared, angry and confused, at the tablecloth. "William, we loved each other, and we still can. I am sorry that my boldness offends your American morality, but we are in Europe, and we are adults."

William shrugged, and looked up. How lovely she is, he thought. Did I want this to happen?

"William, my husband and I have a French marriage. You might say a marriage of convenience. The colonel is sixty years old, from a very old but impoverished family in the Champagne country. His pension from the army is a pittance." She put two fingers under William's chin and forced him to look at her. "He married me for my money, so he can keep his family's lands and their meager wine growth."

"Why did you marry him?" William was ashamed to have asked the question. He felt like a high school freshman on his first date. How sweet their few days in Saigon had been!

"For his good name, *mon ange*, and more important, for French citizenship." Her voice was crisp and a little cold. "We are good friends; I grace his receptions for his boring aristocratic friends with my exotic charm, and of course I pay for them. He 'protects' me from the French government." She paused and sighed. "William, please don't judge me. Times were difficult after we left Saigon."

"No," he choked. "Of course not. I'm sorry."

"My driver will be just outside. Please come home with me."

William got up stiffly. His body ached from the airplane and the stiff chairs of the Defense Ministry. He looked at Khanh and smiled, then bent quickly as she rose from her chair and kissed her. "Of course."

TWELVE

Trai o Bo Song, 13 May 1969

Moser pushed the yoke through the afternoon, his body streaming with sweat in the maddening heat. He was able to stretch his neck down to the trough and lap a few drops of water to slake his thirst, but only at the cost of shooting pains through his arms and shoulders. As the day's heat grew to its maximum in early afternoon he slowed and finally stopped, panting and dizzy, his heart pounding. I am getting weaker, he thought. It must be soon, or I will die while Nan still lives.

Moser hung in the yoke, licking the sweat off first one shoulder and then the other. Midges and tiny bees buzzed around his head. The midges bit fiercely but the bees merely drank his sweat. He looked out across the River Camp and remembered it as it had been when he first saw it. The camp had been a circle of neat huts built on bamboo frames, roofed and walled with nipa, floored with rough-hewn boards a foot above the ground. No trace of any of the huts remained; Nan had forced the prisoners to take the nipa roofs and siding with them to attach to the bamboo frames in the High Camp. The boards had been taken as well, and later nearly all the poles. The only structure left had been the platform, six feet above the ground, where the camp's threshed rice had been stored. The poles had been smeared every few days with the sap of the *lua* bush, which prevented rats and snakes and ants from climbing up to steal the precious rice. Only the poles now stood, ten meters from the pumps, and one was leaning. The platform, woven of thick reeds from the river's edge, was gone. The platform had been Moser's raft.

Moser's head hung in fatigue and despair. How close he had come to escaping this place. He had floated almost to Thailand on the raft; maybe he had even reached it, but the soldiers who found him and brought him back to Major Nan had been Pathet Lao, in their dark blue loincloths and parachute-cloth scarves, with their old French rifles and their long machetes.

And then Nan shamed me and put me here, strapped to the pumps by day and locked in the pit at night, *pour encourager les autres*. Nan loved to spit that phrase, so elegant-sounding compared to the harsh clipped sounds of Vietnamese. I am being punished to encourage the others, thought Moser. Nothing had been further from the truth; the prisoners had lost all will, but of course that had been what Nan intended.

The afternoon shadow fell across the valley and the breeze wafted up from the river. Moser began to plod in his circle and the trickle of water resumed. One hundred and forty-seven days since the tiny, happy-faced Pathet Lao had brought him back and sold him to Major Nan for two AK-47s and a kilo of raw opium. I must have Nan soon, soon.

Maj. Carter Peters led the detail of men sent to harvest rice up the path from the paddy to the muddy overgrown ground that had been the River Camp. He saw Moser, his head down and cords standing out on his neck and limbs, as the big man strained to keep the heavy pump wheel turning. Moser was harnessed to the pump like a crucified man, and every day Carter Peters damned himself because he had done nothing to force an end to his torment. As senior American officer Peters knew he should do something—get the men to refuse to tend the fields at the very least—but he knew Major Nan would simply withhold food and perhaps reinstate the random beatings.

Peters remembered the night Moser had been brought back to the High Camp, bound and blindfolded. He saw the scene nearly every night in tortured dreams. Sometimes he thought he felt Moser's pain as well and twisted in his sleep, pulling against the others to whom he was handcuffed and crying until they woke him. Looking at Moser now he saw it all again, and his throat closed against a sob.

The prisoners in the hootches had been awakened that terrible night by shouts in Vietnamese and the banging of the camp gong. Peters had awakened slowly as the guards entered and unlocked the leg blocks and the handcuffs that bound the prisoners together. The major felt sick and weak, and he sensed that he had been asleep only a few minutes.

The gooks had worked his men all day rethatching the roof of the cookhouse, first tearing off the old nipa thatch with hands soon cramped and bloody and then binding on the fresh fronds. The major's whole body ached and his blood burned with malaria. What now? he had thought, at once irritated and dejected. The guards shouted and gestured: hurry, they said, the commandant commands you to parade.

The prisoners stumbled out into the central packed-earth grinder of the camp. The pile of old thatch had been set alight and the major thought for a moment that they had been awakened to fight the blaze, but the guards hurried them into a ragged line in front of the fire. Major Nan, leaning on his staff, stood with his back to the flames. Before him, on his knees, was a bound man. The major sighed as he recognized Moser, who had escaped four, five days before? The major shook his head in an effort to clear it. When Moser had been gone two days Peters and everyone else figured he'd be halfway to Thailand or dead in the jungle. Peters saw fear on each prisoner's face. Nan's rages since the big man had escaped had been monumental; what would he do to them now?

The guard who had been beating the gong stopped as the Americans were counted. At a command from Major Nan the guard drew a machete from the scabbard hanging from his web gear and thrust the blade into the fire. The commandant stepped forward and began to rage, his English and sometimes French words lashing at the prisoners. The Americans stared back dully; many were half asleep on their feet and all were weak from work, malnutrition and disease. The bound man was jerked to his feet between two guards, then the sergeant untied the man's hands from behind his back and kicked his legs out from under him, swiftly retying his wrists in front of him and then looping the end of the line around his already tied ankles, trussing him like a calf for branding.

The commandant continued to shout, hobbling back and forth in front of the swaying line of prisoners, telling them that escape was dishonorable and futile and rebellion could never be tolerated. Carter Peters looked at the tall Georgian lying in the dirt, tied and blindfolded. What are they going to do to him? the major wondered. I must say something, stop this, but he couldn't find words.

Nan turned and shouted an order to the sergeant, who drew a long curved knife from his belt. The sergeant cut away the rag of a loincloth the bound prisoner wore, and then cut suddenly and deep. The prisoner bucked against the ropes and let out an animal bellow of anger and pain. The sergeant cut again and blood gushed from the wound. Once again the prisoner cried out, then shuddered and was still. The major fought the urge to vomit from his empty stomach. Several prisoners in the line tried to turn away and many gagged, dripping bile from their mouths, but the guards prodded them back into line and made them face the flames and the bleeding man. Major Nan, his face black with rage, squatted and retrieved the machete from the fire and held it up. Its point glowed cherry red in the darkness as he brought it round and pressed the hot point against the wound. Moser bucked helplessly as the commandant staunched the blood flow, the hot blade hissing obscenely, but he did not cry out again. The commandant limped to a place immediately in front of the American major, thrusting the point of the machete under his nose. Peters recoiled from the sight and smell of the black blood sizzling on the blade, but the guard behind him pushed him forward, prodding with his carbine.

"See this and remember," seethed Nan, shaking the point of the machete in front of Peters's eyes. "See this and know there can be no escape from my valley except in death." The commandant dropped the machete at the major's feet and hobbled away. The guards herded the prisoners back to their hootches, leaving the bound man alone by the dying fire.

Peters closed his eyes to blot out the vision and to shield himself as well from the sight of the living Moser he had done nothing to help. Nan would simply have laughed if he had told the men to stop working; the rice and the poppies could wait longer than the men and Nan would win, but Peters felt he should have *tried*.

In some respects the camp life had been easier under the corrupt Lieutenant Mounh, even though he had given the sergeants more freedom to beat the men and showed no concern for the prisoners even as beasts of burden. Mounh was silly and easily ridiculed. Nan stood apart like a wrathful and twisted god. One can always conceive of reaching a corrupt man, and Peters's predecessor as senior American officer, the old colonel who had died, had had some influence on Mounh. Nan was incorruptible, implacable, utterly unreachable. Still, Peters thought as the detail passed the straining Moser and started across the bridge, he, *Major* Peters, should have *tried*.

Ironically, Peters thought, I should have been as ready for this as any man. Peters had taken the one-week SERE course —Survival, Escape, Reconnaissance, and Evasion—in North Carolina before shipping over to Thailand for his first combat tour. In the prison camp phase of the training he had been thrust, unexpectedly, into the role of senior American officer. He felt he had performed no more than adequately, although he had been praised by the instructors at the end of the course, and he remembered being taken in by the tricks the instructors had used to discourage and disorient the trainee prisoners. Resist, conserve the chain of command, keep faith with your fellow prisoners, they had been taught. Peters had done that here in Laos and he felt he had prevented a severe breakdown in discipline. But Nan did not use tricks and he fed and treated the men as well as he could, all except Moser, tortured to shame them all because Moser alone had tried to do a prisoner's duty and escape. Nan did not use any of the devices the SERE trainers had copied from the North Koreans; Nan ruled by simple, enervating, unending despair.

Peters felt the tears streaming down his muddy face and was too saddened to wipe them away.

THIRTEEN

Paris, 13 May 1969

Stuart lay awake in Khanh's bed, listening to the rain lash the silk-curtained windows. The clock on the bedside table read 0530, and it was still fully dark outside. Khanh lay on her side, the back of her neck toward him, her chic short hairdo hardly disarranged on the creamy silk pillowcase. She purred softly, like a contented cat.

Stuart closed his eyes. It was half an hour to midnight, Washington time, and he should feel sleepy, but he didn't. Jet lag never affected him in a rational way; he just didn't feel right for days every time he travelled across time zones, especially moving east against the sun.

He drifted behind his closed eyelids. Love making with Khanh had been intense and sophisticated, Khanh controlling him and taking her pleasure before giving him his own. In Saigon she had seemed innocent and even frightened; now she was a confident woman of the world. He wondered if old Colonel de Farge had taught her, or perhaps a young lover, and jealousy tugged at his heart.

He fell into a deeper slumber and dreamed he was on an airplane, leaving Vietnam. Unaccountably, the aircraft seemed to fly backward, returning him to Nam. He tossed and rolled over, pushing against the pillow, the case of which was becoming damp and slick with his perspiration. No, not me, he thought. He heard the drumbeat of a helicopter and saw the bird rise through its dust cloud, bearing the wounded Moser. Stuart flew with the helo and watched it crash into a hillside in a silent sheet of flame. But Moser hadn't died. Stuart watched Moser thrown free and then he saw Moser in a bamboo cage, tiny for the big man's size. Moser looked up at Stuart, still hovering, and beckoned. Stuart descended toward the jungle and was engulfed by the fetid smells of decay. Stuart willed his body to rise, but it continued to sink. Soon he was face to face with Moser.

"You have come," said Moser. "I knew you would, but it has been so long since I sent for you."

Stuart twisted violently, trying to shake off the image, which he knew was a dream. The silk sheets held him and he tried to cry out, but could hear only a soft moan. Moser pointed to the lock on the cage and then at Stuart.

Khanh shook Stuart awake. "What is the matter?" she asked, her voice sleepy but alarmed.

"Dream," said Stuart. His mouth tasted of copper and he was soaked with sweat. He sat up. "Sorry."

"You cried out in Vietnamese," said Khanh, turning on the bedside lamp.

"I did?" Stuart was puzzled. "What did I say?"

"*Con ran, con ran,*" said Khanh, wiping his face with the sheet.

"I don't know what that means," said Stuart, suddenly cold.

"It means snake. You must have learned the word years ago."

Stuart freed himself from the twisted sheet. Snake? he thought. "I guess so. Khanh, I have to go."

"Why?" Khanh sounded peeved. "Whatever your business is, nothing in Paris opens before nine."

Stuart stood. He was slightly dizzy and still dripping with sweat as the nightmare and malaria passed. "Khanh, I can't tell you, but a friend of mine is waiting, a dear friend. I will walk back to my hotel and dress." Khanh looked sad and skeptical. "I have to; it's very important."

"Stay, William. My driver will be here at seven; he will take you back to your hotel and then on to your appointment."

I cannot stay here lying with this woman while Moser waits in a cage, thought Stuart. "Khanh,—I'm sorry, but the dream—my friend is in great danger, and the matter is very urgent."

Khanh's expression softened. "All right. Will you call me this evening, please?"

Stuart dressed rapidly. "Yes—if I can. I may have to leave Paris today."

Khanh frowned, and seemed about to ask why or to where. Please don't, Stuart willed. "If you do, you will return to Paris before you go home?"

I guess, thought Stuart. "Yes, of course."

Khanh rolled back onto the pillow. "Then I will see you soon, without fail, *mon ange*."

"Yes." Stuart stomped into his shoes and walked from the bedroom into the living room. The Eiffel Tower stood out in ghostly silence across the Seine above the morning mist that clung to the river. I will find the place, Moser, and then I will come for you, he thought. He shook his head and let himself out of the richly furnished apartment.

Marlene brought Stuart drawer after drawer of file cards. They were mostly yellow with age and gave off small, clinging clouds of irritating dust as he searched. He concentrated on sites in the Annamite Mountains, where there were many prominent peaks. Mindful of Colonel de Rennes's warning about security in the archives, he also chose several mountainous areas in North Vietnam so as to lay a few false trails if any of the civilian custodians of the archives noted his work. He doubted anyone would.

At one o'clock the colonel entered the catalogue room and asked Stuart to lunch. Stuart gratefully accepted; his fingers itched and his sinuses burned from the dust. Stuart was pleased that the colonel included Marlene in the party. They walked to a small bistro in the rue de Bellechasse, just south of the Gare d'Orsay, and feasted on oysters and steamed sole. Stuart insisted that the colonel select the wine, and when the meal was finished, paid the bill despite the Frenchman's protests.

Over coffee the colonel asked Stuart how his work was progressing. Almost finished, said Stuart; almost ready to go on to Aix and see the maps themselves.

"Marlene will book you on the train when you are ready to go," said the colonel. Marlene merely smiled, and held William with her large eyes. "Perhaps tomorrow or the day after?"

"There are only a few other areas to check, Colonel," said Stuart, sipping his *café filtre*. "Perhaps I could go tonight, if I could get a sleeping berth to Marseilles?"

The colonel nodded. "Better Avignon, don't you think, Marlene?"

"*Oui*," she said. "Marseilles is closer, but the city is terrible. Better *louer en voiture*—how do you say it, Uncle?"

"Rent a car," said de Rennes. "See Avignon and the surrounding countryside. Be not so obviously on a mission." The colonel touched the side of his nose with a long finger and winked at Marlene.

Stuart smiled. He felt he could trust the aging French officer and his exotic, sexy niece. "Thanks for the advice. Is there an express to Avignon this evening?"

"There is," said Marlene, as Stuart retrieved his credit card. The three of them walked slowly back to the ministry and Stuart went back to the catalogue room.

Aix-en-Provence, 14 May 1969

Stuart took the fast overnight train from the Gare de Lyon in Paris to the city of Lyon. The train departed at 2215. Stuart found a compartment in second class that held only one other passenger. He climbed into the narrow *couchette* immediately after the train left the station. His companion sat staring out the rain-flecked window, drinking Calvados from a bottle in his lap, chain-smoking Gaulloise Bleu cigarettes, and politely refusing Stuart's several suggestions to open a window or at least the door to the companionway.

The train arrived in Lyon at 0520 and Stuart transferred to a slower train to Avignon, which got in at just after 0800. Stuart felt pressed to go on and confirmed his ticket on the even slower train which would carry him down to Aix-en-Provence. He was quite sure that Harry MacAndrew would not approve if he rented a car. He had an hour and a half to kill before the next train's departure, so he walked north from the station through one of the gates in the ancient wall, found a cafe, had a coffee and a croissant, and then walked to the Palace of the Popes. It was a lovely, high Romanesque-Gothic building, but it wouldn't open until ten, so he walked around the grounds and then trudged back to the station. His fellow passenger's black tobacco cigarettes had given him a sore throat and a bad temper.

In Aix, he thought, I will find that place. He was more sure than ever that Moser had given him the Valley of the Shadow, especially since the Annamite Mountains were so jumbled as to make the occurrence of three peaks in line, west to east, very unlikely to be common.

The train to Nice deposited him in Aix just before noon. He took a taxi to the Archives Nationales d'Outre-Mer, France's records of her lost and few remaining overseas possessions, which proved to be a modern building faced in pink stone, six stories tall with tiny slits for windows. The archive was on a campus of university buildings, described as the Faculté des Lettres, that was altogether pretty, with wide lanes lined with trees that were in full flower in the warm spring weather.

Stuart went inside and found the reading room. He presented his short note from Colonel de Rennes and was directed to the reception on the fourth floor. All maps, he was told by a kindly-looking matron, were stored on the fourth and fifth floors. She told him to seek M. Lapin, the curator of the map collections.

Jean-Claude Lapin proved to be a short, somewhat overweight man with tiny reddish eyes and a button nose like his namesake, the rabbit. He wore round spectacles, which he took off and polished on a large, dirty handkerchief as he sized Stuart up. He seemed faintly amused. "You have a list of the old maps you wish to see?"

"Yes. Here is the list of catalogue numbers."

The archivist took the four sheets of handwritten numbers and glanced at them without interest. "I was just going to have my lunch," he said, handing the papers back to Stuart. "Perhaps you would join me, and then we could discuss what it is you wish to find."

"That would be nice, M. Lapin," said Stuart, putting the list back into his briefcase. "Perhaps you will allow me to invite you?"

M. Lapin grinned broadly. "You are most kind, monsieur; may I suggest a restaurant that serves very well the cuisine of Provence? It is called l'Abbaye des Cordeliers; it's in a fourteenth-century cloister. We can go in my poor old car."

Lapin drove slowly through the streets of the old city, his smoky, noisy Deux Cheveaux complaining all the way. When Stuart saw the restaurant he immediately doubted a clerk like Lapin could afford it, at least not often, as the menu, posted out front of the old abbey, was extensive and the prices approached those of Paris. They were seated at a corner table and Stuart asked his guest to order for them both. Lapin immediately addressed himself to the wine list, selected a Côtes du Rhône Stuart didn't recognize, followed by snails, a spicy stew of fish and shellfish, and salads. Lapin talked expansively during the meal about the city of Aix, its Roman past, its July festival, and the wonders of the surrounding countryside. Over pastries and coffee the Frenchman seemed to relax and began to talk of Provence as a special, unique region of France.

"M. Stuart, have you never been to France before?"

"Only Paris, when I was younger," said Stuart. Lapin sipped his small cognac while Stuart stayed with the strong coffee. "My parents brought me; we went also to Chartres."

Lapin leaned forward. "Then you don't know why the south is so important, *hein*, monsieur?"

Stuart smiled. Pedantic, boring asshole, he thought, but best to be on his good side if I am to get through the maps in a reasonable amount of time. "Please tell me."

Lapin raised a stubby finger, pointed straight up. His little eyes shone behind the round spectacles. "The sky. The light. All the great masters of the last century came here to paint the light."

"Which masters, M. Lapin?" asked Stuart, hoping the lecture would not take much longer.

"The best of the Impressionist School, monsieur, the best. Eighty kilometers west of here the Dutchman van Gogh painted the flowers and the fields in the brilliant light. He brooded because the light was so bright he could not capture it all on the canvas. Gauguin came down from Paris to cheer van Gogh up, but they quarrelled because Gauguin wanted to enjoy himself and Vincent just wanted to paint. Gauguin left, and Vincent cut off his ear." Monsieur Lapin paused and took a tiny sip of cognac. He smiled happily at his captive audience. "Van Gogh was quite mad, of course. Perhaps the light did that as well."

Despite himself and his desire to get back to the archive Stuart began to take an interest in the Frenchman's ramblings. William was no connoisseur of fine art, but he liked the Impressionists and he hoped to have time to visit the collection in the Jeu de Paume Museum when he returned to Paris. He smiled at M. Lapin, encouraging him to continue.

"Here in Aix the great Cézanne painted that granite crag that overlooks the city, the Mont Saint Victoire, over and over again, in all of the different lights of Provence. He painted the mountain in the morning, at noon, at sunset, and on cloudy days, the rare ones. Matisse decorated churches in Provence and in the Alps and the great Renoir lived and painted in Cagnes-sur-Mer and is buried there." Lapin finished the last of his cognac and peered sadly at the empty glass. "They all came here for the light, Monsieur Stuart."

"That's interesting, monsieur—"

"Yes, it is, monsieur," Lapin leaned forward, and looked at Stuart's eyes with new force. "It is interesting, monsieur, because while all those artists came here for the light, and while French men and women, plus tourists from all nations come here for the sun, you come here for the darkness and dust of my archive." Lapin's voice became as hard as his eyes. "And I should like to know why."

Stuart fought to avoid looking away from Lapin's eyes. "I can say little, monsieur," he began slowly. "Your government is assisting mine in trying to find certain locations that have been described to us."

"That is rather obvious," said Lapin with a snort.

"Well—" began Stuart, seeking a plausible evasion.

Lapin cut him off. "I do not approve of your war in Indochina, monsieur, as I did not approve of France's. As a young man I was a junior official in the post office, and I served for three years in Saigon."

"I understand," said Stuart. "We—"

Lapin got up quickly, dropping his napkin on the seat. He smiled at Stuart, but his little eyes were still cold. "Thank you for the excellent lunch, monsieur. And now I will show you my maps."

M. Lapin collected a total of fifty-nine maps, which covered and overlapped the areas Stuart had selected from the catalogues in Paris. Lapin loaded the cardboard tubes onto a wheeled cart, guided Stuart to a small workroom, and left him alone, to return to his own work. Stuart sat down at the large wooden table and sighed. The fifty-nine maps made a considerable pile, and even setting aside the maps from North Vietnam, which he had requested as red herrings, the task seemed enormous. Jet lag and the wine from lunch made him want to sleep, but he removed his camera equipment from his grip, as well as the photographs from Georgia and the map sketches the Army Corps of Engineers had made from them, then set out his notes from the catalogues at the Ministry of Defense, which he had arranged in order of the places which seemed most promising. He opened the first of the tubes and went slowly over the maps, searching for terrain features similar to the Valley of the Shadow in the dark mountains of Georgia. The first map yielded nothing; the mountains of the Annamitique Cordillera seemed hopelessly jumbled and the chain itself ran from northwest to southeast, not west to east as the mountains in Georgia. Stuart felt a great welling of despair as he opened the second map. He thought of big Moser as he had been at his side and as he had been in his dream in Paris. The whole enterprise seemed hopeless and infinitely sad. He put away the second map and opened the third, searching carefully with his magnifying glass, his eyes blurred with fatigue and sorrow for the man, the friend, he had lost.

*   *   *

On the fifth map he found the place, and he knew it immediately. Three mountains marching west to east, farther apart than in Georgia but higher, and therefore in the right proportions, with a river between the two easternmost. Stuart quickly measured the exact latitude and longitude and noted the nearby features: a town identified as Xieng Mi to the west and the river called the Nam Mang, a small tributary of the Mekong. Latitude 18 degrees, 6 minutes and 30 seconds north, longitude 103 degrees, 1 minute east. Southern Laos.

Stuart set up the 9mm Minox camera with its copying lens on its folding tetrapod and photographed the area carefully, fighting the trembling of his hands. Everything was as it should be. He carefully returned the map to its tube and then forced himself to examine every other map on his list from the catalogues. There was no other place like the one near Xieng Mi. Stuart packed his camera and all his papers, then returned the last maps to their tubes.

M. Lapin knocked at the door, entered, and announced that the archive was closing. Stuart glanced at his watch and realized that the Frenchman had waited for him: the archive closed at five and it was nearly six. Stuart followed Lapin out of the building. At the front door Stuart thanked the archivist and told him his work was finished, that he would return to Paris in the morning and then to the United States. Lapin smiled his little smile, and then offered Stuart a lift to his hotel. During the brief drive, and when Stuart got out of the tiny car, Lapin said not a word.

FOURTEEN

Aix-en-Provence, 15 May 1969

On the evening of the day Stuart returned to Paris Jean-Claude Lapin decided to treat himself to supper at a small, moderately priced restaurant called the Palais d'Harmonie, near the fountain in the center of town. The restaurant specialized in the spicy cuisine of Vietnam and southern China, and was run by a very handsome Vietnamese widow of indeterminate middle age called Madame Huong. Lapin thought Madame Huong had taken a fancy to him from the rapt way she listened to his little stories of comings and goings in the Archives, and she often offered him a cognac at the end of a fine meal without adding it to his bill. Madame Huong made Lapin feel important—he was too old a dog not to recognize the flattery—and besides, the food was among the most interesting and the best in Aix. Even a southerner like Lapin could sometimes tire of Provençal cooking.

Lapin reached the restaurant a little after eight. There were only twelve small tables and about half were filled. The place was garishly decorated in red satin and black wood. The tablecloths were white with red good-luck lanterns. The air was smoky and fragrant with hot spices.

Madame Huong got up from her stool behind the *caisse* and rushed to meet Lapin, smiling and clasping her hands in front of her bosom. She allowed him to take both her hands in his and kiss the tips of her fingers, in the manner of the old Vietnamese Imperial Court, and then took him to his favorite corner table. Lapin sat and Mme Huong clapped for the skinny young waiter Lapin supposed was her son or nephew; Lapin's favorite aperitif, a sweet Cinzano, was quickly brought.

Madame withdrew to allow Lapin to savor the vermouth and then returned with the menu and the wine list. Lapin waved both away, ordering a half-liter of the house white wine. He invited the *maîtresse* to sit. She perched on the edge of the banquette on the other side of the corner and began to tell Lapin of the special dishes of the evening. She spoke rapid Vietnamese with what Lapin recognized as a Northern accent. He answered in the same language, saying simply that she should choose for him and should join him over coffee after dinner if her duties permitted. Mme Huong smiled at her client and stroked the back of his hand. It was always thus, thought Lapin: our little ritual. How nice it is to be liked and respected, he thought.

Madame served him soft steamed dumplings filled with tiny shrimp and fish paste, seasoned with spicy, strong-smelling *noukmam* as a first course. More soft dumplings filled with fiery hot peppers brought tears to the Frenchman's eyes; he finished the half-liter of wine and ordered another. The principal plate consisted of thin scallions and slivers of pork wrapped in soft rice wafers, which were then fried hard and crisp. Lapin ate with gusto, finishing two whole plates of the crisp flutes. He sighed and patted his tummy. Even in Saigon one could rarely get such delicacies. The benefits of French influence on the ancient Vietnamese culture, he thought happily as his dessert was brought, a thoroughly French *macédoine des fruits* flavored with a dash of Calvados. Lapin dabbed his lips with his napkin and leaned back to give his belly room to relax. He had been treated specially and he knew it. Madame came to the table, following the waiter with the coffee service on a tray. Lapin half-stood and gave a little bow, taking her by the elbow and guiding her to her seat. Mme Huong served the coffee and told the waiter to bring Lapin a cognac. She then spoke to Lapin in her unaccented French.

"Monsieur seems content," she said, her voice low and caressing. "Did my poor kitchen not insult your palate?"

"Everything was superb, madame," replied Lapin, beaming and patting her tiny hand. "This house is so restful after a tiring day, and the meal was truly superb."

"You have been busy. Your important work is so taxing."

Madame's tone carried a hint of disapproval directed, Lapin supposed, at his masters, who did indeed press him. Lapin nodded. "I have much to do; so many of the maps remain uncatalogued. And if that were not enough, this week those fools in Paris sent some dullard of an American agent to bother me and interrupt my work."

Madame Huong's eyes grew wide and her mouth made a little round O. Lapin smiled slightly and sipped his cognac. He had known she would find the story of the American interesting. "An American agent, monsieur? A *spy*?"

Lapin chuckled. Mme Huong glanced toward the bar and the waiter rushed to the table with a fresh glass of cognac. "I don't know what part of the American government he represented; he wouldn't say. Paris just told me to cooperate, so I did." Lapin drew himself up importantly. "Apparently the American's business was far too important to be disclosed to a mere archivist."

Mme Huong frowned in sympathy. "You are their best man. They don't appreciate you enough."

Lapin leaned forward to whisper. "The American was such a fool, madame. He drew out more than fifty maps, but he studied only one. And I know which one!"

Madame clapped her hands once, softly. "You see? They shouldn't try to fool a senior archivist! But how could you know which map he wanted?"

Lapin touched the side of his nose with a stubby finger. "An archivist knows, madame. Most of the maps had at least been removed from their tubes and spread out, though not all. But only one map, madame, *only one*, had been weighted, pressed flat, and studied."

"You could see all that just from looking at the maps?"

"Well, most people might miss the signs, dear madame, but a trained eye is not easily fooled." Lapin paused, basking in Mme Huong's rapt expression. He placed his hand over hers. "And I am almost certain he took photographs of the same map."

"Photographs!" whispered Mme Huong. "The spy had a camera?"

"Well, I never saw one, but just in the center of the map were four slight impressions, in a square. I believe the American had a miniature camera in his document case, and must have had a tetrapod to support it."

"How exciting! Where was this place he photographed?" Mme Huong placed her other hand on top of Lapin's.

"No place, really," shrugged Lapin. "A jumble of mountains in southern Laos. There was a river valley in the center of the square, near the town of Xieng Mi."

The name meant nothing to Madame Huong, but she felt the old fool's story might be important. She would have to send a message to Comrade Ai Quoc in Paris. She squeezed his hand and whispered, "Pray, monsieur, did the valley have a name?"

Lapin smiled. Madame's face was so close he could smell her delicate perfume. He wondered if he had the daring to kiss her. "Not in French, madame, and I don't read Lao." Maybe just to brush her cheek with his lips, he thought. "In Vietnamese the valley was labelled Thung Lung Toi."

Madame Huong released Lapin's hand and stood. Surely Ai Quoc should know of this. Thung Lung Toi, a place of ghosts, of shades of men denied the afterlife. Thung Lung Toi, the Valley of the Shadow.

Madame Huong turned back toward Lapin, who looked puzzled and a little sad. "The coffee is cold, monsieur," she said, smiling. "I will get more, and a little cognac, then you must tell me everything about this silly spy who tried to fool a clever man like you."

Paris, 16 May 1969

Khanh lay in Stuart's arms in the big bed in her apartment. Her face was pressed against his chest and she felt the rhythm of his breathing as he slept. She was wide awake and knew she wouldn't sleep until she sorted out his story in her mind. She had felt a hint of pain when he had entered her apartment with a large and expensive bouquet of roses, full of confidence that had been entirely missing during his visit of three days before, but he wouldn't talk of it, insisting on taking her off to the restaurant at the Hôtel Bristol for a meal she knew he could not afford. He had charmed her as he had at the airport in Saigon, and when he had brought her home he charmed her again, and loved her with delicate touches in all of the best places, and kisses and gentle words, and finally with his smooth muscular body and his urgent strength, sending ecstasy through her in waves, leaving her breathless, speechless, and deeply satisfied, and yet also deeply sad. He would go shortly after dawn, to Orly and to Washington. She knew she would miss him in a way she would never have thought possible on the day he and his red-faced friends had put her and her family on the plane from Saigon to Paris. She knew now as she had not known then that he touched her through her cynicism as no man ever had or would, and she knew that she loved him. Yet he was going toward danger and there was nothing she could do to save him. Khanh wept for a while, silently, against the skin of his gently moving chest, and then she fell asleep.

Stuart awoke with the dawn and slipped quietly out of Khanh's bed. He felt invigorated from the sound sleep; his jet lag had at last departed. He walked across the deep pile carpeting of the bedroom and through the passage to the living room, feeling strong and primeval in his nakedness. Khanh's scent clung to his body, causing a stirring in his loins as he sat on the large carved Chinese rug in the center of the living room across from the uncurtained glass door that framed the Eiffel Tower and began his stretching exercises and then his calisthenics. He grinned as he worked through the routine, and in twenty minutes he was slick with healthy sweat. He felt more alive than he had any morning of his life since he had left Nam, and he was absolutely sure that when he got to the valley where the three mountains lined up he would find Moser and bring him out alive. Absolutely sure.

Khanh stirred and shook off her deep sleep. She heard Stuart in the shower adjacent to the bedroom. She looked at the bedside clock and shook her head. Six A.M., and she rarely rose before ten. Wearily she sat up and then stood, wrapping a silk kimono around her, then made her way, stretching and yawning, to the other shower down the hall. She showered and then applied a careful makeup around her large eyes and her lips. Her creamy skin required nothing. She looked at herself from several angles and was satisfied. Her jaw was set in a firm line of resolve. She tried to smile at her reflection but could not.

When Khanh reentered the bedroom Stuart had all the curtains open to admit the damp, pale dawn. He had a shirt on and his tie knotted, and he favored her with his lopsided grin, followed by a quick but enthusiastic kiss. He sat and pulled on his socks and then his trousers as Khanh selected a dress of an intricate gray and green pattern in heavy silk and stepped into it. She had put on no underwear. She strode across the room and pressed her fragrant belly into Stuart's face while caressing his head and neck. Stuart felt his arousal as he reached around her and stroked her firm buttocks.

"Stay with me," breathed Khanh. "Please stay here."

William sighed as he kissed her through the smooth fabric. "I have to go back to Washington, Khanh, and you have to stay here." He pushed her away gently. "Would that things were different."

"*Mon ange*," Khanh wailed, surprised by her own passion. She pushed William back onto the bed with all her strength, then stepped back, unzipped her dress, let it fall, and then leaped into Stuart's lap.

Stuart tried to hold Khanh but she fought like a bobcat, clutching and scratching, pulling and tearing at his clothing, all the time emitting little cries. She got his trousers and his underpants off and his shirt partially unbuttoned, and then she straddled him and forced him deep inside her. Stuart surrendered to her intensity and watched her as she rode him slowly. Her eyes were closed, her face was flushed and contorted in a look of pleasure or pain, and her head swayed from side to side. The volume and tone of her cries dropped until a single moan issued with each breath, and then she collapsed on his chest and burst into tears. Stuart stroked her short hair and the length of her back, and the crying quickly stopped. She raised her head and he kissed her. Her eyes were still closed but the anguished expression had softened to a small smile. "You had better get ready to go, *mon ange*," she whispered. "I am sure Paul is already waiting downstairs." She rolled off him and got back under the covers.

Stuart showered again quickly and dressed in fresh clothes. He threw the last of his things into his grip. He bent to kiss Khanh on her cheek. She didn't stir. He closed the curtains, returning the bedroom to darkness. Stuart left the apartment and descended to find Paul waiting with the big Citroën.

Khanh awakened again just after nine-thirty. She got up slowly, shaking her head to clear it. She hated having to get up early for any reason and she had not slept well after Stuart departed.

Khanh picked up the silk dress from where she had dropped it on the rug, straightened it, and hung it in the antique panelled wardrobe next to the window. The fog had cleared away and the Seine sparkled in the sunlight. She took a kimono from the wardrobe and wrapped it around her. She rang for her maid and asked for a cup of Vietnamese tea to be brought to her study. She then washed the light makeup off her face and brushed her hair vigorously. What to do about William? she wondered.

Lourdes put the tea tray on Khanh's desk as she entered the study, smiled, and departed. Khanh sat at the Louis XV desk and unlocked the bottom right drawer. She took out the single blue sheet of the postal telegram she had received the afternoon before and smoothed it on the polished leather surface. She took another sheet of paper from the drawer and placed it next to the telegram. The telegram was a series of five-letter groups with no apparent meaning. The other sheet was the decoded version, written in Khanh's fine hand:

FOR COMRADE AI QUOC PARIS FROM HUONG AIX-EN-PROVENCE

SOURCE R REPORTS AMERICAN AGENT EXAMINED AND PROBABLY PHOTOGRAPHED DETAILED MAPS OF AREA NEAR TOWN XIENG MI SOUTHERN LAOS LAT 18 DEGREES 6.5 MINUTES N LONG 103 DEGREES 01 MINUTES EAST. AGENT'S NAME GIVEN AS M. STUART, FN UNKNOWN, PRECISE AFFILIA-TION UNKNOWN. AGENT BELIEVED DEPARTED AIX THIS MORNING BY TRAIN TO LYON OR PARIS. ENDS.

Khanh sighed as she put both sheets of paper back in the drawer and locked it. Why was William going to Laos? Neither the name of the town nor the map coordinates meant anything to her. He had mentioned a friend in danger, perhaps a downed flyer, so she guessed the location might be that of a camp, though she knew nothing of prison camps. But why had the Americans sent someone so guileless and so obviously ill-suited to field work as to be caught by the amateur watchers of the NVA intelligence cell in Aix?

If the Americans are planning to mount a rescue effort Hanoi will want to set a trap, and then the man who got my family out of Saigon, the man who had never asked for anything in return, would die. It would be the third time in her life she had betrayed the only man who had genuinely cared for her, the only man she had ever allowed herself to love.

Khanh closed her eyes and rubbed them with her fingertips to prevent tears from starting. Perhaps I could warn him, she thought, but he would go anyway. I can lose this note, but not forever; Aix would surely inquire again, as it was a major coup for them and they would want the credit if the Americans were foiled. And I am chief of North Vietnamese intelligence in Paris; it is my duty to report this on to Hanoi without delay. I have no right to protect this man, this *imperialist* who has violated my country and will do so again.

The NVA major known as Ai Quoc, the Patriot, let her tears fall. Calling William an imperialist did not make her able to hate him. Whomever she betrayed, men would die.

Khanh made herself drink the cooling tea and calm herself. She had at least a few days to decide whom she would sacrifice.

FIFTEEN

Stuart's plane landed at Dulles a little after noon. He got his car out of the long-term lot and drove directly to the NIS building in Arlington. Major MacAndrew was out to lunch, expected to return about 1330. Stuart took the film from his Minox downstairs to the photo lab run by the Code 30 (Criminal) branch. The first class photographer's mate who ran the lab was a friend of Stuart's and promised to do the film right away and have blowups in an hour. Stuart felt a little tired from the long flight, but he also felt a keen sense of excitement at his discovery and a restlessness to get started on the rescue itself. He was sure Harry MacAndrew would be able to get authorization. The mission shaping up in Stuart's mind would be so small, so easy and so relatively cheap that he felt they could get it organized and done in a matter of weeks. Moser home in a matter of weeks, though he would be weak and sick. Still, thought Stuart, grinning, not much time left for old Clem Watkins.

Major MacAndrew returned from lunch to find Stuart sitting at the desk outside his office, a large, red-striped top secret envelope on his lap. MacAndrew waved Stuart into his office and told his secretary to hold calls. He removed his sport jacket and watched as Stuart shrugged out of his rumpled suit coat. MacAndrew seated himself at the worktable and pulled the envelope toward him. "Your message said you thought you had found something of value, William," said MacAndrew. "You weren't gone long."

"I got lucky, Major. And the French are quite well organized."

MacAndrew pulled the sheaf of photos out of the envelope. The maps were clearly readable in the 8-by-10 glossies. MacAndrew traced the three mountains with his fingers. "Jesus," he said softly. "The scale is different but the alignment is perfect."

"I know," said Stuart, presenting another photo showing more of the area. "It's spooky. It's exactly like he said, exactly like that valley in Georgia."

"And it is right near Thailand," said MacAndrew, scratching his head. "A walk-in for a small team, clear a landing zone, and in come the helicopters. It seems too easy."

Stuart stirred uneasily. MacAndrew clearly was not convinced. "I wondered about that, Harry. Why would they put a camp that close to Thailand? But the Ho Chi Minh Trail is not far to the east, so NVA control of the area is probably complete." He pointed to symbols on the margin of the map. "These marks indicate mining activity; perhaps the Viets are using prisoners to work mines."

Major MacAndrew looked slowly through the rest of the photos. "Only one site. No other promising places?"

"No, sir." William shook his head. "This place fits, and I couldn't find anything else even close."

MacAndrew stood, wincing at the pain in his feet. "I am going to take these to the director. I doubt he will want to see you before tomorrow, so go on home and get some rest."

Stuart stood and picked up his coat. "I want to stay on with this, Major."

"I know you do. We'll talk tomorrow, William."

"I think—I don't know why, but I feel strongly that I should go with the extraction team."

MacAndrew looked at the young officer. His expression was serious, even sad. "One thing at a time, son. See me tomorrow, first thing."

"Aye, aye, sir," said Stuart. He left the office, and suddenly he felt very tired indeed.

Captain Willis set the phone in its cradle and looked across his desk at Major MacAndrew, who had sat smoking in silence as the director spoke with the assistant to the president. "The deal," said Willis, "is as follows. I have to take this to ACSI–Army. John Hermann doesn't want any interservice rivalry nonsense."

"They'll bury it, Director," said Harry MacAndrew, frowning.

Captain Willis waved his hand in front of his face. "Perhaps they won't; young Stuart is right, Harry, it should be a real easy operation and the army could use a success in the prisoner-recovery area."

"But they like flashy, big stuff: paratroopers, clouds of helicopters, the whole nine yards." MacAndrew leaned forward. "I still think they will bury it."

"If they do, the mission comes back to the navy. Specifically, to me."

Harry MacAndrew stood. "How much time do we have to give them to decide?"

"Not long," said the director, getting to his feet. "I have an appointment with a Major General Clifton at the Pentagon at ten-hundred tomorrow. He is in charge of the overall coordination of prisoner sightings and the scheduling of rescue missions. By the time I get there he will have heard from the president's man, and I imagine he will see the need to act without delay."

"Did the president's assistant say the White House was less than pleased at the efforts the army has made up to now?" asked MacAndrew.

"Didn't say it, no, but I think Nixon is pressing," said the director. "He ran on a promise to end the war in six months but the Viets won't deal, and the absolute minimum he can accept is the return of all the prisoners of war."

MacAndrew nodded. "If the army takes the mission I would like to second Stuart to them. His instincts are very good and his record shows him very steady under fire."

"I'll try. I think they would give me that." The director walked around the big desk and walked to the door with MacAndrew. "I will call you as soon as I get back from the Pentagon, Harry. Perhaps you would join me for lunch."

MacAndrew grinned. "Delighted. Give 'em hell, sir."

"I will, Harry," said the old man with a small smile. "I will."

Captain Willis's limousine left the Pentagon and drove slowly north on Memorial Parkway, past the vast Arlington National Cemetery. Captain Willis had been cordially received by General Clifton, who had told him the White House had indeed taken a great interest in recovery of POWs. Clifton had a harried appearance, a result, Willis had concluded while watching the younger man pace his small office like a caged cat, of trying to act quickly to please the White House while still respecting the wishes of the service commanders to plan and prepare with great caution. A rescue mission inside North Vietnam would be extremely difficult even with the best possible intelligence, but the intelligence was never completely reliable and the need to use Vietnamese agents meant it was often compromised as well.

Willis sat back in the soft plush seat and thought about the young major general and his problem. Photos of ragged POWs, mostly looking haggard and with their heads hanging, appearing on American television and in news magazines, had fueled the opposition to the war and given it its new cry, "Bring the War Home." A major demonstration to be called Vietnam Moratorium Day was planned for Washington one week hence, the first major protest in the capital since the very large near-riot on the day of President Nixon's inauguration. The Nixon people were frustrated; the demonstrators demanded an end to the bombing campaign against the North, and the North for its part refused to talk until the bombing was halted. It wasn't hard for many in the administration to conclude that the antiwar activists were in effect aiding the enemy, although Captain Willis knew that extensive surveillance and even infiltration of activist groups by the FBI and other intelligence agencies (including his own) had found no direct link between Hanoi and any of the groups that had disrupted the Democratic Party convention in Chicago the previous year, and who now bayed around the White House.

Captain Willis believed the Nixon people wanted to end the war, and quickly, before it ceased to be President Johnson's war and became their own. Willis also believed, however, that the North Vietnamese felt that if they held out they would get all or nearly all they had fought for because victory was essential to them and not to the United States. Therefore they wouldn't talk unless Nixon gave them something, and what they wanted was an end to the bombing so that they could reequip their large divisions in the southern part of North Vietnam, and in Laos and Cambodia, for the final thrust to Saigon. But Nixon had to keep bombing while his programs of "Vietnamization" and withdrawal of American forces were rushed forward. The bombing continued and the North Vietnamese continued to parade downed flyers, often surrounded by the jeering peasants who had captured them. Nixon, Captain Willis surmised, needed some good news on the POW situation, and he needed it soon. That pressure was felt in Major General Clifton's office and doubtless by the Joint Chiefs. Willis sighed as his car turned into Fort

Myer. Pressure like that made for bad operations. Perhaps that is why Clifton took his copy of the photographs and maps with apparent enthusiasm but no obvious interest. The general had agreed as well to take Lieutenant Stuart on temporary assignment, but had been very vague about scheduling of even preliminary plans. On reflection, Willis decided that Clifton had been almost brusque, rushing through the meeting, doing it because he couldn't afford not to, but without interest.

Something, thought Willis, something very large must be up. And Harry is right: the army will bury Stuart's information.

SIXTEEN

Washington, 17 May 1969

Stuart was assigned a gray metal desk in the ACSI–Army liaison area on the second floor of the B ring of the Pentagon. It had taken him the better part of the morning to get photographed for new passes and to find his way around. Since he was in the Pentagon on temporary duty he was not granted a space in any of the vast but overcrowded parking lots that surrounded the building, and he had had to leave his car in a private lot a quarter mile away and pay the thief who ran it five dollars per day, a not insignificant portion of a lieutenant's pay.

Stuart reported to a Lieutenant Colonel Becker, a General Service Corps officer in a sharply pressed service dress green uniform. Becker was an intense man, compact and handsome with quick blue eyes and a firm jaw. From his patches and decorations Stuart could see the colonel had served in Vietnam with the 1st Cav, had been wounded, and had received the Bronze Star with Combat V. Stuart could see the colonel's eyes run over his own ribbons. The colonel looked impressed but puzzled.

"May I ask, Lieutenant?" said the colonel, after bidding Stuart sit in the small conference room that separated the bullpen from Major General Clifton's large office by the windows.

"The Combat Infantry Badge, Colonel?" asked Stuart, smiling.

Colonel Becker's stiff demeanor seemed to soften. "Exactly. I have never seen a naval officer wear that device."

"I ran an ANGLICO detachment in I Corps, Colonel," said Stuart, suddenly remembering the glory and the pain that had followed. "I was twice assigned to the 197th Light Infantry Brigade."

"Ah-ha!" said the colonel, slapping his thigh and grinning. "I remember, that was the outfit run by that black cowboy who gave the generals in Bien Hoa and Saigon fits. He kept running large-scale operations MACV said couldn't work and sometimes produced dramatic results, finding the enemy where the REMFs said they couldn't be and kicking the shit out of them. What was his name?"

"Gen. Blackjack Beaurive," said Stuart, proudly, remembering the man.

"Right," said Becker. "Well, I am glad to have you here, Stuart. I should admit that when General Clifton told me Navy was sending me an officer to work on a special project within the prisoner-recovery area I thought you would probably get in the way, but clearly you know enough about how the army works to help." The colonel leaned forward and steepled his fingers on the scarred surface of the table. "Tell me about your project."

Stuart hoisted his briefcase up onto the table and took out the photographs.

21 May 1969

"How did your first week in the Pentagon go, William?" asked Harry MacAndrew, pouring a fresh glass from his pitcher of beer as Stuart sat next to him at the bar.

"Slow, Major." William looked around him in the rapidly filling bar. Fort Myer Officers' Club always did a land-office business at happy hour on Fridays. Stuart leaned close and lowered his voice. "Something is going on over there, Major. This Colonel Becker I am supposed to be working with walks away from me in mid-sentence whenever his phone rings, and then he scurries into the general's office, and when he comes out he is always grinning."

MacAndrew nodded and kept his own voice low. "The director has the same impression, but even he can't find out what is up. How are you doing with the planning for the raid on the camp?"

"That's another strange thing. They let me write the whole thing: assault force, ground support, combat air support, and extraction requirements, even signals." Stuart took a sip of beer and looked around them for listeners. "Christ, Major, what do I know about signals?"

"What do you think they are doing?"

"I don't have any idea, but it is not as though they are ignoring me, it's more like they have a great secret, something that amuses them, that they don't want me to know."

"The director tells me that major new funds are about to be made available for prisoner rescue missions," said MacAndrew.

"Not before time. The antiwar people are gathering in greater strength every day around the Pentagon, Major. Troops have taken over perimeter security from the police. So far the kids are just singing and chanting insulting slogans, but I have to tell you, my quarter-mile hike to my car through the crowd twice a day is a spooky experience."

MacAndrew nodded. "I think the Nixon people have to pull a rabbit out of the hat, William, some kind of good news on negotiations, or failing that something on the POWs and the missing."

"Colonel Becker as much as said the same thing, Major," said William. "But I don't understand why they don't want to press forward with our operation. It's perfect for the politicians because it is small and inconspicuous: if it works they can tell the world, and if it fails they can bury it."

MacAndrew smiled wryly. "You have already been in D.C. too long, William."

"Maybe," agreed Stuart, refilling his glass and MacAndrew's. "My guess is the army have some flash operation laid on, something to show they are in control."

"Nixon needs some heroes," said MacAndrew.

"Yes, perhaps," nodded Stuart. "The army does too. Even though they are doing fairly well in the big clearing operations all anybody wants to hear about are the casualties they are taking. Even victories don't help anymore, and the security officer on the general's staff tells me the government expects a quarter million demonstrators on the Mall this weekend."

"The 82d Airborne is on alert down at Bragg," said MacAndrew. "Keep that under your hat."

Stuart frowned. "None of this is getting Moser out of the shit, Major."

"I know, William, and the director knows. Give it another week; if the army won't act or at least take a serious interest, we will get it back." MacAndrew twisted on his stool and looked at Stuart. "Have you given that any thought?"

"The plan I have written will work as well with Navy or Marines as with soldiers, Major, and either way we will need the air force to bring us out because of where the camp is."

"Good," said MacAndrew, sliding off the stool. "I have to see the director in a half hour. Keep planning, William, and keep listening."

"Aye, aye, sir," said Stuart, following MacAndrew out of the crowded bar.

III

NIGHT
CROSSINGS

SEVENTEEN

Washington, 22 May 1969

William Stuart had given up on taking his car to the Pentagon after the third day and had resorted to the bus up the Columbia Pike from Alexandria. The morning was raw with blowing light rain, and the bus slowed to a crawl as it approached the Pentagon. Even at 0730 the antiwar demonstrators were out in force, chanting and singing and pressing against the ranks of weary-looking soldiers, rain glistening on their riot gear and rifles. Stuart abandoned the bus about a half mile from the Pentagon and pushed through the demonstrators, who looked at him, in his black raincoat with the twin silver bars on each epaulet and his white-topped uniform cap, with curiosity, as though they had already taken over the Pentagon and didn't expect to see his kind again. For the most part the demonstrators were young and seemed to be enjoying themselves. The smell of marijuana hung heavily in the damp air.

Stuart found the gate he normally used to enter the building blocked off by barricades and a heavy concentration of soldiers. As politely as he could Stuart made his way to the wooden barricade and showed his identification to a harrassed-looking black MP sergeant. The man glanced at the cards and pointed to the left. "You will have to try the next entrance, Lieutenant," said the sergeant, shouting to be heard above the chanting and laughter of the crowd. "We are supposed to hold this door open for some brass."

Stuart nodded and pushed along the barricade, excusing himself as he went. He stepped over and around people, some of them in sleeping bags. His progress was slow, and by the time he finally made his way into the building he was wet outside, sweaty inside, and forty-five minutes late. The office was supposed to be open at 0800, but since the demonstrations had begun on-time arrival by both officers and enlisted personnel had been impaired. Stuart was therefore somewhat surprised to notice, as he hung up his cap and his raincoat, that everyone in the ACSI subunit to which he was attached was in and working and looked as though they had been in for hours. He walked into Colonel Becker's office, interrupting a conference of the colonel, a captain, and a sergeant first class, all of whom stopped speaking when he reached the door.

"Excuse me, Colonel," said Stuart, backing out of the office.

"No, come in, Lieutenant, the door is open."

"Something up this morning, sir?" said Stuart, smiling and gesturing toward the bustle in the bullpen.

"Ah," began the colonel. The captain and the sergeant looked sharply at Stuart. "Come on in, Lieutenant," said the colonel, nodding as he reached a decision. "Captain, Sergeant, go get us set up in the large conference room. The general will be coming down from JCS in half an hour." The captain and the sergeant left. Each gave Stuart a conspiratorial wink. The sergeant closed the door softly behind him. "Sit down, Stuart," said Becker, smiling. "I'll bet you came in to gig me because I still haven't endorsed your preliminary operations plan for your extraction in southern Laos."

"Well, sir, I just thought I would ask if there was more information the colonel required." Stuart felt he was being gently mocked.

"Come on, Lieutenant, you think we have been ignoring you and your project, and maybe we have," said Becker. "But after today we will be able to give you all the attention you deserve, and plenty of money if needed."

"I knew something was going on," said Stuart cautiously. "Though no one ever said anything."

"Strictly speaking, you aren't cleared for it, Stuart—no need to know. But you are a good man, so I am going to put you in the picture." Colonel Becker paused. "Just say nothing outside this room for at least twenty-four hours, or until the story breaks."

"Of course, Colonel."

The colonel grinned. "Okay. Those CIA assholes have finally done something useful. They have pinpointed the location of the prison camp the press calls the Hanoi Hilton and have confirmed between seventy and ninety POWs in residence."

Stuart jumped to his feet. "When are you going in?"

Colonel Becker glanced at his watch. "The first aircraft should be taking off from the carriers in the South China Sea in less than an hour. Twenty-two-hundred, Saigon time."

Gulf of Tonkin

USS *Constellation* (CVA 64) signalled her screening ships with the omnidirectional blinker on the yardarm. The signal was "000 Foxtrot Corpen 2210," and it told each ship that at 2210, ten minutes from now, the carrier would turn to her left from the present course of 050 to 000, due north, and would then be prepared to launch aircraft. It was a far easier signal to make with flags, but they couldn't have been seen in the darkness. The signal bridges on either side of the carrier's island logged each destroyer's and cruiser's acknowledgement and reported to the bridge when the last answer was in. The screening ships now had just under ten minutes to figure out where the carrier would be just as she made her own turn, and then speed to a location relative to the big ship on her new course—ahead of the carrier, astern, to starboard, or to port—identical to the assigned station in the present screen. It was a complex maneuver, as the *Connie* had a total of eight escorts. Destroyer shipdrivers hated the Foxtrot Corpen, especially at night. Carrier drivers loved it; all they had to do was turn on time and then comment drily on any confusion that ensued among the smaller ships.

The night was calm, bright with stars above broken clouds. The strike would be launched directly at Haiphong, eighty miles to the north, using the wind created by the carriers themselves steaming at flank speed of thirty knots. *Constellation* and her battle group were under the command of the admiral on the smaller attack carrier USS *Oriskany* (CVA 34), steaming with her escorts some ten miles to the northwest.

Connie acknowledged the "station" signals from her escorts that indicated that they had completed the required maneuvers to reorient the screen. At exactly 2210 the great ship turned to the north, heeling slightly as she swung. The officer of the deck used minimal rudder to keep the flight deck as level as possible; it was crowded with aircraft, fully fuelled and armed, though still tied down. The carrier signalled the screen that she was increasing speed to thirty knots. *Connie*'s officer of the deck gave a green deck to Primary Flight Control (PRIFLY), which overhung the flight deck just aft of the bridge, and the Alfa Strike launch began.

The Alfa Strike was the most powerful attack an aircraft carrier could execute, with nearly all available aircraft flying. Since *Oriskany*'s attack was to be coordinated with *Constellation*'s, the strike was a double Alfa, involving 152 aircraft, with only the single squadron of little A-4B Skyhawk attack aircraft aboard *Oriskany* remaining in the hangar deck, since they had no all-weather capability.

With both carrier battle groups steaming north toward the Vietnamese coast, the first aircraft up were the search and rescue helicopters, two CH-53s from each carrier. They would fly close behind the carriers during the launch and then approach the shore during the raid itself to assist pilots who might be forced to ditch. As soon as the forward deck spots were cleared by the helos *Oriskany* started launching her squadrons of F8-U Crusader fighters, armed with cannon and Sidewinder air-to-air missiles, from both bow catapults. *Constellation* quickly launched a squadron of F-4 Phantoms armed with Sidewinder and Sparrow air-to-air missiles from both bow and waist cats. The pace of the launch was like a slow dance, with yellow-shirted aircraft handlers darting under the big machines, guiding them to the cats where the green-shirted hookup men hooked up the nose tows and the holdbacks, then signalling for tension on the cat. Each aircraft's takeoff weight was shown to the cat officer and the pilot, then the cat officer signalled for full power, saw the hookup man jump free, received and acknowledged the pilot's ready signal, and signalled the launch. *Constellation* had her first fourteen fighters launched in nine minutes.

The fighters from both ships would fly to stations close to the coast and establish the Barrier Combat Air Patrol (BARCAP) to track and intercept any North Vietnamese Air Force aircraft that might attempt to attack the fleet. Because the NVAF rarely ventured out over water, and because their sorties at night were normally limited to tracking incoming aircraft for the SAM batteries, the Cruds (F-8s) and Rhinos (F-4s) would take stations aggressively close to the Vietnamese coast and let the strike aircraft fly in beneath them, hoping to spot any MiGs rising from the coastal airfields to follow the bombers.

Next to launch after the BARCAP fighters were the tankers for in-flight refuelling of strike and fighter aircraft. Huge KA-3 Whales and smaller KA-6s took off with all their takeoff weight allowance committed to fuel. These unarmed aircraft would refuel the strike aircraft immediately after they launched, especially the F-4s given a bombing role, as the F-4s could not launch with full bomb loads unless they took off with fuel tanks virtually empty. After refuelling the strike aircraft the tankers would fly out to loiter behind the shield of the BARCAP or wait behind the carriers to land and load up again after the last strike aircraft had gone; then they would proceed out to the BARCAP line to refuel aircraft returning light from the attack.

Next up were the two E2-C early warning aircraft, which would fly between the fleet and the coast. Between them the two aircraft could easily track all friendly and hostile aircraft in a radius of two hundred miles, track any friendly aircraft that might be damaged or lost, and thereafter coordinate rescue efforts. Next, each carrier launched two A-6s carrying electronic countermeasure pods instead of munitions on their underwing hardpoints. The electronic gear was designed to blind and confuse enemy radar and at the same time pinpoint their locations for the attacking aircraft. Then, as the fighter and attack aircraft pilots would say, began the launching of the Serious Shit.

The strike itself consisted of F-4 fighters armed with air-to-air missiles and, in the case of the late-model E aircraft, 20mm Vulcan cannon. These aircraft would lead the bombing aircraft over the target area in a mission frag called MIGCAP, for MiG Combat Air Patrol. The MIGCAP fighters would establish air superiority in the airspace over the entire attack area. Other F-4 aircraft carried bombs and would attack large targets, on this evening the railroad marshalling yards at Haiphong, Yen Vien, and Kep, air bases at Phuc Yen, Kep, and Hoa Loc, all around Hanoi, and the Haiphong petrochemical complex. Following the first waves of F-4s would come the A-6 Intruders equipped with Shrike and HARM antiradiation missiles, which would target and attack SAM sites in the Hanoi–Haiphong corridor and along the coast. Further squadrons of A-6s and the smaller A4-C all-weather attack bombers would follow, with the targets requiring the most precise bombing left to the A-6s, which were specialists in the night attack role. SAM batteries pinpointed at sites 660, 537, and 663, all east of Kep, and 649, south of Hanoi, as well as the railroad switches at Giap Nhi and Kinh No, were targeted for special attention by the A-6s, while the A4-Cs pounded the Hanoi and Haiphong railroad yards.

Last off the carrier decks were the RA5-C Vigilante reconnaissance aircraft, whose photos both at high and low altitudes would help the planners on the carriers to assess the damage. Their pictures would show the results of a devastating raid.

An hour after the first strike aircraft were launched the aircraft began returning. Some had minor damage from flak but only two had been lost, both bombing F-4s, and all four crewmen of those aircraft had ejected over the sea and had been recovered by search and rescue helos, affectionately called Dumbos. Pilots in ready rooms were boisterous as more and more aircraft came aboard the great ships safely. Massive secondary explosions in the freight yards and at the SAM sites, as well as huge fires at the petrochemical plants, were reported and confirmed by the attack pilots, while the fighter jocks told tales of stealthy MiGs (three reported shot down) and the radical writhing maneuvers needed to escape the flying forest of giant SA-2 and SA-3 missiles that rose and pursued on tails of fire. When the last aircraft were recovered a pair of refuelled and rearmed A-6s were launched from *Constellation*, along with a pair of F4-Es. One of the airborne E2-Cs refuelled and followed. These would fly above the task force as it made its way toward open water and also render any assistance needed to the army. As soon as these last aircraft were airborne and formed up the carriers once again reoriented their screens and turned south, speeding out of the confined waters of the Gulf of Tonkin. The double Alfa Strike of 22 May was one of the largest of the war in terms of total carrier-based aircraft launched, ordnance deployed, and targets successfully struck. Hanoi and Haiphong would be without most of their rail links and much of their SAM protection and petrochemical production for months to come. It was an enormously important raid.

But in the larger sense the double Alfa Strike was a colossal diversion. Immediately after the launch of the SAR helos from *Oriskany* four army CH-47 Chinook helicopters in black jungle camouflage livery took off from the forward end of the flight deck and headed for the coast of North Vietnam at an altitude of five hundred feet. They were accompanied by a single UHE-1 gunship configured with command radios and carrying the commanding officer of the army task force,

Lt. Col. Michael Grogan. The army helicopters timed their flight to cross the coast ten minutes after the naval air attack reached its maximum intensity. Their goal was the town of Xuan Mai, forty kilometers west of Hanoi on Highway 6, the place where seventy to ninety American air force and navy pilots had been located by the CIA, confined in the notoriously cruel conditions of the camp called the Hanoi Hilton.

Inside the Chinooks army rangers faced each other on the red web fold-down benches. The rangers wore special night camouflage uniforms and their faces were painted black and green. Each Chinook could carry forty-four troops with full combat gear, but the first two held only twenty each, and each of the last two carried a single squad of twelve men. The group could lose a chopper and still bring out all the troops and all the prisoners. All the rangers carried light battle packs and their M-16, M-79, or M-60 personal weapons. Every man not encumbered with a radio carried a LAW (light antitank weapon). Opposition was expected to be light from the guards at the prison camp and it was believed that reinforcement from NVA strongpoints nearby to the north would be forestalled by the disruption caused by the naval air raid, which at its southwesternmost target was bombing only five kilometers away.

The plan was to land the first two Chinooks in an open area, previously photographed, a hundred meters south of the two buildings that constituted the prison compound. The third chopper would send its squad rappelling down north of the compound onto a road too narrow to land on. This squad would hold the road in case the NVA attempted to send reinforcements from the large army base at Ha Dong or from Hanoi itself. Reinforcements were not expected since targets in Hanoi and Ha Dong were under savage bombardment from the navy and would still be under attack long after the rangers picked up the POWs and left to rendezvous with the carriers. The troops from the first two helicopters would storm the prison itself while their aircraft waited overhead, marshal the prisoners, and then depart. The fourth chopper and its rifle squad were a reserve to be used where needed. The Huey with the colonel embarked was to remain airborne to coordinate the raid and communicate with the navy, and if need be use its machine guns and rockets to support the ground forces.

The rangers had been practicing their assault at a mock-up of the Hanoi Hilton built at Fort Benning, Georgia, since the first pictures of the camp had been brought out of North Vietnam by a Swedish camera crew in October of 1968. The photos had been clear enough to show the buildings and the perimeter fencing around them, the guard towers, the gates, and the road behind. From sun angles and the information from the Swedes that they had visited the camp in the early morning the army had determined the approximate orientation of the camp. The Swedes had given no inkling of the location of the camp and had claimed to have been blindfolded going and coming, but their pictures of pathetic, gaunt men in the rags that had once been their flight suits had stirred the world to ever more protest and elevated antiwar sentiment in the United States to fever pitch. Many of the protestors ringing the Pentagon and streaming into Washington itself for Moratorium Day as the army helicopters sped toward Xuan Mai carried posters, gigantic blowups of the prisoners as seen on the Swedish film, and signs saying "The only way to bring them home is to end the war." The Joint Chiefs thought differently and had convinced the president, frustrated as he was at the North Vietnamese side's refusal to deal. When the CIA reported they had information as to where the Hanoi Hilton was and when photos made by an Air Force SR-71 flying from Kadena Air Base in Okinawa matched the Swedish pictures Operation Night Crossing was authorized, and tonight the rangers' choppers descended toward the darkened camp as their pilots watched the light show of the naval air bombardment a few klicks to the north and east.

Chinooks One and Two (radio call signs: Nightwing One and Two) stooped and landed in the darkened open area, and the rangers poured out and formed fire teams. The camp was dimly lighted around the perimeter fence and in the guard towers, but the buildings themselves seemed completely dark. The Chinooks lifted off as soon as the last rangers were clear, and the door gunners fired long bursts of .50 calibre ammunition into the guard towers. On the other side of the compound twelve rangers slithered down their ropes and set themselves up on both sides of the road where it led northeast. The colonel sat quietly in the Huey as it hovered over the center of the camp. He watched as the rangers engaged the near towers and the main gate with LAWs, and listened to the tactical radio net. Capt. Robby Ferris, with the assault team, reported the rangers were inside the compound and had encountered no resistance. The colonel gave the order to storm the buildings immediately. The operation was ahead of schedule.

Captain Ferris sent a five-man team led by a sergeant into each building. The rest of the rangers inside the compound worked around the outside of the buildings looking for Vietnamese guards. The soldiers holding the road reported no contact.

Colonel Grogan listened intently as the teams worked their way through the buildings, passage by passage and room by room. The reports were all the same: no prisoners, no gooks. Damn! he thought. The fucking CIA did it again.

"Colonel," said the specialist manning the secondary tactical net. "Blocker Three Actual reports he can hear tracked vehicles approaching from the *west*, sir." Blocker Three Actual was Lt. Barry Schwartz commanding the squad holding the road against reinforcements expected from the *northeast*. The colonel thumbed the transmit button on his microphone. "Striker Six, this is Night Crossing Six. Get out of there, Robby, ASAP."

"Roger, Six," replied Captain Ferris. "We will be assembled in the LZ in one minute."

"Sir," said the colonel's RTO, tugging at his sleeve. "Lieutenant Schwartz has vehicle noises from both directions. He thinks tanks, sir."

Lieutenant Colonel Grogan nodded. "Tell Blocker Three to engage the vehicles from the northeast. We will take a look west." Fucking CIA has dropped us into a trap!

Grogan told the Chinooks to land one at a time, the other flying cover with its door guns. He then told the Huey pilot to swing around to the road facing west and to fire an illumination flare. The flare, fired from the 40mm grenade launcher mounted under the Huey's chin, burst a hundred meters in front of the aircraft and hung under its parachute, revealing a landscape of brilliant light and inky shadows. Directly below the flare were two armored vehicles, the first easily identified as a Russian-built PT-76 light tank and the second a four-barreled antiaircraft gun mounted on a light tank chassis called a ZSU 23-4. Colonel Grogan sucked in his breath as the pilot threw the Huey into a violent turn away. The ZSU fired a thick blast of green tracers. The Huey seemed to be completely surrounded by the green fire for just a second, then the pilot dove to treetop level and accelerated into another turn to bring himself around behind the vehicles. "Rockets!" screamed the pilot into his headset. "Rockets!" The copilot gunner nodded and armed the rockets in their pods, a mixture of white phosphorous and the antipersonnel flechette rounds the troops called nails. They hadn't expected armor.

The Huey popped up over the road and slowed. The flare was almost gone but the vehicles could be seen clearly. The ZSU's turret traversed rapidly to the rear as the copilot fired four rockets and then four more, then the Huey pulled sharply upward and banked away from the first burst of green tracer. The yellowish flare of the willy peter illuminated the interior of the Huey as the chopper turned and raced around for another look.

Blocker Three reported putting two LAWs into a light tank, stopping it with a broken track. A tank behind it began pushing the damaged tank and firing past it with its 76mm main gun and coaxial machine gun. Lieutenant Schwartz reported he had seven LAWs left and was fairly well concealed. Colonel Grogan told him to hold and try to hit the second tank to block the road, but also to be ready to pull back to the landing zone.

Nightwing One stooped and landed, with Two hovering above, raking the trees with machine-gun fire from the door guns. The rhythmic, insectlike chirping of the tank tracks in the woods could be heard even over the roar of the CH-47's rotors. The first fire team of rangers was already on board when a PT-76 pushed its gun through the undergrowth on the south side of the LZ and fired. The round struck the tall tail assembly of the chopper underneath the engines. The tail assembly disintegrated and the tail rotor flew up and cartwheeled into the trees. The ranger fire team holding the western edge of the LZ perimeter immediately engaged the tank with LAWs and small-arms fire. The lightly armored vehicle began to reverse back into cover, but a LAW burst under the turret ring and the tank exploded in a bright orange fireball. Nightwing Two landed immediately and Captain Ferris gestured to his load sergeant to get six full fire teams from the assault team—thirty men—as well as the troops and crew coiling out of the burning Number One chopper aboard and out. That would leave him with nineteen men on the ground including Lieutenant Schwartz's squad on the road. The Number Two Chinook loaded and lifted off immediately.

Colonel Grogan monitored the traffic on tactical net as the Huey swung back over the road to the west. Both the PT-76 and the ZSU were stopped and burning. Colonel Grogan broke into tactical to order Schwartz to break off immediately and get to the assembly area. Nightwing Three swung south of the assembly area with Four following, waiting for a call from Captain Ferris. We can still get out, thought Colonel Grogan, and then Lieutenant Schwartz reported that a tank with infantry following had slipped behind his unit and cut half of them off from the LZ. Colonel Grogan ordered Captain Ferris to bring in Nightwing Three immediately and to clear all personnel including himself out of the LZ. The Huey would rocket what tanks it could to the northeast, then pick up Schwartz and his five. Schwartz reported more tanks and trucks on the road. He was down to one LAW.

The navy flight of two A-6s and two F4-Es screamed in over the battle, turning at five thousand feet and radioing Night Crossing Six for instructions. Colonel Grogan gave them Schwartz's position and told them to seek targets up the road toward Ha Dong, away from the line of contact. The commander leading the flight informed the colonel that the carriers were launching additional attack aircraft as fast as they could be refuelled and rearmed. Colonel Grogan acknowledged and then went back to his immediate problem. Nightwing Three descended rapidly into the LZ as Four watched. Captain Ferris, his last fire team, and the six of Lieutenant Schwartz's squad waited for the chopper to land. The Huey moved slowly over the dark road toward the sound and flash of gunfire. The colonel reached forward into the cockpit and grabbed the pilot's shoulder, then shouted into his ear for him to switch to the tactical frequency. The pilot nodded and switched his headset and the copilot's. Now everybody could hear everybody else.

"Schwartz, this is Six," said the colonel. "Where are you and where is the tank holding you down?"

"We are in the drainage ditch to the left of the road as you see it, Six." Schwartz's voice was a strained whisper in the radio. "Next to a solitary tall tree. There is one tank just across the road in the tall elephant grass and scrub trees, and I think another beyond it. There are perhaps a squad of soldiers on this side of the road, and I think they are looking for us."

"You are not actually engaged?"

"Negative, Six. Lying low."

"Okay," said the colonel. He placed a hand on the pilot's shoulder. "Here is what we do. The Huey will come in quick and low and put all its remaining rockets into the grass to the right. Schwartz, as soon as you see us, shoot the bastards on your side of the road and run for the Huey and pile in. I don't want to be on the ground more than ten seconds."

"Roger, Six, understood," answered Schwartz.

"Go," said the colonel to the pilot. The radio crackled again: Nightwing Three was up from the LZ with thirteen men. We are going to make it, thought Colonel Grogan.

The pilot popped up to a hundred feet, then disengaged the turbine from the rotors to autorotate and begin a steep dive to the spot on the road next to the lone tall tree. He angled the nose of the aircraft right as he descended, and at fifty meters of altitude the copilot fired the remaining six rockets in salvos of two. The willy peter ignited the grass and two tanks were briefly visible, then the nearest exploded. Shrapnel and burning fuel splashed over the Huey as its skids hit the ground hard. The pilot immediately reengaged the motor to the rotors, pulled collective, and powered up for takeoff.

The first ranger from Lieutenant Schwartz's squad dove into the main compartment, scrambled across, and ran straight into the colonel. Bodies flew in after him, rolling on the deck like football players after a fumble. At last Lieutenant Schwartz stood in the door, holding both edges. The colonel crawled out from under the soldier and thumbed his mike. "Go, Captain!"

The Huey lifted slowly with the added weight of six more men. The pilot had to pivot the chopper in the ground effect before he could run along the road to gain speed and lift. The Huey started forward as the pilot pulled in more collective. Suddenly, like a whale broaching, a PT-76 tank burst from the high grass at the side of the road, its tracks churning the red earth like water. The thing filled the entire plexiglas nose of the Huey, and as the pilot tried frantically to lift over it, it fired both its main gun and the coaxial machine gun. The main gun round entered the engine intake on the top of the chopper and blew the turbine to hot, jagged pieces that sliced into the main cabin, wounding many of the rangers huddled below. The machine-gun fire killed the pilot and copilot instantly, and Colonel Grogan felt a bullet smash through his shoulder. The Huey crashed back on its skids and tilted over to the right. The tank turned, came right at the aircraft, and stopped, with its track running over and crushing the damaged right skid, causing the helicopter to tilt farther. Colonel Grogan heard a roar overhead and then the staccato multiple crashes of the Rockeye fragmentation bombs the A-6s were dropping on whatever vehicles lay around the bend. Another PT-76 ground around the tank Schwartz's squad had disabled and stopped behind the Huey, and a third emerged from the

same area as the first. A man with captain's insignia pulled himself
out of the commander's hatch of the first tank as infantrymen approached
the Huey from all sides.

Grogan looked around him in the main cabin. Most of the men
had wounds from the explosions of the shell and the engine. Schwartz's
rangers lay sprawled where they had landed on jumping into the aircraft. No man even had a weapon in hand, unless it was pinned beneath him. Resistance was clearly hopeless.

The NVA captain shouted orders to his soldiers, who started pulling
the stunned rangers from the floor of the Huey. The captain crawled
into the aircraft, levelled his pistol at Grogan, and gestured for him
to come out. The colonel still clutched the handset for the PRC-25
tactical radio. He thumbed the transmit key and spoke rapidly, "Nightwing
Flight, this is Night Crossing Six. Return immediately to Seabase. Huey
is down, captured—"

"*Im lang di*!" shouted the captain, lunging across the cabin and
tearing the handset from Colonel Grogan's hand. The colonel put his
hands palms out, a gesture of surrender. The captain aimed the pistol
at his face and pulled him roughly across the cabin with his other hand.
Grogan's wounded shoulder screamed as he bounced onto the road.
The rangers and the survivors of the air crew were all lying face-down
with their hands behind their necks except for two who sprawled face-
up, badly wounded or dead. There were perhaps forty infantrymen standing
around watching. The second and third tanks pulled back out of sight
as the A-6s made a last bombing run up the road. The NVA captain
climbed back into the Huey to retrieve the radio and Grogan found
himself face to face with an older Vietnamese with colonel's red flashes
on his collar.

"What did you say to your men in your last transmission, Colonel?"
said the Vietnamese in careful, French-accented English.

Colonel Grogan did not answer. He looked at the spectacle of his
defeat and bit back a groan. Medics checked each of his men and treated
superficial wounds, and then soldiers marched them off the road surface and into the trees. The two men lying face-up had been checked
by the medics and then loaded into loose black body bags and carried
off. Soldiers with tools taken from the tank were trying to extricate
the bodies of the pilot and copilot from the Huey. Colonel Grogan looked
at the Vietnamese colonel. The man was very thin, with a skull-like

face with high and prominent cheekbones. His hair below his cap was iron-gray and his skin was wrinkled by his smile, which indicated either pity or amusement. Old for his rank, thought Grogan, wincing as a medic cut away his jacket and shirt and put heavy field dressings on his shoulder wound. The medic said something to the NVA colonel and stepped away. The colonel translated. "The medic says your wound is clean. That is good, Colonel, for I regret to tell you that the medical care in the camps is truly appalling."

Colonel Grogan looked back at the faint smile. Was it amusement or pity? Perhaps both. "You knew we were coming."

"Of course," said the thin man, with a dismissive gesture. "But that does not matter now. What did you radio to your men before Captain Nguyen relieved you of this radio?" The PRC-25 lay at the colonel's feet, silent, with the handset in its cradle.

"I told them to return to their base, Colonel," said Grogan.

"Did you?" replied the colonel. He spoke sharply to the NVA captain, who nodded and removed a radio handset from a compartment on the rear of the idling tank. Immediately the roar of a heavy diesel and the creak of tank tracks could be heard to the right, and another of the four-barreled ZSUs rumbled out of the concealing grass and started down the road to the west. "Perhaps you sent them away, Colonel," the NVA officer continued. "Or perhaps you called on them to come and rescue you."

"I may be stupid," said Grogan, waving at the blasted Huey and the bloodstained roadway. "But I'm not fucking suicidal."

"No, of course not, now that you can see our strength. The rangers are famous for their courage and daring, but I doubt you would ask your remaining men to pluck you from the midst of an entire armored battalion, plus those lovely Shilkas the Russians have lent us to try out." The colonel pointed to the ZSU rolling away from them. "But I wonder if they might try anyway?" The colonel called for one soldier to pick up the radio and for another to guide Colonel Grogan off the roadway and under the tall tree.

"They will follow their orders, Colonel," said Grogan. If they received them, he thought with sudden unease. He watched as the ZSU halted about a hundred meters down the road and once again backed into the concealing grass and scrub. If the Chinooks did come it would have to be along the road. The CH-47s were far less maneuverable than the

Hueys. But they had to have heard my last transmission and they know about the armor.

"Perhaps we should listen, Colonel," said the thin man. He plucked the handset from its rest and disconnected it at the jack. He then turned the switch to allow the radio to receive through a small speaker on the front. It was clear that the NVA colonel was thoroughly familiar with the operation of the highly secret PRC-25. "Let us see if they will not come to your rescue, Colonel."

"Captain Ferris?" The crew chief aboard Nightwing Three plucked at Ferris's sleeve. "A/C up here got a call for us from Night Crossing Six."

Robby Ferris made his way to the forward bulkhead of the chopper and put on an intercom headset. "This is Captain Ferris. You heard from the colonel?"

"Roger, Captain," said the aircraft commander. "You better come up here."

Frowning, Ferris put the headset back on its hook and climbed through the narrow passage into the cockpit. The pilot, a major, and his warrant officer copilot sat faintly illuminated by dim red lights from gauges. Ferris squatted in between the two seats. "What do you have, Major?" shouted Ferris. The chopper was noisy even far away from the turbines.

The pilot handed Ferris a padded earphone-headset and waited while he adjusted it. "Very short message. Spoken quickly. Something like 'Night Crossing Flight, Night Crossing Six. Return to Seabase, Huey down.'"

"Can you still get him?"

"Negative." The pilot turned the frequency selector switch. "That's Tac Net; give him a try."

Ferris pushed the button on the bar that held the lip mike. "Night Crossing Six, Striker Six, over." He released the button and waited. "Night Crossing Six, Striker Six, come in Colonel, over." Silence hissed in the headphones. Ferris switched himself back to intercom. "Where are the other CH-47s, Major?"

"Three and Four are here at the assembly point, Captain," said the aircraft commander. "Two was overloaded and proceeded out toward the carriers—should be feet wet by now." Feet wet meant over water, and by implication, safe.

"You're sure he told us to go back to the carriers?" asked Ferris.

"Pretty sure. But he was cut off real abruptly, and now we can't raise the Huey on any of the channels he should be guarding."

Ferris pondered that. "Huey down." Did that mean that the colonel wanted them to break off and leave him? The Huey had been going in after Schwartz, surrounded by armor. Or could the colonel have first said they were all to return to the carriers and *then* been shot down? Captain Ferris didn't like the idea of leaving the colonel and most of Schwartz's team in the shit when he had two helos and better than two intact squads of rangers not five klicks away. "How is your fuel state, Major?"

"Beaucoup. Two hours easy; need less than thirty minutes to get home to *Oriskany*."

"What do you think, Major? Was Colonel Grogan sending us off or calling us back?"

The A/C shrugged. "It was a quick message, Captain, and I was a little busy outflying the green flak just then. Anyway, you are the senior grunt; it's your call." A flight of four A-6s roared in overhead and checked in on the air control net, as did a flight of four F-4s flying higher, the new MIGCAP. The copilot acknowledged their check-in. "At least we got plenty of firepower now," concluded the A/C.

"Right," said Ferris. "Look, can you vector the fast movers out there to overfly the colonel's last location, take a look?"

"No problem," said the pilot. "It was us that dropped the Blocker team there. What are you going to do?"

"First, talk it over with Lieutenant Barnes on the Four bird. But if the bomber spots any living rangers and not too many gook tanks, I want to get my colonel and my men back."

"Airborne," said the A/C, and switched over to talk to the pilot of the Four helicopter.

The last tank backed away from the blasted Huey, leaving it alone in the road. The NVA soldiers pressed themselves into the moist earth around and behind the trunk of the giant tree as two A-6s roared over no more than a hundred feet up, one two seconds behind the other. "They are searching for you, Colonel," said the NVA colonel. "Perhaps your helicopters *will* return."

Sweet Jesus, no, thought Colonel Grogan. Get away, Robby Ferris;

no cowboy shit. He'll go; he is a steady officer. Then, to his horror, the PRC-25 crackled to life.

"Linebacker Three this is Striker Six. The colonel's Huey is down on the road where Blocker was set up. Fast movers saw just the Huey. Fly cover for me while I have a look."

"This is Linebacker Three. Wilco. Standing by."

Colonel Grogan's jaw dropped. This can't be happening. They must see it as a trap! He looked at the NVA colonel to plead. The thin officer's expression no longer held any hint of amusement, only sorrow, pity for a man about to witness a commander's greatest nightmare.

Captain Ferris readied his rangers in the main cabin of the CH-47, poised to go out in three fire teams from open doors on both sides of the aircraft and also out the open ramp in the tail. He then returned to the cockpit and squatted between the pilots. He put on the headset and keyed intercom. "What did the fast movers see?"

"No people, no tanks," said the aircraft commander. "But the road and the sides of the road look torn up, maybe by tracks. Tiger Oh Three—that's the lead A-6—would like to bomb the right side of the road before we go in."

"No. If there are any rangers down there they will be close to the road," said Captain Ferris. "Have the bombers follow us around, ready to blast anything that shows up or shoots from cover. What are the bombers carrying?"

"Tiger reported each A-6 has two five-hundred-pound cannisters of Rockeye cluster bombs and three five-hundred-pound high-explosive bombs," said the A/C.

"Okay. Tell them to follow us and watch our asses. Tell the Four bird to stay high and tight." Captain Ferris fought the fear in his gut. "Take her in hot, Major, but anything moves that could be a tank and we're gone."

The A/C spoke briefly into his lip mike. The Chinook swung over the road and began to descend rapidly toward the distinctive shape of the downed Huey lit up by the rising moon.

I have to do something, thought Colonel Grogan. He could hear the chopper approaching, though he couldn't yet see it because of the overhanging branches. If I run out into the road I could wave them off. The gooks would shoot me, but that would for sure turn my people away. I cannot let this happen. He looked at the Vietnamese colonel, who looked back, his sad expression unchanged. He spoke a single word to the soldiers behind him, and two scuttled up and sat on either side of Grogan, holding him lightly by his arms. "I am sorry, Colonel, that you must see this," said the Vietnamese officer. "But my orders were to inflict as heavy a defeat on your raid as possible."

Colonel Grogan gritted his teeth in anger and hatred. Come on, Robby, see something!

Moonlight filtering through the trees was suddenly interrupted by the shape of the Chinook skimming over the road toward them. The NVA colonel spoke into the microphone of the clumsy Russian radio. The ZSU fired from its concealed position. Hundreds of 23mm cannon shells raked the helicopter from cockpit to tail. The chopper tore apart in midair and then exploded on the road surface as the fuel cells ruptured. Colonel Grogan stood and then doubled over, clutching his stomach. The soldiers made no move to stop him as he crawled out onto the road. Flames from the twisted wreckage rose a hundred feet and lit the entire area. Shapes that had been men tumbled out of the wreckage and lay still in the widening pool of burning fuel. Grogan felt utterly helpless, like a sick old man watching his children destroyed.

The ZSU was on the move, pulling up onto the road behind the wreckage and away from the flames. Grogan saw the Gun Dish radar turning on top of the turret and watched as tracers from the monster's four guns began to sweep upward toward the last remaining CH-47. The helicopter turned and climbed in a frantic attempt to escape the cone of green tracers, but the chopper was well within range and climbing very slowly. Grogan tasted bile.

In the scrub and tall grass across the road machine guns on the concealed tanks opened up, also reaching for the number Four Nightwing, which still flew, against all odds. Grogan stood in the middle of the road, watching the tracers rise from the tanks. He was once again a lieutenant colonel of infantry and he thought with grim satisfaction, keep firing and reveal your positions, the bombers will come back.

"Flak gun, two o'clock, underneath!" crackled the voice of Tiger Oh Three's wingman in his ear. Lt. Cmdr. Bill Conn rolled to his right and saw the tracers. "Take it, Frank; your angle is better."

"Roger," said Lt. Frank Porter. He inverted his aircraft and pointed the nose straight down at the source of the green tracers, a desperate maneuver at fifteen hundred feet of altitude. The bombing angle was zero. His bombardier-navigator armed the three five-hundred-pound iron bombs and pickled them off immediately, then Porter righted the aircraft and sped away to avoid being consumed by the explosion of his own bombs.

Grogan saw the ZSU disappear in an immense explosion, and the miraculous escape of Nightwing Four. The shock wave reached him with a blast of heat and he dove flat on the roadway, driven by instinct and training. He crawled rapidly back toward the NVA soldiers concealed under the tree, a slight smile crossing his lips. He knew what was coming next even before he heard the rising scream of the A-6s as they lined up on the tanks still firing tracers into the night.

The bombers flew over in a simple line-astern formation, thirty seconds apart to avoid being blown away by the ordnance dropped by the plane ahead. Each dropped its full load of five-hundred-pound bombs and the cluster bomb units. Grogan crawled next to the NVA colonel, who had his face buried in the crook of his arm as the foliage above them was slashed and scythed by the metal fragments from the Rockeye bomblets. The ground beneath them shook with the rhythm of an earthquake, increasing as each new load of bombs and cluster munitions detonated in the trees. Showers of leaves and sliced-off branches rained on the NVA soldiers under the tree, and waves of heat and the smells of burning fuel and ammunition washed over them along with the sharp smell of burning foliage.

Grogan grabbed the NVA colonel by the collar and jerked his head up to make him watch the secondary explosions as his tanks in the scrub and grass blew up one by one. As the deafening thunder of repeated explosions was replaced by the roar of fires, Grogan shouted to the NVA colonel. "You stopped a raid today, Colonel, nothing more. You will never defeat us in battle."

The NVA colonel shook off Grogan's grip and sat upright. He looked stricken as he watched the bulk of his battalion burn, but his eyes were hard as he looked at the American officer. "You may well be right, Colonel," he said, evenly. "But in the end it will not matter."

EIGHTEEN

Washington, 22 May 1969

The full extent of the disaster of Operation Night Crossing was known in the Pentagon and the White House by 1100. Stuart's army colleagues wandered about the ACSI offices in stunned disbelief. Conversations started and then ended abruptly. Lieutenant Colonel Becker, who had gone down to Fort Benning several times over the weeks of planning to brief the extraction team, closed himself in his office and sat stunned and silent for over an hour. Every time he closed his eyes he saw another of the faces of the men of the ranger unit, especially those of Captain Ferris, now known dead, and Lieutenant Colonel Grogan, missing and presumed dead as well. Lt. William Stuart left before lunch and went home. He had intended to get his car and drive over to NIS, but in the end he just sat in his living room, staring out at the dripping trees along the creek called Holmes Run, behind his apartment, until it got dark.

At the White House the first concern was damage control. Nothing was said to the press, but the White House press corps rapidly grew suspicious as routine briefings and backgrounders with various members of the president's staff were cancelled or cut short. An ad hoc crisis management assessment committee gathered in the basement conference room of the White House at 1530. The committee was chaired by the Deputy Head of the National Security Council, Dr. Saul Goldberg, previously a professor of political science at Princeton. Other members included Maj. Gen. Joseph Howard, the army's Deputy Chief of

Staff for Operations; Navy Captain Neil Williams, CINCPAC's representative to the Joint Chiefs; Lt. Col. John Paul Gunn, previously senior advisor to COMUSMACV in Saigon; Roland Fisher, Deputy Undersecretary of State for Asia; Philip Arnold, Deputy Director of Central Intelligence for Operations; and John Hermann, Special Assistant to the President. It was their job to summarize the reams of data that had come in and were still coming in by direct teleprinter from *Oriskany* and then to brief the head of the NSC, Dr. Kissinger, and the president.

"Well, gentlemen," said Dr. Goldberg, lighting a cigarette. "What do we tell the president and what does he tell the nation?"

"As little as possible, I should have thought," offered the CIA's Mr. Arnold.

"Won't work, Phil," said Fisher from State. "The North Vietnamese are sure to trumpet this to the world, very likely in time for tonight's news."

"Through their good friends, the Swedes, no doubt," said Dr. Goldberg. "God, what an awful mess."

"We are going to have to hear from the Agency as to how the mission was so completely blown to the NVA," said Major General Howard, looking hard at the thin, ascetic-looking Philip Arnold.

"We will try to find out what happened, General," said Arnold, his voice noncommittal. "We are presently trying to find out. However, you will remember that the report when given to the president listed the foreign nationals who knew about the Agency's locating of the prison camp."

"It isn't just that *they* knew that *we* knew where this place was, Arnold," said General Howard. "They had to know we were coming after it and approximately when. That piece of information should have reached *no* foreign nationals."

"As I have said, General, we are investigating." Arnold pointedly looked up the table at the chairman.

"What are the casualty figures to date, General?" asked Dr. Goldberg.

"Judging by the reports we have from survivors who reached the carriers, as well as reports from the navy fighter and bomber pilots, we had eighteen killed in the downing of Nightwing Three. The crew of the command chopper plus six rangers they were trying to extract, eleven in all plus the commander, are missing and presumed killed," said Howard softly.

"That is out of how many in the entire force?" asked John Hermann.

"Twenty-nine lost out of eighty-one. The Night Crossing force consisted of fifty-six rangers and twenty-five air crewmen."

"Dear God," said Captain Williams, to his folded hands.

The internal White House telephone rang softly. John Hermann picked it up, listened for a moment, and then said, "Put him on. Hello, Bernie." There was a long period of silence while the others watched Hermann nod and grimace and rub his eyes. Finally he broke in, "Okay, Bernie. Hold it a little while. No, I know it will come out. I promise to call you back within the hour." John Hermann dropped the telephone into the cradle as if it were hot. He looked up at the expectant faces of his committee colleagues. "That was Bernard Kohl at CBS. Swedish television is offering him film they just got from Hong Kong via satellite."

"Any chance they'll hold it for a day until we can see it?" asked Dr. Goldberg.

"Bernie Kohl? Are you kidding?" snorted Fisher from State. "He is only telling us to rush us out with a statement *without* knowing what's in it!"

"What the Swedes told him is bad enough," said Hermann. "Footage, all shot at night but with good light, of at least three downed helicopters and what appear to be about two dozen bodies."

"My God," said General Howard, rising and pushing his chair away angrily. "Those men never had a chance. You—" he pointed a finger at the CIA representative, who paled.

"General, please," said Dr. Goldberg, sharply.

"Sorry, sir," said the general, sitting but maintaining his deadly stare at Philip Arnold.

"I am sorry, gentlemen, but it gets worse," said Hermann. "Pictures as well of six to eight men, at least one of whom appears to be an officer, being dragged and kicked through the streets of Hanoi."

The men sat silent for a moment, each with his own thoughts. "We had better begin work on a statement," said Dr. Goldberg.

THE WHITE HOUSE, 1630, 22 MAY 1969

IMMEDIATE RELEASE

AT 2200 SAIGON TIME (1000 EASTERN DAYLIGHT SAVINGS) TODAY ELE-
MENTS OF THE 75TH RANGER REGIMENT, SUPPORTED BY ARMY AVIATION AND
BY NAVAL ATTACK AIRCRAFT OPERATING FROM CARRIERS ON YANKEE STA-
TION, LANDED WEST OF HANOI AT A SITE BELIEVED TO BE THE NOTORIOUS
HANOI HILTON PRISONER OF WAR CAMP. THE PURPOSE OF THE ACTION

WAS TO LIBERATE AND RETURN TO THE UNITED STATES A LARGE PORTION OF THE AMERICAN POWS PRESENTLY HELD BY NORTH VIETNAMESE AUTHORITIES IN BRUTAL AND INHUMANE CONDITIONS SPECIFICALLY FORBIDDEN BY THE GENEVA CONVENTION.

IT IS APPARENT THAT THE ENEMY WAS SOMEHOW FOREWARNED. WHEN THE RANGERS LANDED THEY FOUND NO POWS, BUT WERE IMMEDIATELY SET UPON BY A NORTH VIETNAMESE FORCE FAR LARGER THAN ANTICIPATED. THE RANGERS AND THE ARMY HELICOPTER PILOTS FOUGHT VALIANTLY AND WELL TO DEFEND THEMSELVES AND THEN WITHDREW, BUT AT LEAST TWO HELICOPTERS WERE SHOT DOWN AND THIRTY RANGERS AND TEN HELICOPTER CREWMEN ARE MISSING. SOME OF THESE MAY HAVE BEEN CAPTURED BUT MOST ARE PRESUMED DEAD.

THE PRESIDENT AND MRS. NIXON EXTEND THEIR HEARTFELT SYMPATHIES TO THE FAMILIES OF THE FALLEN HEROES. THEIR MISSION WAS ONE OF MERCY, THEIR DESIRE NOT TO ATTACK BUT TO SUCCOR. THE PRESIDENT ASSURES THE FAMILIES OF THE POWS THAT HIS RESOLVE AND THE RESOLVE OF THEIR BROTHERS IN THE ARMED FORCES TO GET THEIR LOVED ONES SAFELY HOME REMAIN STEADFAST.

THE PRESIDENT HAS REQUESTED TIME FROM THE THREE MAJOR TELEVISION NETWORKS AT 2000 WASHINGTON TIME TONIGHT TO MAKE A BRIEF STATEMENT TO THE NATION.

William Stuart and Harry MacAndrew sat in the bar at the Officers' Club at Fort Myer, each nursing a beer. Stuart had first tried to decline the major's offer of dinner and talk, feeling just too dejected to do either, but the major had given his invitation nearly the force of an order, so Stuart had showered and dressed and driven to the old red-brick club, arriving as instructed not one minute later than 1830.

The film taken by the Swedish crew was aired on "CBS Evening News" with a minimum of comment from Walter Cronkite and then Bernard Kohl. It ran nearly the entire half hour of the broadcast and was far more devastating than expected by either Stuart, who did not know in advance that it would be shown, or MacAndrew, who did. The pictures of the wrecked helicopters and even the double row of covered bodies on the road, long dark shapes with deep shadows caused by the bright TV lights and surrounded by rows of tough-looking NVA regulars, were chilling enough but had a staged, final quality, like the photos of a road accident. A Vietnamese officer, speaking slowly in English, led the camera to a table where American weapons were displayed along with a neat, sad square of the curved "Ranger" patches, appar-ently cut from the shoulders of dead men's uniforms. The officer explained that many of the dead and their uniforms had been too badly burned for the recovery of any identifying insignia or papers.

The second part of the film made the first almost easy to bear. Eight Americans, their arms bound and their eyes covered, were shown marched through the streets of a suburb of Hanoi. Each man had his head bowed as though in shame, and when one of them, with the oak leaves of a major or lieutenant colonel on the epaulets of his torn jacket, tried to raise his chin he was beaten repeatedly on the back of his neck by a soldier with a long strip of bamboo until his chin fell once again.

The captives were lined up in front of a rail yard, where firefighters still struggled to contain soaring flames. Bernard Kohl broke in to say that the Swedes had declared that the damage had been done by navy bombers that same evening, somewhat giving the lie to the earlier White House statement that the raid was a mission of mercy.

An angry crowd of Vietnamese, which had been held back by soldiers and police, was allowed to approach the blindfolded Americans while being addressed by a man identified as the head of the town Communist council. The Vietnamese, including many women and elderly people, spat on the Americans and kicked and punched them. The film ended with a statement read by an unidentified Vietnamese official to the effect that it was pointless to discuss peace with an amoral government that would bomb innocent civilians in their beds and send its soldiers into the very heart of the country to burn and kill. The last five minutes of the news program was a polemic by Kohl, saying that while Nixon had run on a promise to end the war, ill-considered raids like this could only stiffen North Vietnamese resolve, not to mention adding twenty-one names to the roll of the dead and eight more men to the population of the Hanoi Hilton, wherever it might really be.

Stuart and MacAndrew left the bar and went into the dining room at the end of the broadcast, then ordered dinner. There were very few people in the large room, and neither man would later remember what he had eaten or what, if anything, either had said. They returned to the bar at 2000 to watch the president speak. Nixon appeared even more pale and sad-faced than usual, and he spoke quietly of the sacrifice of the brave men and the terrible burden upon their families, which he called upon the nation to share. He reaffirmed his administration's deep desire for peace with honor and announced he was sending Henry Kissinger back to Paris, from whence he had so recently returned, to try again, even to plead with the Communist side to respond to the administration's generous proposals. He then asked God to bless the nation and faded to black. The bartender immediately flipped to a basketball game and fiddled with the volume until he was told pointedly by several officers at the bar to turn the set off.

"Jesus," said Stuart, shaking his head and bowing toward his beer stein. "What a colossal fuck-up."

"Worse than that, from what I hear," said MacAndrew, refilling his glass and Stuart's from the pitcher on the bar.

"What have you heard?" asked Stuart, looking up quickly.

"Off the record," replied MacAndrew.

"Understood, Major."

"The NVA reception committee had tanks, lots of them," said MacAndrew, quietly. There was no one near enough to them to overhear. "More tanks, if you believe the rangers' accounts, than we thought they had in their entire inventory."

"They used tanks at Lang Vei last year," said Stuart, absently, not seeing the significance of the major's story.

"Yes, but not many," said MacAndrew. "We always figured they would hold all armor for the final conventional-war push south."

"After Nixon pulls us out," said Stuart.

"Right, or after Kissinger signs up some phony peace." MacAndrew sipped his beer. "So why would they put all that armor at risk to catch the rangers? The president didn't tell you, but I have it on good authority—off the record—that the rangers knocked out a few of those precious tanks and even some of the new Russian ZSUs we didn't know the NVA had, and the navy bombed the shit out of quite a few more."

Stuart frowned. "What are ZSUs?"

"Mobile, self-contained, radar-guided antiaircraft gun systems. Same chassis and machinery as the PT-76 tanks the NVA has. Very effective." MacAndrew twisted in his seat and looked at Stuart. "But consider my question: why should the gooks put their precious armor at risk to block a small raid?"

Stuart shrugged. "Helos are very vulnerable to tank fire."

"True, but if the gooks had simply wanted to drive the rangers off heavy machine guns, perhaps mounted on trucks, of which they have plenty, would have been just as effective."

"So what is your view, Major?" Stuart was depressed and tired of the questioning.

"First, they had to know the raid was coming. Either the CIA was penetrated, which happens because they have to use Vietnamese nationals for intel gathering in the North, or the whole thing with the original Swedish television crew was staged, so they moved the prisoners out, maybe weeks ago. From the reports we are piecing together from the radio traffic and interviews with the ones who got back, the armor came from all directions around the camp, so it was there in place when the raid began, and not rushed up from Ha Dong or some other base."

"And the NVA let the helos land?"

"Right. That is point number two. The LZ appeared cold, as expected. All the troops got in and even went through the empty prison before anything happened."

"The gooks wanted to catch the rangers on the ground, then surround them with armor and be in a position to drive the helos off."

"That's what I think. A soldier may fall to the ground and fight to the death against overwhelming numbers of other infantrymen, but there is no making a stand in the open against tanks."

"They wanted prisoners, then. Why?"

"Quite simply to test Nixon's resolve. Maybe to make him crazy enough to do *any* deal to get out, to get those men back."

"So what happens now?"

Major MacAndrew sighed. "I may be getting old and paranoid, William, but I just don't believe every one of the quarter million antiwar activists camped out in the rain on the Mall and around the Pentagon is a starry-eyed hippie or a feckless draft dodger trying to prove he has stones after all. Somehow, some of those people are getting the word from Hanoi, and the word now will be to turn up the heat."

Stuart finished his beer and paid the tab. He was suddenly very tired and very sad. "So you think the NVA got a tip, built this crowd here at this time, and now has given them a new reason to run amok. Forgive me, Major, but that *is* a bit paranoid."

MacAndrew shrugged and smiled, a smile of irony and not mirth or joy. "Look at the best alternative explanation, William."

"Which is?"

"That some NVA tank commander, of whom there are very few, William, was out doing a little night training near a recently abandoned prison camp and then pulled the military equivalent of drawing three cards to fill an inside straight."

*　　*　　*

In the basement den of a large country house near Potomac, Maryland, eighteen men and two women met to discuss the schedule for Moratorium Day tomorrow in the light of the news of the disaster at Xuan Mai. The house, really a mansion complete with tennis courts, two pools, and riding stables, was owned by C. Wilson Tagliaferro, a man of great inherited wealth and an affection for left-wing causes of all types. He had lent the house for meetings by the self-appointed steering committee of the massive and now week-long demonstration, but after hearing some of the proposals had discreetly declined to attend the meetings themselves.

Each of the attendees represented a different group or coalition, except there were two representatives of the Students for a Democratic Society, which had unofficially split after the Days of Rage at the Democratic convention in Chicago the previous summer. Most of the people were in their teens and twenties, although the man from the War Resisters' League who was trying to run the meeting was well above the untrustworthy age of thirty. All dressed in the uniform of radical chic: jeans, boots, beads, bandannas, and military surplus jackets. Only two of the participants were FBI informants, which meant security was unusually good.

The heavy hitters of revolution were all represented in Tagliaferro's sunken playroom, and they walked around each other sniffing like strange dogs. The Black Panthers, the Weathermen (various factions), the Student Nonviolent Coordinating Committee (jovially cross-referenced by the FBI as the Nonstudent Violent Coordinating Committee), the Yippies, even a statuesque American Indian with a face like a broadaxe who represented a coalition called simply Hostile Tribes. The rest of the groups represented were less radical and less focussed, and for the most part their leaders here tonight stood in awe of the serious revolutionaries. The Gay and Lesbian Alliance was spoken for by a woman six feet tall with flaming red hair and a swimsuit model's body called only "Red Sister," who talked a great deal and even had the balls to challenge the blacks. The rest were pretty quiet. The issue most discussed was under what conditions during tomorrow's surrounding of the White House and the Capitol was the demonstration to "go red"—get violent.

"The issue," insisted Eric, representing the Weathermen, "is whether we can whip up this humongous mass of low-consciousness pussies to go red under any circumstances."

"I disagree, man," interjected Judy Moon of the Weather Underground.

"Yeah, me too," said Josh of the Weathermen Revolutionary Faction, although it wasn't clear just which of his former comrades he was agreeing with. The milling around continued as the air grew dim with the smoke of tiny hand-held grass fires.

"'Let a hundred flowers bloom, let a thousand schools of thought contend,'" quoted Judy Moon, to no one in particular.

"Look, people," said Art Shamsky, the fortyish, graying representative of the War Resisters' League who was a graduate student at Columbia. "Let's put the question." The young people always let Art put the question. Art liked to think of himself as a natural leader, but he knew the others regarded him as a curiosity, a specimen of the enemy. Art, alone in the room, had fought in a war, in Korea. "We want to radicalize the crowd. Okay, violence can do that, but not if we radicals are seen to provoke it. Most of these people are middle class, bourgeois. Kids taking a break before finals, bored housewives. They see the Panthers or SNCC or the Weathermen punch a cop or a soldier, they will melt away from us like we had the plague."

"So what?" asked the chairman of SNCC, L. "Brotherman" White. "Kick a few pigs around always feels good."

"Off some," hissed Van Camp of the Black Panthers, sitting cross-legged on the edge of the fireplace, a cut-crystal glass of Tagliaferro's bourbon in one hand and a fat joint in the other. "*Off* some pigs." His voice trailed off in a little giggle.

"Oh, shut up, Van Camp," said Brotherman, disgusted to see a black revolutionary look so bad in front of honkies. "Why Huey send you anyway? How come he ain't here?"

"Gentlemen, please—" said Art Shamsky, holding his hands in the air like a referee in a boxing ring.

"Huey's in jail in Oakland," said Van Camp, struggling to his feet and looking mean. "You know that, Brotherman."

"Gentlemen!" shouted Shamsky. The group subsided to sullen murmurs. "Thank you. Now, the other reason violence can't come from our side is that the image, especially the image on television, is of peaceful citizens confronting armed forces of oppression, of a government forced to protect itself with armed force from its own citizens. Now, believe it or not, those soldiers out there in that enormous crowd are going to be scared, and there is a clear image we should try to create for the cameras."

"Surely we don't want them to shoot?" asked Red Sister, who was getting bored and wanted to start an argument.

"No." Shamsky looked at Red Sister's prominent breasts, approximately at his eye level. These kids have no vision and less discipline, he thought sourly. "Although a picture of a soldier butt-stroking a grandmother with his rifle would be nice." His attempt at humor was entirely lost upon his audience, and he realized that these people frightened him with their mindless, undirected intensity. "Seriously, people, the violence, if there is to be any, must appear to come from the soldiers and police. But we can use this thing that happened, this fucked-up prisoner rescue attempt. We can taunt them, tell them how incompetent the army is, how their own officers dream up cockeyed schemes to get young draftees killed."

Eric of the Weathermen spoke up. "Taunting the pigs sure worked in Chicago."

"Right," said Shamsky. "Good point. Some taunting, some jeering, but no physical pushing, and some kid in uniform is gonna explode and take a swing."

"You might get an added benefit," said Judy Moon. "Some of the really scared ones might drop their guns and come over to us."

"It could happen, Judy, but I doubt it," said Shamsky. "Even though these kids are mostly draftees, and even though they might like to drop their rifles and walk away, discipline will prevent them from doing that. The military has its own form of consciousness raising."

"Be called basic training," said Van Camp, with a grin. It was a proud part of his radical resume that he had been drafted but had been discharged after basic as being totally incorrigible and unfit for service.

"So, can we agree, people?" asked Shamsky. "Taunt them for being fuck-ups about to be sent to a fucked-up war by other fuck-ups. Tell your people to watch for the camera crews and try to make something happen, but make sure the pigs swing first."

The representatives nodded and began to shuffle out. A few fists were raised, a few palms were slapped. Everybody agreed that tomorrow was going to be awesome.

Red Sister said goodbye to the group and left by the front door. Her battered VW bus was parked well down the road, away from the other cars. When she entered the van the overhead light did not come on; she had disconnected it. She keyed the ignition and the ancient motor ground to life. "You asleep, baby?" she whispered over her shoulder.

"No," said a small voice from the backseat. A small, plain, mousey-haired woman climbed over the back of the front seat and sat next to Red Sister. Jolene Dinkins was as fervent in her opposition to the war as anyone in the meeting, and more than most. She had been a supporter of the war in a vague, patriotic way until the day just over a year ago when she had stood in the cold wet snow in her hometown of Ellenboro, West Virginia, and watched her baby brother buried with full military honors. She had never accepted that Tommy had been anything other than murdered by the government and the army, and yet she had never marched, never chanted, never been to a meeting, because she worked for the government and she needed to keep her job. She hated herself for serving the fascist machine, as Red called it, but she needed the money to live and to send home to help her parents and Tommy's widow and tiny girl, and there was no work in Ellenboro. Jolene had taken the civil service exam right after high school and had gone to Washington to work in the main post office. She was a good worker and after two years she got a chance to work for another agency, with a promotion to civil service grade GS-4 and the possibility of further promotion. At the time the work of her new employer did not offend her, and she made GS-5 after two more years. Jolene was a watch supervisor and cryptographer at the Central Intelligence Agency in Langley, Virginia.

Red Sister, whose name to her friends was Susan, talked about the meeting just ended as she drove slowly through the Maryland countryside. She made humorous little verbal sketches of the posturing of the silly men. Jolene usually received these reports of meetings she could never attend with animation, but tonight she sat silent as the VW ground on toward the apartment the two women shared in MacLean, Virginia. "What's the matter, baby?" asked Red Sister, reaching over and touching the smaller woman's short brown hair.

"I'm kinda down about those rangers getting killed over there, Susan," said Jolene in a tiny voice. "On account of I knew about it; I encrypted the signal to the embassy in Saigon myself, it was so highly classified."

"But you told no one, dear," said Red Sister, staring straight ahead, her jaw set.

"I told you," said Jolene, looking hard at her friend in the dark car. "I shouldn't even have done that."

"You were upset," said Susan firmly. "Your brother Tommy was a ranger, and you were upset. Besides, I told no one; you know that."

"I don't want the North Vietnamese to win, Susan; I just want our men to come back, to live in peace."

"Of course you do, sweetheart," said Susan, stroking the soft mop of Jolene's hair. "You—and I—are better patriots than the fascists we oppose."

"But you're sure, Susan, that you never told anyone, not even by accident?"

"Of course I am sure," lied Red Sister, smiling despite herself. It had been a fucking triumph when she told them. "Let's just get home and go to bed, baby. It will be a long day tomorrow."

Nineteen

Washington, 23 May 1969

After a week of cool, intermittent rain the dawn of Moratorium Day itself was clear and finally springlike, with temperatures rising through the fifties and a warm gentle breeze from the south. Demonstrators rose early and formed up into their groups, or attached themselves to groups if they had none of their own. The people were mostly young and cheerful, despite soapbox speeches that tried to swing their mood toward indignation and anger. Buses from all over the country arrived in the early hours of daylight and disgorged another hundred thousand of the committed, the passionate, and the merely curious. The Pentagon contingent, the group that had been on station the longest, decamped and streamed across the Fourteenth Street Bridge into Washington. When that bridge was choked with arm-linked marchers groups broke off and marched north on the roads and on the grass that led up the Potomac to the Arlington Memorial and Theodore Roosevelt Bridges. By 0800 vehicular traffic trying to cross from the suburbs of northern Virginia into Washington was backed up for six miles. The assembly point for all of the demonstrators was to be the Lincoln Memorial and the long park called the Mall that ran east all the way to the Capitol. Speeches would be made by the darlings of the movement, songs sung, and prayers offered. A few of the less inhibited disrobed partially or totally and waded in the reflecting pool. When the throng reached its maximum size attempts would be made to ring the White House and the Capitol with human chains tens of people deep. Today was the day the government itself was to be shut down and made to face the people.

William Stuart got off his bus at the Pentagon at 0730 to find the troops in place but the demonstrators mostly gone. The young soldiers looked relieved and a little sheepish to be guarding a nearly empty building from an absent mob. Stuart reached his office and hung up his uniform blouse. The office was stuffy and smelled of stale tobacco smoke. He went down the narrow passage to the coffee urn. On his return he passed the open door of the colonel's office and was waved inside.

"Stuart," said Lieutenant Colonel Becker. "Good morning. Your last here, I assume."

Stuart sat opposite the colonel, who was drinking coffee and smoking a cigar. His expression was tight, a smile of pain under control. "I still have my operation to run, Colonel," Stuart said quietly. "I still need your help."

The colonel shook his head slowly. "'Fraid not, Lieutenant. Everybody in this office, me included, has asked for a transfer to the Russian Front, and will feel damn lucky to get it. ACSI–Army is officially out of the POW rescue business. Unofficially, of course."

Stuart nodded slowly. "Then there will be no objection from Army if Navy takes this one on itself."

The colonel forced a laugh. "Not from me, son, but if I were you I wouldn't hold my breath waiting for approval from Milestone." Stuart looked his question. The colonel looked sad through his cloud of gray smoke. "Milestone is the White House, kid. The covert committee, the guys who turned us happily loose on Night Crossing." The colonel leaned forward and stared at Stuart. "Don't be naive, Lieutenant. Forget your operation. Go back to NIS and chase queers off submarines, or whatever it is you do."

"Colonel," said Stuart, getting to his feet, fighting anger. "This operation—"

The colonel cut him off with a wave of his cigar hand. "I'm sorry, Lieutenant, I was rude. None of this is your fault. Go back to your good cause while I and some other designated fuck-ups go up to the roof to watch the peace creeps burn the nation's capital."

Stuart took the bus back to Holmes Run Park and picked up his car. The traffic aimed at Washington was halted on the other side of the highway. He took a local road map from the glove compartment and plotted a route to NIS headquarters in Arlington that would keep him off of any of the main roads leading into the city. As he got out of his car in the small parking lot behind the headquarters he heard the beat of helicopter rotors and looked up to see two Hueys in army livery fly overhead in formation, their flex guns trimmed in over the skids. He stopped in his tracks and shaded his eyes. There was no doubt. Gunships. Gunships flying over the capital of the leading nation of the free world. He shook his head and hurried inside, wishing he had never seen them.

By 0900 the Mall was completely filled and marchers still came, overflowing into Constitution Avenue and across Independence Avenue. A speaker on the steps of the Lincoln Memorial shouted into the microphone that he could see half a million people. A police spokesman interviewed by a television crew dismissed the number as way too high but declined to offer his own estimate. The signal to begin the blockading operation was given by Art Shamsky. He held a freon-powered horn over his head and gave six short blasts. The signal was repeated by other organizers spread throughout the crowd, and so was passed to the entire throng. The mood was still festive as organizers with bullhorns began leading or herding the willing masses on their errand of peaceful civil disobedience.

The large area of the Ellipse in front of the White House filled rapidly with marchers, who stopped and shouted slogans at the triple row of soldiers standing in front of the wrought-iron fence that separated the great South Lawn from South Executive Place and E Street. Pushing around the curve of the fence, some demonstrators climbed up onto the equestrian statue of General Sherman and several joined the Civil War hero on his bronze horse. The crowd flowed around the outsides of the Executive Office Building and the Treasury Building, which flanked the White House on either side. Once again they were stopped before the rows of armed soldiers. Police, including mounted officers, were massed behind wooden barricades at the various access points to the White House. All of the gates were locked and braced except those at either end of West Executive Place. East Executive Place was outside the wrought-iron fence and was normally open to public passage, but wooden and metal police barricades and extra squads of soldiers extended the perimeter from the White House fence to the Treasury Building. East and West Executive Places were the normal accesses to the White House, and most people with business to conduct entered through the southwest gate into West Executive Place. The uniformed police and supporting soldiers were instructed to maintain normal business access to the White House, but not to hinder the demonstration otherwise.

The crowd did not contest the police positions, but merely flowed farther out, up Pennsylvania and New York Avenues in both directions and along K, Fourteenth, and Eighteenth Streets. The circle could be of any size, and the marchers kept coming. Police in cars and on foot struggled to keep the avenues open against flying squads of young people who linked arms and blocked the arteries at various points until the harried police could return and disperse the human barricades. The first arrests were made and the mood became decidedly less festive.

At the Capitol the scene was repeated, except that the security problem was much more difficult because of the lack of an encircling fence. Buses of the D.C. Transit Company had been brought in during the night and parked nose to tail along the nearly circular drive ringing the building, with troops in ranks confronting the marchers outside the ring of buses. Police fought the demonstrators to keep the main access routes open, especially New Jersey, Maryland, and Pennsylvania Avenues. The steering committee had planned to make a special battleground of Pennsylvania Avenue, since it ran from the White House to the Capitol. The crowd grew so large that all six traffic lanes and the wide sidewalks of Pennsylvania Avenue became engulfed, with police cars halted, surrounded by a sea of people that could not be pushed back because of the crowds surging in behind it. Television crews shot footage from vans as totally immobilized as the police cars, and television helicopters photographed the crowd, as did military and police helos. Police reports flowed into a special command post set up in the Department of Justice Building, which had a fine view of the crowd from its upper floors. The Department of Justice Building was on the south side of Pennsylvania Avenue, roughly equidistant from the White House and the Capitol. The command post was in open-line contact with the White House basement conference room, the security office in the Capitol, the D.C. Metro Police, the U.S. Park Police, which had jurisdiction on federal properties, and the Situation Room at the Pentagon. The decision was made to let the marchers have Pennsylvania Avenue for the time being as long as other access routes into the White House and the Capitol remained open.

Organizers with bullhorns moved among the crowds, seeding radicals among the peaceful. Radicals worked their way to the front ranks and started people heckling the soldiers. Brotherman White found a largely black group of soldiers near the north gate to East Executive Place and gathered a contingent of his SNCC to confront them. Brotherman noticed a TV crew filming from the top of a van parked in Madison Place twenty yards away, and he began to shout. "Hey, little brother, hey, hey! You wanna go to Asia and kill colored people for that white muthafucka live in the big house? Come over and join the revolution!" roared Brotherman through his bullhorn. The white kids took up the "Hey, little brother, hey, hey!" refrain, while the SNCC members pressed forward, shoving the blue police barricades or slipping between them, touching the soldiers, black and white, and looking knowingly at the black troops as the white ones shrank from their touch. "White boy don' even wanna *touch* a black man, little brother," they whispered in the ears of the black troops as they leaned in over the soldiers' rifles, held at port-arms. "Get out that housenigger uniform and join your real brothers!"

A buck sergeant, white, walked behind the lines of his men, speaking softly but insistently. "Steadee–e–e," he breathed over and over again as the marchers crowded and yelled and taunted. The sergeant keyed his short-range radio mike. "HQ, this is Sergeant Hunnicut at North Three. Is Sergeant Major Wilson there?"

"Affirmative, North Three."

"I need him."

"On my way," said another, deeper voice.

The crowd pressed and jostled. Women in the front ranks stuck withered flowers in the barrels of the soldiers' weapons, and in some cases chewing gum. Some demonstrators began to spit on the soldiers. The troops were in their service dress uniforms, the kind a soldier had to have dry-cleaned at his own expense. Some of the soldiers started to press back at the mob. The sergeant could see the muscles in their shoulders bunch as he walked behind them, and he knew he had very little time. "Steadee–e–e," he said forcefully.

An olive drab van drew up in the road behind the soldiers, and another behind it. A squad of soldiers with MP brassards and long billy clubs coiled out of the first van and formed up. The passenger side of the first van opened slowly and a very large, very black man stepped out. Command sergeant major's chevrons, rockers, and wreathed star gleamed on his tightly tailored service dress green uniform, pressed with creases sharp enough to cut paper. His trousers were neatly bloused over mirror-shined black jump boots. Command Sergeant Major Wilson scowled at the yelling crowd as he slowly, carefully placed his polished steel helmet on his clean-shaven head. A D.C. Metro policeman, a thin black man with a bouncing Adam's apple, named Cruthers, followed Wilson as closely as he could without tripping over him. Because the Military Police could not arrest civilians unless martial law was declared, Cruthers was along as a "tap officer"—he would make actual arrests if instructed by Sergeant Major Wilson.

The command sergeant major patted Sergeant Hunnicut on his shoulder as he passed through the briefly opened gate, but his eyes never left the faces of the demonstrators, searching them and finally settling on the now laughing face of Brotherman White. With a flick of a short swagger stick he carried in his right hand, Command Sergeant Major Wilson motioned his MPs and the D.C. cop to pass through the ranks of beleaguered soldiers, following him. He stopped with his face an inch from the man he did not yet know was the chairman of the Student Nonviolent Coordinating Committee and shaped his smooth ebony face into a smile of pure delight, such as one might display to an infant. He and Brotherman were of approximately the same height, but the CSM had at least a sixty pound weight advantage, none of which was fat. Nevertheless, Brotherman didn't back off, and returned the smile. "Well, *hello General!*" said Brotherman, putting his hands on his hips.

"Command Sergeant Major Wilson, *sir*," said Wilson in his parade-ground voice. The rest of the hecklers in the immediate area had fallen silent and backed off a couple of yards. People strained to see what would happen. "May I know your name, *sir?*"

Brotherman laughed. "Call me Brotherman, brother man."

"Well, *Mister* Brotherman, you people are just going to have to move back a bit. You can stand there behind the barricade, and you can sit there, but no closer."

"We have the right to peaceable assembly, and to freedom of speech."

"Indeed. Everywhere but here, *sir*."

"Especially here, housenigger," shouted Brotherman. "*We* are the people, not that long-nosed honkie you be protecting. The government belongs to *us*."

The CSM reached out and took Brotherman's left hand in his right. It seemed a friendly, almost a prissy gesture, but the CSM had the other man's thumb pinned to his wrist. Brotherman stiffened against the pain, but when he tried to pull away the CSM's pressure increased. Brotherman stood still and the pressure eased a little. "You are under arrest, Mr. Brotherman," said Wilson, pleasantly, adding enough of a squeeze to make Brotherman writhe. Patrolman Cruthers squeaked on cue, confirming the arrest, and then backed away. "Nice and legal, Mr. Brotherman," said Wilson, grinning again. "Take him," he said to the first MP behind him. The man stepped forward and secured Brotherman's wrists behind him with plastic riot cuffs. Brotherman was glad to have his thumb released, and his defiance returned in an angry rush. "You can't do this, trash! This a peaceful demonstration! What is the charge?"

"Disturbing the peace," shouted the CSM, in his parade-ground voice. The MP behind him wrote it down and began to lead Brotherman through the soldiers to the second van. Brotherman pulled away and turned back to Wilson, snarling. Their chests just touched. The CSM looked down at his chest as he stepped back a pace and smiled once more. "Add assault," he said to the MP.

"What is this bullshit!" screamed Brotherman, looking wildly at the crowd for help. "Whose peace is disturbed? This demonstration has all the required police permits!" he struggled in the grasp of two MPs.

"Add riot," said the CSM loudly. "And get him out of here." As the two MPs dragged Brotherman back, the CSM stopped them and rested a hand briefly on Brotherman's shoulder. "To answer your question, asshole," he whispered in Brotherman's ear. "Disturbing *the command sergeant major*'s peace."

Brotherman was pulled through the ranks of soldiers and hustled into the van. The CSM walked a few paces into the crowd, now sullen and silent. The marchers parted and gave him a circle two yards wide. Wilson turned around, making sure he was surrounded by the marchers. "Now," he said in his carrying voice, but his tone was even, almost kindly. "You can stay here as long as you are peaceable, but no trouble." The marchers seemed sheepish. "And if there is anyone left who would care to spit on a black soldier, do it now." He waited, turning and looking at the faces of the people around him for a full two minutes. "I thought not. Have your demonstration, then, but peacefully." CSM Wilson turned and marched through the demonstrators and then through his soldiers, his stick tucked under his left arm. "Take over, Sergeant Hunnicut," he said, remounting the lead van. "You handled that just right."

*   *   *

The motorcade carrying the secretary of defense to Washington from Andrews Air Force Base sped up the Suitland Parkway and into southeast Washington. The secretary had just returned from two gruelling two weeks in Southeast Asia, visiting allies in the Philippines and Thailand and consulting with South Vietnamese and U.S. officials in Saigon as well as with senior military commanders in Long Binh, Bien Hoa, and Danang. The results of his tour had been very discouraging and very exhausting. The secretary wanted nothing more than to go to his home in Silver Spring and sleep for twenty-four hours, but he knew the president would expect at least a brief immediate report.

It was just after 1300 when the motorcade crossed over Anacostia Creek near the Navy Yard. The radio car in front with the Secret Service detail was in contact with the command post in the Department of Justice Building as well as with their own HQ in the White House, and were following the police reports of the demonstration. The shortest route to the White House would have taken them up Twelfth Street, under the Mall, and then up Pennsylvania Avenue, but clearly that was out of the question. The command post gave them a route that would take them around the crowd to the east of the Capitol, onto Massachusetts Avenue to the point where it intersected New York Avenue, straight down New York past the Treasury, into the short piece of Pennsylvania Avenue directly north of the White House that the police still controlled, and then into East Executive Place. Police units along the route were alerted and the troops at the gate were reinforced. The secretary overheard the instructions relayed to the driver of his limousine and silently cursed the additional delay.

Sergeant Major Wilson monitored the alert in the Military Police headquarters and noted that the cars would be coming in through Sergeant Hunnicut's sector. Wilson mentally congratulated himself for having lanced the carbuncle that was Brotherman and removed him from the scene. He thought Hunnicut was a pretty good kid, but when the MP reinforcements were loading into the vans he picked up a hand-held radio and decided to accompany them out to East Executive Place.

Van Camp and his small contingent of Panthers moved to the scene of Brotherman White's arrest, thinking to do themselves some good with the SNCC brothers now that the great Brotherman had stomped on his dick. The SNCC kids were surly and embarrassed that their leader had been arrested on TV by a black man, and more embarrassed that they had been so overawed by the command sergeant major that they had done nothing. There were only four of them with Brotherman, they told Van Camp defiantly, and the white kids were having nothing of provoking the troops. Van Camp looked around at the white people, most of whom had backed off several yards and were seated on the sidewalk, chatting like guests at a very crowded garden party. Van Camp motioned his six Panthers from Oakland and San Francisco close to the SNCC kids, who were noticeably more middle class than his ghetto-wise followers. "Well, brothers," said Van Camp, dismissing the white kids with a wave, then pointing at the silent ranks of soldiers and back at the SNCC blacks, "we an army of eleven now, and the first chance we get, we show these honkies and these pigs some revolution." The SNCC four exchanged glances and seemed to shrink together and away from the Panthers, with their tight black jackets, red, green, and black knitted caps, and taut street scowls. "Unless," Van Camp continued, adding menace to each word, "you rather be pussies and *watch* us do it."

The tallest SNCC kid stepped forward and faced Van Camp. He looked scared, so Van Camp smiled. "We are not afraid to get arrested," said the kid.

"Get *arrested!*" laughed Van Camp. "That ain't the half of it."

The secretary of defense looked out the windows of his limousine as it turned into New York Avenue and was surprised to see demonstrators in small groups fully half a mile from the White House. People raised fists at him and some darted across the road, trying to slow the little two-car motorcade. The driver of the Secret Service car ahead turned on the flashing lights concealed in its grille and, as the crowds thickened south of H Street, the siren as well. As the cars turned into Pennsylvania Avenue police on foot and horseback forced an opening in the crowd blocking the way to East Executive Place. The secretary saw people pressed back and winced as a woman fell in the crush. Demonstrators began pushing back at the police, not with apparent aggressive intent, but simply because they had no place to go in the dense crowd. The Secret Service car was forced to slow and then to stop. The crowd pressed against the limousine and people peered at the secretary through the tinted windows. "It's Laird, it's fucking Laird!" shouted one man, his voice clearly audible to the secretary despite the bulletproof glass and extra insulation in the limousine. The secretary leaned forward to instruct his driver to lock all the doors, but he had already done so. Through the windshield the secretary could see a squad of MPs, led by an enormous black sergeant with a swagger stick, pushing through the crowd toward the cars. The Secret Service men were out of their car and were working their way back to the limousine, and then a skinny black man wearing a black jacket and a red, white, and green cap leaped up on the hood. The secretary recoiled into his seat; the man was screaming and pounding on the windshield with the haft of a hunting knife. A Secret Service man, almost to the limousine, was dragged off his feet into the crowd, and another drew his pistol and assumed a combat stance, aiming at the man on the hood of the car. The man gave him the finger and laughed, then went back to pounding on the windshield, producing tiny cracks in the outer layer of glass.

Sergeant Major Wilson reached the Secret Service agent with the drawn gun in a final violent surge through the shouting crowd. He grabbed the man's hand and forced it down to his side. The agent's face was contorted with fear. "Pistol do no good here, man," said CSM Wilson. "Put it away and come with me." Wilson pushed on through the crowd to the limousine, no longer caring who got thrust aside or stepped on as he went. The black Cadillac was being rocked by demonstrators pulling on both sides, but Wilson doubted the six-ton armored behemoth could be overturned. The command sergeant major's target was the thin black man with the colorful knitted cap who was chopping at the windshield. Wilson reached across the hood of the car and grabbed the thin man's wrist, pulling the man toward him and twisting at the same time. The knife fell to the pavement and Wilson kicked it under the limousine. "You come with me, son," said the CSM quietly. "Come on, now." The man struggled in his grasp with surprising strength and spit in Wilson's face, a thick, foul-smelling stream. Wilson noted that the man's pupils were mere pinpoints despite the bright sun of the afternoon. Twenty-two years of discipline momentarily deserted the CSM, and with a roar he lifted the slight black man over his head and hurled him five rows back into the crowd.

Wilson wiped the stinking mess from his face with a handkerchief. His MPs and the Secret Service agents had cleared the crowd from around the cars, and both were slowly moving forward. Once they passed through Sergeant Hunnicut's position the cars sped to the east portico of the White House. The secretary of defense, still shaking from his close encounter with the mob, made his way through nearly deserted corridors to the Oval Office in the West Wing and was admitted.

President Nixon stood with his back to the room, watching the crowd pressing against the soldiers outside the fence at the far end of the South Lawn. Despite the distance and the thick glass the crowd could be heard as a low-pitched, undulating roar. John Hermann, the special assistant to the president, sat in a chair in front of Nixon's desk, a pad in his lap. The only other occupant of the room was Mrs. Woods, the president's secretary, also with a pad, ready to take dictation.

Nixon turned and looked at his secretary of defense. Secretary Laird's face was white and sweaty, and his right eye was twitching. He looked old and ill. Nixon's face registered shock at his friend's terrified appearance, and then the president's jaw firmed and his eyes grew cold. He stepped forward, put his hand on the secretary's arm, and guided him gently to a chair. "John," he said, pointing at Hermann without looking away from the secretary, "call the command post at Justice. Tell Chief Haines and General Davis to take back the streets. And tell Director Hoover I have finally decided to take his recommendation: he can have the ringleaders." He bent to bring his face close to the secretary's. "This has gone quite far enough."

Command Sergeant Major Wilson emerged from the tiny washroom adjacent to the Military Police headquarters, towelling off his face and dabbing at his uniform blouse with paper towels. The first lieutenant standing the watch waved him over to the duty desk and pointed to a row of electric bullhorns on a shelf across the room. "Word just came down, Sergeant Major," said the lieutenant. "Clear 'em back to the Mall. Thought you might like to be one of the people who got to take them the message."

"Be a pleasure, sir," said the CSM. "But they won't go."

"Well, perhaps not, until we give them a little encouragement," laughed the lieutenant. "But you are a remarkably persuasive man, Sergeant Major."

Wilson picked up a bullhorn. "I'll give 'em the president's compliments, sir. But I do hope we have something in mind beyond our one company of MPs to back them up."

"Be assured, Sergeant Major." The lieutenant stood. "The general was most emphatic: the President wants his city back."

"Sir," said CSM Wilson as he left the HQ.

*   *   *

Soldiers with bullhorns fanned out from the White House and the Capitol, all with the same message, which was also broadcast from the roof of the Department of Justice Building and from police cars equipped with loudspeakers stopped within the crowd. The message was that the demonstration could not be allowed to block the streets. The marchers were asked to return to the Mall and assured that once they had done so a delegation of no more than twenty of them would be admitted to the White House to discuss their grievances with a representative of the president. The crowd flung the words back at the speakers, shouting "Nixon, here, now!" The men with the bullhorns marched away, and then soldiers in battle dress began emerging from the basement of the Capitol and advanced to the line of troops ringing the building. More soldiers rushed from the basements of the Treasury and the Executive Office Buildings, formed up on either side of the White House, and advanced on the crowd through the access points. A few minutes later CH-47 helicopters began landing on the lawns in front of both the White House and the Capitol, disgorging more troops and lifting off, apparently to bring still more. At the outer edges of the crowd police sirens announced the advance of more cops. The crowd grew quiet and began to shrink back into itself. The troops advanced to the barricades shoulder to shoulder, passed through the lines of their exhausted comrades, and pressed forward against the crowd. At the edges of the mob, where people could move, people began to run to the supposed sanctuary of the Mall, while smaller military helicopters with guns over their skids and in their doors hovered low enough to blow trash and grit into the marchers' faces. Where it could, the mob began to break up and flee.

Senator William Brush had watched the demonstration from the window in his office in the north wing of the Capitol with a feeling of unease. In the early morning the participants had seemed more boisterous than menacing, and the bullhorn-amplified speeches echoed faintly through the open window without meaning, but Brush knew in his heart that the day would turn ugly. When the mob approached the Capitol to surround it and symbolically cut it off he was able to see the faces in the front rows where the troops confronted the marchers in the open accesses to Pennsylvania Avenue and First Street, and watch as the more radical and the better organized moved among the merely present. He watched smiles and laughter give way to scowls and jeering.

The senator considered going out onto the lawn to talk to the marchers, to tell them he shared their desire to end the war, but he couldn't make himself do it. The faces of the people, the *people*, he thought, frightened him, and the thin line of soldiers between the *people* and the government they had come to jeer seemed too fragile a protection. He was afraid, yet when the troop helicopters landed on the lawn west of the dome and offloaded their reinforcements he was shocked and angered. Yet still he did not go down; he merely closed the window and turned away. He sat at his big desk with his head in his hands and pondered what this dreadful war, which had been begun with noble thoughts and strict limits, had become, and what it had done to the nation. He picked up a pen and began to write single lines on a legal size yellow pad. Almost without knowing it, he began to write a speech as the roar of the helicopters drowned the voice of the people.

In the streets the mob found difficulty in dispersing because of its sheer size. The police plan had been to drive the demonstrators from the White House and the Capitol back to the central and western parts of the Mall, and to contain them around the Lincoln Memorial and the Tidal Basin, west of the museums of the Smithsonian Institution. In the main the plan worked well, as the police and troops advanced slowly, bypassing those demonstrators who sat and refused to move, leaving them to squads of police, following on with vans, who made arrests when they had to. But on the outer edges of the crowd, especially along Pennsylvania Avenue and to the north of the White House, large groups of people broke off from the main body as the police passed and couldn't reach the Mall. Police chased these marchers through residential areas of northeast and southeast Washington, and arrested many whose only crime was running away in terror from the squad cars, the horses, and the helmeted, club-swinging officers.

Red Sister was with one such small group southeast of the Capitol. They dodged through the quiet, tree-lined streets of Southeast, pursued by the sounds of sirens. A police car with twirling roof lights blocked their way on A Street three blocks east of the Supreme Court, and many of the marchers stopped and raised their hands as the police got out, billy clubs in hand. Red Sister fled south on Third. She had good reason to fear arrest: she had handled explosives and other things in a brownstone house in Greenwich Village many times until the place had been busted a month before, and she had never been any more careful than any of the others about leaving fingerprints. Another car blocked Third, so she turned west into Independence Avenue, hoping to reach the safety of the crowd in the Mall. As she entered the path outside the buses she saw that the troops and police who had circled the building had mostly gone. She walked slowly north through the litter toward a small group of demonstrators who stood near a monument to navy officers and men who had died defending the Union during the Civil War. Among them she recognized Art Shamsky of the War Resisters' League with a bloody rag around his forehead. She knew enough about Shamsky to know he would not want to be fingerprinted either.

Senator Brush looked out his window at the setting sun. The crowd seemed quite far away down the Mall. He felt old and ill, and he needed air. He decided to walk to the taxi stand on Constitution Avenue near the National Gallery of Art and get a cab to his home in Georgetown. He had left his car at home because of the demonstration.

The senator left the Capitol by the stairs to the northwest of the Rotunda and walked along the path to the Navy Civil War Monument, where Pennsylvania Avenue began. A small group of marchers sat near the base of the monument. They looked dazed and some appeared to be injured. I should talk to them, thought the senator, but he would have passed them by except that one, a man with gray hair, a beard, and a bloody bandanna on his head, called his name.

"Hey, that is Senator William Brush of Georgia," said the man without inflection.

A Junoesque woman with flaming red hair turned to look. "Hey, Senator," she said, pointing to the bearded man's crude bandage. "Look what your pigs do to the people."

Brush stopped and set his jaw. He *had* to speak to these people, he *did* share their commitment to end the war. "Young lady, I do not support the war. I have spoken out against the war on the floor of the Senate, and—"

"You hypocritical pig!" the redhead screamed. "You helped push the Gulf of Tonkin Resolution through the Senate for that archfascist Johnson!"

Brush recoiled from her fury. The other demonstrators seemed to throw off their weariness and began to crowd around the senator. He took a step back and then another, and held up his hands, palms out, imploring reason. "That's true, I did. But I was deceived! And since the Tet Offensive, I have been a leading advocate—"

"Fuck you, pig!" shouted a young woman, barely more than a girl.

She clenched her tiny fist and struck at Brush's outstretched hands. He took another step backwards. "Go back in there and hide in your Senate! Americans are dying and Asian people are being butchered and American kids and mothers and grandmothers are being clubbed right here in Washington, and all you do is talk! You serve the fascists because you do not oppose them!"

"But—" said Brush, but the girl and the redheaded woman were suddenly gone, running. Brush felt a hand on his shoulder and saw he was escorted on either side by uniformed policemen of the Capitol detail. He looked at them questioningly. "But I—"

"You all right, Senator Brush?" said one. "You want us to get a car to take you home?"

"No," said the senator, shaking his head. "I'll go back up to my office. I have things to do." He felt dizzy and there was a tightness like a steel band around his chest. "I have to make it right."

The two policemen nodded, their expressions at once grave and uncomprehending. Brush made his way back to his office and sat at the desk. The chest pains persisted, but he had had them before. He felt terribly tired. He poured himself a generous measure of bourbon and spilled most of it on the leather top of his desk, his hand was shaking so. He swiped angrily at the spill with the sleeve of his suit jacket and willed his hand to be steady. He then picked up his pencil and began to write.

TWENTY

Trai o Bo Song, 24 May 1969

Moser woke in the darkness, slumped in his tiger cage pit. The muscles in his shoulders and legs had cramped badly during the night. He felt agony in the slightest movement and wished for relief, even in death. He had dreamed about his escape for the fourth night in a row, vivid scenes of rushing water and hunger and joy and despair and humiliation. During the days, while he was lashed to the pumps, he saw his flight again, minute by minute like a grainy silent newsreel. He had no idea why these images were so insistent: he had rarely thought about his escape since he had been brought back by the Pathet Lao so long ago, in a different, cooler season. Somehow the images, with their awful, searing conclusion next to the fire in the High Camp, were sapping the anger that sustained him, that linked him with Major Nan and kept him going toward the day when they would be fully joined in death.

Moser began to move around. He heard the snakes in the darkness and thought to grab one and take its poisonous bite into the endless journey. But he couldn't and he knew he wouldn't. He knew he had to endure until, somehow—

"Get up, Con Trau Duc," called Sergeant Minh from above the pit. "The sun is rising and the rice needs water."

Moser climbed out, his joints and muscles sending rockets of pain through his tired mind. Perhaps I am nothing but a water buffalo. Perhaps I have ceased to be human. Perhaps Major Nan and Sergeant Minh and this place have finally taken away my mind.

Why does no one come to help me?

TWENTY-ONE

The Capitol, Washington, 26 May 1969

The Senate chamber was crowded as Sen. William Brush approached the speaker's lectern. He nodded to acknowledge the president pro tempore, then turned toward the great hall. He looked at the faces of his colleagues and at the press and visitors' galleries above. News that the senior senator from Georgia planned a major foreign policy speech had been spread carefully, and the galleries were full. Rumors were flying that the senator would finally do what he had long threatened to do while Johnson was still in the White House: break with the bipartisan consensus and denounce the war.

Brush's appearance on the Senate floor was greeted by polite applause. He smiled his thanks and smoothed back his mane of silver hair. He placed his speech in front of him on the lectern, handwritten as he had drafted it, with a very few pencilled changes made just before coming down to the floor. He took a pair of reading half-glasses from the pocket of his dark blue suit jacket and perched them on his nose. He looked again at his audience and it fell silent except for a few coughs and murmurs, like a crowd at a concert at the moment the conductor raises his baton.

"My colleagues of the United States Senate," he began, warming up his rich, southern voice. "And my fellow Americans." He raised his eyes to the press galleries. "I have asked the president pro tem and the leaders of both parties to speak today on a matter of highest national importance.

"Yesterday I witnessed one of the greatest demonstrations of the American people's desire to participate in the direction of their destinies, and not merely to be governed. Estimates of as many as five hundred thousand of our fellow citizens, mostly young but many older, men and women of all races, clergy and adherents of all religions, gathered *here*." Brush paused and pointed to the floor in front of him for emphasis. "Gathered *here*, around this building and around the White House, to bring a message to this government. Their message was clear, and they brought it themselves, directly *here*, because they have lost faith in the process of representative democracy.

"My fellow Americans, I watched the demonstration, the peaceful assembly, from my office upstairs here in the Capitol. I felt I should go down and speak to the people, but the sight of the soldiers of this republic with their rifles and their black helmets keeping the people from its elected representatives so repelled me that I did not. Only after the even more shocking sight of troops in battle gear pouring out of helicopters onto the lawn of the Capitol as they might assault a village in *Vietnam*, and then forming up to push the people *farther* away from this arrogant seat of power—" Brush's voice rose on this last phrase, and he paused. The chamber remained silent, the faces of his colleagues expressionless. "—only then did I have the courage to go down and talk to some of the people who remained on the Capitol grounds.

"One of the men in the group had been beaten. Most of the rest were women, young women. One of them reminded me that in 1964, at the request of President Johnson, I managed the passage of the Gulf of Tonkin Resolution through this house. That resolution encouraged President Johnson to bomb North Vietnam and then to land troops in South Vietnam, even though at the time he *insisted* he intended never to send our sons and husbands and brothers to fight and die in Asia.

"I told these young protestors that I had changed my views about the war, and that I had worked tirelessly with the Johnson Administration and latterly with this one to move our national policy toward peace in Vietnam. But they cursed me because I continued to acquiesce and to be part of the government that made the war and caused so much suffering and destruction not only in that unhappy land so very far away but here, at home, and indeed on the Mall and the steps of *this House*. They told me that if I truly wanted the war ended I had to do more than make a few speeches on college campuses; I had to *act* here in *this House*." Brush looked up from his notes and scanned the faces of the senators. Expressions of polite attention, at best. "My fellow senators, upon prayerful reflection, I have come to believe those young people are right and that I do have to act, and I propose to begin today. I stand before you today to repudiate my support for the Gulf of Tonkin Resolution and to call for the Senate and the Congress to repudiate it as well. Furthermore, from this day forward, until the last American troops have left Vietnam and the surrounding countries, I will oppose the war, and funding for the war, and resolutions in support of the war, in my every act." For the first time Brush was interrupted by applause, mostly from the galleries but from a few senators as well. Others looked shocked.

"In the resolution I will place before the Committee on Foreign Relations I will specifically require, and I urge my colleagues to join me in making this the sense of the Senate, that the government of the United States begin serious talks with the other side, proposing a cease-fire for the parties fighting, but that even without a cease-fire we begin the rapid and complete withdrawal of our forces, and that we take no further military actions in prosecution of the war other than those necessary to protect our troops as they depart. The only condition—" The applause in the galleries was louder, and Brush could see interest replacing passivity in the faces of his Senate colleagues.

"The only condition I would insist on prior to our disengagement from this sad and bleeding land would be the prompt return by the other side of all of our prisoners of war."

Once again the applause from the galleries increased. Senator Morse from Oregon was clapping loudly from his desk in the front row. Other senators looked up at Brush in amazement. Several mouthed the word "no," over and over. Brush mopped his brow with his large pocket handkerchief and patted his silver hair. He straightened his notes on the lectern; he was down to one last page. The chamber fell silent. "A couple of days ago, and just before the people came to Washington to demand an end to the war, the president sent a team of men into North Vietnam itself in a bold attempt to rescue some of our imprisoned airmen. The tragic results of this attempt are known to all. That these army rangers were courageous is beyond question. They did what they had to do to honor a soldier's debt to his imprisoned comrades. But, my friends and colleagues, the operation itself was sheer folly, and in the aftermath not only did none of our POWs come home, but eight more of our sons and husbands are now in cruel captivity, and twenty-one more have been added to the sad rolls of the glorious dead. I will include in my resolution—" The chamber erupted with noise: some applause, some angry shouts. The president pro tempore pounded his gavel for a full minute before order was restored. Brush continued, his voice commanding but softer. "I will include in my resolution, and once again I hope my colleagues will join me and make this the sense of the Senate, that adventures of this sort be stopped, and that any being planned be cancelled as an act of good faith. The way to bring our men home from those awful camps is to end this tragic war, and that can only be accomplished by negotiating with the Vietnamese people." There was a smattering of applause. Brush held up his hands for quiet and rushed on. "This war, begun as an attempt to help a small Asian nation escape the crushing embrace of Communism, has become a millstone around the neck of the American nation, dragging us ever downward into a dark valley of killing and death. We should fear the evil in this valley, and we should repudiate it before it consumes the light which is this great nation. That light is the light of peace: peace in all the world, and peace in the streets of this nation's capital." Once again the applause began and Brush raised his hands to hush it.

"I leave you with one final thought," he said, scanning the faces of the senators. "One sad thought. Imagine what the television pictures taken yesterday outside this building will look like on screens throughout the world, in countries that call us friend and ally, and in countries in the Communist grip that look to the United States for hope."

Brush walked from the podium and took his seat. He was exhausted and the pains in his chest returned. The chamber was noisy, but it was hard to tell whether he was being praised for speaking out so strongly or condemned for breaking with the bipartisan support for the president's attempts to achieve peace with honor. Some of both, he thought. But by God, I feel better for having said it.

TWENTY-TWO

Paris, 28 May 1969

Khanh Vu Binh read about the failed American raid on the empty prison camp in the *International Herald Tribune*. The story was accompanied by a photo of American prisoners being marched through Hanoi streets and a list of the killed and missing. She read the list slowly, while holding her breath. She was glad not to find William's name, but even as she read the list again she was anxious. What had he gone to Aix-en-Provence to find?

Khanh wandered around her apartment, trying to decide what to do about William. She had received another postal telegram, from the little cell in Aix, which now reposed in the locked lower drawer of her desk. She felt drawn to it yet repelled, so she stalled, looking out the windows at the Seine, brassy in the hot sunlight, and the passing barges and tourist boats. Damn William, she thought, for placing his fate in my hands, and damn to hell those nosy old women of Aix!

Khanh clenched her fists with purpose and strode into the little study. She unlocked the drawer and retrieved the telegram and its decoded translation. It had arrived this morning along with the *Herald Tribune*.

FOR COMRADE AI QUOC PARIS FROM HUONG AIX-EN-PROVENCE
   GLORIOUS NEWS OF THWARTED IMPERIALIST INVASION! HAS HANOI RE-
SPONDED TO OUR REPORT OF AMERICAN INTEREST IN CERTAIN SECTION OF LAOS
DATED 16TH INSTANT? ENDS.

Khanh took a lined pad and wrote out her response, in block capitals on alternate lines to facilitate subsequent encoding:

HANOI HAS NOT RESPONDED YET. I WILL SEND A FOLLOWUP MESSAGE.

Which means *you* should not inquire, she thought as she encoded the text onto a telegram form. She then took another form and summarized the original report from Aix, downgrading the source code from two (believed reliable) to four (reliability unknown), and gave the message the lowest possible priority, routine. She put her summary into an envelope with some other minor gossip she had collected and sealed it. She rang for her maid and told her to give the completed telegram and the envelope to her chauffeur, Paul, one to go to the post office and the other to the dead drop she used for communications with the North Vietnamese mission. Khanh asked the maid to bring her some tea. God, I hope that report gets filed and lost, she thought, rubbing her temples against a sudden headache. William, my only love, stay away from Indochina!

TWENTY-THREE

Arlington, Virginia, 28 May 1969

Stuart and MacAndrew entered the director's office, passing the elderly secretary, who held open the door and then closed it behind them. Stuart looked around at the oak panelling and the wood-and-leather furniture, the spacious carpeted floor and the three broad windows. There was an oil painting of a naval battle over the long sofa and floor lamps with parchment shades gave a soft light that reflected off polished surfaces. It was hard to believe this office was in the same building as the Spartan cubicles the rest of NIS used, with their battered steel desks and file cabinets and harsh fluorescent lighting. In his year at NIS Stuart had never been in this office and never met the director, nor had he expected to.

The great man pushed himself up from behind his huge desk and gestured MacAndrew to a high-backed leather chair. Stuart was taken by Captain Willis's presence. He seemed very old and very wise, a Washington insider out of Central Casting: flawlessly tailored blue suit, white shirt and club tie, tanned, lined cheeks, and full head of gray hair cut military short. The director motioned Stuart to the long couch as MacAndrew collapsed into his chair. The director pulled a chair over to the low coffee table, across from the two others, and sat. His expression was kindly. Stuart felt sure about what Captain Willis was going to say and he burned with controlled anger. He sat in the low couch and cocked one leg over the other, looking up at the two old men.

"It is good to see you, William," began the director, ignoring the fact that they had never met.

"Thank you, sir," managed Stuart. Get it over with, he thought.

"You have served your country well, Lieutenant," smiled the director, opening a personnel file stamped "Top Secret—BuPers Only" on the cover. "Many decorations. And Major MacAndrew has nothing but praise for your work in your latest project."

Which means Tom Miller pissed on my previous fitness reports, thought William. He had always suspected it. Another "Thank you, sir," came out.

"You are here on extension, William, and Major MacAndrew has told me he can at last let you go back to civilian life. You will be released to the inactive reserve the day after tomorrow." The director paused and smiled his patrician smile. "Is there anything we can do for you? Have you thought about a civilian job?"

Stuart's face reddened. "Sir, I can't *believe* we are simply going to leave Douglas MacArthur Moser in the shit! We—"

"Steady, Lieutenant," said MacAndrew, sharply.

"It's all right, Harry," said the director, mildly.

Stuart fought down his anger. "We owe him, sir. We owe them all!"

"We do indeed," said the director. "Major MacAndrew and I once talked of your operation as perhaps the crowning achievement of our own long careers."

"Then why—"

"Because the operation you were helping to plan is stood down, Lieutenant," said the director. "We work for the navy, which works in turn for the government. The army's tragic losses in Operation Night Crossing have cast a pall over all rescue operations. Surely you heard that the chairman of the Senate Foreign Relations Committee has spoken out specifically against further such missions?"

"But sir!" blurted Stuart, his face mottling again. "We *know* where Moser is! We need a tiny operation. Just because the army screwed the pooch—"

"Dammit, Stuart, shut up!" shouted MacAndrew, starting to rise from his chair. "Remember where you are."

"Yes, sir," said Stuart, ashamed. "I beg your pardon, sir," he said to the director.

The older men regarded him in silence. Stuart fought the urge to fidget. After a minute under the lofty gaze of his two superiors Stuart spoke softly. "So that's it. I am out of the navy and Moser rots in jail."

The director spread his hands, a gesture of shared defeat. "We can't

get the army to look at the project, and to restart it as a navy operation at this point seems impossible, William."

A vision, similar to the one he had dreamed in Paris, of Moser in
a cage beckoning him rose in Stuart's mind, accompanied by a strong
smell of the jungle. He closed his eyes against his despair. The telephone
on the director's desk rang softly.

The director ignored the ringing. He had instructed his secretary
to hold all calls. In a moment the ringing stopped, but the lady herself
appeared at the open door. "Pardon me, Director," she whispered. "It's
the White House calling. Mr. John Hermann."

The director nodded and the secretary withdrew. Captain Willis
crossed to his desk and picked up the phone as it rang once again.
MacAndrew rose and beckoned Stuart to follow him out of the office.
The director motioned them back to their seats. "Yes, Mr. Hermann?"
said the director, then fell silent. Stuart could hear the muffled sound
of speech from the receiver as the director listened without responding.
After a minute and a half the director once again spoke. "At 1:30. Yes,
you may tell the president that I'll be there." He placed the phone in
its cradle without a sound. "That," he said, clapping his hands once
in front of him, "was the special assistant to the president. The president
wants to see me this afternoon, and from the tone of that conversation,
I would say there is a good chance that our off-again on-again operation
may well be on again." He pointed to Stuart and then at MacAndrew.
"Go have one of your conspiratorial lunches Tom Miller complains
to me about and be back here no later than 1330, in case I have to
reach you for specifics." William jumped to his feet. "It isn't guaranteed,
Lieutenant," said Willis, quietly. "But we may indeed need you a while
longer."

"Yes, *sir!*" said Stuart, and followed MacAndrew out of the room.

Captain Willis was ushered into the Oval Office at precisely 1330.
The president stood by the bow window, looking south at a thin line
of demonstrators standing by the iron fence at the bottom of the South
Lawn. John Hermann sat in a blue leather chair next to the fireplace
with a yellow pad on his lap. A fire popped merrily behind the wire
screen, but failed to dispel the air of gloom in the room.

The president turned away from the window and advanced to greet
the director. He smiled his campaign smile, but his blue suit was rumpled
and he looked worried and old. He guided Willis to a chair opposite

Hermann and then sat between them, facing the fire. The president stared at the dancing flames as he began to speak and the reflection of the flames on his cheeks gave his face an eerie, twitching glow.

"Did you see them?" said the president.

"Sir?" said the director.

"The demonstration," said Hermann. "The big one, five days ago."

"Yes, Mr. President," said Captain Willis, carefully. "On the television."

"You should have been *here*!" said the president, waving at a bank of closed-circuit television monitors set up near his desk. His eyes hadn't left the fire. "They reviled me! They insult everything this great republic has stood for, and I am trying to negotiate a peace!" The president fell silent. The director thought to say something to fill the void, but a look on John Hermann's face discouraged him. After a minute the president resumed. "Captain Willis, that hypocritical S.O.B. Senator Brush is telling me I can't do anything but cave in to the North Vietnamese demands, telling the world that the Senate will oppose me as I look for a just peace! Well, I have the votes to defeat his resolution, but think how this looks to the North Vietnamese, and to the world!" The president shook his head. "If Senator Brush has his way the Viets will just sit and wait and watch our will erode, and eventually win without ever defeating us or the South Vietnamese." Nixon looked up and smiled at the director. "I can't let that happen, Director; I have to send the North Vietnamese a clear signal that they will deal fairly with me or suffer unacceptable consequences."

A long moment passed. The president's gaze returned to the fireplace. The director cleared his throat. "Yes, sir," he murmured.

"He even has the gall to dictate to me that I cannot try to bring back my POWs." The President looked quickly at the director. His face was lit by the fire on one side and in deep shadow on the other. A soul divided, thought the director.

Another pause. The director cleared his throat. John Hermann spoke softly. "Mr. President, Captain Willis has proposed a rescue mission, on a rather modest scale."

"I was coming to that," said Nixon, smiling. The director saw only the fire-lit side. "John tells me that you have a mission with a high probability of success and at the same time a low profile during the operation itself."

"We are well along in the planning, Mr. President," said the director, leaning forward. "We could go quickly and quietly with our own resources if we had highest authorization."

"How many men would be at risk? The rescuers, I mean," queried the president.

"No more than eight to ten on the ground; a couple of air crews for the extraction," said Captain Willis.

"So if the rescue failed—I hate to suggest this, Director—any losses could be attributed to normal combat operations and not to a specific rescue mission?"

Willis had a sour taste in his mouth, but he sympathized with the president's dilemma. One more public fiasco and Senator Brush might get enough votes to pass a resolution of censure against the administration's policy of fighting while talking. At least the president is willing to let us try. "Yes, sir, if we use units already in Vietnam; people, if you will, with business in the area."

"Not many people," said the president. "And people who won't talk."

"We can run it that way, Mr. President," said the director. "We would need covert funding and a letter of authorization from you that would allow our man to request and receive assistance from any command in Southeast Asia."

"Have Moorer sign it," said the president, turning toward Hermann, who nodded. Admiral Moorer was the chairman of the Joint Chiefs of Staff. "It can't come straight back here, you see," said the president to the director, looking sad and embarrassed. The director nodded.

"What should be the name on the letter?" asked Hermann. "The one 'acting on behalf and by the authority of' et cetera?"

"The field man will be Lieutenant William M. Stuart, USNR," said the director.

"A man that junior?" asked the president.

"You want this done quietly, with an absolute minimum of people even needing to know, sir," said the director.

The president nodded and returned his gaze to the fire. "Make it so, John," he said, drawing a wrinkled piece of paper from his jacket pocket and smoothing it on his knees. John Hermann got up and left the room. The director started to rise, but the president began speaking, still smoothing the paper, which seemed to be a letter of some kind. "These so-called peace marchers revile us at every turn, Captain," said the president, staring at the paper and shaking his head. "This is the agreed statement they handed to Chief of Police Haines when he went to meet with their self-appointed steering committee." Nixon seemed to be about to hand the paper to Captain Willis, who started to reach for it, but the president snatched it back, refolded it, and put it into his jacket pocket. "I have been in this office barely four months, and already they call me the ugliest compound word in the English language."

"Sir," said the director, wishing he could leave with his good news, fearing the president, in his strange mood, might change his mind.

"Don't they understand the greatest nation in the world can't just— bug out?" said the president, once again seeming to address the fire. Willis fidgeted in silence. The president turned toward him and smiled a little at the corners of his mouth. "But this is not helping you with your delicate and dangerous mission, Director. Bring me back some of our POWs, and do it in such a way that no one will ever know just how it was done, or on whose specific order. Even if the rescue is successful I will never be able to give you or your men anything more than private thanks."

Willis rose. Please let me go, he thought. "Your thanks will mean a lot to those men, Mr. President, but they will go because they want those men back as much as you do."

"Thank you, Director," said Nixon, pushing himself up from his chair. Standing, he seemed to loose the gloomy slump to his shoulders. He shook the director's hand. "Keep me up to date through John Hermann."

"Yes, Mr. President. Thank you, sir." Nixon nodded and returned to the window.

The director passed through the doorway and found John Hermann alone in the outer office. "The letter you requested will be hand-delivered to your office directly from JCS this afternoon, Director," said Hermann. "The boss is really counting on your boys to get some POWs out, to show just how committed he really is to getting all our boys home."

"We will do our best, of course, Mr. Hermann." He paused, knowing he was about to be indiscreet. "What was in that statement that so upset him? He said something about the ugliest compound word?"

"Take your pick," said Hermann, frowning. "They used them both."

IV

THE
VALLEY
OF THE
SHADOW

TWENTY-FOUR

Trai o Bo Song, Laos, 1 June 1969

Moser strained against the yoke, pushing off each step against the coarse decking. The wooden gears squeaked monotonously and the water gurgled into the trough. Moser's head hung down and his eyes were closed against the bright sun of early afternoon. He heard whispering inside his head, a low murmur too faint to comprehend. The sounds of the jungle were reduced in his brain to a low buzz. He plodded on with the measured tread of the *con trau duc*, the water buffalo, his totem, walking forever to nowhere to pump the water so he could have a ball of rice and exist for one more day.

A bird trilled loudly as it flew past Moser's ear. He cocked open his good eye and followed it. It was one of the iridescent blue parakeets that he—

That he used to enjoy. The memory was a sharp reminder of when he had been alive. He closed the eye and took another step. How long ago had he been alive?

You have a purpose, said the voice inside his head, quite clearly now. Moser took another step. He would have shaken his head against the voice's statement, but he lacked the energy.

You are not the water buffalo. You have a purpose.

The voice was sharp, insistent, like the trilling of the bird. Moser stopped and opened his eyes. The water gurgled, then fell silent. The sooty black cobra lay coiled loosely on his log, sunning. The snake was supposed to remind him of something long past. *Con ran mang xa.*

It has been a long time since you said it, said the voice. Could the snake be talking to him from inside his head? wondered Moser. Say it, urged the voice.

Say what? What could matter? Moser took a step forward, another. The water began to gurgle again.

The litany, said the voice. Say it after me. I am Douglas MacArthur Moser. I am not the water buffalo.

Moser's lips moved. He had no voice, but he formed the words in his brain to answer the voice of the cobra. I am Douglas MacArthur Moser. I am an American fighting man. The words coursed through his body with angry energy. He felt his flesh burn from the heat in his blood.

I am a man, not an animal, said the voice. Moser repeated it, stopped walking, and stood as nearly erect as he could. I am Douglas MacArthur Moser, an American fighting man.

Look at yourself, said the voice. Moser hung his head and looked at his filthy body. He couldn't remember when he had last washed carefully, although Trung-si Minh still took him to the river every morning. The red sores on his arms and legs were so numerous as to have merged into strips and patches, and his remaining skin was black with jungle grit. His feet were white and puffy, and they bled. His toenails were mostly missing. A fighting man takes care of his feet, no matter what.

The time will come soon, and you must be ready, said the voice of the snake.

Ready to kill Thieu-ta Nan, thought Moser. I can't die until I release his spirit. He and I will always suffer in this valley unless I release his spirit. He looked at his filthy body with disgust. I am not worthy. I must regain my purpose. I must. His eyes burned with shame and his tears left pale streaks through the mud on his chest. He began to walk, pushing against the inertia of the creaky pump machinery. Tomorrow I will wash. I am a man, not an animal.

They will come, soon, said the voice of the snake, inside his head.

Who? thought Moser. The snake didn't stir and its voice was still. Who will come? Moser tried to concentrate, but it took so much energy. Someone would come and he must be ready to kill Major Nan. But first, tomorrow he would wash.

Danang, 4 June 1969

The chartered Trans International Airways DC-8 touched down with a thump on the long runway of Danang Air Base, shaking Stuart awake from his fitful doze. The plane was completely full, mostly with replacements; new raw meat going to fight the war the government insisted was almost over. Stuart sat in his window seat as the men around him stood in the cramped space and milled around collecting their hand luggage. He had taken this flight before and he knew as they did not that the processing in Danang would take hours and that the first phase, the mustering of the passengers and their assignment to various bays for processing in-country, would take place before anyone would be allowed off the aircraft.

The plane's public address system crackled. "Okay, people, you might as well sit on down again while we figure out who goes where." The men groaned and sat. With the doors open and the air conditioning running from an outside cart the aircraft began to heat up rapidly. "I am Technical Sergeant Swazey and I am your mustering NCO. Welcome to Nam." More groans and some jeers. "Okay, let's get started. First, priority inbound. Colonel Estep?" The air force tech sergeant looked up. An army colonel near the front of the plane stood and filed forward. Stuart noted that he had a briefcase handcuffed to his wrist. Even colonels normally had to go through processing. "Lieutenant Colonel Morris?" called the tech sergeant. Morris had been seated next to Estep and followed him out, attached to an identical briefcase. Good day to be a courier, thought Stuart, yawning and settling in. "We gotta navy type," broadcast Swazey. "Lieutenant Stuart?"

Stuart raised his hand and waited for the two soldiers seated between him and the aisle to stand up to let him pass. This was unexpected, but he supposed NIS had sent word on ahead. Anyway, he was glad to get off the stifling aircraft. He put on his sunglasses as he stepped onto the top of the ladder, but still had to shade his eyes from the fierce glare of the Southeast Asian sun. It, like the heat and everything else about Nam, felt instantly familiar, as though he had never left.

The two colonels were just getting into a gray air force sedan as Stuart reached the bottom of the ladder. Stuart plucked at the shirt of his utilities as his body, accustomed to Washington in late spring, broke into a soaking sweat. He knew from experience that his system would adjust rapidly. The temperature on the apron was well over 110 degrees and the breeze coming in off the South China Sea was humid. Stuart looked inland and saw the thunderheads of afternoon building over the nearby foothills. Their fluffy white tops were brassy in the setting sun.

The sedan sped off. The only vehicle other than the gray buses for the troops was a black jeep with an ident number and no other markings. The jeep was parked under the wing of the DC-8, in the shade. A tall, red-faced, beefy man dressed in unmarked utilities lounged in the front seat, observing as air force baggage handlers removed the passengers' meager luggage from the belly of the aircraft and placed the pieces in rows. Stuart walked around to the jeep and grinned at the big man. "Hello, Hoop."

"Pick your shit outta that mess," said Lieutenant Philip Hooper, the officer in charge of the Danang SEAL detachment. Stuart laughed. It was a pretty typical greeting to expect from Hooper, despite the fact they were good friends and hadn't seen each other since—

Since January 31, 1968, thought Stuart with a start. Since the first night of Tet.

Stuart found his sea bag with three clean utility uniforms, underwear, socks, poncho, and personal items. The uniforms inside were not only clean but starched and sharply pressed. Washington seemed a long way off. He had one other small case. Hooper made no move to help him as he heaved both items into the open rear seat of the jeep. Stuart climbed in. Hooper stared straight ahead, like an enlisted driver with an unfamiliar VIP to drive around, but his impish grin was beginning to flicker around the corners of his mouth. His cap was pulled low against the sun, hiding his face from the nose up. Overlong blond hair tufted from under the cap. "Gee, Hoop, thanks for picking me up," began Stuart, in mock humility. "I had expected to go through shots and assignment like every other poor S.O.B. who gets welcomed to Danang."

Hooper started the jeep and drove slowly from beneath the aircraft. Once on the road to the base perimeter he tilted back his cap and grinned at Stuart, then reached across and punched his shoulder hard enough to hurt. "Day come ole Hoop can't fix this chickenshit air force lash-up, ole Hoop probably blow the fucking place up, and the base security officer knows it." Hooper returned the salute of the sentry at the checkpoint, then the next at the outer wire, and turned toward town.

"I have orders to report to NIS in Tien Shaw," said Stuart.

"Been changed." Hooper drew a piece of telex paper from his shirt pocket and handed it over. "NIS commander says your business is with me. Wouldn't say what."

"I'll explain," said William. "First, however, I wouldn't mind getting quarters and a shower and even a nap. I feel every one of the thirty-two hours since Washington."

Hooper chuckled. "Duty in the World has made you soft, RAMF," he said. "Besides, times here are hard. We have water hours, and showers won't be available until 1800." Hooper glanced at his watch as the jeep bumped through the rutted streets of the ville that separated Danang from Camp Tien Shaw. "That'll be an hour from now, if you haven't reset your watch. You can bunk with the SEALs, but for now I think you should buy me a drink and explain your sudden and unexpected presence in this, the war."

Stuart sighed, but he felt his strength returning. Even the heat had begun to feel good. "The Stone Elephant?"

"Pre–cisely," confirmed Hooper, passing through the gates of Camp Tien Shaw. "The last place I ever did see your pretty face."

Lieutenant Hooper parked his jeep in a space in front of the Stone Elephant Officers' Club in the navy's Camp Tien Shaw. The space was prominently marked "Commanders and above vehicles only." Stuart climbed down, feeling his stiffness from the long flight, and took the smaller case from the back of the jeep. "That'll be safe enough in the jeep, RAMF," said Hooper, amiably. "This isn't Washington."

"I have some papers I will need to explain what we will be doing," said Stuart.

"Who be *we*, boy?" laughed Hooper. "Ain't volunteered for nothing yet."

"You will," said Stuart, and preceded Hooper into the familiar dark, cool bar.

Hooper wanted to sit at the bar, but Stuart led him to a table. Hooper hand-signed a waiter, and the thin Vietnamese brought a large pitcher of beer and two mugs and departed. There were few officers seated at the tables, although the bar was already crowded for the beginning of happy hour.

"So why all the secrecy?" asked Hooper, pouring beer into the chilled mugs.

"What did the NIS guy tell you?" asked Stuart.

"Nothing. Some bullshit about a small operation, so classified he had no idea what it was, only that it involved you and *possibly* my SEALs." Hooper took a long pull at the beer. "I assume, of course, that if SEALs are requested, it must be an operation of critical importance, great danger, and the need for courage, skill, dash, and daring."

Stuart took the letter on Joint Chiefs of Staff stationery from his wallet and handed it to Hooper. Hooper read it quickly and tossed it back. "So it's important. What is it?"

"My orders are to go into Laos and effect the release and extraction of an unknown number of prisoners of war," said Stuart.

" 'Effect the release and extraction'? You even sound like Washington. What does that have to do with me?"

"Because of the political sensitivity of rescue operations—" said Stuart.

"Because the army fucked up on television their Hanoi Hilton raid," corrected Hooper.

"—JCS has directed that this operation be conducted with as few people in the loop as possible. Preferably only people who know each other and who won't talk, either before or after."

" 'In the loop'! Jesus, I used to be able to talk to you," Hooper topped up both mugs. "Drink some beer; tell me some good news."

"That letter from JCS should allow us to travel at will and get whatever assistance we need as we go in and out, while leaving no trail of paper."

Hooper looked at Stuart for a minute without speaking. His expression was grave, even sad. "You're serious, aren't you, old friend?"

"Of course," said Stuart, puzzled.

Hooper reached over and tugged gently at the collar of Stuart's utility blouse. "I was afraid when I saw you at the air base in this outfit that this might not be a social call. But do you really expect to take a walk in the woods? To look for POWs?"

"That's why I'm here. That's why I'm talking to you."

Hooper leaned back away from the table and let his breath out in a whoosh. "We may get our *Newsweek* ten days late, but we do get some information from the World. We also get specific policy directives. The most recent, from MACV to all commanders of all units from first line combat troops down to dental clinics contained a strong and very specific prohibition of 'adventurism' and reminded all of us to stay within stated operational guidelines."

"That is why this operation needed special authorization," said Stuart.

"That piece of paper? Look, Willie, vague special authorizations are a dime a dozen. Nobody is going to help you on some quixotic attempt to find a prison camp contrary to *specific* orders to confine operations while Kissinger and company try to slide us out."

"Not even you, Hoop?" Stuart felt his fatigue becoming anger. "I never knew you to be such a stickler for following orders from the rear."

"Not even me." The big man leaned forward on his elbows. "Look, I am just as unhappy about what the gooks are doing to our POWs as anyone else, but to go on safari with you on the basis of that letter, which just directs commanders to give you 'all assistance required' and in no way covers *your* ass, would be too crazy even for me. You won't even get out of Danang."

Stuart leaned forward. He felt his face flushing. "Hooper, listen to me. I have been living this mission, night and day, for a month. Nonstop, no respite. At every turn some son of a bitch has told me it couldn't be done. First logistics were impossible, then funding wasn't available, then the army or the CIA or whoever fucked up at Xuan Mai, then the peace people took over Washington, and finally a prominent senator made a speech and scared the pants off the administration. But the operation is still on and I am here to carry it through."

Hooper drained his glass and stood up. "Well, bully for you, old son, but count me out. I have plenty of serious work to do, work that is highly destructive to the enemy and is unlikely to get me killed, captured, or if I am real lucky, just thrown out of the navy for disobeying clear and direct orders."

"One of the prisoners believed to be in the camp we are going for is Moser."

Hooper sat down abruptly. His mug clattered on the table. "Moser?"

"Yes, Moser, Douglas M. G Division's gentle giant and sometime bare-knuckle bruiser." Stuart paused. Hooper had been G Division's officer when Stuart had first reported to the *Valley Forge*, and Hooper had been the first to see the merit beneath Moser's silent demeanor. Getting Moser squared away had been one of Hooper's first assignments to Stuart. They had both liked the man. "I owe him, Hoop, you know that," said Stuart quietly, sadly. "And I am asking you to help me."

"I heard he was killed," whispered Hooper, his face distraught. "I heard he went north with you after Tet and was killed."

"He was reported killed, but two months ago his mother got a letter through the Red Cross, and I think I know where he is."

"Where?"

"I thought you weren't interested. This is need-to-know only."

"Fuck you; I'm in, and I am sure a team of my Sealies will volunteer."

Stuart reached down and unsnapped the case beneath his chair. "Best get us another pitcher; this will take a while to explain."

Stuart briefed Hooper with the maps he had and the photographs of the maps he had taken in France, plus the information gleaned from intelligence reports about the disposition of North Vietnamese and Pathet Lao forces in the area. The mission plan was simple: a team of SEALs plus Stuart would fly to Udorn in Thailand, helicopter to the Thai Special Forces camp at Ban Nong Mum, cross the river in rubber boats, and then walk up the Mang River to the site Stuart had chosen as the location Moser had described in his letter. The two lieutenants ate dinner and talked it through. Hooper ticked off the many hazards of the infiltration, especially of being detected in the river valley, which was sure to be populated. They agreed to travel only at night, and therefore that the walk in could take three or even four days. They would have to locate a place for helo extraction, either near the site or downriver. The steep cliffs on either side of the river worried them both.

By 2000 Stuart was too tired to continue. He left the maps with Hooper and crawled under the mosquito netting in the extra bunk in Hooper's hootch. The night sounds of the insects and animals of the Vietnamese night seemed strange to him, but only for a few moments, and then he slept.

Hooper roused Stuart at 0700 and led him to the mess tent for a large breakfast. Hooper had a pad with questions in one column and suggestions for logistics and organization in another. After second cups of coffee Hooper took Stuart back to the SEAL area and into a twelve-man tent. Eight SEALs in black camouflage battle dress utilities greeted them. Each man had a light pack that he was loading with different kinds of gear.

"Adams, Harris, Freinberg, Swank, Chief Bosun's Mate Clark, Ferguson, Corbett, and Ricardo," said Hooper, pointing to each man in turn. Stuart looked at them one by one, trying to attach names to faces. Harris, Clark, and Swank were black and Ricardo a dark-skinned Mexican; the others were white. All looked fit and confident. "These are the lucky ones who will accompany us," concluded Hooper.

Stuart smiled at the men. "You men really volunteer?" he asked.

"Every man in the detachment volunteered," said Hooper. "All forty-eight, including Ramirez, who is in sick bay with bullet wounds in both thighs."

Hooper grinned down Stuart's mocking glance, and stuck his thumb in his own chest. "That's *leadership*, RAMF."

"Eight enough?" asked Stuart, walking among the men, noting their equipment.

"Ten, with us," said Hooper. "You said the only major unit in the area is a company of NVA regulars in Xieng Mi. Ten is more than enough, and as large a unit as I would like to move in the jungle undetected and without resupply."

"Good enough, then, Lieutenant," said Stuart, opening his case. "Equipment as agreed?"

"We have everything we need," said Chief Clark. "Claymores for ambushes, C-4 explosive, detonators, climbing ropes and equipment, one long-range radio and two short, five hundred rounds of 5.56 ammo per man, four collapsible stretchers, C rations and dry rations, water purification pills, medical kit with extra stimulants and antibiotics, plus the normal personal equipment for each man."

Stuart nodded, drew two weapons from his case, and set them on the footlocker next to the nearest bunk. "These are for special circumstances."

The weapons were submachine pistols, less than twenty inches long with their telescoping wire stocks retracted. The twenty-five-round clips protruded below the pistol grips. Stuart withdrew two short, fat silencers from the case and placed one beside each weapon. "In case we have to kill someone without sound," continued Stuart.

The SEALs crowded in to look at the stubby weapons. Hooper picked one up and turned it over in his hands. "Piece of shit," he murmured.

"Steyr MPi 69," said Stuart, ignoring Hooper's comment. "Nine millimeter parabellum, muzzle velocity 1250 feet per second without the silencer, 1000 feet per second with. Made in Austria."

"Piece of shit," confirmed Hooper, putting the weapon down on the footlocker. "Surely you don't suggest we leave our Stoners for these?"

Stoners were an improved version of the M-16, the standard infantry weapon. SEALs and other elite units had been 'testing' them since 1967.

"No, I have only two," said Stuart. "I'll carry one; we might need a quiet weapon."

"SEALs carry knives," said Hooper, his disapproval evident. "Give the other to Ricardo; he is our best man with a pistol."

"Good. Then we can leave your men to finish building their packs," said Stuart, handing one of the Steyrs, two clips, and a box of loose 9mm ammo to Ricardo. "A word outside, Lieutenant?"

"Sure, Lieutenant," said Hooper, and followed Stuart out into the sun.

"Now the hard part," said Stuart, quietly. "I will go over to Danang and wave my piece of paper and get us fragged to Udorn, then we will have to convince the air force to pull us out once we find the camp and secure the prisoners."

"Save your precious paper until we need it," said Hooper, putting his arm around Stuart's shoulders. "I can fix the air force here."

"Good. When will your men be ready to go?"

"They're briefed," said Hooper. "So as long as you are sufficiently caught up on your sleep we might as well go today."

"Today?" said Stuart. Somehow that didn't seem possible after all the waiting.

"Why not?" said Hooper. "Moser be waiting and some RAMF could change his mind if we delay."

"Today, then," said Stuart. "I will go and build a field pack."

"Relieved I be you still remember how," grinned Hooper, as he stepped back into the tent.

Trai tren Nui Cao, Laos

Sergeant Minh saluted Major Nan as he emerged from his hootch in the yellowish haze of the mountain dawn. The weather was warming and the pain in Nan's missing limbs was easier to bear. "How is the *con trau duc* this morning, Minh?" asked the major.

Minh frowned. "The water buffalo seems stronger, Thieu-ta. It is difficult to understand. For the last several weeks he has seemed weak, finally defeated, but today he has the look of hatred back in his eye and he has gone back to his strenuous efforts to clean his body." Minh shifted his feet. He wasn't sure how the major would take the news that the focus of his hatred was regaining strength. "He was fully twenty minutes in the river, squeezing and scrubbing, despite my shouting at him to hurry and get to the pumps."

Nan smiled. What did it mean? When Moser's lassitude and apparent decline had been reported to him weeks ago he had wondered if the water buffalo and he would soon be leaving the valley, their mutilated shades to wander elsewhere. The thought had not disturbed him; karma was karma. Yet the news that Moser's spirit had once again grown fierce did not disturb him either. "Thank you, Trung-si," said Nan, hobbling out into the open area to watch the prisoners begin their Tai Chi exercises under the bellowed guidance of Sergeant Vo. "Perhaps later today I shall go and visit him."

"Sir," said Minh. Feeling himself dismissed, he ambled off to the mess tent while Nan climbed slowly up the hill overlooking the river.

The sun was high as Moser pushed away at the yoke, mentally reciting his litany, trying to infuse his spirit with worthiness. His sweat ran cleanly over his torso as he walked and the former rank smell of his body was missing. The birds' individual calls quickened his mind and he felt better for them. The time was coming when his soul would fly with them out of the valley. The black cobra that had spoken to him, that had told him to prepare, saluted him with its swaying head.

The jungle sounds suddenly ceased and then resumed, but in a muted, insect buzz. The cobra slipped silently from the log and disappeared. Moser stopped walking and the water stopped flowing, and then he heard the swishing sound of men coming up the narrow path that led away to the east. The men passed into his clearing, staring at him without apparent interest. Small, brown men, six of them, barefoot except the leader, who wore high-topped sneakers. All wore purple loincloths and orange or white parachute nylon kerchiefs, and all carried long spears and wore machetes on harnesses over their shoulders. The leader and the drag man at the rear of the column carried AK-47 carbines. Pathet Lao, thought Moser, as the men passed silently by and headed onto the bridge.

Sergeant Vo knocked on the wooden frame of the door of Major Nan's hootch. "The Pathet Lao are here, Major. Colonel Phouang."

The man himself pushed past Vo and bowed slightly, then leaned his carbine against Nan's desk and sat on his bunk.

Nan was angered by the man's insolence. "Colonel" Phouang was a bandit, nothing more, and had no business coming into Nan's camp unannounced—and far less business taking the liberty of seating his filthy loins on Nan's bunk. Nan controlled his face and looked at the little man, who grinned, revealing two gold front teeth of which he was very proud. "To what good fortune do we owe your visit, Colonel?" asked Nan, amiably.

"This camp is to be turned over to me," began Phouang, without any preamble or courtesy. They spoke in French.

"By whose authority?" retorted Nan, curtly. He had known for some time that Phouang had coveted the High Camp with its mature stand of good-quality poppies.

"The order comes from Louang Phrabang," said Phouang, taking a grimy piece of paper from a fold in his loincloth and tossing it onto Nan's camp desk. "It covers several of these camps, but only this one in my district."

Nan turned the paper toward him. It listed several sites including the High Camp, and was signed by Souvanouvoung himself, the head of the Pathet Lao. The document was written in crude, ungrammatical French, but Nan recognized the signature as genuine. The High Camp was underscored on the list and the initials of the Vietnamese "military advisor" in Xieng Mi, Colonel Nguyen, appeared beside it. There could be no question of its authenticity, yet Nan was shocked. He had been told nothing. "I will confer with Colonel Nguyen about—arrangements," said Nan.

"Confer as you like," said Phouang, rising. "I wish you and your people to be gone when I return in four days with the peasants who will look after *my* crops."

"Four days!" exploded Nan. "I can't arrange to move these men in four days!"

"Then kill them here, or if you have become too attached to them leave us a few extra bullets and we will do it for you." Phouang grinned, flashing his teeth. "We are always so short of bullets."

"It is not a question of attachment, Colonel," said Nan, lowering his voice and controlling his anger. "These men are good workers, trained to the poppy."

"We will have no use for them, Major; honest Lao peasants can tend the crop." Phouang walked to the door and turned to face the major. "You are guests in my country, Major, and it is time you went home. Perhaps you will be given a poppy field in *Vietnam*, Major." Phouang strode through the door.

Nan rose, shaking with his anger now that the other man was gone. He hobbled to the doorway and observed Phouang strutting around the camp, pointing out this feature and that to his little escort as if he were already the master of the camp. Nan watched as the Laotians made their tour of the fields above, where the Americans were cutting pods, and then walked back toward him and the road to the bridge. Phouang waved as they passed Nan's hootch, his hand held with the fingers splayed. "*Quatre jours, Commandant*," he sang out. Four days.

TWENTY-FIVE

Royal Thai Air Base, Udorn, Thailand, 5 June 1969

The U.S. Air Force C-130 from Danang via Nakhon Phanon landed at Udorn in the heat of early afternoon. The SEALs carried their gear off the lowered rear ramp, glad to be off the hot, noisy aircraft. They were happier still to be finished with the bumpy passage over the mountains and through the turbulence kicked up as the Southwest Monsoon rolled up over the jagged, cloud-covered peaks. The men and their gear were escorted by air force ground crew to temporary quarters, solidly built structures of wood with framed canvas roofs, which looked like American tract houses. Air force officers in white shorts could be seen playing tennis on two courts on the far side of a shimmering blue swimming pool. "Shit on a stick," spat Hooper. "I been living in tents and hootches for two years. Don't these humps know there is a war on?"

"Steady, Hoop," said Stuart, evenly. "The system is build the officers' club and the pool and the courts, then the quarters, all within budget, then request additional funds for the runways. Get it?"

"I sure as fucking do," said Hooper. "Those pussies—"

"Good afternoon, gentlemen," said an air force captain in a dusty flight suit as he entered the building. "I'm Captain Scirano. Operations officer for the Jolly Greens here."

A man we have to deal with, thought Stuart, placing a hand on Hooper's arm. The man who owned the rescue helicopters—the HH-3

Jolly Green Giants—that the SEALs would need to get out of Laos once they found the camp, or didn't. "Lieutenant Stuart, Captain," said Stuart. "And Lieutenant Hooper, with eight men."

Captain Scirano grinned. "Men with no mission, no frag orders, and in need of our help, we are told." He offered his hand and Stuart and Hooper took it in turn. "We will do what we can, but first the colonel commanding would like a word." He paused and rolled his eyes to the low cinderblock building beneath the control tower. "The colonel is a bit of a bear, but we will get you fixed as soon as he takes his bite."

Hooper told Chief Clark to get the SEALs settled in and then followed Stuart and Captain Scirano into the office beneath the control tower, which served as the command post for the entire air base. They passed between lines of clerks at typewriters and adding machines. Metal desks were arrayed in neat rows, and the air conditioning worked. "Must remind you of fucking Washington," seethed Hooper.

"Take it easy, Hoop," whispered Stuart. "We have to deal with these guys."

"You talk, then, Willie," said Hooper. "You are the Washington diplomat."

Captain Scirano led the two naval officers along the narrow passage between the clacking office machines and into an office, the door of which was stenciled with a black colonel's eagle against its gray paint. He stopped inside the door and saluted. "Colonel Harker, these are the navy officers we were asked to receive. Lieutenant Hooper and Lieutenant Stuart." Captain Scirano did an about-face, winked at the two naval officers, and left the office.

The colonel, a wiry, gray-haired man in a pressed flight suit, with a ruddy face as lined as old saddle leather, looked up from a single sheet of paper centered on his clean steel desk. Stuart and Hooper saluted, hands cupped inward against the brims of their jungle hats. The colonel waved a hand at his uncovered head. "Sit, gentlemen," said the colonel, in a gravelly voice that buzzed with irritation. "And tell me why you are here."

Hooper and Stuart looked at each other. Hooper smiled and nodded, a gesture Stuart took to mean "after you." Stuart looked at the scowling colonel. "We have a classified mission, Colonel. We have to enter Laos in this sector and may require extraction at the end of the mission."

The colonel stared, unblinking, into Stuart's eyes. After thirty seconds he said, "Go on, Lieutenant."

"That's it, sir," said Stuart. "That's all I can tell you."

"Lieutenant," said the colonel, tilting back in his chair. "Surely you don't expect me to risk my assets and my men on no better explanation than that?"

"I'm sorry, sir," said Stuart. He took a copy of his JCS order from his case and handed it across the colonel's desk. "That is all I am authorized to tell you. If you have further questions, may I recommend you call the Joint Chiefs directly."

Colonel Harker read the short note and seemed to study the signature. "JCS? Not MACV?"

"JCS," said Stuart.

"And if I *did* call JCS, what do you think they would tell me?"

"That you are not cleared for it, Colonel," said Stuart. "Sorry."

The colonel pounded a fist into the center of Stuart's authorization and half-stood. "And why the hell am I not cleared for this—in *my* sector, with demands on *my* aircraft?" he shouted.

"I can't answer that, Colonel," said Stuart. "Except to say that to my knowledge only about eight people in the entire world are fully briefed on the mission."

The colonel sat and put the copy of Stuart's letter in a drawer. "Captain Scirano will get you organized and he will help you if he can, not to interfere with the performance of his regular duties." The colonel picked up a pencil and pointed it at the two naval officers in turn. "But if you fuck this up, and if I lose a chopper or a single airman, I will have your balls for breakfast, JCS or no JCS. Is that clear to you, gentlemen?"

"Yes, sir. Clear, sir," chimed Hooper, with his most mischievous grin.

"Dismissed," said the colonel, returning his eyes to the sheet of paper on his desk. Hooper and Stuart rose to attention and saluted. The colonel ignored them, so they about-faced and departed, Hooper closing the door behind them with exaggerated care.

"Hey, thanks for saving your support for the very end, Hoop," said Stuart, chuckling.

"What a prize asshole," said Hooper. "Couldn't you have told him a bit more than that?"

Stuart shrugged. "My orders are to keep knowledge of this op to an absolute minimum number of people. He has no need to know more."

"You're going to have to tell that captain a bit more. Especially about the terrain and those nasty high cliffs along the river gorge."

"I know. I just hope he is a good guy, because we are going to need him."

"The Jolly Green drivers fly where the shit is deepest," said Hooper as they walked toward the hangar set aside for the huge HH-3 helicopters. "Nobody questions a Jolly Green driver's balls."

"I'll brief him. You reckon we should spend the night here?"

"Nights are what we need for movement from now on," said Hooper. "So why waste one?"

"Tonight, then," said Stuart.

"Tonight, aye, laddie," grinned Hooper.

Major Nan climbed as high as he could on the knoll to the east of the High Camp. Tranh, one of the junior guards, puffed along behind with the bulky Russian-made Rl05-M FM radio transceiver. Nan climbed slowly with his bamboo staff, still smarting from the command from the insolent Laotian bandit to give up his camp.

Nan reached the top of the cliff overlooking the river and sat. Tranh set the radio down by the major's feet and began fiddling with the frequency adjustment. There was a natural saddle between the hill and Xieng Mi, making line of sight communications possible, but the signal was rarely clear, especially in the early afternoon, when the electrical storms rose over the higher peaks both east and west. Tranh finished his adjustment and raised Colonel Nguyen's headquarters. When the colonel was brought to the communications shack Tranh passed the handset to Major Nan, who keyed and began to speak. "Greetings, Colonel. Please forgive this unscheduled communication."

"Major Nan has seen our friend Colonel Phouang," stated Colonel Nguyen.

"Yes, sir. He said we are to depart these camps in four days. Is that confirmed?"

"It is. I am sorry; I know you have worked hard."

What Nguyen won't say over the open net, thought Nan, angrily, is that the Lao *moi* take over any mature opium plantation they find, after the hard work of clearing the land and nurturing the young plants is done. "What am I to do with my prisoners, Colonel?"

"I have no orders. Can you march them down to Highway 13, get them to the main base at Pak Sane?" asked Colonel Nguyen.

"That is thirty-two kilometers through the jungle to the highway and another forty-eight kilometers along the road." Nan paused to think about it. "Many would not make it, Colonel." I certainly would not, he thought, grimly.

"I can have you relieved, Nan," said the colonel. "You are a hero of the revolution; you need not suffer such a march."

"I brought many of these men here, I should take them out." And die with them, he thought without emotion. Karma.

"As you wish." The colonel's voice faded and returned as lightning flashed in the distance. "You will be away in time, then?"

"At your order, Colonel. Is there no chance of a delay, just a few more days?"

"No, the order has the highest approval." The colonel paused. He wants to tell me why, thought Nan, but he can't on this radio conversation anyone could overhear. "It is a small price to pay for the aid our Lao brothers give us, Nan."

Nan smiled. He knew, as did the colonel, that as soon as the Americans and their puppets were defeated in the South the Laotians and the even nastier Khmers in Cambodia were to receive prompt attention from the North Vietnamese Army. "Understood, Colonel. Thank you."

"You have done well, Major. Your work will be recognized in the future as it has been in the past."

"Thank you, sir." Nan passed the handset back to Tranh, who terminated the call and picked up the transceiver. He trudged off down the hill, with Nan following slowly. Damn, thought Nan. He thought of the bandit Phouang with his four raised fingers. Sometimes karma was not explanation enough.

Stuart entered the hangar where the HH-3 Jolly Green Giants were maintained. Two of the large helicopters were in the building, with various access covers removed and engine nacelle covers open. Another dozen waited on the tarmac in earthwork revetments. Stuart found Captain Scirano in a small office in the back of the hangar. Stuart knocked on the glass partition and Scirano, talking on the phone, motioned him inside.

Scirano put down the phone. He was grinning happily. "That was Colonel Harker, commenting on his fruitful meeting with you two."

"He didn't seem all that pleased," said Stuart, taking a seat in front of the captain's desk.

"He wouldn't have been no matter what you had told him," said Scirano, leaning back and propping his boots on the gray steel desk. "But you can't really blame the old bastard. We have to fly any mission at any time and we can't plan anything. The maintenance officer left two weeks ago with a perforated ulcer."

"Ugly thing, the war," said Stuart, glad Hooper wasn't along to hear this rear-echelon view of things. "We should brief. You, or others as well?"

"Me first, anyway. When do you leave, and are you asking us to get you there?"

"The team would like a ride to the Thai Special Forces camp at Ban Nong Mum, to arrive at dusk. We're expected."

"Piece of cake. One bird, twenty minutes."

"Good, Captain—"

"Call me Lou, please."

"Okay. I'm William, and Hoop is Hoop, Lou. The problem is getting back."

"I hope you are going to tell me a bit more than you told the good colonel."

Stuart placed his map case on the desk and popped the clasps. Scirano dropped his feet to the floor and straightened up. Stuart raised the lid of the case and removed maps and photographs from beneath the silenced Steyr pistol. Scirano raised his eyebrows in question as he looked at the odd weapon, but got no answer. Stuart pointed to the area of the three mountains in line and the river valley between the easternmost two, which was very lightly circled in pencil. The three mountain peaks were connected by a line, which at the 1:500,000 scale of the chart was almost perfectly straight and almost perfectly east–west in orientation. Stuart pointed to the spot where the line intersected the river. "Lou, we believe there is a prison camp just there. We will go in and find out. If we find any prisoners or are detected we will need to be extracted. If we find nothing we will walk back here and then disappear."

Scirano whistled. "I am sure you guys are aware that prisoner rescue missions are strictly off limits since the army got bushwhacked south of Hanoi."

"We are," said Stuart. "Officially, to the extent anything associated with this is official, we are looking for a super-secret black box jettisoned from a crippled B-52."

Scirano looked at Stuart, a wry smile on his face. "And why, might one ask, would navy SEALs be sent hundreds of kilometers from the sea on a mission like that?"

"Box could be underwater," smiled Stuart in return. *I believe I can do business with this man.* "Just pray you don't ever have to tell that story."

"Roger," said Scirano. "Let me see the map." He pulled it toward him and looked at the point where Stuart had indicated the camp should be. "Looks like a pretty steep gorge nearly all the way up from the Mekong to your objective."

"Right. The only indicated flat spot is right about where we think the camp is." Stuart took a ruled pad out of his case. "Can we start by your telling me about the Jolly Greens? How much radius over an LZ, angles of approach and climb-out? Capacity?"

"Sure. You know much about helicopter operations?"

"Done some vertical envelopment with the marines," said Stuart. "CH-34s and 46s; one ride in the CH-53. And some work with the army: CH-47s and Hueys."

"Okay. In size and type we are closest to the 53, which is based on the same airframe, although it is larger than the HH-3. I need a hundred-foot-wide circle to land safely, although I can lower an extractor cage through canopy from hover; we pick up a lot of pilots that way."

"Some of the people we expect to find won't be in good shape," said Stuart.

"Some of the black boxes," Scirano corrected, smiling. "Anyway, we can send a crewman down for a wounded pilot, and in fact do it all the time, but your problem is going to be numbers."

"Exactly," said Stuart. "If we manage to find a bunch of sick prisoners we are not going to be able to hold a perimeter long enough for you guys to pluck them out one at a time in your Noisy Green Targets."

Scirano laughed. "I heard the navy called us that. Anyway, what we need is a landing zone."

Stuart nodded. "Preferably one big enough to take several helos; we have no idea what we will find."

"Okay. We can carry thirty troops per bird, or fewer if we carry along some riflemen from the Air Police, which I would recommend. Let's say a unit—a frag, if we had real authorization for any of this— is twenty prisoners and or your folks per aircraft."

Stuart took notes. "Got it. Each twenty guys coming out is a separate aircraft. Given the terrain, where would you think we should look for an LZ?"

Scirano looked again at the topographical map. "The gorge is steep, and in that area sure to be triple canopy forest. Your best bet will be a relatively straight stretch of the river itself, but without much current. Better yet would be a long sandbar: we can land in the water, but it is a lot tougher taking off again because of the resistance of water surface tension."

"Will your helos be armed?"

"To the fucking teeth, although we don't like to use a rescue bird as a fighting platform." Scirano pointed to the helicopters in the revetments. Only their rotor heads could be seen. "We are flying the E model, which has 7.62mm miniguns mounted on the sponsons either side in addition to the M-60 door guns the older mods carried. You seen the minigun?"

"Yeah," said Stuart, writing. "The army has them mounted on their OH-6A light helos."

"Five thousand rounds a minute," said Scirano reverently. "Sounds like a foghorn with a sore throat, cuts like a chain saw."

"Good to know," said Stuart. "Although our planning almost requires a cold zone. There are only ten of us and it is very likely some of the prisoners will have to be carried."

Captain Scirano opened a locker behind his desk and produced two cylinders, one survival orange and the other a bilious green. "Once you get into that gorge your radios won't reach us and would likely get you some unwanted attention. These are Emergency Position-Indicating Radio Beacons—EPIRBs—just like the aviators carry. Their signals can be tracked by any aircraft that hears them and relayed to us. The surveillance satellites also monitor the frequencies. What I want you to do when you get where you are going and find us an LZ is to use the green one. It's a special frequency. I'll make sure it is monitored around the clock in addition to the regular freq, which the orange one squawks. As much as eight hours before you want us, if you have that kind of time, give the green one a squawk for each frag—for each bird you want. I will add one for backup, so if you squawk once you get two choppers, twice you get three, et cetera. Then shut the green one down. When you are well and truly ready turn the orange one on and leave it on. If you are in deep shit give me numbered squawks on the green and then turn the orange one on and leave it. The ready birds can get to you in well under thirty minutes, but if you give us the eight-hour-or-less signal we can be flying in shifts and also get some Spads from across the base to fly cover and suppress any bad guys who happen along."

Stuart made another note. "Spads," A-1Es, the old Douglas propellor-driven fighter bombers, could carry a lot of ordnance—bombs, rockets and cannon—and were used by the air force to back up the Jolly Greens because they could loiter in target areas and fly low and slow for precision support much more effectively than jet fighter bombers. "Your colonel give you the Spads?"

"Different colonel over there. Anyway, captains have friends who are other captains," said Scirano. "I am sure it works the same in the navy."

"Got it. The Spads could be a real plus if the evac is slow. Is there anything else you need to know, or I do?"

"No, that's about it," said the captain. "You now know far more about how we operate than do our usual clientele, the shit-scared, shot-down jet jocks. The critical element is the LZ. Get us the biggest, flattest place you can find. You have done enough chopper operations to know how hard it is to hover in Southeast Asia because of the heat, the loads we carry, and in this case the altitude of the LZ."

"Roger, and thanks for being helpful."

"No sweat," said Scirano, standing up and smiling. "I might ditch in the ocean one day—it nearly happened once—and I might need a friend in the navy. Meantime, I'll frag a bird for local training; be ready here in half an hour. It will take your troops to Ban Nong Mum, and after that we will wait and listen and wish you luck."

Trai tren Nui Cao, Laos

Rumors swept through the High Camp that some or all of the prisoners and guards would soon be leaving. Speculation on their destination ran from the major prison camp at Son Tay, west of Hanoi, to locations farther into the Laotian bush. One young air force captain who had been at the High Camp since it was built talked wistfully about a prisoner exchange and going home. The rumors of imminent departure gained credibility when Major Nan ordered the immediate gathering of all threshable rice heads, even immature ones, and a maximum harvest of the opium sap.

Major Peters entered Major Nan's hootch and found the commandant seated behind his little camp desk. Peters saluted. "You wish to see me, Thieu-ta?"

"Yes, Thieu-ta," said Nan, returning the salute. "Sit."

Peters sat on the rough stool and looked at his jailer. Nan's pale, usually expressionless face looked drawn with pain or anguish. Most of the Americans in the camp cursed Nan as a sadistic bastard who made their lives miserable for his personal pleasure, but Peters felt he knew the man better. The two sergeants had definite mean streaks, but in Nan Peters occasionally thought he saw sympathy even beneath his demeanor of utter lack of concern.

"How is the harvest progressing, Thieu-ta?" asked Nan, placing his hands on the desk with fingers interlocked. His tone and his gesture suggested an owner talking to a foreman rather than a camp commandant to a prisoner.

Peters thought the question odd. *Surely he gets reports from the sergeants. It's as though he is asking about the weather.* "The poppies have all been cut and milked, Thieu-ta, even the ones we cut only last month," said Peters, wary.

Nan nodded. *No sense leaving the garden plump for that pig Phouang.* "And the rice is in?"

"Yes. The last is drying and the guards have already threshed and bagged the dried grains."

"We will soon be leaving here," said Nan. "The rumors you have heard are true, at least to that extent."

Peters had expected the news but it startled him nonetheless. Life in the camps with Nan and the guards was hard, but they were used to it. Moving meant uncertainty and Peters felt disturbed, even fearful. "Where will we go?" he said, barely above a whisper.

"That hasn't been finally determined, Major," said Nan. "The Pathet Lao are taking this camp and others we Vietnamese have established in Laos, and turning them into collective plantations, but that does not interest you." Nan paused, studied the air force officer's face and thought he saw worry. *He hates this place but is reluctant to leave it, just as I hate my broken body but do not hurry to death. Perhaps the hill people are right: the forest spirits enter our noses when we sleep and eat away* at our souls. "The first destination will be Ban Namngiap, almost due east of here. I want you to select fourteen of your men, the fittest, to go with you to make up the first unit. It will be a rough march of fifty kilometers, but mostly it will be through a succession of connecting valleys at the six-hundred-meter elevation. Much of the land is cultivated and there will often be paths between hamlets. You should be able to make it in five days or less."

Why is he telling me all this? thought Peters. Prisoners were normally told nothing about where they were going, lest they orient themselves and try to escape. Peters searched his memory for Ban Namngiap on a survival map, but those maps and the preflight lectures that had accompanied them had long ago faded from memory.

Major Nan continued. "Sergeant Vo and two guards will accompany you. When you reach Ban Namngiap you will be turned over to NVA authorities."

"What about the others?" Peters asked. "And what about you?"

"The NVA will send some form of escort for me, and I will take the sickest men with me," said Nan, although he was far from sure even he would ever be sent for. "That is why you should take only fit men."

"I can choose them?" asked Peters.

"Yes. Subject to my approval."

"Morse," said Peters, testing.

"No," said Nan. "He is second senior American officer. He should stay."

Peters thought about his ragged, illness-weakened command, about who was strong enough to stand a march through rugged country carrying food and supplies for at least five days. He named several men and Nan nodded each time. He had thirteen names approved, and once again he tested. "Moser."

Nan shook his head slowly. An expression of profound sadness crossed his waxy face, as if Peters had mentioned the name of a dead loved one of Nan's. "No. Moser will stay with me and we will leave this place together."

"But why, Thieu-ta?" protested Peters. "Moser is strong; Christ, you have had him walking God knows how many miles a day for months."

"He will stay with me, Major. He tried to escape; he would again."

"With Sergeant Vo and two guards watching us by day and locking us down every night? Come on, Major. He has suffered in this place more than any other man."

How little you know, thought Nan. "Choose another, Major Peters. I will want your contingent to be ready to depart tomorrow."

The SEALs waded ashore, Ricardo on point, and slogged up the muddy beach as quietly as possible and into the trees, where they squatted. Each man had his face painted green and black and gray, and each carried his Stoner carbine and a light ruck of a design the U.S. Army had copied from the NVA. Hooper was the last man out of the second rubber raft. The Thai Special Forces soldiers pulled swiftly back into the current and disappeared into the blackness. They would paddle well away from the northern bank of the Mekong before they started their silenced outboard motors. It was only 1900, but the tropical night was inky black. It seemed not only to lack any light, but to absorb it where it did occur.

Hooper squatted in the center of the rough circle. Adams, Harris, and Freinberg moved a few yards out into the jungle to set up security and to preserve their night vision. Stuart spread his detailed map of the area on the back of Ricardo's ruck. Chief Clark illuminated it dimly with a red flashlight.

"We in the right place, Superspy?" whispered Hooper.

Stuart pointed to a spot on the map marked in orange. "The Thai lieutenant said this is where we would be landed," said Stuart. "We walk due west until we find the hamlet of Ban Thabok and cross Highway 13. There is a lake there and we stay to the north of it. Two rivers empty into the lake, which itself empties back here into the Mekong. As long as we keep the lake and the river to the south of us we will find the right river."

"The Nam Mang," said Hooper. "And then we just climb on up the gorge till we find Moser."

"Piece of cake," said Stuart, smiling in the blackness.

Hooper shifted his position as Stuart extinguished the light. "Think the Thai lieutenant knew his shit? You notice *he* didn't come along on this little outing."

"The sergeant on my boat pointed out an island downstream just before we landed. He seemed to be using it as a landmark."

Hooper stood up. The night was noisy with the squeaks and clicks and buzzes of insects and the bats that hunted them. The heat and humidity felt like the interior of a greenhouse and thunder rumbled in the far south. "Well, Navigator, since you are confident of our position we might as well make some distance. As I recall, the first sixteen kilometers are flat and mostly paddy before we start to climb. Shall we endeavor to make the gorge by morning?"

Stuart nodded and put away the map and the flashlight. The SEALs got up silently and picked up their gear. Hooper pointed to Ricardo to resume the point. The men filed into their familiar positions with Adams, toting the PRC-25 secure radio, walking behind Hooper, who took the slack position right behind Ricardo. Stuart walked next to last, two meters behind the chief. Freinberg, a big, happy-go-lucky Jewish kid from Manhattan's Lower East Side who possessed phenomenal night vision, walked the drag man slot, last in line, the tail gunner. Stuart often lost sight of him, but Hooper had told him he let the kid range quite far back. It had saved the team's lives more than once.

Two and a half klicks in, a mere hour's slow, silent walk through the jungle, they found the hamlet, the highway, and the lake. They stayed well away from the village, then angled back to the north shore of the lake and walked on through the darkness. Soon they were walking uphill, the slope just noticeable at first and then becoming steep. The river they followed began to gurgle as it descended and then to rush. The paddy ended and the jungle returned at the beginning of the steep gorge, and they made their camp just as the sky became gray with the false dawn.

TWENTY-SIX

Trai tren Nui Cao, Laos, 6 June 1969

Major Nan lifted himself from his cot with his staff and hobbled to the door. The morning was unusually cool and damp for the spring monsoon season, and his missing limbs throbbed. Once outside he saw Major Peters standing in front of two ranks of men, fourteen in all plus the major. Sergeant Vo and the two guards detailed as escort stood well back from the Americans. The guards looked apprehensive; the prisoners looked worried, even frightened. Nan smiled. Why had he told Peters his destination? He shouldn't have; Ban Namngiap was a short, flat walk from the Thai border. Pak Sane, their eventual destination, was even closer, but it was a major NVA strongpoint. Ban Namngiap was just a river town, a day's drift from the Mekong and Thailand. Did Nan want them to escape? Did he want to take a hand against the inevitability of the Americans' fate? Or did he simply want to make them anxious at the start of their journey, as he clearly had done? Nan didn't know, and somehow it pleased him that he didn't.

Sergeant Vo stepped to the deck in front of Major Nan's hootch, and saluted. "We go now, Thieu-ta?" said Vo in Vietnamese.

"Yes," replied Nan in the same language. "And mind you not a one of these men escapes."

"We will be vigilant, Thieu-ta," said the sergeant, stepping back.

Nan stepped down to the ground then sat on the deck. Every joint in his body burned with the dampness. "Major Peters," he said, beckoning. The gaunt, ragged man shuffled forward two paces and stood silent.

"Major, you must know that once on the trail the guards will shoot to kill any man who tries to escape or even disobeys the simplest order."

"Yes, Major," said Peters, his hollow eyes darting.

"We could handcuff your men and loose-chain your ankles, but that would make the passage through the jungle much more difficult."

Peters nodded, fighting to control his terror. Why should leaving this awful place seem so frightening? He doubted that any of the fifteen men would have the courage to run from the others, or even to leave the familiar guards. Does Nan mean to have the guards shoot us down a few kilometers from camp? Somehow that didn't seem the worst that could happen.

"You will be roped together loosely, around your necks." Nan continued, noting the American's discomfort. "Three meters between each man." Major Peters nodded again. Vo's two guards were already harnessing the first rank of Peters's men. Nan rose, pushing up with his staff. "Goodbye, Major." He turned and reentered his hootch.

Major Peters bit back a curse and then a sob. He was roped into the middle of the single file and then Vo, grinning like a fat Buddha, pointed to the path to the bridge and told the lead man to *di-di*.

Moser stopped his pacing around the pump deck at the sound of men approaching across the bridge. He watched as the men entered the clearing, the POWs roped together, each man with a makeshift rucksack. The weight bowed the men and several seemed to be frightened. Moser wondered what was happening; it certainly wasn't the normal rice harvesting party.

Major Peters stopped when he got close to Moser. The rope around his neck jerked as the man in front of him was brought up short, and the whole procession halted, the men stumbling, bumping into each other. Major Peters called to Moser, lashed to his yoke. "Hey Moser, we are being taken to a place called Ban Namngiap, fifty kilometers east. They are supposed to bring you in a few days."

Sergeant Vo ambled up from his position at the back of the file and menaced Peters with his carbine. "*Im lang di,*" he shouted.

Peters ignored him. "Ban Namngiap, Moser, remember that."

"*Di-di mau len!*" bellowed Vo, poking Peters sharply in the ribs. The lead man moved off, and Peters was pulled along. The POWs followed the path down toward the rice paddy and disappeared.

Moser resumed his walk. His rations had been increased in the past week, with no explanation. Perhaps they are giving me strength for a march, he thought. Why had Major Peters told me the name of a place? It meant nothing to him. Perhaps the time is coming. Perhaps he would have a chance to kill Major Nan on the trail. Ban Namngiap. He locked the word in his mind. Tonight he would ask the snakes; perhaps they would know.

Udorn

Captain Scirano briefed the communications watch supervisors personally, explaining that a special operation was in progress and showing them the approximate location of the SEALs' objective. He told them of the multisquawk signal expected on the frequency emitted by the green EPIRB he had given to Lieutenant Stuart, and ordered them that the Search and Rescue duty officer be informed immediately once the signal was matched with other stations and located. If the special signal was followed by a continuous squawk on the regular frequency the watch supervisors were not only to advise the HH-3 squadron duty officer but also Captain Scirano personally. The four sergeants who ran the watches logged the instructions in their watch books and promised to brief their individual watch teams.

Lower gorge, the Nam Mang

The SEALs resumed their trek up the gorge of the Nam Mang as soon as it was fully dark. The going was difficult; at many places the rock cliffs came right down to the swift-flowing river and the men had to climb the rocks to the bluffs above. The soil was rocky granite with limestone outcroppings and protrusions. Very little of the land was under cultivation, just a few paddies on some of the flatter river-banks and an occasional terrace carved into a hillside. The men made steady progress, with Ricardo or Adams scouting well ahead. They passed two silent, shuttered villages and kept climbing. The river turned occasionally around a cliff or a rock, but in general flowed almost exactly from the north. Stuart estimated they had thirty kilometers to cover from the bottom of the gorge to the place where the three mountains were aligned. When the men halted an hour before dawn he estimated they had covered eighteen kilometers, having passed the halfway point two hours earlier, a tributary that entered the Nam Mang from the east.

The SEALs prepared their daylight defensive position with almost no talking in a shallow, depressed clearing in the dense forest, and then Swank and Ricardo set about preparing their morning meal of spaghetti and meatballs with lima beans over a nearly smokeless fire of C-4 plastic explosive shaved from one of the many bricks they carried.

Hooper walked the perimeter, seeing that the SEALs were well concealed. He returned to the center of the DP and found Stuart cleaning his ugly Austrian machine pistol, its parts lying before him on a green towel. Hooper squatted. "So tell me, Willie, how is life in the World? The peace marchers treating you right?"

Stuart looked at his friend and then back down at the weapon. He slowly shook his head. "I don't guess the ones who just want peace bother me much, Hoop. It's a natural thing to want, as long as this war has gone on. Hell, even a fire-eater like you must be tiring of it."

Hooper dusted off a piece of ground across from Stuart and sat. "I guess I could admit that it were better ended, now that the politicians have given it up," he said slowly. "Can't say I want to be the last man killed or lose the last man, now that Nixon and Kissinger are looking for a way to turn out the light at the end of the tunnel."

Stuart nodded without looking up. He finished cleaning the parts of the Steyr and began to reassemble the weapon rapidly. "I was in Washington for the big demonstration, the Moratorium Day. They had us on alert, first in Arlington and then in the evening after the crowd was scattered, out walking around in the crowd in civilian clothes. Most of the people I listened to seemed generally of good will. Most were badly frightened by the military and police crackdown on the crowd, but many seemed to realize that the radical elements had provoked the government more than they should have."

"Where were the radicals?"

"That night? Gone, so far as we could see. There was a rumor the FBI and the D.C. police were looking for a small number and that arrests had been made."

Hooper picked up one of the clips for the Steyr from the towel, popped the bullets out, and began wiping down each one with Stuart's oiled rag. "What do you make of those people, Stuart? The ones who want to bring the whole system down. Can they really hate the war that much?"

Stuart worked the action of the reassembled Steyr and added a little oil to the bolt, then wiped the exterior of the weapon. Hooper replaced the bullets in the clip and started on another. "Hoop, you know, sure they hate the war, but in a real sense they love it and they need it," said Stuart. "The war and only the war makes them special, justifies every crazy and violent thing they do. The antiwar movement and the radicals' coopting of it gives every misfit a mission and a sense of being morally superior to men like you and me who are too dumb or too morally bereft to see the light."

Hooper put a hand on his friend's shoulder. "You are angry."

"Damn right I am, Hoop!" Stuart raised his voice and Hooper put a finger to his lips. "I saw people after that demonstration, men and women with innocent, honest faces and bandages on their heads, people who had been driven into the police and soldiers by so-called organizers who slipped away when the action started and left the soldiers and police, who were only trying to maintain civil order, look like the bad guys." He gripped Hooper's wrist and looked into his eyes. Stuart spoke more softly, calming himself. "When the war does end, Hoop, and no matter what judgment the nation eventually places on the wisdom of our ever getting into Vietnam in the first place, those self-righteous radicals will slip back into the obscurity from which they came. Then the nation is going to have to examine its conscience, and I predict that many people are going to find themselves needing to explain their actions during the war, especially men our age, Hoop. But it won't be us making excuses, Hoop, nor men like us. It will be the ones who turned against their country in the name of their own self-conferred moral superiority."

Hooper looked at Stuart and nodded slowly. Stuart lowered his eyes and the heat left his cheeks. He packed the cleaning equipment back into his ruck and stood up as Chief Clark approached and whispered chow was on.

Hooper stood, placed his arm around Stuart's shoulders, and pulled him close as they walked to the tiny fire. "I be glad to see you back after all, brother mine," he said.

The meal took only a few minutes, and then the SEALs deployed to their security assignments or to sleep. Stuart and Hooper went over the map. "Another night, then, eh, Willie?"

"Yeah, Hoop," said Stuart. "The worst climb is behind us, if this map is right. Should maybe take only a few hours."

"Then what?" asked Hooper. "Figure we should attack the shit out of the place before dawn, get extracted as soon as it gets light?"

"Maybe. We will have to see what it looks like, how many guards, et cetera." Stuart folded the oilcloth map. "We will have to find a good LZ for the Jolly Greens."

Hooper stood up, looking carefully around the DP. It was well set up and well concealed. Chief Clark ran a tight unit. "Well, I hope this goes well and we find some real live POWs, and then I hope the fucking air force manages to get us out, because I don't mind telling you I will be glad to get out of this place."

Stuart nodded. The dawn light was filtered by the jungle growth above and around them, and the river could just be heard. Daytime insects and animals were waking up and crying out as the night creatures scuttled around in the undergrowth seeking their burrows. "This place is kind of creepy, isn't it?"

"Yeah," said Hooper. "Especially those villages, all locked away, even the animals inside. That Thai lieutenant told me no one ever goes out at night because of the evil spirits."

Stuart chuckled as he spread his ground sheet and rolled into it. "You superstitious, Hoop?"

"Very," said Hooper, with no trace of humor. "I will be very happy to get back to smelly old Danang, where we never have to do anything more dangerous than parachute into Haiphong Harbor at night and blow up piers and docks."

"I don't think I will mind going back to Washington and finally taking off the blue suit forever," said Stuart. "So let's get lucky tonight."

"Be no moon," whispered Hooper. "Good night for witchery."

Stuart actually shivered despite the morning heat. "Cut it out, man."

Hooper chuckled, a low slow rumble. "Sleep tight, Willie. You relieve Ricardo in two hours."

Washington, 6 June 1969

The director of NIS and Major MacAndrew emerged from the director's limousine and entered the Old Ebbitt Grill on Fifteenth Street, just across the street from the Treasury Building. The Grill was decorated in the style of the last century, with a lot of dark wood, cut glass, and green plush banquettes. There was a long bar in the shape of a flattened U on the south end, backed by a mirror. The bar was crowded at noon but the restaurant itself, down two steps to the left of the entrance, was comparatively empty. The maître d' hôtel nodded to the director and led him to his favorite booth, one in a corner separated from other tables by a corridor that led to the kitchen. The location and the noise of waiters rushing in and out of the kitchen made it highly unlikely that their conversation could be overheard. Because of its proximity to the White House the Old Ebbitt Grill was a favorite place of Washington insiders as well as others who aspired to be.

John Hermann crossed the room and sat beside MacAndrew with his back to the room. He greeted the director, seated opposite, and MacAndrew. A waiter appeared and took drink orders. The director asked for a glass of club soda with bitters, Hermann a bourbon and branch water. Harry MacAndrew decided he deserved a Bombay Martini. The waiter raced away. The Old Ebbitt prided itself on its fast service, especially for its more powerful clients.

"Where are they now?" asked Hermann.

"Danang two days ago," said MacAndrew. "By now, most likely inside Laos."

"Most likely?" queried Hermann, turning to look at the tired, ruddy face of the NIS senior section head.

"They're radio-silent," said the director, quietly. "We—no one, that is—will hear from them until they squawk for pickup by the air force."

Hermann nodded, studying Captain Willis. The director is taking this personally, he thought, and like MacAndrew he is showing the strain. "Could they be recalled?" he asked.

"As a practical matter," said Captain Willis, sipping his club soda the waiter had just placed before him, "no."

"A mission like this can have three outcomes, Mr. Hermann," said MacAndrew. "They find nothing and return. They are going into a very remote part of Laos, the Annamite Mountains. Or they may find someone, and then they will find a way to get them out." MacAndrew took a long pull on his martini.

"And the third possibility?" said Hermann, picking up on the tension of the other two men.

"They could disappear without trace," said Captain Willis.

Hermann drank a bit of bourbon, rolling it on his tongue. "The president wants this operation to remain a deep secret," he said, looking first at Willis and then at MacAndrew, "but he doesn't want to lose those men. I hope that was understood."

"It was," said the director, cutting in before MacAndrew could speak. "Those men are good and we have no reason to believe they will be expected. And we are confident the air force will give its usual good effort, despite a squawk JCS received from an unhappy colonel in Udorn."

"So if it works we get some live POWs back," said Hermann.

"And if it gets fucked up it won't become public," growled MacAndrew.

Hermann caught the reproving glare from Willis to MacAndrew. There is tension between these two, he thought. "What about CIA in the area? Are they lending assistance?"

"They have nothing in the immediate area," said MacAndrew quickly.

"How do you know that?" asked Hermann.

"Because they ought to have told us and JCS if they did," said MacAndrew, smiling into his martini.

"But you checked. You informed them," pressed the president's special assistant.

MacAndrew finished his drink and waved to a passing waiter for another round. "I haven't, actually."

Hermann turned to the director. "But surely, Captain Willis, the Agency needs to know, and they have certain assets in the area—"

Willis looked hard at MacAndrew, who sat silent as the second round of drinks was deposited on the table. "Harry, I am afraid that is a detail you left out of your briefing on this operation, both yesterday and today."

"Yes, sir, I did." MacAndrew turned to face the young White House special assistant. "You may not know, sir, but I am a retired army officer, and many of my friends are still on active duty and quite senior now." He turned back to face the director. "There is a quite complete consensus that the CIA compromised the Xuan Mai raid, although no one knows just how."

"But surely the Agency must be told," said Hermann, in a raspy whisper. "They could have operations planned or even in being that could be compromised."

"Young Stuart, if I may say," said MacAndrew, watching the anger in the director's eyes, "felt very strongly that the Agency not be told."

Hermann shook his head. "The president will insist—"

"The Agency will be briefed this afternoon," said the director. "Now let's order lunch."

Maj. Harry MacAndrew eased back into the cushions of the director's Cadillac and let out a sigh. The old man sat beside him and closed the partition between them and the driver. Here it comes, thought

MacAndrew as the director turned to address him. And I deserve it.

"You embarrassed me, Harry," said the director, evenly.

"I'm sorry, sir. I just hoped it wouldn't come up."

"The CIA *must* be informed of any covert military operation in Indochina, Harry, and you have known that for the entire fifteen years you have been in this game."

"Yes, sir. I'm sorry I embarrassed you," said MacAndrew, doggedly.

"But not sorry you didn't inform the Agency." It was a statement, not a question.

"Night Crossing was well planned, sir. The rangers were set up, ambushed."

The director looked out the window as the limousine pulled into Twenty-third Street and turned south toward the Arlington Memorial Bridge. "Well, you will have to inform them now, Harry, this afternoon and without delay."

"Yes, sir." MacAndrew stared out the window. I'll tell them, he thought, everything that John Hermann knows, unless the director tells me otherwise. "I'll phone Langley as soon as we get back to the office."

"Good," said the director somewhat curtly.

MacAndrew looked across. The director was going to say nothing more. The major smiled out the window. John Hermann knew the entire operation, had been briefed by MacAndrew personally, but he had been briefed with a special map that MacAndrew had asked Stuart to make up with the aid of an army cartographer.

The same map MacAndrew would send to the Agency. The one that fudged the location of the prison camp by a good thirty kilometers.

Trai tren Nui Cao, 7 June 1969

Sergeant Minh had the remaining fifteen prisoners out early to complete the last of the poppy cutting. Actually only twelve were available for work, with three in the crude hospital hootch, too weakened by disease to do anything but lie still and wait for death. Minh knew the Pathet Lao could come the next day or the day after; their bannerman hadn't been sure but he had said that Colonel Phouang expected the camp to be in his full control the day after tomorrow and that he expected the Vietnamese and their prisoners to be gone. Minh had discussed this with Sergeant Vo just before Vo had left with his contingent to walk across the mountains to Ban Namngiap. Vo had nearly all the healthy men in his group; Minh doubted that any of the remaining POWs could make a march, except for the fierce *da dai-uy*, the black man, Morse.

Minh heard a shout from the forest and an answering call from the nearest of his guard detail. Minh was surprised to see a squad of NVA regulars, led by Colonel Nguyen, emerge into the clearing. Minh saluted.

"Good morning, Trung-si," said the colonel. "I have come to speak with your commandant. Is he in his office?"

"I think he may be up on the hill near the river, sir," said Minh, pointing across the compound.

The colonel grunted and moved off.

Major Nan watched the colonel and his escort cross the camp and rose to meet them, leaning on his staff. Nguyen waved his soldiers off at the base of the hill and climbed up, gesturing at Nan to sit and sitting beside him. "This is an honor, Colonel," said Nan. "But how did you come through the jungle so quickly?"

"The Pathet Lao have about thirty peasants clearing a road, Major," panted Nguyen, mopping his shiny brow and getting his breath. Nguyen was old and fat; he had been a field commander against the French but, like Nan, was no longer useful to the main struggle. "They have nearly cut through; they should be here tomorrow."

Nan frowned. Trips to Xieng Mi had always been taken by walking upriver and then across the saddle, a difficult trek of fifteen kilometers to cover the nine that separated the two places on the map. "What about the gorge? Surely they can't have bridged it in so little time."

Nguyen chortled, his fat chins quivering. "There is no gorge, only a swale and a stream you can almost step across, and they have indeed bridged that. I suspect that gorge was a convenient invention of our delightful allies' ancestors to confuse the French, one that the Pathet Lao have until now chosen to preserve."

Nan nodded. "But why do they now need this path?"

"Apparently they intend that Xieng Mi become the center of opium export and they plan to expand production greatly."

"They will sell the production to us?"

"They will sell to the highest bidder, like the good socialist brothers they are." Nguyen waved at a fly buzzing around his head, at the same time waving away the thought. "No matter; the junk will end up with the Americans either way. But that little concerns us now, my friend.

The fact is we now have a good road between here and Xieng Mi, or will by tomorrow, and we can take you out."

"It's good of you to come and tell me that, Colonel. Is that the reason for the great haste?"

"No, and that is what I came to tell you. I felt you deserved an explanation as to why Hanoi agreed to so rapid a handover of this valuable property, and at such great inconvenience to you."

Nan pulled his good leg beneath his thin buttocks, stretching the stump with its clumsy prosthesis. He waited silently for the colonel to go on.

Nguyen mopped his face and neck again. His breathing had at last returned to normal. "Hanoi wants you out of here. It seems this place may have been compromised."

"Compromised? How so?" Perhaps one of the few American planes that passed overhead had seen something, he thought. But no, we have always been careful.

"Hanoi said only a report from Paris. Apparently the Americans have been rummaging through the French archives and have photographed maps of this area. So we would have pulled you out even without the sudden rapaciousness of our Lao brothers."

Nan smiled. "You have informed them, of course?"

Colonel Nguyen shrugged. "Hanoi said it was little more than a rumor, from a source of unknown reliability. Why distress them? Besides, with you and the prisoners gone an American incursion into officially neutral Laos would be politically embarrassing if they should be caught by our dear Lao brothers, and if the Americans come in and shoot Colonel Phouang and his band they will be saving us from a future sad task."

Nan got up and stretched. The morning was warming his aching joints. "We will go back to Xieng Mi, then?"

"Yes, tomorrow. Might as well let the Pathet Lao finish their nice road, then I will send litter bearers for your sick. You could leave Sergeant Minh in charge and come back with me today; two of my soldiers can carry you."

"No," said Nan, slowly. "I should stay until the end."

Nguyen stood. "Do as you like. I must say I am impressed by your desire to protect and preserve all your prisoners. Surely you realize some at least are too poorly off ever to be repatriated."

"I know. And that shames me."

"You are a soldier, Nan, an idealist," said Colonel Nguyen,

sharply. "We have been at war too long to have ideals about our enemies."

"The colonel is right, of course," said Nan, sadly.

"What about the giant, the one the men call Water Buffalo?" asked Nguyen. "Surely you had better simply destroy him."

Nan looked at the fat colonel, holding his face impassive. How I wish the water buffalo and I could have died that day so long ago in Vietnam! he thought. How I wish it could end now. Nan saw that Nguyen expected an answer, expected Nan's agreement. "The water buffalo I would save first of all, Colonel."

Colonel Nguyen shrugged. "As you wish; bring him tomorrow. But you know we could never send him home as he is."

"His home is here, Colonel."

"Very well, Major. Have your camp struck and ready to move by ten-hundred tomorrow. Including your precious water buffalo."

Nan saluted. The fat man hopped down the hill faster than Nan could follow. Nan stopped and watched the colonel's back. He doesn't understand, thought Nan. The colonel is a party member and a professed atheist. He has forgotten karma.

Trai o Bo Song, 8 June 1969

"It's here," whispered Stuart. The night was moonless but the river shone with starlight between thin, blowing clouds.

"You sure?" said Hooper. "We can't see your three mountains from this gorge."

"But we are in the right spot if the map is accurate," said Stuart. "And look, there is a bridge at the end of the bend." Stuart handed the night binoculars to Hooper.

Hooper scanned the gorge, quite shallow here compared to farther downriver. "Okay, I see the bridge, and it is the first we have come to."

"Look at the surface, out about twenty meters from the east bank."

"What about it—wait, I see it, looks like a sandbar."

"How wide do you think, how long?"

"Wide?" said Hooper. "Say ten–fifteen meters. Long, easily sixty."

"It's our landing zone, Hoop."

Hooper snapped the glasses down, handed them back to Stuart.

"You could be right, laddie. I am going to send two men up, one each side of the river. If they find anything you best be ready to squeeze off your warning signal on the green EPIRB."

"Ready when you need it."

"Ricardo, Adams!" whispered Hooper. He gave them their instructions: examine the areas on each side of the river to the bridge and beyond. He told them to be gone no more than forty minutes.

Stuart laid the green emergency transmitter on the sand beside his rucksack. This is definitely the place, he thought, suddenly very tired. I just hope Moser is still here.

TWENTY-SEVEN

Udorn, Thailand, 8 June 1969

Technical Sergeant Simon O'Connell stood the 2000–0000 watch in the main communications station in the control tower, two floors below the air base control room itself. Antennas on the roof of the tower fed radio monitors guarding all the frequencies in use by the air force flying over Southeast Asia, and the navy and army aviation freqs as well. Technical Sergeant O'Connell wandered around the big room, watching the three airmen who moved from set to set, changing the freqs over to those prescribed for the new day. It was a very quiet night: almost no missions were up on the clear plastic status board. O'Connell glanced at his watch: 0020. He was bored, tired, and full of air force coffee, so he had to take a piss. His relief, Sergeant Towser, was late as usual.

Two of the airmen on the watch—the oncoming, O'Connell noted sourly, the 0000–0400 crew who worked with Towser—were experienced and settled in near the fighter and strike net consoles. The third, a new man O'Connell didn't even know, sat in the corner near the emergency board, reading a manual. O'Connell approached the airman, an earnest black man, skinny with a pronounced Adam's apple and, it appeared, a proper fear of sergeants.

"What's your name, kid?" asked O'Connell from behind him.

The kid jumped and twisted around. "Washington, Sergeant." The Adam's apple bounced in his thin neck like a thing alive.

"Okay, Washington," said O'Connell, resting a haunch on the table in front of the young airman. "You know what your duties are here?"

242

"Watch the emergency channels," said the kid stiffly, as though reciting. "Tune to direction-finding. Log all receptions."

"And?" said O'Connell, leaning forward.

"Call the duty sergeant, Sergeant."

"Yeah. Well, be sharp, because the duty sergeant is going to run down to the Three level and take a piss."

"Yes, Sergeant," said the kid. Technical Sergeant O'Connell passed to the other side of the room and told the other two airmen he would be right back, then headed for the stairs, his bladder fit to burst.

Washington's head jerked up at the loud buzz from the panel. A light was flashing under a label marked "ALT 3." The buzz stopped after about five seconds. Washington stood and picked up the log under the ALT 3 monitor. There were no entries from the previous two days, which was as far back as the log went. Washington jumped as the buzzer and the light went on again. He knew this was not the emergency channel the pilots used, but he hit the direction-finding button anyway. Once again the buzz and the light ceased after five seconds. Washington logged the signal and put the clipboard down as Sergeant Towser entered the room. "Morning, Washington. Any squawks?"

"Just two, Sergeant, just now. Short, nothing more."

Towser looked at his watch, and at the nearly empty mission status board. The time was 0031. "Probably a test. Ground crews are allowed to squawk a test on the hour and half hour to check the EPIRBs are working." Towser looked around. "Where is Sergeant O'Connell?"

"In the latrine, Sergeant. But the freq wasn't the regular—"

"Log it as a test, Washington. We got any coffee?"

Washington shook his head. Something wasn't right, but he was afraid to say so. He had been in Thailand just three days. He looked across the room as Technical Sergeant O'Connell reappeared, signed the log across, and departed immediately. Washington stared at the ALT 3 light, hoping it would sound off again so he could say something, but it did not. I guess it was a test, he thought, and went back to his basic airman's manual.

The Nam Mang, near Trai o Bo Song

Stuart replaced the green EPIRB in his rucksack after sending the two five-second squawks separated by an equal interval. "You really think they got that?" asked Hooper.

"Yeah," said Stuart, tying down the ruck. "The signal is picked up by aircraft or by satellites, which amplify the signal and help locate it."

"You hope," said Hooper, sourly. "We are going to need the Jolly Greens as soon as we find what we find."

"Well, that's the agreed ready signal. Eight hours or less before we need them, two squawks requests three helos."

Ricardo had reported remnants of a camp on the east side of the river, as well as the strange pumping apparatus. There were no dwellings and he had seen no one, though he reported a strange smell, perhaps of a large animal. He had scouted as far as the bridge approach, and he reported on its iron arches and plank road. Adams had climbed the cliff on the west bank and located the hill camp. It had been silent and apparently unguarded, but smoke rose from a cookhouse and a single dim light burned in one of the hootches. Adams had guessed at a prisoner population of thirty or fewer, so Stuart had squawked for two Jolly Greens plus the backup bird Captain Scirano had promised.

The SEALs established a defensive position in an area of fallen trees that provided good natural concealment. Ricardo and Adams, working under a shielded red lantern, produced sketches of what they had seen and marked in accesses of approach. Hooper and Chief Clark studied the sketches and made their own observations from the river's edge. At 0330, by Hooper's estimate ninety minutes before first light, he gathered all the men and spread the sketches under the night lantern. "I see no reason to be subtle about this," he began. "Ricardo found no one guarding the bridge, so we will go up to the area by the pump, check out whatever Ricardo smelled, cross over, waste the gooks as we find them, and then get the prisoners moving as best we can. As soon as we get them down to the river we will start squawking for the air force." Hooper grinned the grin Stuart recognized as meaning he was frightened and fighting not to show it. Stuart was sure the SEALs knew their commander and would recognize the broad grin as well. Like most brave men Hooper excelled in battle by harnessing his fear, but he was still too proud to show it. "Questions? Suggestions?" Hooper finished.

"Adams said there didn't seem to be many guards," said Harris, who was cleaning his Stoner. "What about reinforcements?"

"The only town near enough to warrant a garrison is Xieng Mi, some nine klicks away," said Stuart. "The terrain in between is severe and there is no road shown on the map."

"Which assures us that there was no road when the French drew the fucking map eighty years ago," said Hooper, cheerfully. "Speed, gentlemen, is what will protect us. We have enough C-4 to blow at least the deck out of the bridge, if not the span. We go over, grease the gooks, grab the good guys, blow the bridge, and fly off to lovely Thailand."

"Just hope not too many of the POWs will have to be carried," said Chief Clark.

"That, too," said Hooper impatiently. His nervous energy was building and he wanted to move. "Let's move out. Ricardo, take the point, Stuart at slack, then four meters, then the rest of us." Hooper slapped a hand on Ricardo's and Stuart's shoulders, propelling them gently forward. "You two have those silenced grease guns at the ready. If there is anyone this side of the bridge I'd just as soon we didn't have to warn the camp on the other side."

"Aye, aye, Hoop," said Stuart, following Ricardo into the jungle.

"The rest of you men look to your knives," whispered Hooper.

Moser was wide awake in his cage. A man had entered his camp earlier, a man who wasn't Sergeant Minh or any other Vietnamese. A man who had eaten cheese or drunk milk, and probably recently: it changed the body's smell. Moser had learned that virtually no Southeast Asian adults ate dairy products; they couldn't digest them. So the man, who had padded around the camp so silently only one so used to the night sounds of this place would ever have known, wouldn't have been Asian.

He must have been American! The thought jangled in Moser's tired brain. The man had approached to within a few meters of Moser's tiger cage; Moser could easily have cried out or even whispered. But Moser had been terrified and now the man had gone. Why was he terrified? Moser shivered in his crouched position, but he could not fight down his terror of the man walking abroad in the night. He listened intently and prayed for dawn.

Trai tren Nui Cao

Major Nan threw off the gray sheet and parted the mosquito net. The night was still and hot, the first real bite of the Southwest Monsoon, and it made him think of the warm coastal plain where he had lived all his life until he had been sent to this awful misty highland. But it was something else that prevented sleep from taking him. He usually slept soundly the five hours he allowed himself, despite his burdens and his pain or perhaps because of them. Tonight he had a sense of imminent danger; perhaps it was Colonel Nguyen's promise to pick up him and the last few men in the morning, the promise of finally leaving this place—but to go where?

Nan strapped on the artificial arm with its chopsticklike hooks and then the gray plastic peg leg. He pulled his staff from beneath the cot and painfully pushed himself upright. The heat felt good but the increased moisture was burning in every joint. He hobbled into the predawn blackness and made his way the few meters to the sergeants' hootch. With Vo gone Sergeant Minh divided the night watches with Corporal Tranh, who dozed in the chair next to the low-burning oil lantern. Major Nan rapped loudly on the wooden doorjamb and Tranh jumped. "Wake the trung-si," said Nan, sharply. "And send him out to me."

Sergeant Minh emerged from his lighted hootch, hitching up his loose black trousers and rubbing sleep from his eyes. His rubber sandals flapped as he crossed the wooden deck. He carried an AK-47 slung over his shoulder muzzle-down. Nan watched him with weary anger. This slovenly brute would never have made a soldier, much less a sergeant, in the main force units of the NVA. As bravely as we talk, and as sure as we are of ultimate victory, the Americans are wearing us down. Minh saluted, sort of. Nan acknowledged with his staff. "The major wished to see me?" asked Minh, yawning rudely.

"Go down and get the water buffalo," said Nan curtly. "Let him wash, then bring him here; we will want him ready with the others when the detachment from Xieng Mi comes to take us away."

"But it is still dark," protested Minh.

"The Trung-si fears the dark?" asked Nan, anger creeping into his voice.

"No–no, Thieu-ta," said Minh. "But he might try to run. At least let me take another guard."

"A sergeant of the People's Army of Vietnam armed with an automatic weapon should be able to control one emaciated prisoner, Minh."

"Yes, Thieu-ta. But do I have permission to shoot him if he does run?"

"Of course," said Nan. Is that how it ends? It didn't seem likely. "Now get moving, Sergeant. I want him up here in time to eat with the others."

*   *   *

Minh stumbled down the hill in the blackness. Fucking major, he cursed, stubbing his toe painfully on an unseen root. Colonel Nguyen had said 1000: what was the need to bring the *con trau duc* up in darkness? Minh realized how much he feared the tall man with the hatred in his one good eye and his unsappable great strength. Getting him from cage to river and then tied to the pumps each morning was scary enough, but to lead him across the river and up to the camp, all by himself and in darkness—the thieu-ta was mad. What if the *con trau duc* entered the river and simply swam away? Well, he could have done that any morning and never had. But he might run as soon as he was out of the pit. Minh's AK-47 caught on a branch and snapped back against its sling, the stock slapping painfully against his ear. He regretted not bringing the Makarov pistol; it would have been easier to point at the giant while releasing the latches on the bamboo grating.

Minh reached the bridge and started across, making no effort to be quiet on the uneven, shifting planks. Fucking thieu-ta.

Trai o Bo Song

Ricardo and Stuart entered the darkened camp, skirting the narrow clearing, one on either side. The rest of the SEALs moved through the jungle a few meters inland, flanking the camp and working their way toward the near end of the bridge. Stuart, on the left, saw the narrow trail that led down to the river and paused to inspect the crude, silent pump with its turntable and its double yoke. There was an animal smell in the air, sharp and strong. It reminded Stuart of the smell of horses, way back home at his parents' house in Virginia, after they had been ridden hard and their sweat allowed to dry instead of being rubbed down. Then he saw the bamboo lattice. "Ssst! Ricardo!" he whispered.

Ricardo came towards him across the clearing, walking sideways and pointing the Steyr machine pistol in front of him, toward the bridge. He nodded when Stuart pointed out the tiger cage, then crouched to provide security as Stuart knelt and crawled forward. Stuart peered into the blackness of the pit and saw nothing. He unclipped the red-lens flashlight from his web harness and flashed it briefly into the hole, then turned it off. A head like a skull had looked back at him, the face black with dirt, the mouth a black hole in the dim red light, and the eyes wide in terror. Stuart was sure of only one thing: the man was white.

Stuart reached for the knife clipped to his web harness and pre-pared to attack the crude fastening of the lattice. Behind him Ricardo gave a low whistle of warning. Stuart turned, looked back, and saw Ricardo beckoning urgently, already edging back into the trees. Stuart stood to a crouch, picked up the Steyr, and moved back away from the pit and its terrified occupant. Ricardo grasped Stuart by the back of his ruck and pulled him down into the undergrowth, then pointed toward the bridge. A dim shadow swung toward them, preceded by the slap of his rubber sandals on the bridge decking. As he came closer the shape of an AK-47 held at port-arms became visible in the dim starlight. Stuart nodded to Ricardo and motioned for him to pull back enough so they couldn't be hit with a single burst of fire. Ricardo slipped deeper into the shadows. Stuart's heart pounded inside his chest as he checked the Steyr to be sure there was a round in the chamber and the cross-bolt safety catch was in the pushed-left position for firing. The Steyr had no selector for single or automatic fire: pull the trigger to the first stop for one shot, pull it all the way through for automatic.

The man clumped off the bridge and walked directly to the tiger cage, looking neither right nor left. He squatted and began to fumble with the pins, his carbine on the ground beside him, all the time talk-ing to the occupant of the cage in soft Vietnamese. Stuart was momentarily puzzled; he had been sure the man in the cage was white. The man finished with the latch, picked up his carbine, and jumped back, pointing the weapon at the hole. The lattice flipped back and the occupant began to climb out. The armed man backed away another step and noisily cocked the AK-47. Stuart had a two-hand grip on the Steyr, the wire stock firmly against his shoulder. Before the prisoner could rise fully from the pit and block Stuart's shot he sighted over the fat silencer and squeezed the trigger. The Steyr gave a tiny flash and a single cough, and then another. The man spun away and fell, losing his carbine and never making a sound. Stuart rushed forward, sensing Ricardo behind him. The man in the pit sprang out with surprising agility and fell to his knees next to the body, cradling it in his arms and venting a low cry of anguish, which trailed off into a keening that sounded like "min, min, min."

Stuart reached the man and shined the light full in his face. The man blinked, seeming not to comprehend. Stuart fought not to be repelled by his appearance, his face beneath the dirt covered with running sores, his clouded eye, his nearly toothless mouth hanging open, but he forced himself to look closer. Hooper squatted beside Stuart as the rest of the men checked the clearing and set up a temporary perimeter. Stuart saw the man as he had been, with full cheeks and brown hair and clear eyes and skin and teeth. "Look at him, Hoop. Sweet Jesus, it's Moser."

"Corbett!" called Hooper softly across the clearing. "Get up here with the medical bag, on the double."

"Hey, Moser," said Stuart, touching the man's face as gently as he could. "Give me the body."

Moser let the man in the black utilities take Minh away. *Minh killed but not by me. Now there can be no escape for me without Nan.*

"Hey Moser, it's me, Lieutenant Stuart, and Lieutenant Hooper, from the old *Valley*. Remember? We've come to take you home."

"Can you talk to us, Moser?" asked Lt. Hooper, as Corbett opened up the medical kit.

Moser shook his head. *Mister Stuart and Mister Hooper, of course he knew them, now they shined their red lights on their own faces.*

"Jesus," said Hooper, rising. "Corbett, Swank, take him down to the river and clean him up as best you can. Use a lot of that carbolic soap and then salve his gook sores. Check him over as best you can, then get him into a uniform. We will have to move out in a very few minutes."

Moser let the two men he didn't know take him down to the river, to the place where he had always bathed. He took one last glance at Minh's broken body, his chest shattered by the two silenced rounds he had heard.

"Poor bastard," said Hooper, watching Moser's bowed frame being led away. "He has forgotten all his English."

Moser's keen hearing picked this up, but still he said nothing. He had not forgotten his English, or his Vietnamese, or even the bits of French he had picked up from Major Nan. He just hadn't spoken a word in any language in over four months.

TWENTY-EIGHT

Trai o Bo Song

Lieutenant Hooper had Adams and Freinberg out on the center of the span packing the plastic explosive charges under the loose boards of the roadway directly over the rusted rails. He himself worked the remaining blocks of C-4 into a single mass to be wedged into the joint where the old iron girders of the top of the south arch met the horizontal capping rail just above the level of the road surface. It should be the weakest point in the span, but Hooper hadn't anticipated an open iron structure and he was far from sure he had enough C-4 to do the job. He knew he didn't have enough to blow both arches, so he put the entire charge on the southern one. At least the charges against the rails should make a good-sized hole in the roadway itself, but Hooper would be a lot happier if he could be sure the bridge would come right down. Adams and Harris were concealed in the trees on the far side of the bridge, watching for any further intruders and digging in claymore mines to cover the team's retreat from the high camp. Corbett and Ricardo worked on cleaning up Moser and feeding him small doses of C rations.

This sucker would crack this rusty old arch, thought Hooper as he wired the block in place, if I had a few sandbags to tamp it, to force the explosive to blow outward into the girder joint rather than dissipate into the air as it would do if left untamped. But I don't have any bags and we don't have time to improvise them and fill them from the beach by the river. Water is even better tamping material than sand because it is totally incompressible. Hooper stood and called softly to Ferguson, standing at the end of the bridge. Ferguson disappeared, then came trotting out onto the span with the body of the Vietnamese guard. Hooper returned to find Stuart going over the maps with Chief Clark. "I did the bridge as best I could," Hooper said, squatting.

Corbett came up from the river's edge. "Hoop, I gotta tell you something," he whispered. His face was twisted with anguish and streaked with tears.

"What is it, man?" said Hooper, putting a hand on the medic's shoulder.

"The guy—Moser. Sir, they–they," Corbett shook more tears from his eyes, and wrung his hands together as though twisting water from a cloth.

"What happened, man?" asked Stuart, gently.

"The gooks cut him," said Corbett, grasping his crotch. "They cut him, sir."

"Oh, my God," choked Stuart. He saw Moser, looking all the more gaunt for being in someone's donated uniform. Time was no man's uniform would have fit his big body but his own. "Oh, my God," he repeated.

Hooper grasped Corbett's shoulders. "You mean they cut off his *balls*?" he whispered.

Corbett nodded, looking at the ground. "He didn't want to take off that loincloth until we made him."

Moser returned to the little group, leaning on Ricardo's arm. He squatted, silent, his expression empty. His skin, where visible, was painted with an orange ointment. Stuart got up and squatted in front of the man who had twice saved his life. "Moser, we are going to get you home. We will leave you here with one man to hold this end of the bridge while we go across and get the others."

"No," said Moser, firmly. He stood up quickly, suddenly infused with energy. He picked up Trung-si Minh's dropped AK-47 and quickly inspected the muzzle and the lock for dirt. "I must go with you to the Trai tren Nui Cao—to the High Camp. I know every building. I know every prisoner and every guard. You might miss someone." Moser's English was clear enough but it had an odd sing-song cadence.

"But Moser, you are not strong," said Stuart, startled by Moser's sudden speech, and more by his determination.

Moser pointed to the pumps with an orange-stained finger. "Every day for months I have walked in circles, pulling the water up from the river to irrigate the rice, yoked to that pump like a *con trau duc*, a water buffalo. I am strong." Moser checked the magazine of Minh's carbine, found it full. "And I must find the commandant before I can leave this place."

"We'll get him for you, Moser," said Hooper, still holding the trembling Corbett. "You rest here."

"No," said Moser. "The commandant is Major Nan. He is a cripple, walks with a bamboo pole. None of your men must harm him; I must find him myself."

Hooper and Stuart looked at each other in silence. Harris came in from the bridge, trailing wire from the claymores and from Hooper's charge at the center of the bridge. Corbett knelt beside him and they attached the wires to separate detonators, then concealed them under a bush. The darkness was fast fading to gray. Chief Clark approached with Freinberg, expecting orders.

"Chief," said Hooper. "Usual patrol order, except Moser will follow Ricardo. Set Freinberg and Harris up here to hold the bridge. Let's move out."

"Aye, aye, sir," said the chief.

Hooper stepped closer to the chief and spoke softly. "Make sure nobody wastes the crippled gook unless in self-defense. He belongs to Moser."

"I'll pass the word, sir."

"As for the rest of the guards, no prisoners."

"Aye, aye, sir," said the chief, his face tight with anger as he moved off to organize the SEALs.

"Sir?" said Moser to Hooper. "What did you do with Trung-si Minh's body?"

"He is going to help us blow the bridge, Moser."

Moser nodded, apparently satisfied, and turned to Stuart, who was packing up the maps. "Could you show me where we are on the chart, sir?"

Stuart spread the smallest-scale map and pointed out the location of the River Camp. Moser put his finger on the spot and then swept it slowly east. There it is, he thought, memorizing the route through the valleys. Ban Namngiap. "Thank you, sir," he said, softly. Stuart looked at the gaunt man sadly as he packed away the maps.

The men shouldered their gear. Ricardo took the point and the SEALs waited for Moser to fall in line, then filed across the bridge, keeping low, pressed against the parapets. Moser paused to look at Minh's body wedged against the horizontal bridge rail at the center of the span, but only for a moment.

Colonel Phouang and his small band had spent the night at the hamlet of Kiou Keo Song Lay, four kilometers upriver from the camp he was to take possession of this morning. The Pathet Lao were barely welcome guests of the villagers, whom Phouang taxed severely. An hour before dawn, as soon as the light was good enough to allow his superstitious followers to leave the shelter of the villagers' shuttered homes, he called his new NCO to get them moving. Phouang was pleased with the new man, Phatang, who had been sent to him from Xieng Mi to become chief of the camp once the Vietnamese were gone along with their diseased American vermin. Phatang had been promoted to the equivalent of sergeant because he had recaptured a prisoner who had escaped from the very camp of the proud Major Nan that Phouang would add to his string of tiny but productive opium plantations. It amused Phouang that in the socialist Pathet Lao army a sergeant still carried the old imperial Chinese title of senior bannerman.

The river valley was easy walking down from Kiou Keo Song Lay; it fell hardly at all. Once the men had finished their simple breakfast of tea and rice balls flavored with fish it would take them less than two hours to reach the camp. They should arrive by 0630 as measured by Phouang's golden Rolex, a "gift" from a pilot Phouang had taken alive and promised to guide to Thailand. Phouang had delivered the man to the Viets, who had paid him the usual five hundred rounds of Russian 7.62mm ammunition for his band's few AK-47s. "Hurry the men," shouted Phouang to Phatang. "I want to see that bastard Nan's face as he stumbles out of my land."

Major Nan got his tea and rice shortly after sending Sergeant Minh to retrieve the *con trau duc*, and then he had Corporal Tranh muster the other prisoners and the remaining five guards, even though it was still dark. Now that they were to leave he found himself eager to be ready, though he didn't expect Colonel Nguyen's force for hours. He collected a guard from Tranh's detail, told him to get the radio from his hootch, and then climbed, the man following, to the top of his hill overlooking the river. He would watch the sunrise one last time over the conical mountain to the east and watch the shadow of that mountain projected on the two higher peaks to the west. When the morning was fully upon the camp he would radio Xieng Mi and check on the progress of the column coming to take them away. He wanted to see the water buffalo in the yard with the others, to see him roped up to make his last march.

Nan sat, the radio hissing beside him, tuned to the frequency Xieng Mi used. He sent the trooper away and opened the pouch he had taken from beneath the cot in which he would never again sleep through the agony of the damp highland night. In the pouch were a half-liter of Chinese *mao tai*, a pungent, fiery spirit, and a crumpled but still sealed packet of Winston cigarettes he had saved for some special occasion. He rinsed his mouth with the fiery *mao tai* and then lit a cigarette. Somehow, he knew, it ends today. There would be no other special occasion.

Ricardo led the advance across the bridge and into the trees, Moser close behind, eager, crowding the point man and making him nervous. Adams emerged from the jungle. The SEALs halted briefly as Adams pointed out the two claymores. Hooper told Adams to fall in behind Moser, and the advance resumed.

The day began to warm even though the sun had yet to appear through the thick mist, which swirled like smoke in the light breezes. The men made a fast passage up the path, which was bare from daily use and slick from the moisture. The SEALs' jungle boots gripped well enough but Moser, barefoot, was the surest of all in the pink mud. Ricardo kept up the pace, the men behind him following normal patrol order, each other man looking right or left in alternate order, with Ricardo concentrating on the ground for trip wires. Adams, behind Moser, took the normal slack man's responsibility for looking for wires or other traps in the trees; he wasn't sure Moser would remember.

Ricardo stopped the column when the cover began to thin rapidly. Hooper and Adams came up to the point. "We there yet, Moser?"

"Yes, sir. Just past that downed tree begins the cleared perimeter."

"No fence? No guard posts?" Hooper had Adams's recon report from hours ago firmly in mind, but he wanted Moser to be thinking about the place.

"There weren't when they took me down, sir, but that was a long time ago." Moser paused and cocked his head. "Morning muster, sir. The guards will be unlocking the prisoners and bringing them out for exercise. You can hear their voices."

Hooper listened, but heard nothing above the clatter of the jungle's awakening day creatures. "Ricardo, crawl up to that log and get a look. Chief, take Adams, Swank, and Ferguson and work around to the south. I'll take Stuart, Moser, and Corbett and come in from the north. If they really are all out in the open, we will just walk in and waste the guards."

"How will I know you are moving, Hoop?" asked Chief Clark.

"As General Custer once said—in a battle he won, Chief, not his last one—'charge to the sound of the guns.' "

Ricardo returned, slipping in the wet clay. "It's like Moser said, sir. I counted twelve prisoners lined up in the middle of the camp and two guards."

"There should be three more prisoners, sir," said Moser. "Must be sick."

"Or dead?" asked Hooper, quietly.

"No," said Moser. "Minh would have told me this morning. He always bragged about the ones who died in the night."

"How many guards should we find?" asked Chief Clark.

"Was eight, plus the two sergeants and Major Nan," said Moser, squinting to concentrate. "Sergeant Vo and two left yesterday with Major Peters and the others—"

"What others?" asked Hooper, surprised.

"Fourteen guys, sir. Major Peters said they were being marched away east, to a place called Ban Namngiap."

"Damn!" said Stuart. "A day earlier and we could have had them all."

"And a day later perhaps none of them," said Hooper. "Sounds like they are clearing this camp." Why? he wondered. Could we be expected? Spotted perhaps, downriver? "So three of ten are gone and one is dead. We should find six, plus the commandant."

"Only two will drill the prisoners, sir," said Moser. "The rest will be in the cookhouse, last building on the left, until it is time to go to the fields."

What fields? thought Hooper. No time for that. "It seems clear to me that this is our best shot, with all or nearly all the POWs where we can see them and the guards in more or less known positions. Chief? Stuart?"

"Yes, sir," said the chief. Stuart nodded.

"Let's do it, then," said Hooper. "Ricardo, you watch from the fallen tree; don't let anyone get between us and this trail."

The chief and his detail moved swiftly into the jungle and disappeared. Hooper followed his two around to the north of the camp. When they reached the edge of the trees it was just as Ricardo had described it, prisoners in the middle with two lone guards, no one even looking out at the perimeter. Hooper told Corbett to take the nearest guard; he himself would take the far one. The fifty-meter range was very short for the accurate Stoner carbine. Hooper told Stuart to call it. When both marksmen were ready he raised his hand and then dropped it. Both rifles cracked at once and both guards were thrown skidding to the dirt. The SEALs emerged from both sides of the clearing at the double, three meters between each man.

Major Nan's jaw dropped when he heard the double crack of the Americans' weapons and saw the two teams of black-clad commandos enter the compound. Nan's vantage point on the hill was far enough above the camp to give him almost a plain view of the action. No one was looking his way, but fear soon replaced surprise. And the *con trau duc* was with them! With a weapon that must have been Trung-si Minh's. Nan shrank back to the edge of the tree line, dragging the heavy radio behind him. He retuned the frequency and called for the NVA camp at Xieng Mi.

Hooper used hand signs to direct Chief Clark and his men to hit the row of hootches and especially the cookhouse on the southern side of the central cleared area. He directed Stuart and Moser to check the barracks and the crude medical hootch. All his men reached the cleared area in a rush, Hooper shouting at the POWs, over and over, "Hit the dirt! We are Americans, U.S. Navy, hit the dirt!"

The prisoners stared, uncomprehending, most with their mouths hanging open. They either stood still where they were or continued with the slow, rhythmic movements of the Tai Chi exercise. A guard tumbled out of the cookhouse and Corbett shot him. A prisoner, a tall black man, was the first to realize what was happening. He began motioning the other prisoners to lie down, and even tackled one.

A volley of automatic rifle fire came from the cookhouse, causing the SEALs in the center area to join the stunned POWs on the gritty earth. Chief Clark emerged at the corner of the cookhouse and tossed in two frag grenades. Firing from the building ceased abruptly and flames appeared in the thatch roofing. Swank moved along the decking in front of the building, Ferguson behind him, backing up, and kicked the door in. He took a long look, then backed out and hand-signed "secure" to the chief, followed by three fingers held up and then passed across the throat. Hooper nodded. Three inside, one outside on the deck. With the two they had shot from the trees all the guards were accounted for except the crippled commandant. Ferguson and Swank were already checking the hootches. They would find him.

Stuart and Moser emerged from the prison barracks. Stuart reported, "No more in the hootches, Hoop. Three guys, real sick, in the hootch at the end."

Nan raised Xieng Mi and reported the attack in progress. It was all he could do; he had no weapon. Xieng Mi gave him another frequency and told him to contact the *trung-uy* (lieutenant) in charge of the recovery party, which Nan was relieved to hear was well on its way to him on the Pathet Lao's new road. Trung-uy Ky promised to separate two squads of infantry to rush forward to attack the Americans before they could leave the valley.

Chief Clark organized a perimeter defense for the camp, necessarily thin because he had so few men. Three of the collapsed stretchers were broken out and assembled. They were made of aluminum tubing and nylon netting, and had originally been designed for mountain climbers. The sick men were strapped in as gently as could be.

Hooper looked over the prisoners. Even the twelve who could walk were in a very bad way, their heads bowed as they shuffled into something like a single file. Any thoughts he had had of arming them with the guards' weapons to augment his force vanished. Only the black man who had first understood his command for the prisoners to hit the dirt had any expression at all. The man approached Hooper and saluted, standing as straight as he could against hunched shoulders, which seemed to pain him. The man's sunken eyes glowed with anger or madness.

"I am Lt. Martin Morse, U.S. Navy," said the black man, hoarsely. "The senior American officer."

"Lieutenant Hooper, Danang SEALs, commanding," said Hooper. "Your men look all in."

"Yes, sir," said Morse. "Major Nan sent the healthy ones away, all except me, to march east. I doubt many will make it; none of us is really well."

Jesus, that is an understatement, thought Hooper sadly. He guessed that Morse, without the stoop, would have been at least six feet tall, but now he couldn't weigh more than 120 pounds. And he was one of the healthy ones! "Why did they leave you here, Morse?"

"I was second senior. Major Nan insisted I stay."

Hooper nodded. He looked around. The chief had gathered the prisoners into a bunch—there was no military description for it—and was calling in the perimeter troops. Nothing for it, thought Hooper. We will just have to herd them down to the river in one thick, slow-moving, and very vulnerable mass.

He turned back to Morse, who seemed to be awaiting an order. "Think you can use that AK, Morse?" said Hooper, pointing to the weapon lying next to the dead guard on the deck outside the burning cookhouse.

"I am no infantryman, sir. Better I replace one of your men as a litter bearer."

"You can handle that?" said Hooper, doubting it but not wanting to be unkind.

"Yes," said Morse firmly, his hoarseness gone. "In fact, let me detail five others of my men to release yours to use their weapons. You would be surprised what we can carry; since we have been here we have been little more than beasts of burden."

Hooper smiled. He was glad the prisoners wanted to be part of their own rescue. "Make it so, then, Lieutenant Morse."

Moser came around the rear of the hootches. "We are going now, Moser," said Hooper.

"But sir, I have to find Major Nan!" said Moser, fear in his voice.

"He probably left yesterday, Moser. Anyway, we have to get these men down the hill and then get the hell out."

"I'll just look around once more sir, and then I'll catch up."

Hooper saw the unit begin to move down the hill toward the path, Chief Clark in the lead. The POWs had indeed taken up the three litters, and the chief had deployed the SEALs to fight if they had to. "Fall in, Moser. We need your help with the other men. Getting them home is more important than Major Nan."

"Aye, aye, sir," said Moser, turning and shuffling off toward the receding column. Nan had not left the valley, of that Moser was certain. He would have killed me or taken me with him. Nan is here and I will find him.

Stuart waited for Hooper at the edge of the clearing. "Go ahead, Willie; I'll be the tail gunner," said Hooper, slapping his friend on the shoulder. "And, to quote the legendary Captain Lewis of the Two-Twenty Six Marines as he unbuttoned his fly while standing on the bar in the CABOOM Club* during the summer dinner dance, 'let's say hello to the Air Force!' "

"Already done," said Stuart, moving off behind Moser. "The little jewel is squawking away inside my ruck and has been ever since the chief formed the prisoners up."

"Well, so far so good, me lad," said Hooper, relieved at finally being on the way out of the spooky valley. "Let's just hope the helo jockeys don't tarry long over their morning coffee."

Udorn, Thailand

Captain Scirano ran up the stairs to the communications room and entered. He could hear the buzzer of the emergency frequency across the room. By the time he reached the side of the duty sergeant, Technical Sergeant Crimmins, the squawk had already been triangulated and plotted on the huge wall chart that covered all of Indochina from the Ca Mau Peninsula at the southern tip of Vietnam to the Chinese border with North Vietnam. Scirano looked at the spot: southern Laos! Where the SEALs were going! "Sergeant, any companion squawks on the alternate we set up?"

Sergeant Crimmins reached for the log under the ALT 3 frequency. "Not on this watch, sir." He flipped the page up. "Holy shit! Two squawks, five seconds apart. Logged as a test at oh-oh-three-one."

"Who logged it off?" said Scirano, looking over the duty sergeant's shoulder.

"Washington, the new kid," said Crimmins, frowning.

"And who the fuck had the watch?" roared Scirano.

"Sergeant Towser."

"Damn!" cursed Scirano. "That lazy son of a bitch Towser will lose his stripes for this and worse, will likely get some brave men killed!" Scirano balled his big fists and fought for control. "Call operations, Sergeant. Tell them I need three birds turning up by the time I get back down there. Tell whichever pilot is sitting in the ready chopper that I am taking his and give him this position; he'll lead the second sec-

*Clark Air Base Officers' Open Mess, in the Philippines.

tion of two as soon as we get crews aboard. Call the Air Police duty NCO and tell him to send two squads to the pad with full field packs. Then call the duty officer of the Spad squadron and ask him to get something over that position."

"Yes, sir," said Crimmins, saluting Scirano's fleeing back. He turned to his watch section and saw they were already making the calls as ordered by the captain. Crimmins thought about Sergeant Towser, a happy-go-lucky guy but always a bit of a fuck-up. He winced as he thought about what Scirano would do when he got back, and worse, what the rest of them might have to do to Towser if Scirano didn't get back. The captain was an immensely popular officer, held to be the bravest pilot in a squadron where all were brave, and Towser was sending him out to dust a commando unit out of the shit with his pants around his ankles.

Trai o Bo Song, Laos

Phouang heard the light gunfire from across the river just before he reached the old camp where Nan had kept his single prisoner in the tiger cage. He held up his hand and halted the unit. Senior Bannerman Phatang came up behind him. Both men squatted. Phatang whispered, "What do you think is happening, Colonel?"

"Maybe Nan is shooting his prisoners," said Phouang. That would make sense with most men, he thought, but not with Nan. "In any case, we had best split up and approach the lower camp with caution."

Phatang nodded. He looked back at the meager squad: eight men, only four with AK-47s, including himself. Phouang had his U.S. aviator's .38 special pistol with five rounds. Two men carried old French MAS-36 bolt action rifles, which, with their corroded ammunition, were probably as dangerous to the men who carried them as to an enemy. Total 7.62mm ammunition for the AKs among the four who carried them was 404 rounds. All the men carried knives or machetes and the two men with no firearms at all carried spears. Yet each man looked proud and eager. All but two were teenagers. "May I suggest, Colonel, that I take four and approach up the trail through the rice paddy while you take the route over the hill, which will allow you to command the bridge from the north?"

"Good," said Colonel Phouang, delighted to have a man with actual fighting experience in his command. "Split the weapons equally. If you find nothing show yourself to me and I'll come down. I would still like to be at the High Camp as quickly as possible."

Udorn, Thailand

Lieutenant Colonel Billy Yocum, commanding officer of the 2d Squadron, 1st Air Commando Wing, was in the ready room across the airfield from the Jolly Greens when the call came in from Sergeant Crimmins that the Rescue squadron wanted a scramble of Spads. At forty-three, Lieutenant Colonel Yocum had been flying variants of the A-1 since before it was the A-1. In Korea the sturdy piston-engined Skyraider had been designated the AD, or Able-Dog, in the pre-NATO phonetic alphabet. Billy Yocum had finished pilot training in the Army Air Corps just too late to get into War Two, but he had flown throughout the Korean War, hitting all kinds of targets and earning several commendations. In 1952 his squadron made history, flying cover for Navy ADs as they torpedoed a dam.

Lieutenant Colonel Yocum listened to the airman on duty as he logged the frag from across the air base. Billy rubbed his knuckles through his stubble of gray hair and grinned his crinkly-faced grin. The airman looked up. "You be taking this one, Colonel?"

Yocum had been in the air force twenty-five years. Last year he had missed selection for full colonel for the second time. This was his third tour in Southeast Asia and at the end of it he would be forced to retire. "Damn right, Airman. Who else is ready?"

"Captain Collins and Lieutenant Dooley in the bunkroom, along with your backseater, Lieutenant Harada."

Yocum liked Harada, a cheerful Hawaiian of Japanese extraction, although he disliked the idea of the extra crewman on what before Vietnam he had flown as a single-seat aircraft. But all those newly added black boxes did need tending to, and therefore the E model had two seats. Collins and Dooley were good, steady men. "Blow the horns, Airman," said the colonel. "I'll be out by the aircraft; make sure Harada knows anything more that comes in about what we are supposed to be doing."

"Roger, sir," said the airman, pressing buttons that would sound horns in the pilots' bunkroom off the ready room and also down in the hangar, where the crew chiefs would check out the A1-Es and roll them out. Four minutes later, and before the first Jolly Green reported airborne, the two Spads took off into the morning fog. The aircraft carried mixed ordnance loads. In addition to the four wing-mounted 20mm cannon they carried napalm cannisters, 2.75-inch rockets in pods, and high-explosive bombs on the external hardpoints, as well as a four-hundred-pound fuel tank on the centerline point to increase their loiter time over target. The A1-Es could carry as much as eight thousand pounds of external stores, but Yocum's aircraft were well below that limit.

Eight minutes later the two-plane section crossed the Mekong, though they never saw it in the low hanging fog, and proceeded north on a compass bearing. Mountain peaks jutted above the clag and the fog shrank into the deeper valleys as the day warmed. It was going to be a beautiful morning, Yocum thought.

TWENTY-NINE

Trai o Bo Song, Laos, 8 June 1969

"I smell gooks," whispered Freinberg from his dug-in AO in the heavy undergrowth twenty meters due east of the eastern end of the bridge.

Harris was dug into a shallow fighting hole in the bushes near Moser's tiger cage, four meters southwest of Freinberg and downhill. "Which side?" he whispered back.

"Uphill," said Freinberg, adjusting his position and squinting through the foliage. "The last little puff of wind."

Harris had walked enough jungle trails with Freinberg to take his observation seriously, even though the saucy New Yorker was a known practical joker. He considered the situation. They had two claymores dug in, one facing east into the jungle and one southeast down a trail that led to some rice paddies. To the north was a hill crest, and that direction hadn't seemed a promising access of approach to the camp or the bridge. Besides, the team had brought only four clays and two were guarding the other end of the bridge. Since the gunfire from the other side had ended ten minutes ago Harris had expected the team back by now. No way those few shots fired could signal anything but a quick SEAL victory.

"See anything, Freinberg?" he called, softly.

"No, but a moment ago I thought I heard voices."

"Gook?"

"Not English, man," whispered Freinberg. "And sure as hell not Yiddish, and that's all the languages I know."

Harris agonized. He was a second class gunner's mate; Freinberg a torpedoman's mate 3d. Harris was in charge even though Freinberg had been in the bush longer. One thing was sure: if the enemy had a machine gun or even a couple of automatic rifles on that hill they could prevent the team from recrossing the bridge. Freinberg would have to go up and look. "Hey, Freinberg? Got frags?"

"Yeah," came the reply. "You want I should do a little recon-by-fire of the hilltop?"

"Yeah—wait!" Harris looked down the path to the rice field. A single figure squatted in the path fifty meters away and twenty meters in front of the claymore attached to Harris's detonator. The man was backlit by the morning sun rising behind him; a very poor position, Harris thought. He was wearing loose-fitting clothing that looked purple in the sunlight and had a scarf of orange parachute cloth around his neck. He held an AK-47 in front of him, its butt grounded, and he was perfectly still. He appeared to be listening. "Freinberg," whispered Harris, cupping his hand in front of his mouth to divert the sound away from the solitary figure. "I got a gook on the path. Stay put."

"What are we gonna do?" said Freinberg, hoping the jungle's clatter was preventing the gooks from hearing them.

Harris just didn't know. How many were there? What kind of equipment did they have? Freinberg would never get across the clearing to the ridge without the still figure seeing him. Lieutenant Hooper's lectures on combat leadership rattled around in Harris's brain. Never be afraid to make the decision. Strike first and hard. Learn what you can and then *act*. Harris looked down the trail. The man was still in exactly the same spot, still as a tree trunk, but there was another man with him who looked like he had a fucking *spear*!

"Harris?" whispered Freinberg. Harris heard the tightness in his voice. "I definitely hear people talking on the hill."

"Look, we gotta sit tight unless they make a move on the bridge," said Harris, doubting his decision even as he made it. "When the lieutenant comes down he will call us from the other end of the bridge. I'll blow my clay and take these two out, then you go for the ridge, me behind you. That'll warn the L T, and he'll get us out."

Freinberg chuckled. "Good plan, man."

Udorn, Thailand

Captain Scirano had his three HH-3E Jolly Greens turning up and crews assembled when he saw the flight of two Spads lift off and turn to the north. The ready bird's crew had been on the aircraft, and the backup crew was out of the bunkroom behind the main hangar in two minutes. Even the men of the third crew, who had to be shaken out of their cots and get themselves dressed before being driven to the pad, were in their aircraft in under ten minutes. The Jolly Green crews were used to waking up quickly. Scirano checked his watch. Fourteen minutes since the first squawk of the EPIRB. Those navy guys could be in it up to their noses!

"Sergeant!" he shouted across the hangar. "Where are those fucking Air Police?"

"I got 'em on the horn, Cap," shouted the sergeant, over the noise of the helicopter engines. "He says ten minutes. He says we promised him some warning."

"We did, Sergeant, but we didn't get it. Tell Captain Baxter to load them in the Two and Three birds; I am going up."

The sergeant gave him the thumbs-up signal and spoke into the cupped telephone. Scirano climbed into the right seat of the HH-3 and slammed the door. He added power, pushed the cyclic stick forward, and added collective. The 22,000-pound helicopter taxied fifty meters on its tricycle landing gear, then lifted off into the mist. Two minutes later it was heading for the Laotian border at 4,000 feet and 140 knots. "Check the machine guns as soon as we cross the Mekong," said Scirano to the copilot, First Lieutenant Eaves. "We could be a gunship today."

Trai o Bo Song, Laos

Chief Clark stopped the ragged column in the cover of the forest well short of the bridge. Hooper came up with Moser tagging behind him. The chief sent Ricardo crawling up to the end of the bridge. Moser watched him, remembering his own night crossing of the span on his way downriver, so long ago. He suddenly felt consumed with anger and he knew he could never leave this place while Major Nan lived.

Ricardo hand-signed "clear" from the bridge. Hooper dropped to the ground and crawled forward. Ferguson and Swank came up and took positions on either side of the bridge pathway. The morning was hot as the mists burned off and quiet enough that they could hear the dense cloud of flies that fought for position on Sergeant Minh's body. Hooper raised himself to a squat, his hand on the parapet. "Harris!" he shouted. "Clear over?"

"No, sir!" came the reply, followed immediately by the boom-and-hail sounds of a claymore detonating. Moser rose up and pointed at two figures in loincloths and orange scarves kneeling on the ridge to the left of the other end of the bridge. "Pathet Lao!" he shouted, and ran onto the bridge, firing his AK-47 from the hip. The Pathet Lao troops opened up on full auto, spraying the bridge. Hooper took a round under the collarbone and was thrown backward into Swank. Ferguson and Ricardo started across the bridge, shooting at the ridge from which the Pathet Lao had now disappeared. Stuart came up and knelt next to Hooper, who was breathing shallowly and whose eyes were closed. A steady trickle of blood from the corner of his mouth indicated the bullet had punctured a lung. Stuart pulled a battle dressing from his ruck and taped it quickly in place. Hooper needed hospital. Stuart looked up and saw Freinberg and Harris charge up the ridge. Moser, at the other end of the bridge, poured fire into a small group of Pathet Lao who came up the path into the camp. The crump of fragmentation grenades on the ridge was followed by a short, high-pitched scream, and then all the firing ceased.

Stuart motioned the chief forward. "Get everybody over ASAP, Chief," he said. "Get them down to the river and rig smoke flares on both ends of the sandbar."

The chief nodded and turned back to the POWs, who had stood silently through the short firefight. Ferguson led them across. Swank and Stuart helped Hooper to his feet. He opened his eyes and spat out a mouthful of blood, pinkish and bubbly. "Lung?" he gasped.

"Yes. Sucking chest wound," said Stuart. "Don't talk."

Moser walked down the path to the rice paddy he had walked so many miles to irrigate. He recognized the Lao who had captured him on the Mekong, even though he had been blown nearly in half by the claymore. He turned over the other three bodies, including the two he had shot. All were dead. He saw this as a good sign: The snake had brought this Lao back to me and soon he would bring Nan. Moser picked up a spent cartridge case and pressed it into the wooden stock of the AK, making two neat circles. Time to keep accounts, he thought, putting the brass case in a pocket. He then stripped the bodies of ammo for the AK and put that in his pockets as well.

Hooper was gasping and choking on his blood by the time Swank and Stuart had him over the bridge. "Stop," he wheezed. "Put me down where I can see the bridge."

"We have to get you down to the LZ, Hoop," said Stuart.

"Order," choked Hooper. "Down. Here." Swank was already letting Hooper down, so Stuart had to comply. "Rifle," wheezed Hooper, now resting on his stomach. His voice was clearer. "Detonators."

Swank uncovered the detonators for the claymores on the other side of the bridge and the charge at the center of the span, and put them in front of Hooper. Stuart unslung Hooper's Stoner and placed it in front of him. "Hoop, let me get you down to the beach."

"Shut up," said Hooper, with a liquid cough. "Listen. You talked air force. I want you down there to bring in helos."

"Yes, sir," said Stuart, knowing his friend was right. "But lie quiet; as soon as we establish communications with a helo I'll come back with a litter."

"Go now," said Hooper, squirming to get a clear view across the bridge. "Take everyone."

Moser squatted in the bush near the bodies of the Pathet Lao. The world was different when he spoke English with the Americans. Now he seemed as before, connected with the spirits of the place. But no longer Con Trau Duc. Nevermore Con Trau Duc. Moser stood and followed the others down to the river's edge. He heard the aircraft approaching from far away downriver and knew he had little time.

Lieutenant Harada, sitting behind Lieutenant Colonel Yocum in the lead A1-E, switched to the short-range UHF frequency that Captain Scirano from his following Jolly Green had radioed that the SEALs would guard. Colonel Yocum reported a bridge up ahead and climbed into a higher circle. "Trident, this is Wildcard Leader," said Harada into his lip mike. "Do you copy? Can you see Spads? Over."

"Roger," crackled the radio. "You are overhead. We are south of the bridge on the east bank. Where are the helos?"

"Behind us, maybe fifteen minutes back," said Harada. "You got company?"

"We expect it," said Stuart. "Check the camp just west of the bridge and the roads north."

"Roger, we'll have a look and confirm your location to the rescue birds." Harada reached forward and tapped Yocum on the shoulder. The colonel nodded, indicating he had heard, pulled the Spad out of its circle, and headed west.

Trai tren Nui Cao

Major Nan saw the first squad of NVA soldiers enter the camp near the poppy field. They were cautious and came slowly, well spread out, weapons covering the entire camp. All the buildings on the south side of the camp were burning or smoldering. Nan got up and hobbled down the hill, leaving the radio. He waved to the soldiers, gesturing for them to hurry. They saw him but paid no attention. Instead they crouched and waited, staring at the sprawled bodies of Nan's guards. Nan reached the center of the camp and stopped, red-faced and out of breath. The troops stayed at the poppy field and didn't descend until the lieutenant came forward and walked down to Nan.

"What happened, Thieu-ta?" said the lieutenant, saluting.

"Commandos of some sort, Trung-uy," said Nan, panting. "They took the prisoners and went back down to the river. There was firing there only a few minutes ago."

Two propellor-driven aircraft roared over from the east. The soldiers melted into the jungle before they passed overhead. Nan and the lieutenant merely stepped beneath the smoldering roof of Nan's hootch. "Those are the bombers the Americans send out ahead of their search and rescue helicopters," said the lieutenant, shading his eyes.

"Do you have antiaircraft weapons?" Nan asked.

"The other squad has a DShK machine gun. If we can get it to a vantage point we might get a helicopter."

"There are two paths," said Nan, fighting his fear. The water buffalo must not leave him! "One goes to the bridge, just there." He pointed east and the lieutenant nodded. "There is another, near that dead tree, which leads down to the river. The only place a helicopter could land, other than right here, would be down on a broad sandbar in the river itself."

"Good," said the lieutenant, waving his men forward at the double. "I'll send this squad to the bridge and the other, with the machine gun, down the other path. Either should have a clear shot at a descending helicopter."

"Hurry, please, Trung-uy," urged Nan. "I will wait for the second squad."

"Thank you, sir," said the lieutenant, backing away. He shouted orders to the first squad and they started cautiously toward the path. American troops often mined trails behind them and commandos nearly always did. By the time the American bombers returned overhead all of the first squad was under the trees.

When Stuart reached the river the chief had both ends of the LZ marked with smoke grenades, rigged and wired to triggers in his position on the beach. He wouldn't set them off until the helos showed up. The POWs were all together near the riverbank, concealed in the trees, and the SEALs had established a small defensive perimeter. Stuart keyed the hand-held UHF radio. "Wildcard Leader, Trident. Any word on the helo?"

"First bird reports eight minutes out, two more after," said the radio.

Shit, thought Stuart. Those guys should have been ready to fly after I sent the squawks on the green EPIRB! I wonder if the fucker malfunctioned? "Tell them we may be able to get everyone on one bird, Wildcard," said Stuart. "Tell them we have twenty-six total, three sick in litters and one badly wounded."

"Wilco," said the voice. "Any sign of the bad guys, you let us know pronto."

"Trident out." Stuart clipped the radio to his web gear. Ricardo and Corbett were assembling the last of the aluminum and nylon-net litters. The SEALs had already decided to go get Hooper whether he liked it or not, and then Freinberg would take over the clays and the bridge charge. Freinberg was, among his many other strengths, the team's fastest runner. Stuart saw no reason to overrule them. As long as he ran the LZ he was following his orders, and he wanted his friend out on the first helo, no matter what.

*   *   *

Moser watched all these preparations from the clearing, his hand on the yoke of the pump. He then turned, slung his rifle, and walked back to the bodies of the Pathet Lao. He picked up the biggest, a boy who might weigh 140 pounds, and, carrying him went back to see Lieutenant Hooper. He found him breathing more easily and alert, his hands on the detonators. Moser stopped. "Goodbye, sir. Thank you, and thank Mr. Stuart."

"What do you mean, Moser?" said Hooper, slowly. "Get your ass back down the hill."

"Helo be along in a few minutes, sir. Some a your guys be comin' up for you with a litter."

"Good, Moser, now get down there. I want you out first."

"I can't go back with you, sir. Not—the way I am."

Hooper looked up at the big man with the sad, ravaged face. The lieutenant spoke slowly, gently. "Moser, look, maybe what they did to you seems worse than death, but it isn't. People will look after you; you will get better."

Moser squatted and laid the dead Pathet Lao in the dirt, gently. "Mr. Hooper, you remember way back when we was on the *Valley Forge*? 'Member when I passed the test for third class, an' nobody thought I would?"

Hooper looked at the gaunt man, his orange-painted face cracked with a bittersweet smile. Hooper noticed that the sing-songy cadence had left Moser's voice and he once again sounded like the Southern man he was. "Sure, Moser. We were all proud of you."

"Since that day, Mr. Hooper, the onliest thing I ever wanted to be was a chief gunner's mate. You ever know a chief gunner's mate with no balls, sir?"

Hooper almost choked at the sadness of the thought. "Moser, for the last time, get down and report to Lieutenant Stuart. That's an order."

"No, sir, I'm sorry. But you know skinny old Trung-si Minh's body ain't going to be enough to hold the blast; I heard you talking to Mr. Stuart. So I will put this little fella on top of him. And then I have to go and find Major Nan." He stood and picked up the body. "Goodbye, sir."

Hooper pushed himself up on one elbow and took up his rifle. His chest screamed with pain. "Moser," he spat blood. "So help me God, if you take one step toward that bridge, I will shoot you in the leg. You are going *home*!"

"You won't do that, sir. You know I can't go back." Moser turned and walked onto the bridge. Hooper watched him as he placed the body over the other, packed it in, and then walked off the far end of the bridge into the jungle, never once looking back.

Major Nan directed the second squad of NVA troops to the path that led down to the river, and then hobbled across the camp and climbed painfully back up the hill to the spot where he had left the radio. If he crawled all the way to the limestone outcropping at the top he could see into the river gorge, but he was afraid of the American planes. He sat with his back to a big tree and turned up the radio. He closed his eyes and thought of Moser—now that he was free, Nan no longer thought of him as the *con trau duc*—flying away from the valley in a big green helicopter while Nan remained. Somehow he couldn't see it ending that way.

The radio clicked and whispered. The first NVA squad was nearing the bridge.

Moser moved quickly up the path toward the High Camp, stopping every few meters to listen. Fifty meters up from the bridge he heard the slap of rubber sandals on the pink clay and muted voices talking in Vietnamese. He left the path, climbed up a small knoll, and lay down behind a fallen tree. One end of the tree was off the ground, suspended by its upturned roots. Moser unslung his AK, thumbed the selector to single fire, and pointed it beneath the tree at the trail below, sighting in on each man's head as he passed. The first two men were crawling, probing the undergrowth with strips of flattened bamboo for mines or wires. They won't find our claymores, thought Moser, seeing what would happen in his mind's eye. Mr. Hooper would let as many gooks as would come get at least as far as the middle of the bridge, then he would blow the clays and afterwards the bridge itself. If those gooks stay as bunched as they are they would be lucky if even one survives.

Moser counted twelve men and then no more. He listened another minute, then cautiously emerged onto the trail, heading west toward the High Camp. Where was Thieu-ta Nan hiding? The snake would tell him soon enough. Moser cocked his head; in the distance he heard the wop-wop of a helicopter. Good, he thought. Soon the SEALs and the other prisoners will be away from this place of fear and death and only I will remain, locked in spirit with Nan.

A voice spoke to him in his brain, in English. You are quite mad, it said. You could go back now and go home. Moser savored the thought; it amused him. How could my English-speaking side possibly understand? He smiled and pressed onward toward the perimeter of the High Camp.

Lieutenant Hooper heard the sound of the approaching helicopter as he saw the first soldier, dressed in dark green fatigues and with branches stuck into the netting over his conical helmet, emerge onto the far end of the bridge. After the man had taken three cautious paces a second man came forward, clinging to the south parapet as closely as the first cleaved to the north one. Each man held his AK-47 at the ready as he inched forward, one man taking two steps, and then the other one. Hooper could see no men behind these two, but knew they would be there.

NVA, thought Hooper. The first team. He wound the two detonators to make sure they were tight. Come along little friends, he thought. Death is all we have to offer today and it is too good for you, so swift and clean, but it will have to do.

Captain Scirano horsed the big helicopter into the gorge, still cursing himself for being so late in starting. His copilot, Lieutenant Eaves, was talking to the navy lieutenant, Stuart, who was ready to coordinate the extraction. So far the major problem reported by Stuart was one man bleeding, but Scirano had flown to enough emergency beacons to know that with as much time as the enemy had had to get organized it was unlikely that he would show himself until he had a shot at the big green helicopter. Scirano made the last turn over the river, saw the bridge and the sandbar, and called the color of the SEALs' smoke, green both ends. Scirano called the Spads to make sure they were loitering above and behind him, then gritted his teeth and split the needles for a high-speed autorotate into the LZ.

Hooper waited until the two-man fire team reached the bodies that covered the major explosive charge. The first man cradled his AK and reached down to grip the dead Lao by the back of his shirt, presumably to turn him over. Hooper couldn't let him do that: Moser was right, the extra corpse would greatly enhance the tamping factor and thus the value of the explosive against the iron arch. Hooper turned the screw detonator to the stop and heard the crack of one claymore on the other end of the bridge. They must have found the other clay, Hooper thought fleetingly. The NVA soldier at the center of the bridge let go of the dead Lao and took a step backward. Hooper twisted the handle of the second detonator. The center of the bridge exploded with a roar, sending a blast of heat back to Hooper, singeing his face and hands. The soldier in the center of the bridge was blown straight up, tumbling end over end among boards and fragments of boards from the crude roadway. Hooper closed his eyes and tried to squirm backwards as grit and spinters, some burning, rained down on him. He opened his eyes in time to see the soldier splash into the river below, surrounded by much debris. The southern arch of the bridge was twisted and the cap rail broken at the point of the explosion, but the bridge had not gone down.

Ricardo squatted in front of Hooper and pried the detonator from his hands. Strong hands grasped Hooper's shoulders and hips and turned him over as Corbett and Freinberg rolled him onto the litter. "Time to go, sir," said Corbett. "Helo's coming in."

"I didn't get it down," said Hooper, fighting to stay conscious. "There's NVA on the other side; they will be able to cross."

Corbett and Ricardo picked up the litter. Freinberg laid Hooper's Stoner along his leg and tightened the straps. "I'll slow 'em down, sir," said Freinberg, taking up Hooper's former position on the ground. The litter moved off as the air filled with the roar of the descending helicopter's engines and rotors. Freinberg squinted to see through the smoke and dust that obscured the other end of the bridge. Men moving? he wondered. He steadied the Stoner, fired three rounds into the smoke, and got back a fusillade in return. Shit, he thought. As soon as that helo lands I'll give them a full clip and then *di-di* for the river.

Captain Scirano dove the big helicopter into the narrow gorge, lining up on the smoke flares which, the navy told him, marked a long sandbar, although he couldn't yet see it. He reengaged the turbines to the rotors and added a little power and collective to flare into landing. There was a loud crash to his left, then several reports farther aft. Scirano looked at Lieutenant Eaves and was appalled to see him slumped in his harness with half his face shot away. Scirano fought for control of the helicopter as the crew chief's voice in his headset announced "Machine gun ten o'clock." Scirano had to twist the bird around to climb out of the valley; the bridge in front of him made a forward pull-up impossible.

As the helicopter turned around the axis of its rotor the door gunner on the right side could see the tracers from the machine gun rising like successive bursts of bright darts. He aimed his M-60 machine gun at the approximate center of the upcoming tracers and fired a long burst, fully half a belt. The machine gun on the ground ceased firing. Captain Scirano got the shuddering aircraft moving downriver and clawed his way up and out of the gorge.

The crew chief, Sergeant Kelly, pulled the young airman back inside, away from the M-60. The gunner was black, but his face looked ashen. "You might just have saved this bird, Jefferson," said the crew chief.

On the beach the SEALs opened fire at the spot on the opposite bluff from which the tracers had come and received heavy small-arms fire from many concealed positions on the opposite bank. The machine gun, silenced momentarily by fire from the Jolly Green, opened up again and soon drove the SEALs off the beach and back into the trees. Stuart's radio crackled as Hooper was brought into the area on the litter and placed in a shallow depression with the POWs. Stuart keyed the radio. "This is Trident. Say again, over."

"This is Wildcard Leader, Trident. The chopper has one dead on board, the copilot. Pilot says the crew chief is in the left seat to operate the miniguns and that the bird is still flyable, but he wants us to take out the machine gun across the river from you. Can you mark his position? Over."

"Only with our tracers," said Stuart. "The MG is about twenty meters south of the bridge and maybe a third of the way up the cliff. We are also taking small-arms fire from the bridge itself."

"Roger. I can't bomb that bridge, it's too close to your position. My wing man will fire some rockets at the far end and dust 'em with twenty mike-mike while I roast the hillside."

"Roger, Wildcard, good shooting," said Stuart into the radio.

"Get your men well down, Navy," said Colonel Yocum as he levelled his Spad and started his shallow dive, checking that his wing man was in formation higher and to his right quarter. "This napalm could blow back."

"Roger, Wildcard." Stuart shouted to the men to cease fire and take cover as the Spads flashed overhead.

Freinberg had seen the helo get hit and climb out, and had a bird's-eye view of the exchange of fire across the river. The gooks on the other side of the river had rolled a big, irregular log onto the bridge deck before the smoke of Hooper's charge cleared and were advancing behind it, using it as a moving shield. Freinberg knew he couldn't stay much longer. He unclipped a frag grenade from his web gear, speculating on how far he could throw it accurately. He heard the Spads roar in from behind him, suddenly overhead and then gone before any results from their run could be observed, but then a salvo of rockets struck the opposite end of the bridge, red flares of high explosive and yellow-white blossoms of searing hot white phosphorous. Napalm ignited on the far bank, long, spreading smears of red and yellow flame, each ending in an angry column of greasy black smoke. The bridge in front of Freinberg shuddered and moaned as ancient rivets sheared and popped, the arches buckled, and the bridge fell into the river in two pieces. Freinberg stood and was pushed back a step by the searing heat riding the shock wave from the napalm. Definitely *di-di* time, thought Freinberg, as he ran toward the beach.

The hillside was still crackling with napalm fires and the smoke had not cleared when Captain Scirano came barrelling into the gorge, this time much lower, just above the water. He stamped in major right rudder to kick the bird around the bend of the river, then chopped his power and pulled just enough collective to make a landing instead of a crash. He was relieved to see the SEALs splashing toward the HH-3, pushing black-clad men and carrying four litters. Sergeant Kelly and the two door gunners were quickly out of the aircraft and helping.

Stuart counted the men as they went aboard. Suddenly he realized Moser was not among them. He ran to the helo and shouted to Hooper. "Hoop! Where the hell is Moser?"

"Gone," said Hooper, hoarse from choking. "Get in the helicopter."

"Gone!" shouted Stuart, his face contorted with rage. "What the fuck do you mean *gone*! I didn't come all the fucking way out here to get him—"

Hooper pulled his arm from beneath the strap on the litter and grabbed Stuart by the collar of his utilities. With surprising strength, he pulled Stuart's face to within an inch of his own. "You fucking came out here?" said Hooper, drooling aerated pink blood. "You fucking RAMF, you came out here and you are going back! You have been spat on and reviled in the World, how the fuck do you think it would be for him?" Hooper's chest heaved as he coughed up a continuing froth of blood.

"That everybody?" interrupted the air force crew chief as Freinberg bounded aboard. "No," said Stuart, turning.

"Yes, Sergeant," said Hooper, gesturing.

Sergeant Kelly grabbed Stuart by the collar of his shirt and his belt and threw him into the aircraft. The gunners manned their weapons. Sergeant Kelly spoke into his lip mike, which was attached to the forward bulkhead by a long cable, then stepped unhurriedly aboard and slid the door shut. Captain Scirano pushed the cyclic forward, powered up, and pulled collective. The Jolly Green rose through the smoke over the ruined arches of the bridge and turned south for Thailand, the two Spads following.

Stuart sat next to Hooper's litter, his head in his hands. With the doors shut the helicopter was quiet enough for men to talk. Hooper reached out and grasped Stuart's shoulder, and pulled him down so he could hear. "I tried to make him go down to you, William," said Hooper, his voice slow and sleepy. "I really did. It was his decision alone to stay."

Stuart nodded, rubbed his eyes and took a deep breath. "I guess I lost sight of Moser himself in all this. It became a quest."

"For Moser, it may still be a quest," said Lieutenant Hooper, and then he finally let himself pass out.

THIRTY

Trai tren Nui Cao, Laos

Major Nan watched the big green American helicopter lift out of the gorge, its door gunners spraying the jungle until the aircraft was clear. The jungle fell strangely quiet, the birds and the monkeys and the insects silenced by the roaring and crackling of the brief battle, and Nan heard the helicopter for a long time. The fires started in the jungle by the napalm and the rockets burned low; the vegetation was green and soaked from the morning mist. The smoke rising to the plateau where Nan sat brought the sickly-sweet smell of burned meat. Nan wondered whether any of the trung-uy's men had survived.

He pushed himself up with his staff and hobbled down to the tree where he had left the radio. He was about to pick up the handset when he saw a flash of iridescent green slide through the grass next to the radio. Nan swiped at it with his staff. The green bamboo snake hissed at him but retreated into the bush, sliding rapidly over the exposed roots of the tree. Loathsome creatures, thought Nan. Snakes were said to take up the spirits of men who died but whose bodies were never buried or cremated, of men who died at sea, and of men who were mutilated, before or after death. Nan shuddered. He tuned the radio to the Xieng Mi frequency, picked up the handset, and pressed the transmit button. He asked for Colonel Nguyen and was told to stand by.

Gradually the buzz of the jungle returned. The sun rose free of the mist, above the eastern mountain, and it felt hot across the commandant's shoulders. A deep shadow fell over Nan and he felt a sudden chill. He turned and saw Moser, looking more gaunt than ever in a borrowed uniform. In his left hand Moser carried an AK-47 and in his right, writhing and coiling around his wrist, the *con ran xanh o bui tre*, the deadly green bamboo snake. Nan's jaw dropped in terror and he pushed himself backwards, away from the man to whom he knew he was finally to be joined.

Moser watched Major Nan scrabble backward on his ass, pushing himself along with his good arm and good leg. Moser walked slowly, keeping pace, maintaining the distance between them at about one meter. Why does he try to get away? wondered Moser. Surely he has seen this moment.

Nan's back fetched up against the tree and he could go no farther. He slumped, exhausted, drained, and resigned to his fate. His fear ebbed away as the American came almost to his feet and squatted. The American set the rifle carefully on the ground. The snake continued to writhe, hissing obscenely, in the man's orange-painted right hand.

"*Toi khong phai la con trau*," said Moser, softly, gently. "*Toi la con ran. Cung vi con ran do ma so menh cua chung ta lien nhau.*"

Nan's terror returned in a rush. Moser had spoken to him in his own voice, right down to the clipped Vinh accent. He had never heard Moser utter a word in Vietnamese, and now he had pronounced Nan's death warrant in a perfectly structured sentence, each tone flawless.

Moser shook the green bamboo snake free of his wrist and dropped it on Major Nan's chest. Nan swiped at the animal feebly with his good arm, but the agitated snake sank his fangs into the bulging artery on the side of Nan's throat, shaking along its body as it pumped in the venom.

Moser stood and stepped back. He said the sentence again, not for Thieu-ta Nan, whose eyes were becoming opaque as he died. He said it in English, perhaps, he thought, to tell Mr. Hooper and Mr. Stuart and the others why things had to be as they were and why he had stayed in the valley with Major Nan.

"I was never the water buffalo," he said, watching Nan's limbs twitch one last time and then be still. "I was the snake. It is with the snake that our fates are joined."

The bright green snake slid off the dead major's chest and raced into the forest. Moser picked up his AK-47 and headed north. Mister Stuart's map had shown a wide place in the river a few kilometers up, where Moser could probably ford.

V
LOVED
ONES

THIRTY-ONE

Nice, France, 14 July 1969

Stuart walked down the ladder of the Air France Caravelle behind a slow-moving gaggle of children clustered around a very attractive Frenchwoman. He spotted the French police officer standing next to a dark blue Citroën parked in the shade of the terminal building, though the man was not in uniform and the car was unmarked. The man had the look of a senior policeman: the military bearing, the careful, observant eyes. He wore a blue linen suit that looked expensive and carried a broad-brimmed panama hat. Stuart was dressed in a suit of tan linen with a definite French cut that he had had tailored in Saigon way back in the war. He saw that the policeman's gaze was locked on his as he descended and knew he had been made as well.

Once clear of the bottom of the ladder Stuart walked around the young mother and her brood and headed straight toward the blue car. The plane had been full and the terminal was crowded with people taking the long weekend holiday, and he was glad he wouldn't have to queue up with the others in the hot Mediterranean sun.

The policeman smiled at Stuart as he approached. "I am Captain Lambert, Sûreté Nationale. You will be the mysterious M. Stuart?"

"Yes, sir. William Stuart," said Stuart. They shook hands. The cop had a look of complete competence: a weather-lined face, deeply tanned, blond hair silvering at the temples, pale blue eyes, and a hard body. I'll bet he was, or is, a paratrooper, Stuart thought.

"Give me your luggage claim checks," said Lambert. "Then we will go and have a drink on our famous promenade des Anglais."

Stuart had a hanging bag and a small soft leather case on a shoulder strap. "No checked luggage, Captain."

"Good," said the Frenchman. "Then I don't have to go scowling into the cargo area to intimidate the baggage handlers."

Stuart grinned. "I doubt that French baggage handlers can be intimidated or speeded up, even by the Sûreté."

"You're quite right, of course," said Lambert, opening the back door of the car and tossing Stuart's light luggage inside. "Let's go get that drink, then, and you can tell me whatever you plan to tell me."

The cafe where Lambert took Stuart was actually on the rue du Congrès, just off the promenade near the casino. Lambert ordered wine from a vast list and then suggested a light lunch of omelettes and crisp salads of bitter lettuce. It was just after three o'clock when the waiter left them with their coffee. The policeman had conducted the conversation like a tour guide, regaling Stuart with the history of Nice, its architecture, superb weather, and beautiful women, both tourist and local. It was clear the man enjoyed his posting, which he told Stuart he had held for three years. "Paris is the jewel of France," he said. "For a Frenchman, of the world. But the winters are so long and so gray there, while here it is always hot or at least warm."

"I wish I had more time to see the area, Captain," said Stuart, wanting to get the unpleasant part of this meeting—the lying—done before he began to like the Frenchman too much. "But as you know I have an errand."

"In which I am to assist you and ask no questions, and in return for which you will give me something Paris wants." The Frenchman smiled his easy smile and lit a black-tobacco cigarette.

"That's it," said Stuart. "Sorry about the mystery, but there it is."

Lambert shrugged, as if to say it didn't matter. "What do you want me to do?"

"Drop me at a taxi stand and give me a number where I can reach you tomorrow."

"Where are you going?" asked the policeman. Stuart had been told specifically not to be evasive about his destination; Harry MacAndrew had told him the French would surely have him followed, whatever the deal was.

"Cagnes-sur-Mer," said Stuart. "A hotel called Le Cagnard."

"That's in Haut-de-Cagnes, the old city," said Lambert, getting to his feet in one smooth movement. "I'll drive you there myself; it's unlikely a Niçois taxi driver would ever find it." Stuart started to protest, but the Frenchman cut him off. "Don't worry, I won't interfere with you: I have my orders. I also have an excellent reason of my own for driving you. I live in the village of St.-Paul-de-Vence, just north of Cagnes in the foothills. If you want nothing more of me than a lift I will go on home and celebrate the holiday with my family."

The owner of the restaurant rushed to the table, beaming, and handed Lambert his panama hat. Stuart noticed that no bill had been presented for the lunch, but thought it might be better not to remark on the fact. "If it is really no trouble," said Stuart.

"It isn't," said Lambert. "We will have to pass by my office and get my old Renault, though. My official Citroën will never get through the narrow streets of Haut-de-Cagnes."

"Sounds interesting," said Stuart.

"It's lovely," said the policeman, guiding Stuart out into the brilliant sun.

Lambert drove from Nice to Cagnes-sur-Mer along the coast. At every traffic light they stopped at they observed a stream of people, many of them young and beautiful women in tiny bathing suits. "All day long they go back and forth," said Lambert, as part of his running description of the passing scene. "Onto the beach, and then over to a cafe for a *citron pressé* or a cassis, then back."

Stuart watched the women in wonder. It made the war seem savage and distant and sweaty Washington seem sterile, even absurd.

"You will notice the beach here isn't like America, or for that matter, Spain," said Lambert. "Instead of sand, a gravel of sea-smoothed stones."

"Looks uncomfortable," said Stuart.

"It isn't," Lambert said. "You dig around a bit, make a depression for your hips and shoulders, and it is quite comfortable." Lambert turned off the coast road and up a long ramp onto a broad street. On the left was a racetrack and on the right a line of cafes and restaurants, including one red-and-gold-painted facade that advertised Chinese and Vietnamese specialties. "This is Cagnes-sur-Mer," Lambert said. "We will have you at your hotel in ten minutes."

Stuart sat silently as Lambert weaved through the heavy traffic and began to climb toward the thirteenth-century château that overlooked the mostly modern resort city. If he *had* a room in the Cagnard he would have taken a nap this afternoon gratefully, but he didn't. He had arrived in Paris only yesterday, expecting to find Khanh there, but the CIA man in the embassy told him she had gone to Cagnes to take the sun while her husband attended a meeting of winegrowers in Dijon. Stuart had thought he would have two days to talk to Khanh before he had to give the information to the French, but now he had only this day, and there had been no way to find him a room anywhere nearby because of the holiday. Where he would lay his head that evening was a problem yet to be solved.

The streets became narrower as the little Renault ground up the steep hill in second gear. At the château itself high walls of stone and mortar rose on both sides of the road, which was barely inches wider than the little car. Corners were right angles, and the walls bore marks and bits of paint where cars had not quite made a clean passage. Lambert proceeded very slowly, sometimes stopping and backing up in the tightest turns. The road seemed only to get narrower and darker as high walls shut out the sun. Ahead, Stuart could see that a house had been built right over the road, making a bridge. Lambert stopped just before it. "Le Cagnard," he said, pointing at a narrow doorway where a young man in a starched white jacket appeared.

"That's a hell of a road," Stuart said, emerging from the car and stepping onto the ancient stones.

Lambert said something to the porter in rapid French. The man took Stuart's two cases and ran up the stairs and into the building. Stuart walked around the car to the driver's side. "Actually, the narrowest part is still ahead, at the bottom of this hill," said Lambert. "You see why we Europeans like little cars."

"Thanks for the lift, Captain," said Stuart.

Lambert handed him a card. "My telephone in St.-Paul is written on the back. You won't neglect to call." It wasn't a question.

"Tomorrow, Captain Lambert, without fail."

The policeman put the little car in gear. "Enjoy your stay in Haut-de-Cagnes, monsieur."

The little car made an echo as it passed under the building. Stuart followed his luggage into a dim stairway.

Stuart located the reception, a tiny room up a winding staircase. The common rooms of the hotel, a spacious lounge and the dining room,

which had a balcony with a sea view, were very elegant and at four
P.M., deserted. The owner of the hotel, a large, fiftyish blonde woman
with a very businesslike air, greeted him in the lounge and Stuart explained
that he had just come from Paris with an urgent need to see Madame
de Farge. The woman spoke to Stuart in clear, wonderfully slow French,
nothing like the rapid-fire slang of Paris, and Stuart replied as best
he could in the same language.

Madame de Farge was out, it seemed, but was expected for dinner. Where was monsieur staying? Stuart explained his predicament.
Madame was sorry; her house was full. Perhaps she might notify Stuart
of a last-minute cancellation or departure? Of course, but all her guests
for the weekend had arrived; it was Bastille Day weekend, monsieur.
In the meantime she would have her assistant phone some other hotels down in Cagnes-sur-Mer. Her tone made it plain that anything she
might find would be far inferior to Le Cagnard. Stuart thanked her
profusely and repeated wistfully how much he would have preferred
to stay at the famous hotel. Madame smiled beautifully.

She likes me, he thought, as he went out into the street to take a
walk around the ancient town. He was glad he had worn a suit, even
though it was hot.

On the top of the hill was the château itself, a relatively small fortified
tower now in use as an art gallery. The streets were all narrow, though
few as narrow as the one leading to Le Cagnard. Some of the streets
had broad steps and many tunnelled under the ancient buildings. Many
places had views of the sea and others of the Alpes Maritimes, which
rose quite abruptly a few miles inland. The air was filled with the perfume
of the many flowering bushes and vines that covered ancient stone walls,
and with the twittering music of hundreds of the tiny, swooping swallows
the French called *hirondelles*. The larger streets were lined with smart,
small restaurants and a few shops. Apparently all the old structures
had had their exteriors preserved. Some of the buildings had dates inscribed
on their lintels from the thirteenth and fourteenth centuries.

Stuart found a tiny cafe near the château that had three tables inside and three outside. Stuart sat outside in the sun and removed his
jacket. He ordered a Kronenbourg beer and yawned, fighting the jet
lag. Such a beautiful place and such a sad errand, he thought.

The *patron* shook Stuart gently, waking him with a start. The day
was much cooler and the bright sunlight gone behind high clouds. Stuart
got up and paid his bill, mumbling an apology. The man seemed not
to care. Stuart's watch told him it was nearly seven o'clock. He was

stiff from the metal chair but refreshed, except for a sour taste in his mouth. He walked quickly back to Le Cagnard and found madame behind the counter. She smiled at him around her half-glasses, which had a lanyard around her neck. She was talking on the phone, so he smiled back and waited.

The innkeeper hung up the phone and made a note in the book in front of her. "Monsieur," she began, in her wonderfully clear French. "Madame de Farge has returned, just a few minutes ago. She is now resting. She asked me to tell you that she wishes you to join her for dinner."

"I shouldn't wish to intrude," protested Stuart.

Madame looked over her glasses with a coquettish pout. "But monsieur, madame was clearly delighted to hear you were in Haut-de-Cagnes. Clearly she does not consider herself imposed upon, especially since otherwise she would be dining alone."

Stuart tried not to look flustered. "Then I accept," he said.

Madame leaned across the counter, conspiratorially. "Monsieur, I still have not a room and I have found nothing in the town, though some calls remain to be returned. I will have the maid show you to my own apartment, where you can bathe and rest for a bit."

Oh God, thought Stuart, for a bath and change. "Madame is too kind, but I shouldn't impose so much on your hospitality."

"*Zut!*" said madame, making a pushing motion with her hands in front of her ample bosom. "It is no trouble at all; give Lisette ten francs *pourboire* for the effort of changing the towels. You are tired from your trip and the heat of the afternoon, and you have all your luggage, so why not?"

"Thank you very much, madame." The maid, Lisette, emerged from the office with Stuart's two pieces of light luggage.

"Besides, I am sure you will want to look your best for dinner with such a beautiful woman, monsieur," said madame, with a twinkle in her eye that made her look ten years younger.

"Of course. Madame is too kind."

"Madame de Farge will be dining at nine, on the terrace," she said. "But you must join me for an aperitif at eight-thirty, and I will tell you if I have found you a room."

"Thank you again," Stuart said, savoring the thought of a hot bath and another short rest. "Until eight-thirty, then."

"In the small bar, downstairs," said madame, returning to her ledger.

*   *   *

Stuart found the proprietress alone in the little bar one level below the dining room. He had exchanged his rumpled linen suit for a dark blue blazer and gray slacks. The owner had changed from her blue wool skirt and white silk blouse to a tightly fitting black silk dress that flattered her full figure. Stuart wondered where she had changed, since he had occupied her rooms. "What will you drink, monsieur?" she asked, rising and going behind the bar.

"Champagne, if madame will join me."

She nodded her approval and withdrew a bottle of Moët from the fridge. She opened it quickly and efficiently, with the slightest pop and no spill. Holding the bottle in one hand, she scooped up two crystal flutes in the other and led Stuart to a small table next to an open window with a flower box. It was still quite light outside. "Monsieur looks quite refreshed," she said.

"Yes. The bath was wonderful. Thank you again."

Madame looked pleased. "I hope you will enjoy our Provençal cuisine, monsieur. My personal recommendation tonight would be the baby lamb chops."

"That is what I will have," said Stuart. They clinked glasses and sipped the wine.

"Good," said the woman. "Now, as to accommodations, the best I could find is in a small hotel in town. It isn't very good, but I booked it for you."

But I'll be here, thought Stuart, because you will have a vacancy. The thought saddened him. "Fine," he said. "I'll get a taxi after dinner," he said.

"Here is the name and address," she said, handing him a card. "If, perchance, you should end up staying here—" Madame paused dramatically. She thinks Khanh might take me to her bed. But that won't happen this time. "—it will be no trouble to cancel. The owner of the hotel is the most odious Englishman."

"Madame is too kind." She really was, he thought. It was almost embarrassing, but he supposed Khanh had said something to her.

Madame took the tiniest sip of champagne. "And now I must take you to your table. It is my very best and I always save it for Madame de Farge when she is here, but she is always a little late and my other guests will pester the captain if they see it is vacant."

"Fine. I'll guard it for her."

"Just so, monsieur." Madame rose and he followed her. "I will have the champagne brought to your table."

Stuart sat alone. The view from the terrace was spectacular, and he studied it to fight his panic. He was still angry from the reaming Harry MacAndrew had given him on his return from Thailand, and angrier still at the Naval Intelligence Command for knowing about Khanh for years and not bothering to tell him, even though they knew he had seen her in Paris in May. And he was angry at Khanh for deceiving him, but somehow he knew that that anger was kept on a slow boil inside him to rationalize what he would do, and that he didn't really believe in it.

How could he tell her such a thing without devastating her? He had gotten her to France in the first place. Would she cry, make a scene? No, she wouldn't. Look at the view, he told himself, taking a long pull at the champagne. It's unlikely you will ever see this place again.

The view from the terrace was of the yellow limestone cliffs, running down to the sea, that were the very end of the foothills of the Alpes Maritimes. The sky was pale blue, dotted with crimson clouds as the sun set invisibly behind the yellow cliffs. There was a cleft in the limestone that allowed the narrow road to reach the château, and the ridge beyond held a solitary white house with a red-tiled roof. The road was lined with poplars and tall palm trees, and at the end of the ridge, where it dipped steeply to the coastal plain, there was a single pine, very tall and perfectly conical in shape.

The sea darkened from its daytime azure to an inky blue as the evening shadows filled the valley. The lighthouse at Cap d'Antibes lit up with its double flash. The valley cooled. Vehicles coming up the steep road were barely audible. The swallows, swooping after flies in the dusk, twittered musically.

"William," said Khanh, placing a hand lightly on his shoulder.

He got up quickly and looked at her. She was wearing a dress of pale green silk, cut to bare one shoulder, and a double string of large pearls. She hugged him around his neck, pressed her body to him tightly, and presented one cheek for a formal kiss, then the other. "You look lovely," he said, and felt awkward.

She pushed him away and sat down opposite him. "What a nice surprise to see you, *mon ange*," she said, taking his hand in both of hers. "But how did you find me here?"

"I—the embassy traced you here."

"The *embassy*?" she laughed. "My, how very official!"

"Khanh, we have to talk," he said, feeling the perfect heel. All of the indignation he had hoped would get him through this scene had disappeared with the first touch of her cheek.

A waiter arrived and placed bowls of chilled vichyssoise in front of them, and another brought wine glasses and filled them from a bottle he first showed to Khanh. Seeing that William was surprised at the abrupt arrival of the first course, Khanh explained. "I never bother with menus here, *mon ange*; they know what I like and I seem always to be a bit late."

The vichyssoise was delicious, fragrant with leeks and chives. Fuck it, he thought miserably, might as well leave it till after dinner. Might even try to enjoy seeing this woman he had loved and maybe still did.

Khanh chattered gaily about the shops and restaurants in the various towns between Cannes and Nice, and about the beautiful homes and vistas in the mountains. Khanh went to swim in the sea occasionally, but she did not lie on the beach because her delicate skin burned quickly. The rest of the courses came in quick succession: lamb for Stuart and a poached fish for Khanh. During dessert, *île flottante* for both, the fireworks started to glow and pop over Cap d'Antibes, to the delighted oohs and ahs of those diners privileged to be seated on the terrace. The view from Khanh's table was perfect. Stuart watched the rockets burst around the lighthouse and saw the rockets hit the bridge in Laos, and he thought of Moser.

"You look sad," said Khanh. Stuart turned toward her and saw she was studying him. Her own expression had lost its joy. "Surely my presence does not depress you so?"

Stuart winced. "Khanh, we—"

"I know." She stood. "You said before, we have to talk." He got to his feet, wanting to reach for her, to tell her somehow that it could all be fixed, but he knew it could not. "Come along," she said, pulling a black shawl over her shoulders. "We will have coffee in the lounge. It's cold for me here." He reached out to take her arm, but she was already threading her way between the tables. By the time he reached the door of the dining room, past the beaming waiters, captains, and the maître'd, she was halfway down the stairs.

He found her seated on a banquette, giving orders to the waiter behind the bar for coffee and cognac. The waiter scurried away and the lounge was empty for the two of them. Stuart sat next to her and once again she smiled. "Now what is so bloody sad that you sat there like a lump all evening?" she asked.

Suddenly his rage returned, burning low. Suddenly he wanted her to feel the hurt that he felt, that so many of his friends felt, seduced and deceived by her country.

And by her. Yes, it had to be personal. "Khanh," he said. "You are going to have to leave France."

Her eyes widened but she did not otherwise show surprise. "That's absurd," she said evenly. "France is my home. I am a French citizen."

"You are also an officer of North Vietnamese military intelligence, spying on the French. That makes you a traitor to your adopted land."

Khanh tried to laugh, but it sounded forced, brittle. "*Mon ange*, how silly!"

"Comrade Ai Quoc," Stuart said. "Used to be one of Uncle Ho's aliases, didn't it?"

"William," she said, placing a hand on his thigh. "Even if this were true and could possibly be proved, I have done no harm to France and I am married to the scion of an aristocratic and influential family. I will not be arrested and I will not leave France."

"Tomorrow," Stuart said, ignoring her last statement, "the government of the United States will place in the hands of the French government certain information it has gathered about your activities over many years. The U.S. will also request your extradition from France to the U.S. to stand trial."

"France will not allow the extradition of a French citizen," Khanh said, beginning to get angry. The gall of the Americans, she thought.

"Perhaps not, though you might in the end wish they would." Stuart saw the color rising in her cheeks. "Information will also be supplied implicating you in the murder in 1953 of Capt. René Cellini, of the French Army."

Now she laughed heartily. "Oh, *mon ange*, in 1953 I was ten years old! Captain Cellini did some things for my father, and pestered my sisters and me."

"He was murdered in your garden. Your father paid a substantial bribe to quash the investigation."

"But I didn't kill him!" she protested. "It was never even suggested at the time; my parents had a party that evening, many people were there, powerful people. This Cellini was involved in the black market and had many enemies."

"You and I both know that in our business what is the truth is not as important as what can be proved," he said slowly, watching her, wanting the charade to end. "I understand the Agency's case is most convincing." She started to speak but he held up his hands and continued. "How does the influence of your aristocratic husband stack up against that of Captain Cellini's family?"

"I have no idea who his family could be." It was clear from her tone of voice she thought it unlikely they were aristocrats. "With a name like that—"

"His father is the mayor of Marseilles," said Stuart. "His uncle is the head of the Union Corse."

The Union Corse was southern France's version of the Mafia. Khanh gave a little cry and slumped, hiding her mouth with her hands. "They would kill me," she whispered.

"If you stay in France, probably if you stay anywhere in Europe or the Middle East."

"But where would I go?" Tears brightened her large eyes in the candlelight.

"Tonight, just out of France, to avoid arrest. Do you have your car here?"

"Yes. Paul drove me down from Paris; he stays with a cousin in the town."

"You can be in Italy in an hour or in Switzerland in a bit more," he said, placing his hand on her shoulder. "But don't stay in either place. You could go home to Vietnam, or perhaps to another socialist country."

She broke down completly now, crying and pounding her thighs with her tiny fists. "But I am *French*! I *loathe* Hanoi, and can you imagine me living in Budapest, or Sofia, or *Moscow*?" She took a handkerchief from her handbag and dabbed at her streaking makeup. When she opened her eyes her look was cold. "Why are you doing this to me?"

"I'm not, as an individual, Khanh," he said. "The U.S. government is, because you are dangerous. But I will tell you that an operation of mine was blown, and a good friend I went to rescue is still missing and probably dead, and another good friend of mine is in the hospital with a very bad wound. The CIA has information that intelligence on my operation was passed to Hanoi through Paris."

"I had no choice. I tried to kill that bit of intelligence and when

I couldn't I tried to delay it, to discredit it," she said. "You won't believe that, of course."

"We know that," he said. "That is why we are giving you a chance to run."

"Oh, God, the irony of it," she said softly. "*You* were the source of that report! It originated in Aix-en-Provence, while you were at the archives. I tried to hold it up, but in the end I had to send it through, because Aix wanted an answer."

Stuart's moral indignation shrivelled as he remembered Aix and the inquisitive archivist. If I had been more careful Khanh's life could have been left alone; the CIA had been content just to know who she was and what she did. He was as much to blame as she for Moser being missing and Hooper shot. Fucking Nam, he thought. Nothing is ever clearly right or wrong. "I'm sorry," he said. It sounded awfully lame. "But I need to know why you did it. Your family did well out of the French and better out of the Americans, and, as you say, you now feel more French than Vietnamese."

"Because I can never cease to be Vietnamese; none of us can," she said, softly, looking away from him. "Vietnam will never know peace until all the foreigners leave; we have been occupied for nearly a thousand years."

"But why help the Communist North?" he said. "The Americans would not stay as colonialists."

"That is what the Chinese said, for a thousand years. Then the French said it, and then the Japanese, and then the French again, and now you and your puppets." She paused. "One day very soon you will know these things. For now, accept that the Communists, as brutal as they are, are better than the corrupt cliques that govern the South." She looked at him now and there was only sadness in her expression. "My family taught me that. We did well because we were part of that corruption."

Stuart nodded and looked at his watch. Nearly eleven. "You had better call your driver, Khanh."

She touched his face. He was at once attracted and repelled. "Can't we be together until morning? Surely the French police are not to receive this information you bring at the stroke of midnight."

She knows I am more than a messenger, thought Stuart. So be it. "You know as well as I that the police will have an informant in this hotel, who by now will have reported to the police that we were seen together. The French have agreed to leave me and anyone I see alone until tomorrow—an hour from now—but that is all." She looked so lost. "You must go, Khanh."

She reached out and took both his hands. "In time you will forgive me?"

"I hope so," he sighed. He wanted to weep for her and for their innocence, long dead.

"Come up and make love to me before I go."

Stuart shook his head, looking at the carpet. He knew that if he touched her and closed his eyes he would see Moser's ravaged, orange-painted face. He felt her rise and walk past him, followed by the breeze of her perfume. He got up and went into the street, up the hill to the château. He took deep breaths of the cool, dry air and watched the last of the fireworks display. When he returned madame stopped him and told him that Mme de Farge had had to leave: a family emergency in Paris. Madame asked if Stuart had been the bearer of the bad news, and he acknowledged he had.

"Well," said the lady. "At least it is best to get such news from a friend."

She gave him Khanh's room for the night. Khanh had insisted, and it was paid for.

Captain Lambert took Stuart's call at his home at 0800 the following morning. Stuart asked if he could have a lift to Nice–Côte d'Azur Airport and deliver what he had brought on the way. The police captain agreed and found Stuart on the steps of Le Cagnard twenty minutes later with his luggage.

Lambert drove to the airport in silence, his jaw set. He parked the Renault in a security zone and turned to look at Stuart. Stuart handed him the large, wax-sealed envelope without a word. The Frenchman tossed it into the backseat of the little car without apparent interest.

"You're not going to open it?" Stuart asked.

"Paris told me to get it from you and to send it on." Lambert tried for his easy smile, but failed. Clearly Paris had told him a good deal more than that. "It isn't likely the matter concerns Nice, is it, monsieur?"

Not any more, Stuart thought grimly, if Khanh made it out of the country. "No."

"Where do you go now, Monsieur Stuart, back to Indochina?"

"Yes, with one stop at Fort Benning, Georgia."

Lambert brightened, though something still bothered him. "You are a parachutist?"

"Not yet," said Stuart. "I will be, if I pass the basic course."

"I was a parachutist myself," said Lambert. "And I was in Vietnam."

"What did you think of it?"

"It was a beautiful place, very exotic," said the policeman, smiling at the memory. "I was very young at the time and terribly frightened. All I did was count the days until I would be shipped back to France, but when the day finally came, I stayed." He turned and looked at Stuart, appraising him. "I was there until Dien Bien Phu, in 1954."

"I see," said Stuart, sharing the sadness. Vietnam was still a beautiful and a deadly place.

"What will you do when you go back?"

Stuart wasn't supposed to talk about it, but he felt he owed the Frenchman something more than official evasions. "I'm to have a unit. You would call it a commando. We have new information as to the possible locations of small prisoner of war camps in rural North Vietnam and Laos."

"You will go in after them? Behind the lines?"

Yes, thought Stuart. "We will . . . coordinate."

Now the policeman's easy grin returned. A weight seemed to have been lifted from him. Stuart couldn't imagine what is was. "Go well, my American friend," said Lambert. "I am confident the parachute training will make *coordination* much more effective."

Stuart flushed as his lie was exposed. He was glad he would never be interrogated by Captain Lambert. "Just so," he said with a smile.

Captain Lambert opened the door of the little car and got out. A Caravelle taxied toward the terminal, its two engines loud in the warm morning. He pulled Stuart's cases from the backseat, leaving only the red-sealed envelope. The plane stopped, the engines died, and passengers began to emerge onto the stairs. "Your flight, monsieur," said Lambert. "I bid you good journey, and safe home."

"Thank you, sir," said Stuart. "You have been very helpful."

"A pleasant duty, monsieur," said Lambert, handing over the cases. "You may wish to know that your very lovely dinner partner of last evening crossed over into Switzerland at eight minutes past midnight this morning."

Eight minutes past, thought Stuart. He knows he should have detained her, and he didn't. That's what made him uptight. "Thank you very much, Captain," said Stuart. Thank you for letting her go, he thought.

"A Frenchman, monsieur, even a policeman, would not deny a gentleman eight more minutes with a beautiful woman." Lambert gave a little bow, got in the car, and drove away. Stuart picked up his cases and walked into the terminal.

THIRTY-TWO

Bung Kan, Thailand, 15 July 1969

The Thai police sergeant was jolted awake by the rapping of a man's hand on the counter. The policeman sat up and stared at the gaunt figure silhouetted in the dim predawn light that seeped through the door of the small border post. The man—or the ghost, thought the Thai, rubbing his eyes—seemed impossibly tall, even though he was stooped. He was dressed in a black loincloth and two canvas bandoleers of ammunition. He carried an AK-47 in his left hand the way a normal-sized man might carry a stick. The man coughed deeply and spat out the door, then leaned over the counter. The Thai policeman rose slowly out of the wicker chair in which he had been dozing.

"You speak English?" rasped the visitor.

"A–a little, yes," said the sergeant, straightening his uniform and lighting the coal-oil lamp. He saw that the man's arms and torso were covered with sores, and his left eye was clouded and nearly closed.

"You the po–lice?" the man probed, pointing with a dirty, swollen finger.

"Yes, this border station, Bung Kan," said the sergeant. "What can do for you?"

"I got Maj. Carter Peters, U.S. Air Force, and seven men outside, plus the dog tags of seven more who died on the way." The giant reached into his loincloth, pulled out a bunch of dog tags, and dropped them on the policeman's counter with a clatter. "The major be grateful you call the air force in Udorn, get 'em send a helo. These men need hospital."

"You—you come over river?" gasped the sergeant. Nothing like this had ever turned up at the sleepy post in his two years. "How?"

"In boats, from Pak Sane," said the visitor. "Please make the call."

The sergeant shook his head in amazement. The Mekong was deep and swift between Bung Kan and the Laotian district center at Pak Sane, flooded by the summer monsoon. He picked up the microphone of the ancient AM radio, called the police headquarters in Udorn, and repeated the tall man's message. The headquarters asked a single question. The sergeant looked up at the visitor who looked like a ghost and repeated it. "What you name? Who you?"

"Douglas MacArthur Moser," said the man, softly. "Gunner's Mate 3rd Class, United States Navy."

The USAF Jolly Green Giant from Udorn picked up the small group of POWs from a flat paddy behind the Bung Kan police station as soon as the morning fog lifted. The crew watched as Moser helped each man in turn into the helicopter and made sure each was seated comfortably. Many of the men seemed unaware of their surroundings, but each seemed comforted by Moser's touch and his soft words. The crew chief of the aircraft asked Moser to surrender his weapon, and Moser did so upon the promise that it would be locked in the squadron armory and kept for him. The helo, with its sad but precious cargo, lifted off in the hot, brassy dawn of the Mekong and flew the short distance to Udorn, landing at the hospital pad. All nine men were immediately admitted into the hospital's critical care unit. The commanding general of the American forces on the base was informed and decided against any release of information outside of air force channels until more was known as to who the men were and how they came to be in Thailand.

All of the men were very sick, suffering from malaria of various types including the often fatal cerebral strain, also dengue fever, malnutrition, and dysentery. Every man suffered from skin diseases and fungal infections. One man had pneumonia and another cholera. Treatment began immediately but slowly, as each man's strength had to be built up with food and fluids.

Moser was more robust than the men he had brought out from Laos and more alert, but in many respects he was the sickest by far. In addition to all of the fevers the others had, Moser had parasites in his liver, his lungs, his left eye, his gut, and even in the pericardium, which envelopes the heart. The minimal care given prisoners by the Vietnamese barefoot doctors had kept parasites at bay, as had the sanitation requirements of the camps. The barefoot doctors' herbal medicines had not cured the jungle fevers, but had mitigated the damaging effects of high body temperature on the brain. Moser had been far from such care for a very long time. The air force doctors shook their heads when they read Moser's lab results. The parasites would soon kill the man unless treated, but the fevers had so weakened him that the toxic medicines needed to kill the parasites could not be administered lest they kill Moser themselves. The air force doctors decided the best course would be to try to clear the worms from Moser's gut, and if he survived that, try to feed him up to give him strength for the rest of the treatment. The consensus among the doctors was that Moser would die, probably within days. Only one of the prisoners Moser had rescued was critical, and his prognosis was far better than Moser's.

The facts of the escape and rescue were reported to Washington through the very limited and highly classified channel set up for Lieutenant Stuart's operation five weeks before. The administration was elated to have another batch of POWs returned from Laos, but appalled by the medical reports of the men's condition. The story was kept under wraps until the men could recover and be debriefed. The possibility of an emaciated American officer denouncing the war effort or pleading sympathy for his former captors was thought too great a risk to run in the tense summer of 1969. Such things happen, especially when a prisoner or hostage is first freed. Best have the men interviewed quietly by military psychiatrists, it was decided, as soon as they were able. The story would be managed carefully, under direction of the White House staff.

After three weeks of treatment at Udorn all but one of the Pak Sane POWs were stable and well enough to be flown to the main recovery hospital in Atsugi, Japan. Only Moser and the man recovering slowly from cholera remained. Moser's response to food and fluids and very limited treatment for the parasites surprised the doctors. He gained weight rapidly and the heartworms and the liver flukes largely disappeared without toxic treatment, seemingly expelled by the man's growing strength. His skin lesions cleared up, although they left leathery scars. Fungal infections necessitated the removal of all of his toenails, but on other parts of his body the lesions responded to paints and ointments.

An eye specialist flown in from Hawaii examined Moser's clouded eye and determined it was irreparable, and that the parasites within could migrate up the optic nerve and destroy sight in the other eye. The eye was removed and Moser was given a black patch over his bandage. The patch was made by the nurses out of silk from an undergarment. The gentle patient was a favorite of the nurses, with his slow, Southern drawl, which seemed thicker every day. He never complained, though the nurses knew how ill the medicines made him feel. With the patch and his nearly toothless smile he looked like a wizened old pirate. The nurses knew as well about his mutilation and they whispered about it among themselves, pitying the man. Reconstructive dentistry and other rehabilitation would begin in Atsugi, but nothing could ever be done to make Moser a whole man again.

By the time Captain Holtz, the cholera patient, was shipped to Atsugi Moser was up and around, walking around the hospital grounds and eventually as far as the Jolly Green squadron armory, where he sat and talked with the air force armorer, Master Sergeant Allen. Allen gave Moser his AK, which the sergeant had logged in by serial number, noting the thirty-one circular marks pressed into the wooden stock. Moser stripped the weapon to its tiniest components and cleaned each thoroughly, then oiled and reassembled it, honing the crude stamped parts to smooth the action. At first Sergeant Allen was a bit put out: he had soaked the weapon and cleaned it when it had first come in. But then, with no prodding from anyone, Moser began going through the inventory of M-60 door guns, cleaning and repairing even the ones that had virtually lived in the armory. Moser did the work like the master gunsmith he was, but he tired easily, and many nights the armorer drove him back to the hospital in his jeep, the big man fast asleep.

The story of the prisoners of Pak Sane finally broke right after Labor Day, when a correspondent from *Time* happened upon the wife and sons of one of the former POWs on a plane from Honolulu to Tokyo. She told him she was going to see her husband, who had been shot down and listed as missing in action ten months before. The reporter went and talked to the former POW, who told him about the big man Moser, who had slipped into the camp at night, got them out, and sent them walking toward the river, then ambushed the NVA patrol that came out after them. Moser had then caught up, guided the POWs to a broad river, and stolen the boats to cross the swift waters. The pilot's answers were vague; he still couldn't remember the escape completely. The correspondent flew to Bangkok and then to Udorn, and pieced the story together. Moser himself would say little, but his tired old face with its eyepatch of black silk made the cover of *Time*.

Once the story was out politicians of all opinions on the war embraced Moser as a hero, even as a man of peace. Nobody told Washington about the thirty-one circles pressed into the stock of Moser's AK. Sen. William Brush, claiming Moser as a patriotic son of Georgia, trumpeted that Moser's selfless disregard for his own safety and determination to rescue fellow prisoners deserved the nation's highest honor, and he lobbied the White House for the Congressional Medal of Honor. The White House liked the spin on the story: it was apparent from the correspondent's editorializing, as well as comments from the few people the air force allowed to speak to Moser, that the hero had no intention of bad-mouthing the war, the armed forces, or the president of the United States. The president agreed that Moser should get the Congressional, but saw red when Senator Brush told the press that he, the senior senator from Georgia and Chairman of the Senate Foreign Relations Committee, had volunteered to go in harm's way to Thailand to present the medal himself.

Nixon seethed to John Hermann: "I want to present that medal myself, John, in the Oval Office and before cameras."

"The report we have on the man's condition indicates he is gravely ill and may die any day," said the special assistant to the president. No follow-up medical report describing Moser's swift and continuing recovery from his illness had been sent to Washington; none had ever been requested.

"Then get the navy to send someone," said the president, pacing. "Do whatever you have to, but keep that son of a bitch from Georgia the hell out of it."

"Yes, sir," said Hermann. "Why don't I ask Captain Willis at NIS? He got us the last prisoners, and I recall Moser's name was on the report as having been sighted by the SEAL team but not recovered."

"Good," said the president. "Anyone but Brush."

Hermann phoned Captain Willis and explained the president's wishes. Willis laughed and said, "I have just the man, none more deserving. If you can have the medal and the citation delivered here today I will put it in the hands of Lt. William Stuart, who leaves from Dulles tomorrow on his way to Tan Son Nhut."

*   *   *

Moser continued to strengthen and the doctors began to think about transferring him to Japan. Moser took long walks with the nurses and kept up his work in the air force armory. His weight recovered from 150 to 185 pounds, but he still looked gaunt and indeed was 55 pounds lighter than when he had first been captured. He and Sergeant Allen took repaired M-60s to a makeshift test range set up just outside the perimeter wire, and Moser even fired a few rounds through the AK. Moser had brought in nearly a hundred AK-47 rounds with him and Sergeant Allen asked him why he didn't fire off the lot, since Moser would not be allowed to take the carbine with him as a trophy. MACV forbade the taking of any automatic weapon out of the war zone. Moser smiled and said maybe someday he would do just that.

The doctors decided to send Moser to Atsugi as soon as the naval officer arrived and gave him his medal. Moser smiled and said he reckoned he would be ready by then. Once the news spread that Moser would be getting the Congressional from his old commander, a man Moser described as his best friend, the big man became even more of a pet of the hospital staff and they let him eat more than his diet called for. He seemed to want to get as strong as he could before the lieutenant came.

William Stuart arrived in Saigon on September 10 and stayed one day, checking in with MACV. He had priority travel orders at least until he delivered the president's thanks and the medal, so he got scheduled on a flight from Tan Son Nhut to Udorn via Bangkok. The Air Force informed Udorn that the lieutenant would arrive at 1400 on September 11.

The mood in the hospital and in the Jolly Green Giant squadron was festive. The nurses obtained the biggest suit of battle dress utilities they could find from the Air Police unit, got Moser to put it on, and pinned it up. A Thai seamstress who worked in the hospital kitchen altered the uniform, and the hospital laundry starched and pressed it crisp enough to suit General Westmoreland himself. Moser smiled shyly through all of the commotion, but his mind seemed to be elsewhere. In the evening the hospital staff had a party for the big man, complete with a cake with one candle. The helicopter squadron supplied the booze. Moser was forced to make a speech. He spoke softly, his Georgia hill country accent very pronounced, and said how he would miss all the good folks at Udorn when he went on to his next duty. He looked down at the table and the cake, and a tear dropped down the cheek below his good eye. The party grew very quiet, and then Moser asked for a prayer for absent comrades.

On the morning of the 11th, Moser got up early as was his custom. He ate a monstrous breakfast and then put on the new uniform and new boots. The uniform fitted well, but Moser saw that he would burst out of it if he ever got back to normal weight. Moser went across the base to the Jolly Green squadron and checked out his AK-47 with all his remaining ammo. "Gonna finally shoot that up, Moser?" asked Master Sergeant Allen.

"Gonna shoot it up, Sergeant," Moser replied with his nearly toothless grin. He headed out into the misty sunlight and walked to the gate where the makeshift firing range was set up. The air policeman on guard duty waved him through. Everybody on the base knew Moser, the man who came from the jungle with rescued pilots, the man who would get the Congressional.

Moser walked out to the line of target stakes and paused, his hand resting on top of one marked 150 meters. He turned and looked back at the sprawling base, watched as a flight of two A1-Es took off and curved north. Then he turned and walked toward the jungle, some three hundred meters away, in an easy, ground-eating stride. The gate guard, Airman First Class Perez, shouted after him. "Hey, Moser! You ain't supposed to go no further than the range without a pass." Without turning Moser gave a lazy wave of his arm. "What the fuck," said Perez, reaching for the phone in the guard shack and dialing the office of the Sergeant of the Guard. By the time they answered Moser had disappeared into the trees.

A search party was organized and sent out within thirty minutes, aided by helicopters from the Jolly Green squadron. The jungle canopy was thick, and although they would search until dark they would find nothing. Airman Perez was braced by the Air Police officer of the day, and by an irate major who was the base public affairs officer and who was in charge of the medal presentation ceremony that had just lost its star attraction. Perez took all the abuse he could and then asked, simply, "What was I supposed to do, sir? *Shoot* Moser?" When the distraught major finally stormed out Perez repeated the question to his sergeant. "Was I fucking supposed to shoot him, Sarge?"

"No, Perez, of course not," said the sergeant, who was pissed off at everybody for raining out his morning. "You did okay."

Fuckin' A, thought Perez, flushing with anger. Shoot fucking Moser. Moser was a *legend*. Shoot a fucking legend. Shee–it.

Lieutenant William Stuart stepped off the Air Force C-130 at Udorn at precisely 1400. He left his gear on the aircraft, since it was continuing to Danang later in the afternoon, and carried only the plush-lined mahogany box containing the medal. He was met by the base commanding general and the major from public affairs, both of whom had been seeing their careers flash before their eyes since Moser had disappeared. The general explained their "little problem" and described the extensive search then in progress. The major handed Stuart a sealed envelope, addressed in Moser's familiar block capitals to "Mister Stuart." Stuart tore it open and read the single sheet:

DEAR MISTER STUART

   I AM SORRY ONCET AGIN FOR RUNNIN OUT ON YOU. I GUESS I ALLUS BIN MORE TROUBLE THAN I BIN WORTH, BUT YOU IS MY FRIND AND I THINK YOU WILL UNNERSTAND. I KNOW WHERES A LOT MORE CAMPS WITH A LOT MORE OF OUR GUYS IN THEM, AND THATS BETTER WORK FOR ME THAN ANYTHING I COULD DO IN THE WORLD. SEND THE MEDAL TO MY MOMMA, SHEEL LOOK AFTER IT FOR ME.

   AGIN, I AM REEL SORRY ABOUT ALL THE TROUBLE YOU AND MISTER HOOPER AND ALL THE GREAT PEOPLE HERE IN UDORN WENT TO.

                              MOSER, D. M. GMG 3 USN.

The general read the note over Stuart's shoulder. "Don't worry, Lieutenant," said the general confidently. "We'll find him."

"Not if he doesn't want you to, General," said Stuart, putting the note back in its envelope. "And this says he doesn't."

William Stuart flew on to Danang at 1500, without waiting for the conclusion of the search.

Douglas MacArthur Moser never returned to any area under U.S. control. He is still listed as missing in action.